ANTHONY LYVEDEN

ANTHONY LYVEDEN

BY

DORNFORD YATES

WARD, LOCK & CO., LIMITED

LONDON AND MELBOURNE

Library Editions of " Anthony Lyveden "

First Published	.	.	1921
Reprinted	.	.	1922
Reprinted	.	.	1923
Reprinted	.	.	1925
Reprinted	.	.	1928
Reprinted	.	.	1929
Reprinted	.	.	1932
Reprinted	.	.	1935
Reprinted	.	.	1939
Reprinted	.	.	1942
Reprinted	.	.	1943
Reprinted	.	.	1944
Reprinted	.	.	1945
Reprinted	.	.	1947
Reprinted	.	.	1949

MADE IN ENGLAND
Printed in Great Britain by The Whitefriars Press Ltd., London and Tonbridge

TO

ELM TREE ROAD

whose high walls, if they could talk,
would tell so many pretty tales.

CONTENTS

CONTENTS

CHAPTER I

THE WAY OF A MAN

MAJOR ANTHONY LYVEDEN, D.S.O., was waiting.

For the second time in three minutes he glanced anxiously at his wrist and then thrust his hand impatiently into a pocket. When you have worn a wristwatch constantly for nearly six years, Time alone can accustom you to its absence. And at the present moment Major Lyveden's watch was being fitted with a new strap. The pawnbroker to whom he had sold it that morning for twenty-two shillings was no fool.

The ex-officer walked slowly on, glancing into the windows of shops. He wanted to know the time badly. Amid the shifting press of foot-passengers a little white dog stuck to his heels resolutely. The sudden sight of a clock-maker's on the opposite side of the thoroughfare proved magnetic. Pausing on the kerb to pick up the Sealyham, Lyveden crossed the street without more ado. . . .

Twenty-one minutes past three.

Slowly he put down the terrier and turned eastward. It was clear that he was expecting something or somebody.

It was a hot June day, and out of the welter of din and rumble the cool plash of falling water came to his straining ears refreshingly. At once he considered the dog and, thankful for the distraction, stepped beneath

9

the portico of a provision store and indicated the marble basin with a gesture of invitation.

" Have a drink, old chap," he said kindly.   " Look. Nice cool water for Patch." And, with that, he stooped and dabbled his fingers in the pool.

Thus encouraged the little white dog advanced and lapped gratefully. . . .

" Derby Result ! Derby Result ! "

The hoarse cry rang out above the metallic roar of the traffic.

Lyveden caught his breath sharply and then stepped out of the shelter of the portico on to the crowded pavement. He was able to buy a paper almost immediately.

Eagerly he turned it about, to read the blurred words. . . .

For a moment he stood staring, oblivious of all the world.   Then he folded the sheet carefully, whistled to Patch, and strode off westward with the step of a man who has a certain objective.   At any rate, the suspense was over.

A later edition of an evening paper showed Major Anthony Lyveden that the horse which was carrying all that he had in the world had lost his race by a head.

*   *   *   *   *

By rights Anthony should have been born about the seventh of March.   A hunting accident to his father, however, ushered him into the middle of the coldest January ever remembered, and that with such scant ceremony that his lady mother only survived her husband by six and a half hours.   When debts, funeral and testamentary expenses had been deducted from his father's bank balance, the sum of twenty-three pounds nine shillings was all that was left, and this, with the threat of royalties from one or two books, represented the baby's fortune.   Jonathan Roach, bachelor, had risen to the occasion and taken his sister's child.

Beyond remembering that he did handsomely by his nephew, bred him as became his family, sent him to Harrow and Oxford, and procured him a commission in the Royal Regiment of Artillery before most of the boy's compeers had posted their applications to the War Office, with the living Jonathan Roach we are no further concerned.

The old gentleman's will shall speak for itself and the man who made it.

THIS IS THE LAST WILL AND TESTA-MENT of me, Jonathan Roach, of 75 Princes Gardens, in the County of London, Esquire. I give, devise, and bequeath all my real and personal estate of every description unto my nephew Anthony Lyveden abso-lutely, provided that and so soon as my said nephew shall receive the honour of Knighthood or some higher dignity. . . .

Anthony received the news while the guns, which he was temporarily commanding, were hammering at the gates of Gaza. He read the letter carefully twice. Then he stuffed it into a cross-pocket and straightway burst into song. That the air he selected was a music-hall ditty was typical of the man.

Curiously enough, it was the same number that he was whistling under his breath as he strode into Hyde Park this June afternoon.

Patch, who had never been out of London, thought the world of the Parks. After the barren pavements, for him the great greenswards made up a Land of Promise more than fulfilled. The magic carpet of the grass, stuffed with a million scents, was his Elysium. A bookworm made free of the Bodleian could not have been more exultant. The many trees, too, were more accessible, and there were other dogs to frolic with, and traffic, apparently, was not allowed.

When he had walked well into the Park, Lyveden made for a solitary chair and sat himself down in the sun. For a while he remained wrapped in meditation, abstractedly watching the terrier stray to and fro, nosing the adjacent turf with the assiduity of a fond connoisseur.

For nine long months the ex-officer had sought employment, indoor or outdoor, congenial or uncongenial. The quest was vain. Once he had broached the matter haltingly to an influential acquaintance. The latter's reception of his distress had been so startlingly obnoxious that he would have died rather than repeat the venture. Then Smith of Dale's, Old Bond Street—Smith, who had cut his hair since he was a boy, and was his fast friend—had told him of Blue Moon.

There is more racing chatter to be heard at the great hairdressers' than almost anywhere else outside a racecourse. Some of it is worth hearing, most of it is valueless. The difficulty, as elsewhere, is to sift the wheat from the chaff.

According to Smith, Blue Moon was being kept extremely quiet. Certainly the horse was little mentioned. Lyveden had never heard his name. And thirty-three to one was a long price. . . .

Lyveden pricked up his ears, and Smith became frightened. He was genuinely attached to his young customer, and knew that he was in low water. He begged him not to be rash. . . .

After some careful calculations, which he made upon a sheet of club note-paper, Lyveden came to the conclusion that thirty-three birds in the bush were better than one in the hand. Reckoning a bird at one hundred pounds and Lyveden's available assets at the same number of guineas, who is to say he was wrong?

At twenty minutes to five on the eve of the Derby, Lyveden handed a protesting Smith one hundred and one pounds, to be invested on Blue Moon—" to win only." The odd note was to bring Smith his reward.

A big bookmaker whom Smith was shaving as usual, at a quarter-past six, accepted the commission, pocketed the notes with a sigh, and gave the master-barber forty to one.

Four thousand pounds—in the bush.

That his thirty-three nebulous birds had become forty before they took flight, Anthony never knew. A man whose sole assets are a Sealyham, a very few clothes, and twenty-two shillings and sixpence, does not, as a rule, go to Dale's.

"Young fellow, come here."

Patch came gaily, and Lyveden set him upon his knee.

"Listen," he said. "Once upon a time there was a fool, who came back from the War. It was extremely foolish, but then, you see, Patch, he was a fool. Well, after a while he began to feel very lonely. He'd no relations, and what friends he'd had in the old days had disappeared. So he got him a dog—this fool, a little white scrap of a dog with a black patch." The terrier recognized his name and made a dab at the firm chin. "Steady! Well, yes—you're right. It was a great move. For the little white dog was really a fairy prince in disguise—such a pretty disguise—and straightway led the fool into Paradise. Indeed, they were so happy together, the fool and the dog, that, though no work came along, nothing mattered. You see, it was a fool's paradise. That was natural. The result was that one day the fool lifted up his eyes, and there was a great big finger-post, pointing the way they were going. And it said WAY OUT. The dog couldn't read, so it didn't worry him; but the fool could, and fear smote upon his heart. In fact, he got desperate, poor fool. Of course, if he'd had any sense, he'd 've walked slower than ever or even tried to turn round. Instead of that, he ran. Think of it, Patch. *Ran*." The emotion of

his speech was infectious, and the terrier began to pant.
" Was there ever quite such a fool ?   And before they
knew where they were, the two were without the gates.
And there "—the voice became strained, and Lyveden
hesitated—" there   were . . . two   paths . . . going
different ways.   And by each path was a notice-board.
And one said NO DOGS ALLOWED.   And the other
said NO FOOLS ALLOWED.   And there were only the
two paths, Patch . . . going different ways. . . ."

The approach of a peripatetic tax-collector brought
the allegory to an end.

Anthony paid for his occupation of the chair in
silence, and the collector plodded off at a tangent in
the direction of his next quarry.   This appearing to be
an old lady, he presently altered his course.   With a
caution bred of experience, he would approach her
from behind.

A convenient clock struck four, and Lyveden rose to
his feet. . . .

Two hours later he descended the area steps of a
mansion in Lancaster Gate.

The change in his appearance was quite remarkable.
The grey suit, soft hat, golf collar and brown shoes,
which he had worn in the afternoon, had been put off.
In their stead Lyveden was wearing a bowler hat,
black boots, a single collar, which stood up uncomfort-
ably all the way round his neck, and a dark blue suit.
The latter was clean and had been carefully brushed,
but it was manifestly old.   Besides, it was obvious that
the man who made them had meant the trousers to be
worn turned up.   Their owner's present disregard of
such intention argued his humble respectability.

Arrived at the foot of the steps, Anthony thrust a
relieving finger between his throat and the collar for
the last time, raised his eyes to heaven, and rang the
bell.

After a moment or two the door was opened by a

fair-haired girl in a print dress. Her sleeves were rolled up, and her hands and arms dripping.

" Afternoon, miss," said Lyveden. He was determined to do the thing properly. " Your lady still wanting a footman ? "

The girl stared at him. Then—

" I dunno," she said. " Better come in, an' I'll see."

Anthony thanked her and entered. She shut the door and flung down the passage and out of sight. A second later a momentary burst of chatter suggested that she had opened the door of the servants' hall.

For a minute or two nothing happened, and Lyveden stood in the passage with his hat in his hand, wondering whether his engagement was to rest with the butler. Then a door opened and closed, and a girl dressed as a parlour-maid appeared upon the scene. She was walking slowly, and seemed to be endeavouring to extricate something from the depths of her mouth.

" Come in answer to the ad. ? " she queried.

" That's right," said Lyveden.

" Oh." She leaned against the wall and regarded a wet forefinger. " Got a bone in me gum," she added abstractedly.

Anthony wondered whether he was expected to offer assistance, but, deciding to risk a breach of etiquette, assumed a look of anxiety instead.

" How rotten ! " he murmured.

The girl looked at him curiously. Then—

" 'Addock, too," she said. " An' that's easy, reelly, as fish goes. But there, I ain't got much use for any fish, 'cept salmon. Shall I say you're 'ere ? "

" Yes, please, miss. I've no appointment."

" You're the firs', any way," was the comforting reply.

She left him standing.

The inspection to which during her absence Lyveden

was subjected was only less trying than the open
secrecy with which it was conducted. Heads were
thrust into the passage to be withdrawn amid a
paroxysm of giggling. Somebody was pushed into full
view to retire precipitately amid an explosion of mirth.
Preceded by stifled expressions of encouragement, a
pert-looking lady's maid strolled leisurely past the new-
comer, opened the back door, closed it, and returned as
haughtily as she had gone. She was applauded ridiculously. . . .

Anthony swore under his breath.

At last the parlour-maid reappeared, finger in mouth.

"Somethin' crool, this bone is," she vouchsafed.
"Come on."

Anthony followed her gratefully upstairs and presently into a small withdrawing room upon the first
floor.

From an expensively hideous couch Mrs. Slumper
regarded the fruit of her advertisement.

She was a large vulgar-looking woman of about fifty
summers. Whosesoever the hair of her head, it was
most elaborately dressed and contained five combs.
Anthony counted them. She was enclosed in a dress
which was at once highly fashionable and painfully
unbecoming, and the pearls which rose and fell upon
her tremendous bosom were almost too good to be true.
From beneath the short skirt a pair of ponderous legs
terminated in all the anguish of patent-leather shoes.

Anthony bowed.

" 'Oo 'ave you bin with ? " said Mrs. Slumper.

"If you take me, madam, this will be my first
place."

Mrs. Slumper choked with emotion.

"Firs' place ! " she cried. "Want ter try yer 'and
on me ? " She looked round savagely. "Where's me
lorenets ? " she added furiously.

Much as a victim-to-be might hand his dispatcher

the knife, Anthony plucked the eye-glasses from beneath a cushion and put them into her hand.

His action took the wind out of her sails. Anthony saw this, and hastened to press his advantage.

" I know it's unusual, madam, but I'm quite willing to leave at the end of a week without wages, if you're not satisfied."

Mrs. Slumper grunted with astonishment.

" Wot wages joo ask ? "

" Seventy-two pounds a year, madam, and—er—all found. And one afternoon a week," he added boldly.

Mrs. Slumper blinked at him curiously.

" You don' look ser bad," she said grudgingly. " An' I'm sick an' tired of tryin' for a footman, or I'd see yer further. 'Owever. . . ." She looked up sharply. " Will yer put that in writin' abaout the week ? "

" Certainly, madam." And, with that, Lyveden stepped to a bureau and wrote his undertaking upon a sheet of note-paper. He was about to affix his signature, when it occurred to him that footmen do not write at their mistresses' bureaus except privily or by invitation. He flushed furiously. There was, however, no help for it now. The thing was done. Desperately he signed his name. He handed the paper to the lady humbly enough.

Mrs. Slumper sighed.

" In course," she said, " we 'ave things very well done. The butler's aout naow, or I'd 'ave 'im up. But you'll 'ave ter wait, an' open the door, an' clean the boots, an' come aout on the car. I've got some noo livery—never bin worn yet—did ought ter fit you a treat. An'—'ow soon kin yer come ? " she demanded suddenly.

" To-morrow evening, madam."

" Or-right."

Anthony bowed himself out.

If the parlour-maid had not been on the landing, he

would have leaned against the wall and covered his face.

The girl glanced at the door he had just closed.

" Ain't she a little dream ? "

Anthony grinned.

" Might be worse," he ventured, endeavouring to steer between the respective sandbanks of disloyalty and odium. " I've got the place," he added ingenuously.

The girl stared at him.

That Anthony did not appreciate why she had remained upon the landing was to her incredible.

" I 'eard," she said loftily.

Anthony felt crushed.

At his suggestion she let him out of the front door.

" See yer to-morrow," she cried.

" That's right, miss."

Anthony passed down the steps and walked quickly away. Before he had covered a hundred paces, he stopped and turned up his trousers. The sartorial forfeit to respectability had served its turn.

When Mr. Hopkins, the butler, returned a little unsteadily at a quarter to ten to learn that his mistress had engaged a " proper toff " as his footman, he was profoundly moved.

*　　*　　*　　*　　*

A visit to the West End offices of *Dogs' Country Homes, Ltd.*, which he made the next morning, satisfied Anthony that, by putting Patch in their charge, he was doing the best he could. There was a vacancy at the Hertfordshire branch, less than forty minutes from town, and he arranged to lodge the terrier there the same afternoon. For the sum of a guinea a week the little dog would be fed and housed and exercised. A veterinary surgeon was attached to the staff, which was carefully supervised. Patch would be groomed every day and bathed weekly. Visitors were welcomed, and owners often called to see their dogs and take them out for a walk. It was quite customary.

Lyveden emerged from the office a little comforted. He spent a busy morning.

Deliberately he went to his club. There he wrote to the secretary, resigning his membership. When he had sealed the letter, he looked about him. The comfort—the luxury of it all was very tasty, very appealing. He regretted that he had not used it more often. There was a time when he had thought the place dull. Blasphemy! In his hungry eyes the house became a temple —its members, votaries, sworn to go sleepily about their offices—its rooms, upholstered shrines, chapels of ease. . . .

The door opened and a footman came in.

The silver dream shivered into a million flinders.

After the generous atmosphere of Pall Mall, the reek of the " old clothes " shop was more offensive than usual. The six pounds ten, however, was worth fighting for. Then some cheap hosiery had to be purchased —more collars of the bearing-rein type, some stiff shirts, made-up white ties, pinchbeck studs and cufflinks. As he emerged from the shop, Anthony found himself wondering whether he need have been so harsh with himself about the collars. After all, it was an age of Socialism. Why should a footman be choked? He was as good as Mrs. Slumper—easily. And she wasn't choked. She was squeezed, though, and pinched. . . .

He lodged his baggage—suit-case and hold-all—at the cloakroom, and took Patch to lunch.

It was by no means the first time that the Sealyham's lunch had been the more expensive of the two. Often and often he had fed well to the embarrassment of his master's stomach. To-day he was to have liver—his favourite dish. Upon this Lyveden was resolved.

The pair visited five restaurants and two public-houses in quest of liver. At the eighth venture they

were successful. At the sign of *The Crooked Billet*
liver and bacon was the dish of the day. So much a
blurred menu was proclaiming from its enormous brass
frame. Before the two were half-way upstairs, the
terrier's excitement confirmed its tale.

Of the two portions, Patch consumed the liver and
Anthony the bacon. This was rather salt, but the zest
with which the Sealyham ate furnished a relish which
no money could buy.

Then came a ghastly train journey. Mercifully Patch
could not understand. . . .

A mile and a half from the station, the Dogs' Home
stood in a pleasant place under the lee of a wood. Fair
meadows ringed it about, and in the bright sunshine
the red-brick house and out-buildings looked cheerful
and promising.

Slowly the two passed up the well-kept drive.

With his little white dog in his arms, Anthony Lyveden was shown everything. A jolly fair-haired girl—
the superintendent—conducted him everywhere. The
dogs—all sizes and shapes—welcomed her coming. Of
Patch she made a great deal.

" You must be very proud of him," she said to
Anthony.

" I am. And—we're great friends. I hope he won't
fret much."

" A little at first, probably. You'll be coming to
see him ? "

" Once a week, always," said Lyveden. " Oftener
if I can."

Presently they returned to the office, where Anthony
paid four guineas and received a receipt. Patch was
entered in a big book, together with his age and description. Another column received his owner's name and
address. The girl hesitated.

" We like," she said, " to have the telephone number,
in case of accidents."

" I'll send it to you to-night."

The entry was blotted, and the girl rose. The formalities were at an end.

Lyveden picked up his hat.

Patch greeted the familiar signal joyously. Clearly the call was over. It had been a good visit—the best they had ever paid. No other place they had been to was full of dogs. Yet to be out and about with his master was better still. He leapt up and down, rejoicing.

Anthony caught him from one of his bounds, held the white scrap very close and let him lick his nose. Then he bade him be a good dog and handed him to the girl. She received him tenderly.

" I'm very much obliged to you," he said. " Good day. I'll let myself out. It—it'll be better."

One more caress, and he passed out into the hall— blindly. There had been a look in the bright brown eyes that tore his heart.

For a moment Patch fought desperately. Then he heard a door opened and listened intently. A draught swept, and the door closed heavily. With a sudden wrench he was out of the girl's arms and across the shadowy hall. For a moment he stood sniffing, his nose clapped to the sill of the front door. Then he lifted up his voice and wept bitterly.

*   *   *   *   *

In the long mirror, half-way up the front staircase, Major Anthony Lyveden, D.S.O., surveyed himself stealthily.

" Not much the matter with the kit," he said grudgingly.

That was largely because there was nothing the matter with the man.

Six feet one in his socks, deep-chested and admirably proportioned, Lyveden cut a fine figure. His thick dark hair was short and carefully brushed, and his lean face was brown with the play of wind and rain and sun. Such features as his broad forehead, aquiline nose, and strong well-shaped mouth, would have distinguished any countenance. Yet the whole of it was shapely and clean-cut, and there was a quiet fearlessness about the keen grey eyes that set you thinking. As a footman he looked magnificent. But he would have killed any master stone dead. Royalty itself could not have borne such a comparison.

As we have seen, the strain of the last fortnight, culminating in Blue Moon's failure and his parting with Patch, had played the deuce with his temperament. The man had gone all to pieces. That, now that a week had gone by, he was himself again, the following letter will show. It will serve also as a record, and so, gentlemen, spare both of us.

DEAR TOBY,

Before you sailed you were urgent upon me that I should constantly report progress. Nine months have gone by, and I have not written once. Still, my conscience is clear. Hitherto I have had no progress to report.

Now, however, I have news for you.

You are friends with a footman, Toby. You need not deny it, because I know better. You see, I have been in service for one week to-day.

My mistress is indescribable—a very mammoth among women. Except during prohibited hours, her replica may be seen behind the saloon-bar of any public-house in, say, Bethnal Green. Below stairs she is known as " the dream-child." My master appears to have married, not so much beneath him as beyond him. He is " something in the City." This is as well, for he is nothing in Lancaster Gate. I like him rather.

You would get on with the butler, who is addicted to drink. The ladies of the servants' hall are rather trying, but mean well. The chauffeur is a most superior man.

In fact, except that he has been twice convicted of felony and continually boasts of his successful desertion from the Army in 1917, there is nothing against him. My work would be comparatively light if the unfortunate resemblance, to which I have alluded above, were less pronounced. In a word, the butler's working day finishes at 2 p.m., and on two occasions I have had to repair to " The Blue Goat " as late as seven-thirty to hale him out of the tap-room in time for dinner. His carriage in the dining-room, when he can hardly see, is one of the wonders of the world.

Of course I go out with the car—usually to a wedding. The solemnization of matrimony, especially if one of the parties is of noble birth, draws the dream-child as a magnet the steel. Need I say that she is an uninvited guest? Yesterday, at the wedding of a young Marquess, she was stopped at the doors. " Lef' me card at 'ome," was her majestic reply. Before they had recovered she was in the aisle. Having regard to her appearance, I am of opinion that such conduct is libellous.

On Monday she gave what she calls a " Serciety Crush." This was well attended, chiefly by aliens, many of whom wore miniature decorations, to which, I fear, they were not entitled. These were, I fancy, hired with the dress-coats to which they were fastened. That they enjoyed the viands is emphasized by the fact that, prior to their departure, several of the guests concealed about their persons such delicacies as the flight of time alone had prevented them from consuming. But for the indisposition of the butler, I should have spent a most amusing evening.

Little altercations between my master and mistress are of frequent occurrence. Occasionally they appeal to me to settle the dispute. Once I actually took the liberty of separating them. Indeed, as recently as yesterday evening the dream-child, who had been keeping up her reading, observed that " the rilewise was thinkin' of givin' up the narrer gorge."

" Gage, me dear—gage," says Mr. Slumper.

"That's right," says his wife with hideous irony. *"Put yer betters to rights, Schooly. Ugh, I wonder yer dare! An' wot do you know about it, you hugly worm?"*

Stung to the quick by the painful accuracy of this appellative, her husband was understood to mutter that he had rather be an ill-favoured worm than an overdressed parrot with a swollen head.

Only waiting to throw a glass of water in his direction, the dream-child demanded my ruling in a voice shaking with indignation.

I immediately declared in favour of *"gouge"*—a decision for which Mr. Slumper, to whom victory is even more terrible than defeat, will thank me yet.

Of such is my life. Either Saturday or Sunday afternoon I go off duty. Then I dive into the country and visit my dog, who is well cared for. We spend a hilarious few hours, and Lancaster Gate is never mentioned. In the servants' hall, by the way, I am credited with a delicate wife—an impression which I have taken care not to correct, for where there are gathered together eight single ladies, les avantages de mariage *cannot be over-estimated.*

And now I must take up the tea.

If ever you receive this letter, find time to reply. I know I have spoken ill of your hand-writing, but I take it all back.

Bien à toi, vieux sot,
ANTHONY LYVEDEN.

Anthony, then, was surveying himself, if you remember, in a long mirror. He had just taken up the tea. He was taking a second look at what he could see of his back, when the front-door bell rang. Even at this elevation there was no mistaking its deep peremptory note. Lyveden descended the stairs.

He opened the door faultlessly to find himself face to face with a man who had been his first servant when his battery had been in France.

For a moment the two footmen stared at one another.
Then—

"Glad to see you, Walters," said Lyveden heartily.

"Same to you, sir," said Walters, touching his hat.
"An', beggin' your pardon, sir, is Lady 'Elen at 'ome ? "

"There's no Lady Helen here," said Lyveden.
"This is Mrs. Slumper's house."

"Oh, very good, sir," said Walters jerkily. "Sorry
to 'ave troubled you, sir." He touched his hat and
turned away nervously. . . .

Anthony continued to hold the door open till the car
should have passed on.

Walters was making his report. It appeared that
this was unsatisfactory, for a moment later he was again
at the door.

"Excuse me, sir, but would you speak to my lady ? "

Lyveden descended the steps.

From the luxury of a smart landaulette a dame of
some consequence regarded him shrewdly. She had, of
course, witnessed the comedy upon the steps.

"Who lives here ? " she demanded haughtily.

Lyveden drew himself up.

"Mrs. Slumper, madam."

His statement was received with an irrational
suspicion.

"Indeed ! I didn't know that Lady Helen Amiens
had let her house."

"Neither, madam, did I."

The great lady stared at Anthony, who looked straight
ahead. Then—

"I—I beg your pardon," she murmured.

Anthony bowed and turned on his heel. As he passed
Walters, who was standing wide-eyed, the latter
touched his hat faithfully.

When the car had passed on, Anthony closed the
door thoughtfully. It had not occurred to him that
the house had been hired as it stood. Certainly the

Slumpers had given no hint of such a state of affairs.
Probably they felt it to be beneath their dignity. It
being no affair of his, Lyveden decided to keep his own
counsel.

*   *   *   *   *

Two days later Anthony visited Patch for the second
time.

The same relentless train that had rushed the two down
to Hertfordshire that dreadful Thursday had become
an easy-going friend. By pocketing his lunch, Lyveden
could catch it with anything under five minutes to
spare. This gave the two another three-quarters of
an hour.

Their second meeting was a replica of the first.

Anthony was admitted, announced his desire, and
sat down in the dim hall. Presently a brisk familiar
step made itself heard—firm little paws meeting the
tough linoleum squarely—and Anthony rose to his feet.
Out of a passage came Patch readily, the fair-haired girl
behind him bidding him go ahead. For a moment he
looked about him. Then he saw Lyveden, stiffened
and stood stock still. The next second, with his body
clapped to the floor, he had darted sharply across and,
laying his head sideways, crouched at his idol's feet—an
adoring suppliant, craving to be raised.

" Why, Patch——"

The white scrap quivered and flung up a panting
visage. Lyveden stooped and gathered him in his
arms. The terrier licked his face frantically. Then he
squirmed like a mad thing till he was down, tore to a
basket of logs, and of his strength brought a billet
gripped in his big mouth and laid it at Anthony's feet.

The girl laughed merrily.

" What did I tell you ? " said Lyveden. " It's just
the way of his heart. I must always have a present
when I have been away."

Lord and squire went for a wonderful walk. The

woodland and meadows of Hertfordshire fairly beggared
the Parks. . . .

Tea at a tiny inn sunk in a dell through which a
sleepy lane trickled between high banks—tea in the
pocket garden under sweet-smelling limes, where stocks
stood orderly and honeysuckle sprawled over the brick-
nogging, brought back old days of happy fellowship,
just to outshine their memory.

From the cool of the house came on a sudden the
click of metal and the swift whirr of wheels. Somewhere a clock was in labour—an old, old timepiece, to
whom the telling of the hours was a grave matter. A
moment later a thin old voice piped out the birth of a
new period.

Five o'clock.

Peacefully Lyveden expelled a cloud of smoke. He
need not be moving for another quarter of an hour.
Upon the warm red bricks at his feet Patch lay dozing
after his dish of weak tea.

"Could you give it me in the garden?"

The fresh clear voice floated out of the doorway just
in front of my lady herself. Arrived there, she stood
for a moment looking pleasedly round. It is doubtful
whether the old woodwork had ever before framed such
a picture.

There was nothing remarkable about the dress, except
her wearing of it. There is a grace of carriage that will
make purple of sackcloth. Still, the gown was well cut
of fawn-coloured stuff, which her stockings and shoes
matched. Her face was generous—proud, too, yet
tender and very beautiful. The soft rose of her cheeks,
the misty blue of her eyes stood there for gentleness,
the curve of the red lips for pride. Wisdom sat in her
temples under the thick dark hair. Strength herself
had moulded the exquisite chin. And a rogue of a
dimple was there to mock the lot of them—the print
of the delicate finger of Laughter herself, set in a baby's

cheek twenty-five years before. A tiny watch upon a silk strap served to enhance the slenderness of a white wrist. Against the dark cloud of hair, which they were setting straight, the pointed fingers stood out like living statuary. Lifted elbows gave you the graceful line of her figure : the short skirt, ankles to match the wrists . . . .

Looking upon her, Lyveden forgot the world. He may be forgiven, for she was a sight for sore eyes.

Having set her hair to her liking she put on her hat, pulling it down with a fine careless confidence such as no manner of mirror could give.

She had not seen Lyveden when Patch, counting her Irish terrier an intruder, took him suddenly by the throat. . . .

In an instant the place was Bedlam.

My lady hovered about the combatants, one hand to her breast, the other snatching frantically at her favourite's tail : Lyveden leapt to his feet and, cramming his pipe into a pocket, flung himself forward : the mistress of the inn and her maid crowded each other in the doorway, emitting cries of distress : and the now ravening flurry of brown and white raged snarling and whirling upon the brick pavement with all the finished frightfulness of the *haute école*.

Arrived at close quarters, Anthony cast a look round. Then he picked up the pair anyhow and swung them into the water-butt two paces away.

For a moment the contents boiled, seething as if possessed. Then, with a fearful convulsion, the waves parted and the water gave up its prey. Two choking, gasping, spluttering heads appeared simultaneously : with one accord four striving paws clawed desperately at the rim of the butt. The fight was off.

Intelligently the girl stepped up on to a convenient bench, and Anthony lifted the Irish terrier out of his watery peril. As was to be expected, he shook himself inconsiderately, and Anthony, who was not on the bench, was generously bedewed. Then Patch was hauled out by the scruff of his neck. . . . So far as could be seen, neither of the dogs was one penny the worse. There had been much cry, but little wool.

Lyveden turned to my lady and raised his hat.

" I'm awfully sorry," he said. " My dog was entirely to blame."

" D'you mind controlling him now ? " she said coldly.

Lyveden called Patch, and the Sealyham trotted up, shaking the water out of his ears as he came. Wet as he was, the man picked him up and put him under his arm.

" I hope your dog isn't hurt," he said quietly. " I'm very sorry."

The girl did not deign to answer, but, stepping down from her perch, summoned her terrier and strolled down the little greensward with her chin in the air.

Anthony bit his lip. Then he turned on his heel and, clapping his hat on his head, tramped into the inn. A moment later he had paid his reckoning and was out on the road. After all, he reflected, Patch wasn't to blame. He had acted according to his lights.

When he was out of sight of the inn, Anthony sat down by the wayside and dried his terrier's ears with his pocket-handkerchief and the utmost care.

*　　*　　*　　*　　*

The rain was coming down in sheets, and, in spite of the mackintosh which he was wearing above his livery, drops were beginning to make their unpleasant way down Anthony's neck. His feet had been wet for hours. The violence of the language employed by the press of grooms and footmen huddled about him at the doors of the Opera House suggested that their plight was no less evil.

It was a big night, and of " the distinguished audience " Mr. and Mrs. Slumper were making two. They were inexpressibly bored, but that was beside the point. By occupying two stalls, Mrs. Slumper was sure they were doing the right thing. A box would have been better, of course, but there had been some difficulty, and Slumper, being a weak-kneed fool, had been bluffed into taking the stalls. Mrs. Slumper would like to see the clerk who could bluff her. By dint of concentrating upon her grievance, she had worked herself into a passion by the end of the second act. . . .

It continued to rain copiously.

At last flunkeys appeared and set the inner swing-doors wide open. A blasphemous murmur of relief went up from the company of servants.

" Bet yer my gint's fust," squeaked a little bow-legged Cockney. " 'E's a fair winner, 'e is." A pompous prelate appeared in the lobby, walking with an air of having just consecrated the building free of charge, and followed by a nervous-lipped lady and a deacon who looked like a startled owl. " There y'are ! Wot 'd I s'y ? " he added, turning to scuttle off to his car.

" Ser long, 'Arry ! " cried somebody. " See yer at Ciro's."

There was an explosion of mirth.

The rain, the discomfort, the waiting—three familiar malefactors—all in a moment discomfited by a sudden guffaw, reminded Lyveden vividly of his service in France. His thoughts ramped back to the old days, when there was work and to spare—work of a kind. Of course, the competition was not so keen. . . .

People were coming fast now, and the entrances to the lobby were getting choked. Attendants were bellowing big names, innumerable engines were running, the police were shouting orders, gears were being changed.

" Number a nundred and one ! " thundered a voice.

" Right ! " cried Anthony, elbowing his way out of the crush.

He made his way quickly to where he had left the car.

The information that his employers were awaiting his services was received by the chauffeur with a volley of invective, which dealt more particularly with Mrs. Slumper's pedigree, but touched lightly upon a whole variety of subjects, including the ultimate destination of all composers and the uses of rain.

It was full five minutes before the limousine was able to be brought close enough to the entrance for Anthony to leave the running-board and advise his master. When it was next in order but two, he stepped on to the pavement and struggled towards the entrance. As he was about to tell an attendant to summon " 101," a car slid into position, and the fellow set his hand on the door.

" Forty-six waiting ! " he bawled.

A glance at the steps showed the approach of quality —all cloaks and soft hair and slim silk stockings—the attendant threw open the door and Lyveden stood still.

The taller of the two women was the second to enter the car. As she stood waiting, she glanced round quickly. Her eyes met Anthony's, rested a moment of time, and then swept on without a flicker. . . . A second later the door had slammed upon her high heels.

Lyveden was left to feel the blood come flaming into his face, to wonder whether my lady had known him again, and to stuff the breath of an exquisite perfume into the same reliquary as held the picture of a tall dark figure setting her hair to rights in the mouth of an inn.

*　　*　　*　　*　　*

Upon the next Saturday a particularly smart wedding was to take place. Anthony, who had seen the announcements, was prepared for the worst. Sure enough, on Friday afternoon as he was clearing the table of tea—

" I shall want yer to-morrow," said Mrs. Slumper. " I 'ave to go to the weddin' o' that there Finnigan boy. I'm sure I'm sick o' crushes, but 'er ladyship would never fergive me if I diddun show up."

Anthony hesitated with the tray in his hands.

" Mr. Hopkins is taking Sunday, madam, so I can't go out then."

" I can't 'elp that," was the testy reply.

" I don't wish to inconvenience you, madam, but, as it was arranged that I should always have——"

" Subjec' to *my* convenience," snapped Mrs. Slumper. " That's wot I said." She had said nothing of the sort. " An' am I to go pushin' orf to a dandy crush without a servant ? Hopenin' me own dores, an' fetchin' me own car, an' wot not, jus' like a common beggar in a 'ired fly ? Look 'ere, young man, I didn't ought to 'ave took you at all, reelly. Wot with no refs an' no experience, yer might 'ave walked the soles orf of yer perishin' boots before yer got into a 'ouse like this. But I gave you a chance, I did. An' if you think ter try an' turn me own words agains' me an' talk 'igh about contrax, yer kin jus' shove orf." She regarded him furiously. " Ugh ! I'm fed up with the bunch of yer. Nasty, ungrateful swabs ! I serpose yer kin 'ave Monday, can't yer ? "

" I will take Monday, madam."

The malevolent pig's eyes followed him in silence till he was out of the room. . . .

It was on Monday, then, that Lyveden called for his dog.

His decision to revisit the scene of his encounter with my lady was not fully formed until it was time to act upon it. He had deliberately walked in the direction of the inn, so that, when the hour came, he could, if he chose, indulge the inclination of which he was wholly ashamed. Honestly, he reflected, he had not a good word to say for the girl. (Observe, please, that the fact that the pleasaunce was to his liking did not weigh with him. The little inn and its curtilage had become but environs.) She had been unreasonable and worse than churlish. There was no getting away from it—she had been aggressively rude, administering a rebuff though he had made no advance. To pile Ossa upon Pelion, she now knew him for what he was—a flunkey, acting the gentleman and sporting a dog. And was not that a dainty dish for him to digest, sitting under the lime-trees in full view of that garden doorway which nine days ago had been so honoured? That, of course, was the trouble. Anthony had seen a picture which he could not forget. The girl had done her best to efface it, but had only succeeded in clouding a sunny memory.

With something of the *mauvaise honte* with which a player of " Patience " corrects a mistake he has made by restoring some cards, Anthony took Ossa off Pelion, said to himself, " I don't believe she recognized me," and, walking into the inn, desired the mistress to bring him some tea.

By the time he had finished his meal he had sunk so low in his own eyes—lost so much self-respect, that the rest did not seem worth keeping, and he inquired whether anything had been seen of the lady whose dog his had fought, in much the same spirit of recklessness as moves a bravo to toss his last piece to a beggar.

" She had tea here the day before yesterday, sir," replied his hostess. " All alone, with her little dog. I don't think he's none the worse, sir. Thank you. Good day, sir."

Anthony left the house like a man in a dream. . . .
Why had she come?

To this question the answer which his heart vouchsafed was vain and a vanity. His head, however, gave

innumerable replies—all of them obvious and none of
them flattering. A hundred times Reason drove Hope
headlong, but always the baggage returned. . . .

By way of relieving his feelings, Anthony cursed Mrs.
Slumper with earnest bitterness. He began to feel that
there was much in what the chauffeur had said about
her forbears. At the time he had secretly deplored his
epithets, but now. . . . Certainly he had misjudged
the fellow. He was quite right.

As for Patch, he had never been paid so little attention. Not that he cared. The country was full of
scents. . . .

By a quarter past seven Lyveden was back at Lancaster Gate.

The first thing he saw below stairs was the library
silver, which he had cleaned that morning and the
parlour-maid should have restored to its place. Without
waiting to change, he picked up the tray and carried
it upstairs, intending, if the room was unoccupied, to
replace it at once.

As he gained the hall, the twitch of an inserted latch-
key came to his ears. Then pressure was put upon the
front door. This, however, remained fast shut. The
key was withdrawn violently, reinserted, and wrenched.
The pressure upon the door being maintained, the lock
was jammed. Whosoever was there had lost his temper
and was kicking against the pricks. This was unlike Mr.
Slumper, but it could be nobody else. Lyveden set
down his tray and stepped to the door. . . .

His master came in with a rush, stumbling. Anthony
caught him, and he recovered his balance. There was
running sweat upon his face, which was all grey, and he
was shaking fearfully. Holding on to the furniture as
he went, he tottered as far as the library, clawed at the
switch by the door, missed it, and swayed out of sight
into the black of the room.

Anthony stood spellbound. The spectacle of a bunch

of keys dangling idly from the keyhole of the door, which he was still holding open, brought him to his senses, and, drawing the key from the lock, he closed the door swiftly and ran for brandy. . . .

Mr. Slumper was sitting in the dark, with his head plunged between his knees. At Anthony's coming he started up and would have gone back, but the seat of his chair catching him under the hocks, he subsided again almost immediately. Anthony went to his side and held the glass to his lips. As he drank, his teeth chattered upon the rim of the tumbler, and some of the spirit ran over his chin. Twice he made a gesture for more. After the third dose he had swallowed more than a tumblerful. . . . Presently he began to look less grey, and the trembling abated. In three or four minutes he was quite calm. Anthony was about to ask if he should help him upstairs, when he spoke suddenly.

" Shut t' door."

Anthony did his bidding. When he came back, his master had a letter-case in his hand.

" What are your wages ? " he said.

" Seventy-two pounds a year, sir."

Mr. Slumper put a hand to his brow and knitted this wearily, as if the effort of calculation was more than he could bear. Then he took out two five-pound notes and two one-pound notes.

" There's twelve pound," he said slowly. " One month's wages, and another's in lieu of notice."

Anthony stared at the money.

" I haven't been here a month yet, sir."

His master waved aside the objection.

" Only honest servant I've ever had," he said shortly. " Gentleman, aren't you ? Never mind. Couldn't let you down. Others can go to hell, but not you. And now—better clear out. Right away. Get your box and go. Don't let the others see you. Give 'em the slip."

" But—but won't you be dining, sir ? " said Anthony desperately. He was trying instinctively to grapple with a situation which had put him upon his back.

At the mention of dinner Mr. Slumper laughed hideously. The brandy was getting into its stride now, and colour was beginning to climb into his cheeks.

" Dining ? " he croaked. " Dining ? "

In a deliberate, imperturbable tone a clock upon the mantelpiece chimed the half-hour, and the laugh snapped off short. The next moment the man had Lyveden's arm in a grip of iron.

" Listen," he breathed. " I'm broke . . . ruined . . . got to run for it. Couldn't stand gaol at my age. It ain't pretty, I know, but I'm fifty-nine, Lyveden, fifty-nine." The tense utterance broke into a whimper. " An'—an' that's too old for prison, Lyveden, an' they wouldn't give me a chance. The lawyers 'd make it out bad. You can gamble with others' money as long as you win, Lyveden, but you mustn't lose . . . mustn't ever lose. There's a law against that."

All the soldier in Anthony came to his aid.

" Are you going now, sir ? " The other nodded. " Shall I get you a taxi ? "

" Yes." Mr. Slumper jerked a contemptuous head at the ceiling. " She'll have to go with me," he added thickly. " Can't leave the old fool."

" I'll keep your keys, sir," said Anthony, " to let myself in."

With that he was gone.

Mrs. Slumper was in the midst of a very delicate operation, to wit, the obliteration of her natural complexion—obsequies which not even her maid was permitted to attend. Consequently she was anything but pleased when her husband entered the room. Such procedure was out of all order and convenience. That he came in suddenly and without first knocking upon the door was insufferable. She turned herself round on her seat, bristling. . . .

There was no time for a scene, and, when Mrs. Slumper hurled herself against Necessity, she fell back bruised and broken.

When she would have screamed, a hand was clapped over her mouth, breaking her false teeth, and all her stifled shrieks, queries and expostulations were literally cuffed into a whimper. Five minutes later, toothless, half-dressed and trembling, she thrust a few things into a dressing-case, struggled into a fur coat, and passed with sagging knees downstairs, clinging to the arm of a bully whom she had known as a worm.

Lyveden was waiting in the hall, beside him his case and hold-all—what belongings he had thrust into them anyhow. He was intending to see the couple into the cab and then go quietly away, for he was determined to avoid the loathsome saturnalia with which his colleagues were certain to signalize the *débâcle*. When the two appeared, he started involuntarily. He had been prepared for violence, he had expected tears. . . . The vision of a blubbering idiot, that mowed and mumbled, its wig awry, its dreadful face blotched, like a clown's, with paint, swaddled from head to toe in gorgeous furs, leaning desperately upon the very reed it had broken—this was unearthly, hellish. He found himself praying that it might not visit him in his dreams. . . .

It is to his credit that Anthony, having helped Mr. Slumper into his hat and overcoat and Mr. and Mrs. Slumper into the taxi, flung his own kit upon the canopy and accompanied the fugitives to Charing Cross.

The horror of that drive revisited him for months. The awful pregnant silence, broken only by the sound of rapid irregular respiration, gave to the cab the air of a death-chamber.

Arrived at the station, by his advice the two remained

in the taxi whilst he procured tickets which would take them to the coast by the first available train. At the booking-office he learned, to his inexpressible relief, that they had but ten minutes to spare. He bought the tickets feverishly. . . .

As his master emerged from the cab, Lyveden perceived with a shock that his nervousness had begun to return. Terror was riding behind, coming up, overhauling him fast. The blood which had flooded his face had begun to recede. The hand that received the tickets and change was trembling. In a fever of anxiety the ex-officer hustled his charges towards the platform. . . .

People turned and stared as they passed. One woman screamed. . . .

At the sudden cry Mr. Slumper started violently. His face was very pale now, and there were tiny beads of sweat upon the side of his nose. His mouth was working painfully. It was a question whether they could board the train before he collapsed. The idiot upon his arm could have shambled another mile.

They came to the barrier.

Anthony had no ticket and could not pass, but he put them into the queue and steered them up to the gate.

The passenger behind Mr. Slumper turned suddenly and brushed against him. At the touch on his shoulder the poor devil started frightfully and drew in his breath with a hoarse whoop. The face that he turned to the offender was a wet grey. . . .

In front of them there were only two, now—one. They were in the jaws of the barrier. . . . Mr. Slumper had not the power to present his tickets, and the inspector took the pasteboard out of his shaking hand. He clipped it and handed it back, staring. Mr. Slumper fumbled, and the tickets fell to the ground. He stooped drunkenly, and the inspector put a hand under his arm.

'Gent ill 'ere, Joe," he threw over his shoulder, apparently addressing a colleague, whom Anthony could not see. "Give 'im a 'and up the platform."

Anthony heaved a sigh of relief.

The next moment he saw a burly station-constable— presumably "Joe"—step into view and put a broad arm tenderly about his master's back . . .

Mr. Slumper stiffened and stood quivering with the peculiar vibration of a wire that is taut. The ridiculous figure attached to him stood still also, rolling its head foolishly.

"Come along, sir," urged the official in a kindly tone.

Mr. Slumper stopped shaking, took out his handkerchief, and wiped his face. Then he turned to the speaker.

"It's all right," he said. "*I'll go quietly.*"

Anthony turned on his heel and walked out of the station.

There was no more to be done.

CHAPTER II

THE WAY OF A MAID

A FOOTMAN looked out of an attic in Eaton Square with his pen in his mouth. After a moment's reflection he returned to his letter, added a sentence or two, and signed his name. Then he restored its cork to his bottle of ink, blotted the lines he had written, and, gathering the flimsy pages into his hand, leaned back in his loose-limbed chair with the consideration which that exacting skeleton required of its patrons, and proceeded to read.

This, then, is our chance ; and, since Lyveden will be none the wiser, let us forget our manners and look over his shoulder.

DEAR TOBY,—

By extracting a promise that I would write to you you did me a good turn, for, while my first report was rendered from a sense of duty, I am making this one with a sense of relief—a somewhat scandalous admission. Of course a really good footman would keep his mouth shut. But then I am but an indifferent lackey.

To say that I left my first place would be untrue. In fact, the place left me—rather tragically, as it happened : which reminds me that I must withdraw anything which I have written to you in disparagement of my late master. The poor man had worries I did not know of, and behaved to me very handsomely at the last, remembering that I

*might have troubles, when he could not think straight, so
sore were his own.*

*For a week, then, I became a country gentleman, living
with my dog at a little inn where no ways met. By the
end of that time I had got me another place.*

*Yes, sir, I am in the service of the Marquess of Banff,
sir. There are times when I go powdered. I have even
hobnobbed with the scarlet livery of Royalty. I am, I
assure you, a very deuce of a fellow.*

*With the Marquess, who resembles an irritable baboon,
I have little to do. The marchioness—a strong woman
is also, mercifully, too much engaged upon works of
supererogation, which, in a rich bass, she styles "her
manifold duties," to observe my existence. Lord Pomfret
Fresne, however, a gilded youth with three thousand a year,
finds me extremely useful. I bet for him, I make appointments for him to have his hair trimmed, I retain stalls
for him, and occasionally I admit him to the house at an
unlawful hour. In fact, he is a confounded nuisance.
He is impertinent, grossly ignorant, and a niggard.
Moreover, Toby, he hath an eye whose like I have seen
before—once. Then it was set in the head of a remount
which, after it had broken a shoeing-smith's leg, was cast
for vice at Kantara in 1917.*

*"Lyveden," says he one day, "you're a gentleman,
aren't you?"*

It seemed easiest to say "Yes."

"Why?" says his lordship.

"It's a family failing," said I.

"How beastly! You mean, like drink?"

"Exactly, my lord. We never mention it."

*"No, don't," says he. "My mother's very hot on that
sort of thing. Hullo!" He peers into a gold cigarette-
case. "I had four pounds in here. I'll swear I had."*

*Considering that I had found the case in the library,
and had restored it to him five minutes before, his ejaculation was not in the best of taste. His lordship, how-*

ever, must whet his point upon the grindstone of insult.

"*You're not hard up, are you?*" *says he.*

"*I can pay my way, my lord.*"

"*Well, I know there was four pounds there, because——*
No. Wait a minute. It's all right. I remember I put
it in my coat. Which reminds me—I want a couple
of stalls at Daly's. You might ring up and get them.
How much is the pit?"

"*I'm not quite sure, my lord. It used to be half-a-*
crown."

"*Half-a-crown!*" *cries he.* "*I thought it was a*
shilling."

"*That's the gallery, my lord.*"

"*Oh, yes. Well, I can't afford the pit, Lyveden, but*
you can go to the gallery if you like," *and he produces a*
shilling.

I shake my head.

"*I'm much obliged to your lordship, but I seldom go*
out."

"*Right-o,*" *he says, with ill-concealed relief.* "*Don't*
forget those stalls."

It is pathetic, Toby, but it is true. And when I was
at Harrow, his eldest brother, who is one of the best, was
my fag.

When I say that, compared with the butler, Respect-
ability itself seems raffish, you will understand. He is a
monument, massive, meaningless, and about as useful
as a fan in a cyclone. Yet the household revolves about
him. He came in, I fancy, with the spittoon. . . .

And now I will show you that the cassock of the
confessor has indeed fallen upon you.

Listen. I have been disdained—given the cold shoulder.
Such a beautiful shoulder, Toby. Such a shoulder as
Artemis presented to Actæon. But there was good reason
for that. It fell on this wise. I sat in a garden and
mufti and looked at an aged doorway, thinking how fair a
frame it would make. And when next I looked, lo! there

was the picture, all warm and smiling, her little white hands about her dark, dark hair. I was overwhelmed. I would have slain dragons, levelled castles, broken the backs of knights for her sake. But before I was given the chance, I was given the shoulder. Now mark how a malicious Fate maketh a mock of me. But three days later I run full tilt into my lady, I, the same Anthony Lyveden— but with my livery on. In case that should not be enough, I presently return to the inn, to learn that I have missed her by forty-eight hours. Veux-tu m'en croire?

Beneath the unfair strain my poor vocabulary broke down. Indeed, I soon had no alternative but to repeat myself, thus violating what I know to be one of your most sacred rules.

Assez, j'en finis.

You are so distant and it will be so long before this letter reaches you, that it requires an effort steadily to regard you as a confidant. Already that impression of you is fainter than it was when I picked up my pen. A reply from you, Toby, would do much to revive it—would, in fact, turn into substance the shadow with which I am, rather desperately, cheating my common-sense.

A toi, mon beau,
ANTHONY LYVEDEN.

Having addressed this letter to Australia, Lyveden made the best of an enamelled basin and a mirror, which was not quite so good as one which, once upon a time, his servant had purchased in Port Said for five piastres. Then he put on his very expensive plum-coloured coat and descended twelve flights of stairs.

Five minutes later he opened the front door, confessed to an irreverent gentleman in blue and yellow that "Ole Flat-Feet" was at home, and, after conducting them to the first floor, ushered "The Honourable Mrs. George Wrangle, Miss Wrangle, Miss Sarah Wrangle" into the presence itself. With a contempt for tradition, the Marchioness not only extended to each of the ladies her large right hand, but withheld no one of its fingers.

The identity of the guests was then communicated to the butler, whose supervision of the service of tea depended upon the visitor's position in the table of precedence. That of Mrs. Wrangle, apparently, fell dismally short of the standard which the great man imposed, for, upon hearing her name, he stared indignantly upon a cat which was cleaning itself upon the hearth of his parlour, and then resumed the perusal of the *Morning Advertiser* in contemptuous silence.

Without more ado, Anthony repaired to the pantry. Five minutes later he and the second footman took up the tea.

" Is Lord Pomfret in ? " said the Marchioness.

" I will see, my lady," said Lyveden.

" Desire him to come in to tea."

" Very good, my lady."

Lord Pomfret had just returned from a luncheon-party, and was preparing to attend a *thé dansant*. His mother's command was abusively received. At length—

" Tell her I'm out, Lyveden."

Anthony hesitated.

" Her ladyship was very definite, my lord."

" D'you hear what I say ? "

" Very good, my lord."

The scepticism with which his mistress received Anthony's report was distressingly obvious. Also the faces of Mrs. and Miss Wrangle fell noticeably. Indeed, the bell which summoned Lyveden to speed their departure rang but a few minutes later.

As they descended the stairs, Lord Pomfret emerged from the library, cramming cigarettes into his case with the dishevelling manipulation of the belated swain.

The encounter was not a success.

Reason suggested to Mrs. Wrangle that the episode could be far more effectively dealt with if and when the offender became her son-in-law. Impulse, however, clamoured for immediate and appropriate action. Between the two stools her display of emotion fell flat. As for Pomfret, the knowledge that he had just induced the lady's footman to go for a taxi did not contribute to his peace of mind, and his manners became conspicuously devoid of that easy grace which should have gone with his title.

After the mechanical issue and acknowledgment of a few ghastly pleasantries, Lord Pomfret muttered something about " hearing his mother calling " and fled with precipitate irrelevance in the direction of the back stairs, leaving Mrs. Wrangle speechless with indignation and bitterly repenting her recent indecision. She swept past Anthony as if she were leaving a charnel-house. Her daughters, who took after their father, walked as though they were being expelled. . . .

When their mother found herself confronted with the choice of leaving without her footman or awaiting that gentleman's successful return from the mission upon which he had been dispatched, it required their united diplomacy to deter her from there and then returning to lay the outrageous facts before Lady Banff.

Mrs. Wrangle's complaint, however, was posted that evening.

By the time it arrived, Lord Pomfret had prepared his defence. This he conducted so skilfully that the Marchioness, who believed in red justice, sent for Lyveden and told him two things. The first was that in future, when she sent him for anyone, he would be good enough to look for them before returning to say they were out. The second was that when he was told to fetch a cab, he would be good enough to do so, instead of persuading other people's servants to do his work. Lord Pomfret, who was present at the arraign-

ment, supported his mother dutifully. Anthony said
nothing at all. Four and a half years in the Army
had left their mark.

*   *   *   *   *

If Lyveden was a Conservative, so was his dog. For
the two there was only one walk in all Hertfordshire,
and that, after six fair miles, brought them thirsty or
wet, as the weather might order, to the shade or shelter
of *The Leather Bottel*. This was, in fact, Anthony's
country house. Here for one glorious week the two
had shared the same bed. Heaven only knew when
such a prolonged visit would be repeated. It had cost
two whole pounds, and, do what he would, Anthony
could save very little out of his wages. Of his six
pounds a month the Dogs' Home took four precious
guineas. Then there were railway fares at three shillings
a time—twelve shillings a month. Teas, clothes, and
a little—a very little—tobacco had to be paid for. It
was a tight fit.

With his back to a beech tree, Lyveden thought
upon these things. The weather, perhaps, invited
Melancholy.

Without the wood a sudden shower was falling down
from heaven, drenching anew wet pastures, thinning
the mud upon brown lanes, poppling upon the washed
highway. Dainty scale-armour of a million leaves
protected Anthony. Ere this was penetrated, the
fusillade would have stopped.

It was more than a month now since he had seen
the lady. At the moment he supposed gloomily that
she had gone out of his life. Considering what his life
was, it was just as well. (Melancholy smiled to herself,
sighed sympathetically, and laid her dark head upon
Anthony's shoulder.) His thoughts flew over the
blowing country to Eaton Square. The squalor of
his bedroom rose up before him. The walls were
peeling, and upon one there was a vast brown stain.

The floor was bare. The cracked American cloth upon the chest of drawers made this a washstand. The fact that the *ensemble* had lost a foot made it unsteady. True, some one had placed a Bradshaw under the bereaved corner, but the piece listed heavily. The Bradshaw, by the way, was out of date. In fact, its value as a guide to intending passengers had expired on the thirty-first of October, 1902. That looked as if the chest were an antique. Three of the china knobs, however, which served as handles were unhappily missing. Then there was a flap beneath the window which, when raised, arrested the progress of such smuts as failed to clear it in their descent to the boards. (Melancholy smothered a laugh and laid a wet cheek against her victim's.) The smuts were devilish—the terror by night, the arrow that flieth by day. Anthony believed in fresh air. Also he believed in cleanliness. His twofold faith cost his convenience dear. He had begged a dust-sheet from the housekeeper with which to cover his bed during the day, and regularly, before retiring, shook an ounce of soot out of his window. The bed, by the way, was overhung by the wall, which, for some reason best known to those who built it, deserted the perpendicular for an angle of forty-five, three inches from Anthony's nose. The candlestick had seen merrier days : that there might be no doubt about the matter, it said as much, announcing in so many words that it was "A Present from Margate." . . .

Scaramouche Melancholy fairly squirmed with delight. Then she turned upon Anthony eyes swimming with tenderness, put up consoling lips. . . . The entrance of Polichinelle, however, cudgel and all, in the shape of a little white dog, dragging a bough with him, spoiled her game. Harlequin Sun, too, flashed out of hiding—before his cue, really, for the shower was not spent.

Scaramouche fled with a snarl.

At Polichinelle's obvious request, Anthony seized
the spare end of the bough, and the two tugged with
a will—an agreeable tourney, which was always eventually settled in the lists of Frolic itself. And, whiles
they strove, Harlequin danced in and out the trees,
with magic touch of bat making the mizzle shimmer
and the meadows gleam, and finally, with rare exuber-
ance, breaking his precious colours overhead, to say
the masque was over and bid the racing winds hustle
away the fretful scenery and clear the stage of sky for
his possession.

Master and dog made their way to the inn jubilantly
enough.

As he devoured his tea, Lyveden thought again of
the girl—more cheerfully. Indeed, he made bold to
decide that she was interested in him. That such
interest sprang from the loins of Curiosity he admitted
readily. Its origin did not matter ; the trouble was to
keep it alive.

It is obvious that he himself was more than interested. He was, I suppose, in love. At the moment
when he had looked upon her for the first time his
heart had leaped. Instantly the man knew that he
had seen his maid. He had no doubt of it at all, but
was quite positive. If a million Archangels had
appeared and with one voice told him that he was
wrong, he would have shaken his head with a smile.
His heart had leaped, and there was an end of it. He
just *knew*. In view of the prospective failure of so
many Archangels, it is not surprising that my lady
herself, whatever she did, would not be able to erase
this impression. Consequently though she had behaved
to his face with a manner which it was a Quixotic
courtesy to style " disdain," Anthony never wavered.
For a second of time he had seen beyond the veil—
at least, his heart had—and, now that he knew what
it hid, all reinforcement of that veil was out of date.

My lady might line it with oak, with brass, with masonry miles thick—and all her labour would be in vain. All the same, Anthony hoped devoutly that she would do nothing of the kind. . . .

With a sigh he drank to their next meeting.

Then he called the terrier and set him upon his knee.

"My fellow," said he, "listen. In these very precincts you committed an aggravated assault upon an Irish terrier. I don't blame you. He probably deserved it. But—he belongs to the lady—my lady, Patch, the only lady in the world. And she didn't like it, my boy. She didn't like it at all. So remember, if ever we meet her again, you mustn't fight. I don't want to be hard on you, but you mustn't. Of course, if you could show him a little courtesy—indicate a scent which will repay investigation, or something—I should be exalted. But I don't press that. A strictly non-committal attitude will serve. But aggression—no. Patch, I trust you. I know it's difficult for you to understand, but you'll be a good dog and try, won't you? For my sake, Patch?"

Whether the Sealyham in fact appreciated the nature and gravity of the request is a matter which cannot be decided upon this side of the grave. The fact remains that when, upon entering the grounds of the Dogs' Home some thirty-five minutes later, he encountered that very Irish terrier, looking rather sorry for himself and attached to the end of a long lead, he walked straight up to him and bestowed upon him as generous a greeting as his nostrils and tail could convey.

Anthony could hardly believe his eyes. . . .

At the other end of the lead was a kennelman, who spoke quickly and to the point.

"Beggin' your pardon, sir, but I wouldn't let 'im talk to 'im. 'E's not very grand—this little dog ain't. I think it's only a chill, but we've hisolated 'im, in case . . ."

D

Patch was summoned peremptorily, to come running wide-eyed. Happily in his sight his master could do no wrong ; otherwise it is possible that he might have thought himself hardly used and love's labour lost indeed.

Anthony passed into the hall, thinking furiously.

With Patch under his arm, he spoke to the fair-haired girl in charge of the office.

" I've seen a dog out there that I recognize—an Irish terrier. He's not very well, your man said. May I know whose he is ? "

" Oh, yes. He belongs to Miss French—Miss Valerie French. He's a nice little dog, isn't he ? "

If Anthony Lyveden had reflected, it would have occurred to him that his informant had been, as they say, " very quick in the uptake." The truth was that less than a week ago Miss Valerie French had recognized Patch and had asked the same girl for the name of his owner.

" He's a beauty," said Anthony. " Does she keep him here all the time ? "

" When she's in London," said the girl. " I expect you've seen her. She's very often down."

Anthony nodded.

" I think I must have," he said.

Then he made much of Patch and handed him over.

" See you next week, little Patch. Next Saturday. Only a week from to-day. Good-bye, little fellow."

He ruffled the tousled head with a last caress, smiled at the puzzled brown eyes, and turned away. . . .

There was no sweet sorrow about these partings. They were purely abominable.

At the very hour that Lyveden walked heavily down the wet lanes on his way to the station, Valerie French, who was to dine early and go to the play, was sitting before her dressing-table in an apricot kimono.

The evening sun stared into her bedroom mercilessly

and found no fault in it. It was a broad low room, full of soft colours and the warm glow of highly polished wood. Walls, curtains, and carpet were all of powder-blue ; an old rose fabric covered what seats there were ; an apple-green coverlet filled up the symphony. That taper elegance which modern craftsmanship can give mahogany was most apparent, lending the usual suite unusual comeliness. A great pier-glass flashed in a corner, upon a little table beside a deep chair a bowl of roses sweetened the London air, above the well-found bed dangled an ivory switch.

If the chamber was fair, so was my lady.

Looking upon her beauty, as she sat at the glass, Valerie French might have felt very proud. But, if we pry into her mind, it will be seen that her thoughts were otherwise occupied. Indeed, the fixing of her hair—usually so simple a matter—was making her knit her brow. The fact that the soft dark tresses had been washed that morning made them unruly. In vain the pointed fingers strove to secure and order them to their mistress's liking. . . .

At length, with a sigh, she brought her hands to her lap.

Then she made a mouth at the reflection of her labours.

" I look like his Sealyham," she said.

* * * * *

It was on Monday morning that Lord Pomfret suggested to Lyveden the propriety of putting a pound each way on Slip Along.

" I don't suppose the swine's any good," said his lordship moodily. " But he'll probably start at twenty, so I may as well have a dart. I forget who told me about him."

" Very good, my lord," said Anthony.

To receive this commission, he had been summoned from the drawing-room, whose floor he was engaged in leathering to the requisite degree of lustre. He had had to remove an apron, turn down his sleeves, and put on his plum-coloured coat. So soon as his lordship, who was yet at breakast, released him, he would reverse the procedure and return to his floor.

Lord Pomfret peered muttering into his cigarette case. Then he plucked out a ten-shilling note and flicked it across the tablecloth.

" That's all I appear to have," he said sulkily. " I'll have to owe you the thirty shillings."

Anthony braced himself.

" I'm afraid I haven't any money at all, my lord." The other looked up sharply.

" What ? . . . Oh, nonsense, Lyveden."

Anthony said nothing. He was not anxious to repeat the lie, but he was determined not to lend to Lord Pomfret. That the loan would lose itself was much too probable, and the construction of his slender resources would not stand such a strain.

" Of course you've got thirty shillings. But you don't like parting." Lord Pomfret laughed rather nastily. " I'll pay you back, man, if that's your trouble."

" I haven't the money, my lord."

The youth stared at Anthony furiously. Then—

" Oh, go to hell ! " he said thickly.

Anthony picked up the note and placed it beside his lordship. Then he left the room and returned to his work.

Lord Pomfret was exceedingly wrath. In fact, he brooded over the incident. This augured ill for Anthony. The cold fact that in due season—to be precise, at eleven minutes to four that same afternoon— Slip Along won his race easily did not improve matters. That he started at thirty-three to one was still less digestible. . . .

When his lordship read the news at half-past five,

he broke into a cold sweat. Then he bit savagely at the nail of his favourite thumb. Considering that, so recently as that morning, he had reluctantly decided that that toothsome *entremet* must be allowed to go unmolested for at least a week, his action was indicative of an emotion which knew no rules. That he made no mention of the matter to Anthony, was the ugliest omen of all.

Two days later the second footman called Anthony, who was crossing the hall.

It was a fine July morning, and the famous square was full of sunlight and clear-cut shadows and the soft swish of leaves. All this could be marked from the hall, for the front door stood wide open, and a fresh cool breeze came floating into the mansion, to flirt with the high and mighty curtains upon the landing, jostle the stately palms, and ruffle up the pompous atmosphere with gay irreverence. The air itself would have told you the hour. The intermittent knocks of a retreating postman declared the time even more accurately.

" 'Ere's a letter fer you, mate," said the second footman. " ' A. Lyveden, Esquire,' it says, all bald-like. No C.M.G., no B.F., no nothin'. I should 'ave a raow abaout this."

Anthony came grinning.

" P'r'aps their *Who's Who*'s out of date," he said. The other shook his head.

" It's the deecay of menners, mate," he said sorrowfully, turning to resume the sorting operation upon which he was engaged.

The letter bore the postmark of a village in Hertfordshire, and proved to be a communication from the Dogs' Home at which Patch was lodged.

DEAR SIR,
I am sorry to inform you that your Sealyham has con-

tracted distemper. There is at present no reason to think that he will be seriously ill, and the veterinary surgeon is quite satisfied with his condition.

Yours faithfully,

N. DAWES,

Supt.

Anthony stared at the sheet as it had been a death-warrant. It must be remembered that Patch was all that he had in the world.

The second footman, who had been perusing a post-card addressed to the Marchioness, placed the missive upon the top of his mistress's letters and fell to whistling softly between his teeth. When he glanced round to see Anthony so still, he stopped his fluting in the midst of a bar.

" Wot's up, mate ? " he said eagerly. " 'Ad some bad noos ? "

Anthony folded the sheet and put a hand to his head.

" My little dog's ill," he said. " He's down in the country, and—it's rather worrying."

The other looked at him curiously. Then—

" That's the worst o' dawgs," he said sagely. " Yer goes an' gets fon' of 'em, an' then they gets run over, or dies, or somethin'. Cats is the same. My sister's little gurl 'ad a kitten with one eye. Thort the world o' that cat, she did. 'Adn't got no use fer dolls nor nothin'. ' Moses,' she called it. One day a bull-terrier does it in." He paused dramatically, raising his eyes to heaven with an air of reminiscent resignation which spoke volumes. " Me sister thort the kid'd go aout of 'er mine. In the en' they 'ad to send 'er away."

Anthony listened to the anecdote with what politeness he could, hoping desperately that time would prove its irrelevance.

" Poor little girl," he said quietly.

" But she got over it orright, mate. Same as wot you

will. You see. 'Sides," he added, with the gesture of one who adduces a still stronger argument, " 'e ain't dead yet. Don't you meet trouble 'alf-way, mate. It ain't good enough."

For this philosophy there was much to be said, and Anthony did his best to practise it. When he had sent a telegram, asking to be informed daily of his dog's progress, and advised by wire or telephone if there was any danger, he felt more comfortable. The day, however, dragged heavily. . . .

Happily Lord Pomfret made few demands upon his patience. For all that, his lordship had formed a new habit, which Anthony—partly because he was preoccupied, partly because he had but two eyes—failed to observe. This was a pity, for while it was not a pretty habit, it happened to concern Anthony pretty closely. The trick was this. So often as he and Lyveden were in the same room, his lordship's watery eyes would follow the footman wheresoever he moved.

It may be urged that a cat may look at a king. True.

But if a cat were detected in the act of looking at a king as Lord Pomfret Fresne had come to look at Anthony Lyveden, it is safe to predict not only that the animal would be afforded no further opportunity of inspecting his majesty, but that in about two minutes he would, like poor Moses, be put to sleep with his fathers.

* * * * *

By the same post which so discomfited Anthony, came to Miss Valerie French two letters, one at least of which must be set out.

> c/o Joseph Bumble, Esq.,
> The Shrubbery,
> Hawthorne.

DEAR VAL,

Send your pal along. The Bumbles will jump at him. As for us, if our present colleague wasn't under notice to leave, we should be. Of course he can have his dog here

*Haven't I got José? And if a parlour-maid can keep
one,* d'autant plus *a footman. Pending the dismissal
of the colleague referred to, Anne and I have to do more
than we should, and are a little bored with Life. George
has the best time with the car, but we make him help in
the house. When are you coming to Bell Hammer?
George and I were there on Sunday, and it looks topping.*

Love from us all,

BETTY.

The other dispatch was from Printing House Square.
Its envelope, being opened, was found to contain three
other envelopes, each bearing the same superscription,
viz., " Box Y 779, c/o *The Times.*"

Valerie opened them eagerly.

They were, all three, applications for the post of a
gentleman-footman.

After satisfying herself that no one of these was signed
by Lyveden, Valerie tossed them aside unread. Then
she propped herself on her elbow and poured out a cup
of tea.

That Fate buffets her favourites is sometimes true.
Here we catch the baggage red-handed. With one
cold relentless palm she threatens to take from Anthony,
who hath not, even that which he hath : with the other
she is strawing blossoms upon what is to be his path.
With her right hand she robs the beggar, with the left
she prepares for him a bed of roses.

The lady of Anthony's heart loved him. It is no
good beating about the bush. Pity may be akin to
Love, but Interest is the boy's first cousin. Whether
her heart had leaped, when she saw him, is not for me to
say. She looked upon him, saw that he was good,
made up her mind—and that was settled. The fact
that she immediately turned her back upon him has
nothing to do with the question, but may, if you please,
be construed as confirming her plight.

Had the round world been ten thousand years younger, when she and Anthony looked the one upon the other in the garden of *The Leather Bottel*, he would have put his arms about her, and she would have suffered him, and there in the shadow of the little inn this tale would have come to an end.   That it did not so end then and there is the fault partly of a crop of conventions, which have in so many years increased out of all belief and now stand bristling between Impulse and Action, and partly of the contrariness of women, which is, we know, very ancient, but not so old as all that.   It is these two marplots, which you must bless or curse, gentlemen, as the fancy takes you.

Valerie French, then, was trying to bring Lyveden into smooth water.   She had already earmarked a congenial billet at The Shrubbery, Hawthorne.   The difficulty was to make Anthony apply for the post. Since Mrs. Bumble could hardly be advised to ask a footman to quit the service of the Marquess of Banff, Valerie, who was determined to remain incognito, had recourse to the Press.   Her advertisement for a gentleman-footman appeared daily.

When my lady had drunk her tea, she turned to the telephone.   After a little delay, she was connected to the Dogs' Home in Hertfordshire.   Presently the superintendent spoke. . . .

' Miss French's Irish terrier was not too grand.   He was coughing a little.   There was no real cause for anxiety, but he was not out of the wood.'

" I'll be down this afternoon," said Valerie.

She was as good as her word.

And since, to her grief, the little brown dog was nothing bettered, but rather grew worse, she visited him the next day also and the day after that.

And so it happened that she was at the Home on Friday, when Patch's condition gave rise to such uneasiness as presently decided the superintendent to tete-phone to his master. Indeed, the fair-haired girl had discussed with Valerie the advisability of so doing.

" Mr. Lyveden's a busy man, I fancy, and we hate worrying people. But he's simply devoted to the dog, and he's pretty bad."

" I think," said Valerie slowly, " I think he ought to be told."

" Perhaps you're right, Miss French," said the girl. " I'll go and ring up."

She slipped out of the hospital, through the garden, and presently into her office.

It was perhaps ten minutes before she could speak with London. Then—

" Is that Lord Banff's house ? " she inquired.

" Yes. Who are you ? " said an unpleasant voice.

" Oh, can I speak to Mr. Lyveden ? "

" *Who ?* "

" Mr. Lyveden."

An exclamation of surprise came to her ears. . . . Then an oath. . . . Then a smothered laugh. . . .

The girl frowned with impatience. At length—

" Hullo," said the voice.

" Can I speak to Mr. Lyveden ? " she repeated.

" No, you can't. He's—he's out."

" Oh ! Well, it's rather important. Could you give him a message ? "

" Try me," said the voice.

" Will you tell him that his dog is not so well ? "

" What dog ? "

" *His* dog. His Sealyham. Mr. Lyveden will understand."

" Oh, will he ? " said the voice. " And where do I come in, Mabel ? "

For a moment the fair-haired girl stared at the instrument. Then she flushed angrily and rang off. . . .

At the other end of the line Lord Pomfret replaced his receiver with a hideous leer.

The superintendent returned to the hospital.

" Did you speak to him ? " said Valerie.

" No, Miss French. He was out. I had to leave a message."

Valerie rose to her feet.

Observing her movement, the Irish terrier rose also and got shakily upon his legs. The effort set him coughing again, poor fellow, and he had to submit to the paroxysm before he could wag his tail. How stiffly this moved, his mistress, whose eyes were full of tears, did not remark. Nor did she notice the suggestion of impotence about his hindquarters. With her practised eye, the fair-haired girl noticed both symptoms and bit her lip.

Valerie caressed her favourite and turned to a grey-headed kennel-man who had just entered the room.

" Are you going to wash his face ? "

" Yes, ma'am."

The Irish terrier was plainly pleased to see his old nurse.

" How is the little Sealyham ? "

" 'Tis a sick dog, ma'am."

Valerie turned away.

The superintendent escorted her back to the house.

" I'll be down to-morrow morning," she said.

" Very well, Miss French."

As she walked down the drive, Valerie wondered miserably whether she was treading it for almost the last time.

* * * * *

When upon Saturday morning Anthony received no bulletin from Hertfordshire, he did not know what to think. In the ordinary way he would have telegraphed, but telegrams cost money, which he really could not afford, and he was, in any event, to visit the Dogs' Home that afternoon. . . . He decided to do nothing. All the same, he was far from easy, for

Friday morning's report had said that his terrier was not so well.

He went about his work abstractedly, glancing at the faces of the clocks times without number.

At five-and-twenty minutes past two, just as he was going to change, Lord Pomfret sent for him. Anthony ground his teeth. The man was his evil genius.

Mercifully the interview was a short one.

His lordship produced two pounds and curtly instructed the footman to expend the money upon the purchase of roses.

"They've got to be good ones, and you ought to be able to get stacks for two quid. I shan't want them till to-morow morning, so they've got to be fresh. You'd better get them as late as you can, and put them in water directly you get in. That's all."

"Very good, my lord."

Lord Pomfret returned to the perusal of *La Vie*, and Anthony stepped to the door. As he was passing out—

"Lyveden," said his lordship sharply.

"Yes, my lord."

"I shall want to see the bill."

Anthony hesitated, inwardly raging. Then—

"Very good, my lord," he said huskily.

Ten minutes later he was out of the house.

Along the road of Life goes bowling the coach of Destiny, and we poor passengers inside know neither whither we are being borne nor how long shall be our journey. Now and again the horses are pulled up, the door is opened, that grim guard Fate calls out a name, and one of us climbs pitifully forth, to pass with faltering steps into a sable hostelry. We that are left behind peer after him curiously. . . . Then the door is slammed, with a lurch the coach is off again on its eternal wayfaring, and we poor passengers inside sit betwixt hope and fear, wondering vainly what the next mile of road will bring to each of us.

Climb up upon the box-seat, gentlemen, if you will see what is to become of Anthony : so I am with you, you will not be sent packing.

Look how he is being borne unwitting over the Bridge of Care, into the Valley of Love, by Thicket Perilous, clean through the Waters of Anger to where the white road curls over that grey upland, and we can see it no more. As well for Anthony that he has not our knowledge. The next league or so will play the deuce with his emotions. . . .

One last look, gentlemen. Can you see that cypress there, tall by the wayside, down in the Valley of Love ? We will descend there, by your leave, for the driver will pull up his horses and the coach will stop. A dog has to be set down—a little dog, gentlemen, with rough hair and as soft brown eyes as ever you saw. . . .

Anthony covered the distance between the station and the Dogs' Home at a good round pace. In fact, he was somewhat out of breath when a maid admitted him to the house and, leaving him in the hall, went in search of the superintendent.

As the fair-haired girl made her appearance, his heart began to beat furiously.

" How's my little dog ? " he said jerkily.

The girl looked grave.

" I'm afraid he's pretty bad, Mr. Lyveden. He's naturally very strong, and we hope that'll pull him through. We ought to know one way or the other within twelve hours."

" I see," said Anthony dully. " When I didn't hear, I hoped——"

" Didn't you get my telephone message ? "

Anthony shook his head.

" When did you ring up ? "

" Yesterday. I spoke to somebody—a man, and

asked him to tell you. I don't know who it was."

Anthony went very white.

"I fancy I do," he said grimly, and drew in a quick breath. "And now may I see my dog?"

The fair-haired girl led the way to the hospital.

The building, which stood by itself, was as fresh and cool as a dairy, and a faint clean smell of sanitary fluid rose from its tiled floor. In the hall were a table and a watchman's chair. Half a dozen rooms led out of the hall. The girl went straight to the door of one of these, turned the handle gently, and the next moment they were in the little chamber. This was full of light and air, for the French windows, which gave on to a broad veranda, were wide open. Upon the garden beyond the sun was shining gloriously.

By the side of the great square basket set in a corner Anthony fell on his knees.

"Why, Patch . . ."

The little scrap tried gamely to leap for his master, but his strength failed him, and he fell sideways on to the pine shavings. Lyveden gathered him gently into his arms and let him lick his face.

"Did you think I was never coming, Patch? Did you think I'd forgotten my little dog? My poor little fellow . . . my little boy. . . ."

The laboured breathing slipped into a cough, and Lyveden laid the terrier back on the shavings. There he got to his feet and coughed desperately. The exertion seemed to exhaust him, for, when the fit was over, he lay down where he stood, keeping his eyes upon Anthony and now and again moving his little tail.

The fair-haired girl, who had gone, reappeared, followed by the grey-headed kennel-man bearing a deck-chair.

"I expect you'll like to stay with him for a bit," she said pleasantly.

Anthony thanked her, and she left him alone.

For Patch's sake, Anthony sat very still.

Considering that he had been afoot since half-past five, it is not surprising that after a little space he fell asleep.

Queer idiotic fancies bestrode his dreams : what was impossible came naturally to pass : earth became wonderland, and no one wondered. Patch and Miss French lay in sick beds upon respective mantelpieces : Lord Pomfret had come to mend the telephone, and his tool-bag was full of roses—the scent of them filled the room. Anthony himself was forging a two-pound note upon a page of Bradshaw, and was terribly afraid that it would not pass muster : something weighty depended on this, and all the time the scent of the roses was hindering his efforts : it came between him and the paper, so that he could not see : he brushed it away angrily, but it came back. . . .

He awoke suddenly, for no reason.

Patch was lying very still, breathing more easily. His eye met Anthony's, and the tip of a red tongue came into view.

The faintest suggestion of perfume was in the air. This was so slight and fleeting that Anthony, after a little, charged it to his imagination and thought no more of it.

Presently he rose and, setting his hat on the chair, where Patch could see it and so expect his return, strolled out on to the veranda.

From the depths of an easy-chair Valerie French lifted her eyes from *The Times* and smiled very charmingly.

"I'm glad you've come out," she said. "I think it's a mistake to sit there too long at a time."

That Lyveden felt perfectly at ease with her, and neither started nor spoke constrainedly, is worthy of note. It is, in fact, the best possible evidence that his belief in their affinity was well founded.

" You're quite right," he said. " After all, the great
thing is to be on the spot. I'm afraid this means that
your dog is ill."

Valerie looked away.

" He's worse than Patch," she said slowly.

" I'm awfully sorry."

As he spoke, Anthony remembered how the dogs
had met in the drive a week ago. That, then, was how
Patch had come by the sickness. Her dog had infected
him.

Valerie looked up suddenly.

" I'm afraid I was awfully rude at the inn that day,"
she said quietly. " It was rotten of me."

" No, it wasn't," said Lyveden quickly. " You were
startled and upset and——"

" I've said all that to myself—several times. But
it won't wash. It was just rotten, and I'm very
sorry."

Had she been other than my lady, Anthony would
have felt like a beggar whose feet a queen was washing.
As it was, he felt like a king.

" I knew you never meant it," he said.

" Why ? "

" Because it wasn't like you."

" How could you know that ? " said Valerie.

" I don't know. I suppose I guessed. I suppose
. ." Anthony hesitated, and the colour came into his
cheeks. " I think I know you too well."

Valerie French nodded, as if she had received a reply
which she knew to be correct.

" You're very fond of your dog," she said.

" He's all I've got."

" All ? Haven't you a single friend ? "

" Not one," said Anthony.

A little cough came to her vigilant ears, and Valerie
rose to her feet. As she came to the window, she
stopped and looked at Anthony with a quiet smile.

"I don't think you ought to say that," she said gently. "Not since you know me so well."

Long after she had passed in, Lyveden stood gazing at the threshold from which she had spoken. . . .

The veterinary surgeon was with Patch.

After a tender examination, he rose to his feet, and Anthony introduced himself.

"He's a fine little dog," said the other. "And he makes a good patient, but I'm afraid he's in for a bad time." He turned to the kennel-man. "Have you warned Williams and Minter?"

"I have, sir."

"That's right. From now on, he mustn't be left."

"Will he have some brandy, sir?"

"Not yet."

In answer to Anthony's questions, the surgeon spoke plainly.

"He's getting steadily worse. That will go on for anything from six to twelve hours. Then one of two things will become apparent—either that he will recover, or that he can't."

"What about my being with him?"

"If you like to be near, sir, yes. As to being in the room—he's a highly-strung little fellow, and in the circumstances I don't advise it. Of course, if there was any sudden change . . ."

"I'm in your hands," said Anthony. "I'll leave my hat here. Then he'll know that I'm at hand."

"You couldn't do better, sir."

The surgeon was patently glad of an owner who would do as he said.

Anthony stooped to touch the damp muzzle. . . .

Then he stole gently away.

Out on the verandah he made his plans. Not for fifty Marquesses would he leave ere the change had come. He decided to telegraph to the butler. Perhaps they would understand. Any way, it could not be

E

helped. If he were to be dismissed, he would try again. Only the fear of unemployment had kept him in Eaton Square. The very thought of Lord Pomfret made his blood boil. Perhaps, even if they said nothing, it would be better to leave.

He picked up my lady's *Times*. . . .

The trouble was that the demand for men-servants seemed rather small. Married couples, apparently, were all the rage. Of course he was getting good wages. The substance might not be toothsome, but it was better than shadow. At least, you could get your teeth into it.

WANTED.—A gentleman-footman : country : good wages : would be allowed to keep dog. Box Y779, c/o The Times. E.C.4.

Anthony stared at the lines as if they were unreal. . . .

Then came the flutter of a frock and herself stepped on to the veranda. Mechanically Anthony set down the paper as if it had been contagious.

Valerie did not speak of her terrier, nor did she ask after Patch. Instead—

" If we went up to the house," she said gravely, " I think they would give us some tea." Together they left the veranda and passed through the pleasant grounds. " I've got a room in the village," she added, " and I've sent for some things for the night. Will—will you have to go ? "

" No. I shall stay. I can make shift." He smiled " The Army's a good school."

" Do you wish you were back ? " said Valerie.

" I don't think so. A school has its drawbacks. If I were back in the Army, I couldn't be staying to-night."

Without thinking—

" You like to be your own master ? " said the girl, and could have bitten her tongue in sunder.

Anthony winced. Then—

" Yes," he said slowly, " I do."

Valerie thought frantically. Then—

" That's the best of being a man," she said. " Take our two cases. You have your own establishment—at least, I suppose you have—your own chambers, your own servant. I live with an aunt. If I broke away and set up a separate menage, I should be talked about. To be her own mistress and excite no remark, a girl must be in penury."

Anthony's heart seemed to have stopped beating. The murder was out. From my lady's words it was plain that she did not know his calling. She had not recognized him, then, that night with his livery on. Fool ! He might have known that she would not— could not hobnob with a lackey.

Instead of combating her statement, he made some knock-kneed reply. . . .

For setting wheels within wheels, you cannot match Fortune. After all, she has made trochilics her hobby through all the ages. Look at her handiwork here. Jill knows Jack for a flunkey and seeks to dissemble her knowledge, for fear of bruising his heart. As for Jack, when Jill stumbles upon his secret, he curses his luck : now that he believes it inviolate, he is in despair.

Tea was served to them in a quiet parlour. It being their first meal together, their friendship should have grown fat. Instead, it lost weight steadily. They were ill at ease—both of them. To make things worse, Anthony began to feel that he was an impostor.

He walked with her to the village and sent his telegram. Later they dined together. They dared not go far away, and the landlord of a neighbouring inn was persuaded to serve eggs and bacon. This he did with an ill grace, and, that there might be no mistake about his annoyance, charged for it in the bill. Anthony paid the amount as if it were nothing, and Valerie French writhed. . . .

Afterwards they strolled in the garden and sat upon the veranda. The hours which should have been so wonderful went by lack-lustre. Between the two a phantom barrier had been set up.

As ten o'clock was striking, Valerie was fetched.

When the summons came, they were in the garden, and she left Anthony without a word. Desperately sorry for her, miserably fearful for himself, he followed as far as the steps of the veranda. . . .

Twenty-five minutes passed, perhaps half an hour. Then there was movement in the chamber. A door was opened. The lights, which had been low, were turned up.

A moment later Valerie appeared at the window, putting on her gloves.

As she came to the steps, Anthony rose out of the shadows.

" May I see you back to the village ? " he said.

She just inclined her head.

They passed in silence out of the starlit garden on to a pale grey road. The hedgerows on either side loomed up out of the darkness, blacker than night. A lane led down to the village, leaving the road on the left. It was the shortest path. As Lyveden started to turn, Valerie laid a hand on his arm.

" Not that way," she said unsteadily. " It was our last walk together—Joe's and mine."

Then she burst into tears.

In a flash the barrier that had stood between them was done away.

Anthony put his arm about her instinctively. She caught at his shabby lapel and clung to it, sobbing piteously. They must have stood so for five minutes or more.

When she was better, they walked on slowly, Anthony talking as naturally as if she had been his sister. All his constraint was gone.

" Don't I know how you feel ? Oh, my dear, I'm so grieved for you. I know, I know. . . . Everything you do, every way you turn, calls up some piteous memory. But it'll pass, dear, very soon. . . . Time's very merciful. . . ."

They came to the sleeping village and the door of the house where she was to pass the night.

" Sleep well," said Anthony, and put her hand to his lips.

Valerie dared not speak. For a second she hesitated, inarticulate. Then she leaned over and set her cheek against his.

The next instant she was gone.

* * * * *

Patch turned the corner of danger just before cock crow.

With his heart singing, Lyveden went for a walk. He chose the old way—the way he had trod so often with Patch by his side and Valerie in his heart. My lady had filled his cup. The knowledge that Patch would live had set it brimming. He saw the dawn up and felt jubilant. He found new beauties of Nature at every step. His sympathy with my lady was a thing detached. It could not cloud his happiness. Eaton Square was forgotten. There were only she and he and Patch in all the world. . . .

He came to *The Leather Bottel*, borrowed a razor of an old groom, and presently took a bath under a pump. Later he sat long over a joyous breakfast.

When he came back to the Home, there was Valerie. She just ran to meet him.

" I'm so glad, I'm so glad," she said. Then her lip quivered, and she turned away.

Anthony's heart smote him for his late selfishness.

For as good cause to congratulate her, he would have given anything.

They went up to Town together by the same train.

The feverish haste with which she climbed into " a third " was almost comical.

Arrived at the terminus, Lyveden handed her out. Since it was Sunday morning, the station was quiet. Indeed, except for a crowd of " theatricals "——

Anthony remembered the roses which Lord Pomfret had told him to purchase with an unpleasant shock.

As if a switch had been turned, all the uncertainty of his future rose up in a cold black wave. The hopelessness of their friendship stood out brutally. The thought that he was an impostor came pelting back, to set his ears burning and—the barrier that had stood between them crashed again into place.

Mechanically he saw her into a cab and told the driver to go to a house in Mayfair. Then he took off his hat.

" I hope," he said lamely, " I hope you'll get home all right."

Valerie looked at him curiously. Then she put out her hand.

" I shall never forget your kindness," she said gently.

*   *   *   *   *

When Anthony, some fifty minutes later, opened the front door to admit Lord Pomfret into his father's house, he saw that his hour was come.

For a moment the youth glared at him with the eyes of a snake. Then—

" Oh, you're back, are you ? " he snarled.

He entered the house, and Anthony closed the door.

" I'm very sorry, my lord, about the roses." He held out the two pound notes. " I entirely forgot them."

Lord Pomfret snatched the notes out of his hand. Anthony turned to go.

" Here ! " Anthony stopped in his stride, hesitated,

and then turned back. " What d'you mean, ' you forgot ' ? It's a lie. This is the second time you've let me down, you wash-out. And if you think——"

" My lord, I tell you——"

" Don't dare to answer me," raved the other. " I won't have it. Listen to me. My mother doesn't approve of servants who stay out all night—even if they *are* gentlemen. I'll bet you're ready to pitch a hell of a tale, but it's no good, Lyveden. D'you hear ? It's no good. You see, I answered the telephone on Friday, when your lady-friend rang up about the dog. . . . I know that dog, Lyveden, I've had one myself. And, what's more, I happened to be at Marylebone this morning. . . . Yes. That was a bit of bad luck, wasn't it ? So next time you want a week-end——"

Anthony hit him full on the mouth.

The other reeled backward, tripped over a rug, and fell heavily. He was up in an instant, and came at Anthony, bellowing like a madman.

Anthony, who was now quite cool, hit him between the eyes.

For the second time Lord Pomfret went down.

Again he got up, to hurl himself at his assailant, mouthing obscenity.

Anthony side-stepped and hit him under the jaw as hard as he could.

Lord Pomfret fell flat on his back and lay perfectly still. . . .

The silence was broken by the sound of a dry laugh.

Anthony swung on his heel, to see the Marquess of Banff in the library doorway.

" He's got a lot to learn yet," observed that noble-man, glancing at his recumbent offspring. " A deuce of a lot." He put up his eyeglasses and stared at Anthony. " If I'd known you could box, you should have given him a hour a day. Too late now. You'll have to go, of course. What are your wages ? "

"Six pounds a month, my lord," stammered Anthony.

The Marquess took out a note-case and extracted six notes.

"Does he owe you anything?" he said, peering.

"No, my lord."

In silence the money passed.

"Better get out at once," said the Marquess shortly.

"I'm—I'm very sorry, my lord, that this should have happened."

"Tck! I heard what he said. I don't blame you. If you want a reference, you can give my name. That'll do."

Anthony bowed and left him. The sprawling figure was showing signs of life. He passed through the hall quickly.

Half an hour later, his baggage in hand, he descended the kitchen stairs.

At the foot of these he encountered the second footman.

"'Elp!" said the latter. "Don' say you've got the bird, mate?"

"Got it in one," said Anthony.

"But 'oo——"

"The Marquess."

The fellow exploded.

"It's a perishin' shame!" he cried. "It's a——"

Anthony stopped him.

"No. He treated me handsomely. I—I bought it."

"You didn't never sauce 'im, mate?"—incredulously.

"Not exactly. You'll see." He put out his hand. 'So long."

The other stared at the fingers before accepting them. Then—

"So long, mate," he said dazedly.

Anthony let himself out.

The second footman's inability to comprehend the

matter continued until a quarter-past one. It was at that hour that he did as he had been told, and carried Lord Pomfret's luncheon up to his room. . . .

The condition of his lordship's countenance was most illuminating.

CHAPTER III

THE VOICE OF THE TURTLE

SITTING in the garden of the little Hertfordshire inn, Anthony drafted his application with the utmost care. All the time he tried to keep a tight hand upon his hopes—unruly and mettlesome fellows, which more than once had carried him into the meadow of Expectation before he knew where he was. There the going was splendid—till you came to the sunk fence. . . .

His letter, when finally settled, was comprehensive enough.

> c/o " *The Leather Bottel,*"
> *Nr. Malory,*
> *Herts.*

SIR (OR MADAM),

I beg to offer myself for the situation advertised in yesterday's issue of "The Times."

I am twenty-nine, unmarried, a little over six feet in height, healthy and very strong. I have no physical defects.

I have just quitted the service of the Marquess of Banff. My departure was directly due to my inability to give such satisfaction as one member of his lordship's household required of me, but the Marquess, who is familiar with the facts, was so good as to say that, if and when I needed a " character," he would himself speak for me.

I left the service of my previous employer because that

gentleman was going abroad, and so had no further need of a footman. That was my first situation.

I am accustomed to wait at table, answer the door, go out with the car, take care of silver, clean boots and knives, and carry coals : and I am ready to do anything that may be required of a man-servant. I have no objection to wearing powder.

I have been receiving seventy-two pounds per annum, but since, if I come to you, I may bring my dog with me, I shall be content with a much lower wage.

The dog in question—a Sealyham—is now recovering from distemper, and will not be fit to travel for another week, by which time I shall be ready to enter your service.

Should you desire to see me, I will come for an interview at your convenience.

I enclose a stamped addressed envelope, and shall be very grateful if you will inform me without delay if you are already suited.

> *I am, Sir (or Madam),*
> *Yours obediently,*
> *A. LYVEDEN.*

Sunday, July 25th.

That he was an ex-officer, Lyveden deliberately omitted to mention ; that he was a gentleman, he trusted that his style and handwriting would suggest. Had it been possible, he would have applied in person, not of self-confidence, but because he could have made plain one point, at any rate, upon which in a letter he feared to insist. This was that to have his dog with him he was willing to do his work for a shilling a day.

It was not until after his tea that Anthony fair-copied his letter. When it was signed and sealed, he slid it into a pocket and, telling the mistress of the inn that he would like his supper at eight, took up his hat from the settle and strolled out into the sweet-scented lanes.

Half a mile distant a pillar of lichened bricks stood by itself at a corner where two ways met. Here was enshrined a miniature once-red door—a toy of a door, to gladden a child's heart and set his fancies whirling, and be remembered, with another half-dozen of trifles, so long as he lived. A slot in the door received His Majesty's mails. Anthony, who had used the box before, strolled leisurely in its direction, and, as he went, contemplated, first, the sweetness of emancipation, and, secondly, the drawbacks of having but four pounds seven shillings and a penny between himself and thraldom.

A painstaking adder of figures, I have audited the gentleman's accounts and found them correct to the farthing. He must pay for his terrier's sickness and have four guineas in hand against the dog's board and lodging, in case, after all, he was to stay at the Dogs' Home. For a shilling he gave to a beggar, because he was poorer than himself, I can find no receipt, but hope it is filed in heaven. An eight-shilling meal stands out, among eightpenny teas, as a rare extravagance. . . .

Lyveden was about to commit his dispatch to the posting-box—in fact, his hand was outstretched—when, to the amazement of a cock-robin who frequented the pillar for company's sake, and had seen more letters posted than there were feathers upon his back, he hesitated, exclaimed, stared at the letter with knitted brow, and then thrust it back into his pocket.

The truth was that Lyveden had thought of the lady.

He strolled no farther, but walked—and that furiously. There were times when he strode. By the time he had covered eight miles and was on his way back, he was tramping wearily. He visited the Home and learned that his dog was mending. For fear of exciting the patient, he would not go in, but promised to come the next day. Then he passed on, hardly noticing whither he went, but turning mechanically, when he had covered five miles, wrestling with arguments, grappling with circumstances, and finally setting himself by the ears for a lovesick fool and a varlet in coat-armour.

Her dog, housed at the Dogs' Home, had brought her to Hertfordshire. Now that the poor little fellow was dead, Anthony flattered himself that he (Lyveden) might possibly bring her so far. And if he were to take this situation in the country—Heaven only knew where—she would come to seek him in vain, and would go empty away. That even if he stayed and she found him, and came to care for him, she would eventually go still more empty away, was a still uglier reflection. . . . Anthony was honourable, and there was the rub of rubs. That the shoe which Fate had tossed him was a misfit was nothing : that his sense of honour was chafed was intolerable.

" Now, Naaman . . . was a great man with his master and honourable . . . but he was a leper."

After some consideration, Anthony decided grudgingly that, on the whole, leprosy was worse than footmanhood, though less degrading. After further consideration, he decided that, until he could be rid of his uncleanness, he was in honour bound to see my lady no more.

That it took him seven miles to work out this simple problem may seem ridiculous. Possibly it is. In any case it is highly illuminating, for it shows that the love which he bore Miss Valerie French was worth having.

When he posted his letter at a quarter to eight, the cock-robin, who had been brooding over his late transilience, was greatly relieved.

* * * * *

Upon the second day of August the one-fifteen from Waterloo, or what was left of it, rumbled in the wake

of three other coaches—country cousins, these, that
had never seen London—up the long blue-brown valley
at the end of which lay the station of Mockery Dale.
It was tremendously hot, for the afternoon sun was
raking the valley from stem to stern, and since what
little breeze there was blew from the south-east, the
fitful puffs passed over the dip in the moorland and
left it windless. This suited the butterflies admirably.
Indeed, from all the insects an unmistakable hum of
approval of the atmosphere rose steadily. Anthony
could not hear it, any more than he could hear the
lark which was singing merrily at a vast height above
the shining rails, for the rumble of the composite train,
but he saw and marked the sleepy smile of the valley,
noted with satisfaction its comfortable air of content-
ment to be no part or parcel of a frantic world, and held
his terrier Patch to the dusty window, that he might
witness the antics of a couple of forest ponies, which
were galloping away from the train and kicking up
contemptuous heels at the interloper in an ecstasy of
idle menaces, clown-like in their absurdity.

Patch saw the impudent frolic and, panting with
excitement, evinced an immediate desire to leave the
carriage and deal summarily with the irreverence, but a
second later the sudden demands of a French bull-dog,
sitting pert in a dog-cart which at a level-crossing was
awaiting the passage of the train, superseded the ponies'
claim upon his displeasure. The alien was scolded
explosively.

A moment later the train had pulled into the station,
and Lyveden and Patch got out. They were, it
appeared, the only passengers to descend.

The only vehicle outside the station was a Ford car,
rather the worse for wear. Sitting as drowsily at the
wheel as the exigencies of the driver's seat would
permit was a man of some thirty summers. From his
appearance he might have been a member of the club

to which, till recently, Anthony had belonged. His soft felt hat was cocked extravagantly over one eye to keep the sun at bay, and his country suit was, fortunately, of a cloth which age cannot wither nor custom stale, but whose like has not been woven since the ill-favoured and lean-fleshed kine came up out of the river of War.

As Lyveden appeared, carrying his luggage and preceded by Patch—

" No need to ask if you're for The Shrubbery," said the driver of the Ford lazily. " Shove your things in the back, will you ? "

Anthony set down his suit-case and touched his hat. " Very good, sir," he said.

" Here," came the airy reply, " you mustn't ' sir ' me. I'm the comic chauffeur —your fellow-bondsman, to wit. Name of Alison." He extended a firm brown hand. " Not to put too fine a point upon it, I'm overwhelmed to meet you. With the slightest encouragement, I shall fall upon your neck. The last footman was poor company, and took two baths in three months. My wife didn't try to like him. She's the parlourmaid."

Anthony took the other's hand like a man in a dream.

" I can't believe it," he said simply. " Is this a legpull ? "

" No blinkin' fear," said Alison. " We're all in the same boat. What a topping dog ! "

Anthony felt inclined to fling his hat upon the ground and yell with delight. Instead, he thrust his baggage into the car and, stepping in front of the bonnet, took hold of the starting-handle.

" Is it safe ? " he said, straddling. " Or will she go round with my hand ? "

" Well, we do usually get some one to stand on the step," said Alison, " but, if you like to risk it . . ."

A moment later they were hurtling along a white-brown ribbon of road that sloped sideways out of the valley and on to the top of the moor.

Alison chattered away light-heartedly.

"You see in me," he said, "the complete chauffeur. With my livery on and two thousand five hundred pounds' worth of Rolls-Royce all round me, I'm simply *it*. My only fear is that, when you turn out beside me, the whole perishin' concern will be caught up to heaven. However, I really think you'll be happy."

"I believe you," said Lyveden.

"Of course, I don't do much indoors, but Betty says the housework's nothing. Anne agrees. She combines the duties of housemaid and my sister. Oh, we're all in it, I warn you. Of course, we do old Bumble and Mrs. Bumble proud. They deserve it. They're very kindly and easy-going, and we always try and give them just a shade more than they have a right to expect. He's a retired grocer and proud of it. Plenty of money, no children. Very little entertaining. We have more visitors in the servants' hall than they do in the drawing-room. . . ."

The lazy voice purled on contentedly till the car leapt into a village gathered about the road.

"Hawthorne, I take it," said Lyveden.

"Brother," said Alison, "I will not deceive you. This is indeed that bourn from which no commercial traveller returns, for the most potent reason that none ever comes here. Thank Heaven, it's off their beat. The Shrubbery's half a mile on."

Two minutes later they swept up a shady drive, past the creepered front of a well-built house, and into a small courtyard.

As the emotions of the car subsided, a Cocker spaniel made her appearance, squirming with affection and good-will, and offering up short barks of thanksgiving by way of welcome.

"Hush, José, hush!" cried a pleasant voice, and

the next moment Mrs. Alison appeared in a doorway, wearing the traditional habiliments of a smart maid-servant with a perfectly natural air.

When her sister-in-law, similarly attired, followed her into the yard, Anthony felt as if he had been pushed on to a stage in the middle of a musical comedy. . . .

Not until his introduction was over, Mrs. Alison had shown him his room—a simple sweet-smelling apartment, all pale green and white and as fresh as a daisy—and they were all four seated in a cool parlour about a hearty tea, did the feeling of unreality begin to wear off.

" There'll be just us four," said the housemaid. " The cook's a villager, and doesn't sleep in. She and her daughter, the kitchenmaid, feed together in the kitchen. They're a very nice pair, and seem to think more of us than they do of the Bumbles. It's really as good as a play. We pay the girl a shilling a week on the top of her wages, and for that she lays our table and serves our meals. I expect George has told you about the Bumbles. They're really two of the best."

" By the way," said Anthony, " oughtn't I to be reporting for duty ? "

" Plenty of time," said Mrs. Alison. " I'll ask when I clear away tea. They'll want to see you, just to say they hope you'll be happy more than anything else. And now do ask some questions. I'm sure there must be hundreds of things you're simply pining to know."

Anthony laughed.

"To be absolutely frank," he replied, " I'm still a little bit dizzy. I've been on my beam ends so long that to suddenly fall on my feet, like this, is disconcerting. I've sort of lost my balance."

" Of course you have," said Alison, lighting a pipe. " Bound to. I feel rather overwrought myself. Let's go and cry in the garage."

" Don't take any notice of the fool," said his wife.
" By the way, there's one thing I ought to tell you,
and that is that Christian names are the order of the
day.   Off duty it's natural ; on parade, since we three
glory in the same surname, it's unavoidable.   I'm
known as Betty, my sister-in-law's Anne, and that
with the pipe is George."

" And I," said Lyveden, " am Anthony—at your
service.   This with the hungry look "—he picked up
the Sealyham—" is Patch.   As the latter is convales-
cent, all his days lately have been red-letter, and
celebrated by the addition to his rations of a small dish
of tea.   Whether such a scandalous practice is to be
followed this afternoon must rest with his hostess."

" I think," said Betty, " as he's a *bonafide* traveller
. . ."

José, the soft-eyed spaniel, profited by the Sealyham's
privilege.   It was impossible that she should not receive
equal consideration.

" You must forgive my staring," said George Alison,
gazing upon Anthony, " but you just fascinate me.
To think that you're not going to suck wind when
drinking, or clean your nails with a fork, is too wonderful.   Your predecessor's habits at table were purely
Johnsonian."

Betty shuddered at the allusion.

" If he'd been decent," said Anne, " I could have
borne it.   But he was just odious.   The idea that we'd
come down in the world fairly intoxicated him."

" It's true," said George.   " And when Val wrote
and——".

A vicious kick upon his ankle silenced him abruptly.

" I beg your pardon," said Anthony, who had been
busy with Patch.

" I was saying that—er—if you value your dog, and
he's only just over distemper, I shouldn't let him run
loose just yet.   José's a terrible huntress, and she's

sure to lead him astray. Stays out all night sometimes."

" Right oh ! " said Anthony cheerfully.

It was manifest that Patch was going to have the
time of his life.

When Betty returned from ushering their new footman into the presence of Mr. and Mrs. Bumble, she
reviled her husband as he deserved.

" I forgot," he pleaded.

" Forgot ! "—indignantly. " Well, if you forget
and mention her name again, I'll—I'll prick your tires."

" Any way," said George, " my withdrawal was little
short of brilliant. You'll admit that ? Incidentally,
her *protégé*'s an improvement on little Halbert, isn't
he ? I think we ought to have an appropriate supper
to-night in his honour. What about killing the padded
calf ? "

Betty kissed him behind the left ear.

* * * * *

Long before Anthony had received his livery from
the tailor at Brooch, he had settled down to his nice
new life with heartfelt gratitude. The old zest of living
had returned to him to stay. It was no longer necessary to make the best of things. From labouring in
the trough of oppression he had been swept into waters
more smooth than any he had dreamed of riding—a
veritable lagoon of security and content.

At first, so long had he been mishandled by Fortune,
that, like a cur that has been accustomed to ill-treat-
ment, he viewed her present bounty with suspicion.
Had she poured for him the wine of comfort to dash
the cup from his lips ere it was empty ? That would
be just like the jade. He scanned the sky anxiously
for a sign of the coming storm, and, finding it cloudless,
saw in this calm some new miracle of treachery, and
feared the worst. He was afraid, selfishly, for Mr.
Bumble's health. The man was pink and well nour-

ished. Anthony thought of apoplexy, and, had a medical book been available, would have sought a description of that malady's favourite prey. Mrs. Bumble was also well covered. Anthony hoped that her heart was sound. On these two lives hung all his happiness. He reflected that motoring was not unattended by peril, and the idea stayed with him for half a day. Had he not been ashamed, he would have laid the facts before George and besought him to drive carefully. . . .

As the days, however, went placidly by and brought no evil, the smoking flax of his faith began to kindle, and his suspicions to wilt. His mind shook off its sickness and began to mend rapidly. Very soon it was as sound as a bell.

His temporary lapse from grace, above related, was so innocuous that it need not be counted to his discredit. His was the case of the pugilist who slipped on a piece of peel and felt unable to rise : had the place been a ring, instead of a pavement, he would have been up and dancing within ten seconds. So with Anthony—had Fortune frowned, he would have laughed in her face. It was her smile that made him cower. And, so long as she smiled, what mattered it if he cowered ? Had Homer never nodded, gentlemen, till it was past his bed-time, neither you nor I would ever have heard of it.

If Betty had indeed affirmed that the housework to be done at The Shrubbery was nothing, she was guilty of hyperbole. All the same, the house was an easy one, and such labour as its upkeep entailed melted, beneath the perfectly organized attention of herself, Anne, and Lyveden, as snow beneath the midday sun. The three had more legitimate leisure than any three servants in England, and no residence in Europe was better kept. Mr. and Mrs. Bumble, of course, were in clover. It followed that Anthony Lyveden had much time to himself. Naturally companionable, he spent most of this with his colleagues ; nevertheless, there were days when he liked to change his clothes, call Patch, and walk off into the forest with only the little dog for company. It was then that he could think of my lady. . . .

He always associated her with the open air. Never once did he picture her cribbed in a room. For him she was a creature of the country-side, sun-kissed, folded in the arms of the wind, with the pure red wine of Nature singing through her delicate veins. . . . Thinking of veins, he recalled the faint exquisite blue of those which lay pencilled upon the back of her cold little hand. He remembered the line of them perfectly.

The vein, then, gave him the hand ; the hand, the arm ; the arm, the shoulder. He reconstructed her piecemeal with a rare faithfulness, till by the time he was on the moorland overlooking the smiling valley, where the railroad went shining away into the old world, there stood his lady beside him, complete, glorious, the freshening breeze behind her moulding her soft raiment to the shape of her beautiful limbs, her eyes shining, her lips parted, one little hand touching her dark hair—just Valerie.

So for a brief second she stood by his side. Once she swayed towards him before the mirror of Imagination shivered, but only once. Mostly it flew to flinders almost before she was come.

Anthony hungered for a sight of the girl desperately. Had this been offered him upon the understanding that he appeared to her in livery, he would still have jumped at the chance. From this may be gauged the degree of his hunger. He was, in fact, starving.

Consequently, when one ripe September morning— all dew and mellow sunshine and the lowing of cows— Betty tapped a letter with a significant forefinger and announced that it contained an invitation to a quiet little dance, Anthony, amid the general enthusiasm, displayed no more interest than politeness demanded and no curiosity at all.

Betty addressed herself to him.

" It's from Lady Touchstone. I was at school with her niece. They live at Bell Hammer, a beautiful place about five miles from here. You're included, of course. I saw her last week, so she knows all about you. It's because of her niece's birthday. Only about eight couples, she says, and no strangers."

" Except me," said Anthony.

" You won't feel strange long," said George. " Berry and Co. are sure to be there, for one thing, and they'll wrap their arms about you in about two minutes. They live at White Ladies. Some of them came to tea here the day you went over to Brooch."

" I don't think I'd better go," said Anthony. " It's very kind of Lady Touchstone, but I'm not much of a dancer, and——"

His protest was overruled uproariously.

" And he can't say he hasn't any clothes," said George, " because I've seen them."

This was true. Out of the spoliation of his wardrobe Lyveden had clung to a dress-suit, much as the orphan who lugs her carpet to the pawnshop clings pitifully to an old miniature, remembering happier days.

Anthony coloured at the allusion, and Betty came flying to his assistance.

" What a shame ! " she cried. " Why should he go if he doesn't want to ? And, for all we know, none of us may be able to accept. We've got to get leave first, and then we've got to ask if we can have the Ford." She paused to glance at the time. " Ten to eight, and you haven't washed the yard yet. Don't sit there, George. Get a move on. You chauffeurs ! " She fairly drove him about his business.

All the same, before the day was over she had

wheedled a promise from Anthony that, master and mistress permitting, he would go to the dance.

The Bumbles were duly approached, and consented readily to the projected exodus, asking solicitously if a quarter to ten would be early enough for the four to leave The Shrubbery, and offering the use of the Ford before this was sought. Considering that they were not upon the visiting list of Lady Touchstone, or, for that matter, upon that of any other of their domestics' friends, their readiness to facilitate the excursion must be accounted to them for righteousness of a calibre rare indeed.

The night of the dance came, and the stars with it. All the company of heaven twinkled and flashed out of a windless sky. No solitary breath of air rustled the silence of the woods. Summer was dying hard. Yet in the bottoms there lay—sure sign of Autumn—little hoary pools of mist, just deep enough to swathe the Ford and its complement of would-be revellers in a wet rush of frozen smoke, and make the girls thrust their pink fingers beneath the rug, and Anthony his hands into his coat-pockets.

For all that, for Lyveden the five miles to Bell Hammer were covered too soon. He liked to feel the rush of the wings of Night upon his temples, to mark the untroubled slumber of the country-side, gaze at the velvet dome fretted with silver. Moreover, he was almost dreading the dance. Had he not given his word a week ago, he would—speaking vulgarly—have stuck his toes in and seen his companions to the edge of the pit before he followed them into the mansion.

For a mansion it was.

Though the night was moonless, Anthony could see that. That it was a beautiful specimen of a " Queen Anne " residence he could not perceive. Indeed, almost before the car had been berthed close to the shadowy elegance of a tremendous cedar, the front door was opened, and a great shaft of light streamed out into the darkness.

The guests passed in.

The monstrous deference of the footman who received Anthony's coat and hat gave a disconcerting fillip to the latter's uneasiness. As a respectful butler preceded the party upstairs, he felt as if he were being conducted to a scaffold.

"Captain and Mrs. Alison, Miss Alison, Major Lyveden."

Anthony braced himself.

The next moment—

"How d'ye do?" said Valerie, with a quiet smile. "I'm so glad you could come. How's Patch?"

With a whirling brain, Anthony tried to say that Patch was very well.

"Let me introduce you to my aunt," said Valerie, turning to a lady whom Anthony seemed to have seen before. "Aunt Harriet, this is Major Lyveden—Lady Touchstone."

Anthony bowed dazedly.

"You were very good to Valerie," said the lady, "a little while ago. I've heard about it. And how do you like service? I always said that, if my father had put his money into railways instead of ships, I should have become a cook-housekeeper."

"It all depends," said Anthony, "on whose service you're in. I like yours very much."

Lady Touchstone laughed.

"You'd make a good equerry," she said. Then she turned to glance down the gallery. "You must meet Mrs. Pleydell," she added. "Ah, there she is. Come." They stepped to the side of a tall dark girl with a most attractive smile. "Daphne, my dear, this is Major Lyveden—from The Shrubbery. Amuse him, and he'll flatter you. You see." The tall fair man who had been sitting with Mrs. Pleydell offered

Lady Touchstone his arm. She put it aside with a frown. "I'm not so old as all that, Jonah," she said. "You may take me to the hearth, if you please, but not like a grandmother."

With a crash an alcove belched music, and in a moment all the winking length of the gallery was throbbing with ragtime.

Mrs. Pleydell and Anthony trod the measure with a will.

When it was over, she led him to a tall window with a deep-cushioned seat.

"You were out," she said, "when I came the other day. To make up for it, you must come to White Ladies. It's a pretty walk, and we'll take you back in the car."

"You're very kind," said Anthony.

"If you talk like that," said Daphne, "I shall invite you for the week-end. And now would you like to talk shop, or shall I tell you about my new dress?"

Anthony hesitated, and the girl laughed merrily.

"I'm a past-mistress of blackmail," she said. "My husband taught me."

Anthony joined in her merriment before clearing his throat.

"My first place," he said, "was in Lancaster Gate."

"I know," said Daphne eagerly. "North of the Park. Go on."

Before they parted, they had danced two more dances together.

Then he spent a quarter of an hour with Betty and another like period with Anne. After that, before he could get to Valerie, he was handed to a little fair damsel, all big grey eyes and masses of golden hair.

"Major Lyveden—Miss Mansel."

"Isn't Daphne nice?" said that lady. "I saw you dancing with her. She's my cousin."

"I envy you both," said Anthony.

Jill Mansel stared at him gravely.

" That's very nice of you. Yes, I'd love to dance this. Look. There's Adèle. Isn't she lovely? I think she's like a flower. She's going to marry my cousin. She's an American without an accent. You are tall, aren't you? You're all tall here to-night, except me. It makes me feel a dwarf."

" And us, ogres," said Anthony.

Jill laughed delightedly.

" You are nice," she said. " Valerie said you were. Look at Berry dancing with Daphne, and pretending he's bored stiff. When are you coming to White Ladies? "

She prattled on contentedly, asking questions innumerable, but requiring no answers.

Lyveden enjoyed himself.

After they had sat out a little, Valerie came towards them with the man called Jonah.

" Since you won't ask me," she said to Anthony, " I must throw myself at your head." She turned, smiling, to Jill. " Jonah is bored with me, dear, so I'm going to heap coals of fire on his head and restore him to his little sister." She returned to Anthony. " Now, then." Thus addressed, he offered her his arm soberly enough. " There's some supper, I know, downstairs, because I ordered it myself."

They made for the great doors, Anthony tongue-tied, and she hailing others to follow them.

As they passed down the broad staircase, he remembered the reason of the party, and begged to congratulate her. My lady thanked him with a quiet smile.

" We've got a lot to talk about," she said. " You and I. And there'll be too much noise at supper, so it must wait. Afterwards I'll send for a coat, and we'll walk in the garden. That's the best of a birthday. I can do as I please."

Her promise of his peaceful possession after supper made the meal, so far as Lyveden was concerned, an

Olympian banquet. The assemblage, indeed, was remarkable, and the hostess—a very Demeter—must have been the oldest present by some twenty years. The sprightliness of Hermes alone, in the guise of the man called Berry, kept a lively table in roars of laughter. Yet, full as his cup was, for Anthony the old Falernian was to come. . . .

As good as her word, when the others were straying back to the gallery in response to the lure of a lullaby valse, Valerie led Lyveden to a lobby and let him help her into a chamois-leather coat. A cloak of Irish frieze was hanging there, and she bade him put it about his shoulders against the night air. Anthony protested, but she just stamped her foot.

"It's my birthday," she flashed.

Anthony donned the garment, and she opened a garden-door. A moment later they were walking upon a wide terrace at the back of the house.

"Well?" said Valerie.

"It is my bounden duty," said Anthony, "to remind you that I am a footman. Now that you know, it's very easy to tell you."

"And what if you are?"

"Well, if we happened to visit the same house, I should go in by the tradesmen's entrance."

Valerie tossed her head.

"You might go in by the back, but if you weren't shown out of the front door, *I* shouldn't visit that house again."

Anthony sighed.

"Then your visiting-list would shrink," he said, "out of all knowledge. How did you know my calling?"

"Did you think I didn't recognize you that night?"

"At first I was uncertain. That I thought you must have. Then you misled me, and made me think you hadn't. Why did you do that?"

" I don't know," said Valerie. She could not tell him the truth. " It seemed easier. How did you come to The Shrubbery ? "

" I wasn't happy where I was, and I saw the Bumbles' advertisement. It seemed meant for me."

That it was meant for him, and that she and not the Bumbles had paid for its insertion, Valerie thought it unnecessary to state.

" We're fated to be brought together," she said.

" How did you know I was at The Shrubbery ? " Valerie raised her eyebrows.

" Betty's my oldest friend," she replied.

Lyveden swallowed the *suggestio falsi* without a thought. Indeed, so soon as she had spoken, his mind sped back, bee-like, to suck the honey of her previous words : " We're fated to be brought together." Fated. . . .

The moon was up now, and he lifted his eyes and gazed at its clear-cut beauty. A power, then, greater than he had ruled against his resolve. Why ? To what end ? It was very kind of the power—at least, he supposed it was—but what was to come of it ?

He had wandered straight into her arms. Very good. But—he and she could not stroll upon this terrace for ever. The relentless rubric of Life insisted that he must move—whither he chose, of course, but somewhither. The truth was, he did not know which way to turn. His heart pointed a path, certainly— a very precious path, paved all with silk, hung with the scent of flowers, shadowed by whispering plumage. . . . His head, however, beyond denouncing his heart as a guide, pointed no way at all.

Anthony wanted desperately to do the right thing. Fortune, it seemed, was at her old tricks. Here she was handing a palace to a beggar who had not enough money to maintain a hovel. It would not have been so hopeless if he had possessed " prospects." With these in his pack, he might have essayed the way his heart showed him. They were, however, no part of a footman's equipment. . . .

Anthony began to wonder what became of old footmen. One or two, perhaps, became butlers. As for the rest . . .

Valerie, too, was in some perplexity. She was wondering, now that she had her man here, how best to deal with him. Pride and honour make up a ground which must be trodden delicately. One false step on her part might cost them both extremely dear. Her instinct was to take the bull by the horns, Anthony by the arm, and Time by the forelock. The last of these was slipping away—slipping away. She was actually twenty-six. In a short fourteen years she would be actually forty. Forty ! For a moment she was upon the very edge of exercising the privilege of a sovereign lady who has fallen in love. All things considered, she would, I think, have been justified. Something, however, restrained her. It was not modesty, for modesty had nothing to do with the matter. It was not the fear of rejection, for she was sure of her ground. It was probably a threefold influence—a rope, as it were, of three stout strands. The first was consideration for Anthony's pride ; the second, an anxiety lest she should beggar him of that which he prized above rubies, namely, his self-respect ; the third, an innate conviction that while the path of Love may look easy, it is really slippery and steep out of all conscience.

Thus absorbed in the delicacy of their relationship, they stepped the length of the terrace in silence. Then—

" I don't know what you're thinking about," said Valerie, " but I should like to."

Anthony shook his head.

" I'll tell you a story instead," he said. " If you like, that is."

" Please."

She turned and leaned her arms upon the stone balustrade, overlooking dim lawns and, beyond, the pale ghost of a great park that seemed to stretch and roll unlimited into the depths of a distance which Night had bewitched.

"There was once," said Anthony, "a frog. He wasn't much of a frog, as frogs go. In fact, with the exception that he had no home and no friends, he was a very ordinary frog indeed. One day when he was sick and tired of being alone, he went out and bought a tame minnow. Considering how poor he was, it was very reckless, because it meant that there were now two mouths to feed instead of one, but the minnow and the frog became such great friends that that didn't seem to matter. At last, sure enough, the day of reckoning arrived. The larder was empty, the minnow's appetite was as healthy as ever, and the frog was down to his last penny. So, after a lot of thought, he left the minnow playing in a quiet pool, and went out to earn some flies. By dint of toiling very hard all day, he managed to earn enough to keep the minnow and himself, but it meant that the two had very little time together, and that was a shame.

"Well, one day the frog got back to the pool a little earlier than usual, and, chancing to lift up his eyes, there seated upon the bank he saw a real live Princess. What the frog thought, when he saw her, may be imagined. What he felt doesn't matter. Enough that he was profoundly moved. So moved that he almost forgot to give the minnow his flies. And long after the Princess had risen and gone away, the frog kept thinking of her, and thinking, and thinking. . . . And then, all of a sudden, he began to wish, as he had never wished before, that he wasn't a frog.

"Now, vain desires are the most persistent of all.

"The frog wished and wished, and cursed himself for

a fool, and wished again. . . . At last he could bear it no longer, so he went to a water-rat who was so old that he was said to be wise, and sought his advice.

"The water-rat was painfully outspoken. 'Once a frog, always a frog,' he said.

"'Always?'

"'Always. Unless you can find a Princess and persuade her to kiss you.' And, being an old rat, he chuckled at his own joke.

"But the frog didn't see anything to laugh at. He just became so excited that he could hardly float, and then he turned round and started to swim back to the pool as hard as ever he could. . . .

"By the next morning his excitement had somewhat abated. Of course he was tremendously lucky to have found a Princess. (Being an optimist, you see, he assumed that she would reappear.) But it was quite another matter to persuade her to kiss him. Still, he didn't give up hope, and every day he raced and tore after the flies, so as to get back early to the pool.

"Then one day the impossible thing happened.

"There was the Princess again on the bank of the pool, and when the frog put up his nose and fixed her with a bulging and glassy eye, she smiled at him. Very haltingly the frog swam to land and crouched at her feet, and, before he knew where he was, she had stooped and kissed him.

"The frog just shut his eyes in ecstasy and gloated upon the fulfilment of his desire. It had happened. His wish had been gratified. The change had come. He was no longer a frog. For the first time he began to wonder what he was. Probably a Prince. Oh, undoubtedly a Prince. All clad in gold and silver, with a little fair moustache. He hoped very much that he had a fair moustache. But he wouldn't put up his hand and feel, for fear of spoiling it. He wanted to look at himself gradually, beginning with his feet and working upwards. He began to wonder what sort of boots he had on. He decided that he was wearing soft gold boots, with silver laces. . . .

" Cautiously he opened one eye and glanced at his right foot. He was quite wrong. It wasn't a gold boot at all. It was a queer-looking boot, all smooth and shiny and shaped—well, rather like—like a frog's foot. In fact, if he hadn't known that he was no longer a frog, he would have said—— A frightful thought came to him, and he opened both eyes, staring frantic-ally. . . . Then he sprang to the edge of the pool and looked himself in the face. . . . He stood gazing so long that the minnow, who had been watching him, thought he was ill, and leaped out of the water to attract his attention. At last the frog pulled himself together and flopped back into the pool anyhow. . . .

" And, after many days, during all of which the minnow was a great comfort, he came to realize that frogs should know better than to lift up their eyes, and should busy themselves with fly-earning, and be thankful for the air and the sun and the mud at the bottom of pools, and, last of all, look forward to that sun-bathed marsh where the flies are fat and plenteous, and there is no winter, and whither, at the end of their lives, all good frogs go."

There was a long silence. Then—

" Poor frog," said Valerie, standing upright and turning.

" It's very nice of you to say so," said Anthony, falling into step. " But he richly deserved it."

" And what happened to the Princess ? "

" Oh, she went the way Princesses go, and enriched the memories of all who saw her, and in due season she married a Prince."

" Didn't she ever think any more of the frog? "

" No," said Anthony.

" Then why did she kiss him ? "

They had come to the garden door by now, and, as she spoke, Valerie set a hand on the latch.

" Out of pity," said Anthony. " She had a sweet, kind heart, and she was sorry for him because he was a frog."

" I don't believe it was out of pity at all," said Valerie. " I'm—I'm sure it wasn't."

" It must have been," said Anthony. " Why on earth else should a Princess——"

" Because it pleased her to kiss him," said Valerie, with the air of a queen.

Anthony looked at her with undisguised admiration.

" You're a real Princess," he said, " any way."

Valerie let go the door-handle and laid her hand on his shoulder.

" Why did she kiss him ? " she demanded.

" Out of—because it pleased her."

The hand touched his cheek, and Anthony caught it and put it to his lips. As he let it go, the slight fingers caught his and, before he could stop her, Valerie had stooped and kissed them.

The next instant the door was open, and she was inside.

*   *   *   *   *

Mr. Albert Morgan was working feverishly.

Time was getting on, and the plate-chest had proved unexpectedly stubborn. To know where it was had been a great help, of course, but during his service at The Shrubbery it had been kept unlocked. Somewhat unfairly, he cursed the parlourmaid, who, he assumed, was doing his work, for " a suspicious ——."

Curiously enough he had no idea that his late colleagues were not in the house. He believed them to be sleeping peacefully in the servants' quarters. For considerately placing the pantry distant from these, it might have been thought that the architect of the house would receive Mr. Morgan's commendation. On the contrary, of his zeal appropriately to execrate the former's memory, the ex-footman employed most regrettable language, and this for the simple reason that the stone sill of the pantry window projected rather farther from the wall than Mr. Morgan, when in the act of lifting his knee, had believed to be the case.

With the exception of this painful incident, his ingress had been effected with the acme of ease. This was due to the foresight, patience, and unremitting care with which he had severed the bars and removed the spring of the window-catch during his last fortnight in Mr. Bumble's employ.

After the refractory plate-chest had been made to disgorge, Mr. Morgan had visited the drawing-room. By the time he had garnered what precious metal was there, his two capacious bags had become extremely heavy. So much so, that he almost regretted that he had not brought a friend. The reflection, however, that to present a coadjutor with half the proceeds of a robbery which his brain alone had conceived and made possible, would undoubtedly have shortened his life, made him feel better. Cautiously he made for the stairs and, guiding himself with his torch, began to ascend.

There were some snuff-boxes in a cabinet which stood on the landing. It was unthinkable that he should go without these. The piece was kept locked, but he had often gazed at them through the glass. One of them was of silver-gilt—possibly of gold. Mr. Morgan licked his thick lips.

It was upon the door of this cabinet, then, that, torch in mouth, he was working feverishly. Time was getting on. . . .

As if in answer to the subdued crack with which the door at length yielded came the noise of the insertion of a key into the lock of the front door. Mr. Morgan started violently, thrust his torch into a pocket, and stood extremely still.

The door opened and the admitted moonlight showed him the entrance of one—two feminine apparitions, followed by that of a man. For a moment they stood in the hall, speaking with one another in an undertone. What they said Mr. Morgan could not hear—their voices, too, were too low to be recognized—but he had no doubt at all regarding their identity. Seven weeks of their fellowship had blessed (or cursed) him with a familiarity with their style and proportions such as no manner of wraps and tricksy half-lights could subvert. With a full heart and twitching lips, Mr. Morgan dwelt blasphemously upon the several destinies for which, to his mind, their untimely appearance had qualified them.

" What are you going to do about the door ? " whispered Betty. " We can't leave it open."

" Well, we can't shut it," said George, " can we ? "

" Put it to," Anne suggested. " He won't be more than a minute or two, and when he comes he can just push it open."

The truth of the matter was that José and Patch, who had gone a-hunting, had not returned when the party had left for Bell Hammer. It was possible that, during their absence, the dogs had come back, and Anthony did not like to think that truant Patch might be wandering around the house, seeking admission in vain. Consequently, after the car had been noiselessly bestowed—out of consideration for their employers' rest, the four had alighted before they left the road and had man-handled a silent Ford up the drive and into the garage—Lyveden had bidden the others go on, and had started off upon a visiting patrol, the objectives of which were the several entrances to the residence. If Patch was anywhere, he would be crouched upon one of the doorsteps. . . .

Anne's suggestion seeming reasonable, her brother

secured the Yale lock so that its tongue was engaged, and, quietly closing the door, followed his wife and sister a-tiptoe through the hall and past the baize door which led to the servants' quarters.

As they passed the foot of the stairs, Betty remarked the shaft of moonlight shining upon the landing, and Mr. Morgan's black heart stood still. When her husband reminded her that in less than four hours it would be her privilege to prepare Mrs. Bumble's tea, and added that, if she felt lyrical, he felt tired and footsore, Mr. Morgan, had his emotions included gratitude, would have thanked his stars.

Such devotion, however, would have been premature.

Though he did not know it, his stars in their courses were fighting against him.

The moment the baize door had closed behind his late colleagues, he made silently for the stairs. Of the snuff-boxes he thought no more. The man was rattled. His one idea was to pick up his traps and be gone. He was even afraid any more to employ his torch. Besides, the moonlight, to which Betty had drawn his attention, was asserting itself fantastically.

Step by step he descended the staircase, trying frantically to remember which of the treads would creak under his weight. Faithfully to ascertain which of them possessed this important peculiarity had been one of the last things he did before quitting Mr. Bumble's service. Was it the fifth or sixth ? He hesitated, then avoided the fifth gingerly, and hoped for the best. . . . Beneath the increased pressure the sixth stair fairly shrieked. Mr. Morgan skipped on to the seventh and broke into a cold sweat. Again he was confronted with the choice of the eighth or ninth. After a moment of agonized indecision, he decided to miss them both. . . . Man but proposes. In his anxiety he missed the tenth also and slithered incontinently into the hall. . . .

More than a minute passed before the knave dared
to pick himself up. The last five stairs had been rough
with his hinder parts, but his physical pain was
nothing to the paroxysm of mental torment which
the noise of his fall had induced.

Trembling with apprehension, he groped his way to
his bags. Of these, one had to be strapped, for the
catch of its lock was broken. He knelt down with his
back to the door, fumbling. . . .

A sudden step upon the gravel immediately outside
the front door almost congealed his blood. That peril
could blow from that quarter he had never imagined.
Once again he remained where he was, as still as death.
Unless the new-comer was there because his suspicions
were aroused, there was a chance that Mr. Morgan might
yet escape notice. Who the new-comer might be, he
had no time to speculate, for, without being unlocked,
the door was pushed open. Mr. Morgan marked the
phenomenon, and his hair rose. Then a man stepped
inside and stood still. . . .

Mr. Morgan held his breath until his lungs were
bursting and his head swam, but the man never moved.

The fact was that Anthony was staring at the same
shaft of light which had attracted Betty's attention.
This, however, was no longer appearing upon the landing, but in the hall, which, with the exception of that
corner which contained the crouching ex-footman, it
was doing much to illuminate. From this it would
appear that the arresting beam, so far from emanating
from the moon, was none other than Mr. Morgan's evil
genius, following him about wherever he went. It was,
in fact, his torch, which in his confusion he had thrust
glowing into his pocket *the wrong way up*. That one
end must protrude, he knew, for the brand was longer
than the pocket was deep. He had, of course, no idea
at all that it was advertising his presence and slightest
movement so very faithfully. . . .

It became impossible for Mr. Morgan any longer to restrain his breath. He therefore expelled it as gently as he possibly could, inhaling a fresh supply with the same caution, and wondering dully whether it was to be his last. The suspense was unbearable.

Anthony, of course, was perfectly satisfied that the light was thrown by a torch. The source of the latter, however, was shrouded, not only in mystery, but in a darkness which the very light of the beam served to intensify. He continued to stand still.

There never was such a case.

Anthony, who knew the value of waiting, was prepared to stay still indefinitely. Mr. Morgan was afraid to do anything else. Clearly, if they were not to remain where they were until dawn, there was need of a *deus ex machina.*

He arrived then and there in the shape of a little white dog with a black patch. He was extremely wet, and there were burrs in his coat and mud upon his beard. His tail was up, however, and his gait as sprightly as ever.

As if it was upon his account that the door had been set open at this unlawful hour, he entered boldly, passed by Anthony in the gloom, and then stood still like his master, staring at the mysterious beam. But not for long. For Patch, curiosity was made to be satisfied. Stepping warily, he moved forward to investigate. . . .

When first Mr. Morgan realized that something was smelling him from behind, he made ready to die. Then, so tenacious is the hold we mortals have upon life, he gave an unearthly shriek and sprang from his bended knees for the drawing-room doorway. . . .

When Mr. Bumble and his chauffeur, the one in his night attire and the other in a vest and a pair of dress trousers, appeared upon the scene, Anthony was kneeling upon Mr. Morgan, who was lying face downwards upon the drawing-hearth and dealing as fluently as a sheep-skin rug would permit with Anthony's birth, life, death and future existence. As for Patch, his services no longer required, he was rolling upon the sofa in an absurd endeavour to remove the burrs from his coat.

All of which, gentlemen, must undeniably go to show that the master who suffers his servants to go a-junketing will have his reward ; that a woman knows better than a man what course he should shape ; and that there is much virtue in hunting, even though it keep the hunter afoot till four of the morning.

CHAPTER IV

THE GOLDEN BOWL

WITH Monseigneur Forest, other than in his capacity of uncle and counsellor to Miss Valerie French, we are not concerned. It is necessary, however, to record that the dignitary was no fool. He was, in fact, a very wise man, able to understand most men and women better than they understood themselves. With such understanding, naturally enough, went a rare kindness of heart ; the addition to these things of a fine sense of humour argued a certain favouritism on the part of a Providence which bestows upon ninety-and-nine mortals but one virtue apiece, and to the hundredth but two. Monseigneur Forest was, I suppose, a man in a million.

A letter of some importance, which his niece had sent him, reached him in Rome ere October was old.

DEAR UNCLE JOHN,

I want to see and talk to you very badly, but I can't leave England just now. I suppose you guess what is coming. I can see you smile. You're quite right. I've fallen in love.

Listen. I was out with poor little Joe in the country, and went to an inn for tea. And there was a man in the garden. I didn't know he was there till his dog and Joe started scrapping, and then he ran up to separate them. The moment I saw him—I don't know how to tell you.

I just felt floored. . . . Then—instinctively, I suppose, for I hardly knew what I was doing—I tried to cover up this feeling. I was furious with him for knocking me out. Can you ever understand? And I was pretty rude. He took it wonderfully and just apologized—Heaven knows what for—and cleared out. The moment he was gone, I could have torn my hair. I actually went again to the inn, to try and find him, though what I should have done if I had I don't know. . . .

Then I saw him again—not to speak to—as I was coming away from the Opera. Now hold on to something—tight! He was in livery—a footman's livery.

Yes. It made me jump, mentally, for the moment. Of course, I'd never dreamed of that. And then I realized that he must be down on his luck, and I felt so sorry for him I could have cried. As a matter of fact, I did cry. And then, all of a sudden, I knew that I loved him.

We met properly a week or two later by accident—on his part. You must forgive me. If you knew him, you would. And now we know one another properly, and he's in service quite close to Bell Hammer, with George and Betty Alison—didn't you meet them at Christmas? Lost all their money, and went out as chauffeur and parlour-maid. Anne, George's sister, is there, too. And he came to dinner the other night, and Aunt Harriet likes him, and we're—well, great friends.

And I don't know what to do. You see, he's terribly proud and honourable, and, to him, being a footman matters very much indeed. Of course it doesn't really matter in the least, but he would never look at it that way. And all my money, instead of making everything possible, as it might, only makes things worse.

What is to be done?

I can't blame him. Indeed, I'd hate him to feel any other way, and yet. . . . If only the positions were reversed. Then it would be too easy. As things are, it's a deadlock. And I love him so, Uncle John. I

*suppose you couldn't possibly come. I have a feeling that
you would straighten things out.*

Your loving niece,

VALERIE.

*P.S.—I'm so terribly afraid he'll disappear or some-
thing. He's like that.*

Monseigneur Forest read the letter with a grave
smile. Then he read it again very carefully, looking to
see if there was anything unwritten between the lines.
Only once did he raise his eyes from the note-paper.
This he did meditatively. Before returning to the
letter, he went farther and raised his eyebrows. . . .

The cause of this elevation is worthy of note. It
was, in fact, none other than the reference to Anne—
and yet not so much the reference itself as the manner
in which this was made. The prelate, you will remember, was no fool.

For that matter, he was not a god, either. Consequently, the counsel which he presently offered his
niece had to be communicated by the material channel
of the " common or garden " post, and was, in fact,
nearing Modane when Valerie rounded the edge of a
belt of Scotch firs in Hampshire to come upon Anthony
Lyveden regarding an old finger-post in some perplexity.

As my lady came up, Lyveden uncovered and pointed
to a weather-beaten arm, upon which the words FRANCE
4 MILES were still discernible.

" Can you help me ? " he said.

Valerie smiled.

" I think so. This is a very old post—over a hundred
years old. You know Hawthorne ? "

" I ought to."

" Well, once upon a time the village was called
France. But during the Napoleonic wars the name
was changed. For obvious reasons."

"And they forgot to alter this?" said Anthony, nodding at the cracked grey wood.

Valerie shook her head.

"No one would do the work. You know they used to bury suicides at the cross-roads? Well, one was buried here. That was when—when the post was set up. . . ."

A little shiver accompanied her words.

"I see," said Anthony. "The body was staked, wasn't it? What a barbarous old world it was! I don't wonder they were afraid of the place."

"It's supposed to have been an old usurer who came from these parts and had ruined all sorts of people in his time."

"And why did he kill himself?" said Anthony.

"I forget. There was some mystery about it. I remember an old, old shepherd telling me some of the tale, when I was a little girl, and my nurse came up in the middle and scolded him and snatched me away."

"Quite right, too," said Anthony. "And if she was here now, History would probably repeat itself." With a sweep of his arm he indicated the country-side. "Was this your nursery?"

Valerie nodded.

"In the summer." She hesitated. "I'll show you my window, if you like. It's the best part of a mile, though."

Anthony laughed and turned to summon his terrier.

"Patch and I," he said, "have at least one afternoon a week. As long as I'm back in time to lay the table. . . ."

A moment later he was stepping along by her side.

It had not occurred to him to ask what "her window" might be. If she had offered to show him the mouth of hell, he would have assented as blindly. Whither he went and what he saw did not matter at

all, so he was to be in her company. All the same,
his instinct pulled him by the sleeve. Hazily he
reflected that to retrace such steps as you have taken
along the path of Love is a bad business, and that the
farther you have elected to venture, so much the more
distressing must be your return. And he would have
to return. In the absence of a miracle, that journey
could not be avoided. For an instant the spectre of
Reckoning leaned out of the future. . . . Then Patch
flushed a stray pig, and Valerie laughed joyously, and
—the shadow was gone. Cost what it might, Anthony
determined to pluck the promise of the afternoon with
an unsparing hand.

He had walked in the direction of Bell Hammer for
the same reason that had caused Valerie French to bend
her young steps towards Hawthorne. Each drew the
other magnetically. It was not at all strange, therefore, that they should have met. Neither, since the
attraction was mutual, is it surprising that the effect
of each other's company was exhilarating to a degree.
Together, they were at the very top of their bent. If
the man trod upon air, the maid was glowing. His
lady's breath sweetened the smell of autumn ; the
brush of her lord's jacket made the blood pelt through
her veins. Grey eyes shone with the light that blue
eyes kindled. Each found the other's voice full of rare
melody—music to which their pulses danced in a fierce
harmony. The world was all glorious. . . .

Here was no making of love, but something finer—
nothing less, indeed, than the jewel natural, uncut,
unworked, unpolished, blazing out of a twofold crown
that sat, yoke-like, upon their heads for all to see.
Since, however, they met no one, the diadem was
unobserved. . . .

So Jack and Jill passed with full hearts by yellow
lanes into the red-gold woods, and presently along a
bridle-path that curled mysteriously into a great sunlit

shoulder of forest, where the driven leaves fussed over their footsteps, and the miniature roar of a toy waterfall strove to make itself heard above the swish and crackle of the carpet the trees had laid.

"I'll tell you one thing I've learned," said Lyveden.

"What?" said Valerie.

"That what you do doesn't matter half as much as who you do it with. I found that out in the Army. The work didn't matter. The discomfort, the food, didn't count—comparatively. It was the company you had to keep that made the difference."

"'Better is a dinner of herbs,'" quoted Valerie.

"Exactly. And it's the same now. I don't say I'd pick out a footman's job, but there's nothing the matter with the work. Everything depends on the other servants. My first two places nearly broke my heart: with the Alison crowd——"

He hesitated, and Valerie completed the sentence.

"Everything in the garden is lovely," she said slowly.

"Comparatively—yes. Of course, it's—it's only a back garden."

"Is it?"

Anthony nodded.

"Entered by the back door and approached by the back stairs. You can't get away from it."

"I can," said Valerie. "Speak for yourself. It's you who can't—won't get away from it. They say that in Russia there are noblemen sweeping the streets. If one of them was a friend of yours, would you turn him down because he carried a broom? Of course you wouldn't."

"No, but——"

"But what?"

"The first duty of a servant," said Anthony, "is to know his place."

Valerie stood still and looked at him.

" I wonder you don't call me ' miss,' " she said, shaking her head gravely.

" Very good, miss," said Lyveden.

" That's better," said Miss French contentedly, slipping an arm through his. " And now, if we leave the path and bear to the right, in about two minutes we shall come to my window."

The two had been climbing steadily, but another fifty paces in the direction Miss French had indicated brought them to the foot of a steeper ascent than ever. This was, in fact, a broad natural bank, some thirty feet high. The careful negotiation of a tiny path, followed by a plunge into a thicket, where the stubborn protests of boughs had to be overruled, landed them in a dwarf clearing, which the density of the surrounding *bocage* rendered a fastness.

Valerie stepped to the far side and parted the branches.

" Look," she said.

They were upon the lip of a heather-edged bluff which fell sheer for perhaps two hundred feet into a pinewood. Beyond, by mammoth terraces, the glory of the forest sank step by colossal step into the purple distance, from which distant in turn a thread of silver argued the ocean. There never was such a staircase. The grandeur of its proportions diminished the rolling world. The splendour of its covering made colour pale.

Anthony gazed spellbound. At length—

" I didn't know there was such a view in all England," he said.

Miss French smiled. Then she moved cautiously forward, till she was clear of the bushes, there to sit down upon a billowing cushion of heather which grew conveniently about as close to the edge of the bluff as it was prudent to venture. Abstractedly Anthony followed her and, after a glance about him, took his seat by her side upon a patch of gravel.

" I'm in your debt," he said simply.   " Deeper than I was before."

Valerie nodded at the wonder of landscape.

" I'll make you a present of this," she said.   " What else do you owe me for ? "

Anthony spread out his hands.

" Your society," he said.

" You've paid for that—with your own."

" Your pity, then."

" I've never pitied you," said Valerie.

" You've stooped," said Anthony.

" I've not stooped," was the fierce reply.

" We won't argue it," said Anthony.   " I owe you for your—your interest, at any rate.   You've been good enough to interest yourself in my——"

" Aren't—you—interested ? " said Valerie, staring into the distance and seeing nothing.

For a long minute the man sat motionless, not seeming to breathe.   Then—

" Yes," he said slowly, " I am.   And that's the devil of it."   With a sudden jerk he was on one knee beside her and had caught her hand.   " Oh, lady, don't you see ?   That's what kills everything.   Am I interested ?   Good God, I'm—I'm crazy !   I can think of nothing else.   You blot out everything in the world.   Whatever I do, or say, or think, you're always there.   There's nothing but you, you, you !   And you ask if I'm interested ! "

A wandering puff of salt air swooped out of the windless sky, ruffled his thick dark hair, and was gone, panting.   A gull sailed close to them, circled, dipped and sped seaward with a smooth rush.   The league-long shadow of a cloud swept stately over the gleaming woods, driving the sunlight before it, itself driven before the twin of its prey. . . .   The silver wire of silence became more and more tense.   Each second gave another turn to the screw.   Valerie began to tremble. . . .

" And that," said Lyveden at last, " that's why we can't be friends. I can't be your friend because I love you ; and I mustn't love you because——"

" Why ? "

" Because it's out of the question," he flashed. " Don't tempt me, Valerie. You know it is. I'm crying for something that's utterly, hopelessly, laughably out of my reach. I haven't the right to the moonlight, and I want—the moon."

He stopped suddenly and dropped his head, ashamed that he had let his passion ride him so recklessly, limp after his outburst, sick at heart for the truth of his words.

Valerie sat very still, exultation and anxiety fighting for a grip on her heart. Anthony had told his love, raved of her, called her by name. (Anxiety's claw-like fingers began to yield.) The very intensity of his utterance declared his conviction that he must give her up. The exceeding bitterness of his tone rang too true to be ill-founded. (Exultation's clutch weakened, and Anxiety took a fresh hold.) Of a sudden Valerie felt persuaded that Time could win her battle, could she but gain his aid. As if to establish this persuasion, the reflection that the old fellow had straightened more crookedness than any other minister of love came to her hotfoot, and then and there she made up her mind to court him. She yearned to put her arms about her man's neck, but felt that somehow that way lay ruin. Anthony being what he was, it was all-important that she should not show him her hand. He had seen— should see a card or two, certainly. That the rest were the same, card for card, as those he had just flung down, in his present mood he must on no account realize. Such knowledge were fatal. He would, presumably, kiss her, and then call Patch and walk out of her life for ever. So long, however, as he did not believe her lovesick, he would—well, he would

not disappear, at any rate. There are who lay hold
on hopelessness rather faster than they lay hold on
life. . . .

" Anthony, dear," said Valerie, " let's—please don't
let go of my hand—let's look for a way out. You know,
I think——"

What she would have said should not matter to us.
We have peered into her brain-pan. The sentence,
however, was never completed, and that for a reason
which shall pass muster.

On perceiving that Valerie and he were moving,
Anthony for a moment of time suspected an earthquake.
Almost instantaneously he appreciated that, while it
affected him pretty closely, it was a much smaller
matter—nothing more, in fact, than the giving way of
that portion of the cliff upon which the two were disposed. It was typical of the man that he neither swore
nor cried out, and of the soldier that he thought and
acted simultaneously. . . . By the mercy of Heaven,
he was, as you know, upon one knee. Had he been
sitting, like his companion, they must have gone with
the avalanche. As it was, they were able, after a
painful silence, to hear this crash evilly with a dull roar
into the pinewood.

The echoes rumbled curiously into the distance, and
a startled medley of cries rose from all manner of birds,
which soared out of their shelter, dismayed and whirling.
One bird was fairly gibbering. Miss French and Lyveden both noticed it. Valerie found herself wondering
whether it had lost its wits.

For the perfection to which their senses focussed
these and other very ordinary things, their plight was
responsible. It has been said that the faculty of
observation is never so pronounced as when the
observer is face to face with Death. Anthony and the
lady were looking him in the eyes. The pair of them
was, in fact, hanging in space, dangling two hundred feet

up, with an inch and a half of ash-plant between them and Eternity.

With his right hand Lyveden was grasping the slender trunk of a sapling which grew three feet to an inch from the new edge of the bluff. As he was, arm and all, at full length, it follows that from the breast-bone downwards the whole of him was over the cliff. Valerie was altogether in mid-air. She was directly suspended, with her back flat against Anthony, by the latter's left arm, which if he had released she would have fallen plumb into the pinewood. . . .

In a quiet voice Lyveden was speaking.

" Try and free your right arm."

Providentially, the girl's elbow was on a level with the edge, and at the expense of a torn sleeve she was able to work the arm free and on to the heather. This, when pulled, came away in her hand. Her fingers scratched upon the gravel frantically. No handfast was there. After a moment they abandoned the search.

" Now the other arm."

This was pinioned by her supporter's. By dint, however, of almost dislocating her shoulder, she managed to disengage it.

Again she waited for instructions.

None came, however, for Anthony could not think what to do. She could not turn, and he could not turn her. Neither could he haul them both up. He had not the strength. As it was, the strain upon his two arms was frightful—too frightful to last. . . . If she could have held herself for five seconds, he could have dragged himself up and the girl after him ; but she could get no shadow of hold upon the ground. And all the time his arms were tiring—both of them—tiring rapidly. . . .

The muscles under his arm-pits were aching unbearably, and there was a queer tingling in his right wrist.

As he looked at this, he saw how it was quivering. His
left arm was quivering, too. He could feel it. He
realized with a shock that this was a movement over
which he had no control. Nature, apparently, was
rebelling against his will. . . . And his fingers, crooked
about the trunk of the sapling, were getting hot—
making the bark greasy. . . .

Convulsively he sought foothold for the thirtieth
time, but, except for tweaking the agony in his chest,
the effort was vain. Desperately he blinked the sweat
out of his eyes. . . .

Patch appeared upon the scene, snuffing the ground
casually enough. His surprise to see his master in
so strange an attitude was unmistakable. After a
moment's reflection he decided that the position was
that required by the rules of a new game in which he
was intended to participate. He therefore made ready
to play, and, lowering his head to his paws, put up
his nose and barked joyously.

" Come here, Patch," said Anthony.

The tone was not that of the playground, and the
terrier obeyed mechanically—circumspectly, too,
though, for he disliked heights.

Anthony addressed his companion.

" When he's near enough, take hold of his collar.
Hang on like grim death. Listen ! My arm's giving
out. I'm going to let you go while I pull myself up.
It's the only chance. You're light, and he'll stick his
toes in. Put a strain on him now, so that he's
ready."

" I shall pull him over," said Valerie.

" No, you won't, dear. Do as I say. Quick ! "

He almost screamed the last word.

The moment he felt the strain, the terrier resisted
wildly. Planting his forefeet against the heather-roots,
he refused with all the instinctive terror of the dumb
animal, straining every muscle of his little thick-set

frame to avoid a closer acquaintance with that horrible brink. . . .

Very gently Anthony lowered his companion till her arm was resting upon the turf and the edge of the cliff was in her arm-pit. Then—

" Only a second, sweet," he said quietly, and let her go. . . .

With a frightful heave he was on his stomach . . . on his thighs . . . his knees . . . feet. He turned, staggering.

His back hunched like a cat's, Patch was sliding forward.

In a flash Lyveden had stooped, caught Valerie's arm with both hands, dug in his heels and flung himself backward. . . .

The three landed in a heap anyhow.

The moment he was at length detached from Valerie, Patch retired a good score of paces from the edge of the bluff. He had had enough of cliffs for the rest of his life. His master's interpretation of games was usually brilliant. This last was an exception. He could see nothing in it.

*   *   *   *   *

Betty Alison laid her hand orderly upon the green baize, with the complacent air of the player who is presenting his or her partner with all the essential factors of Grand Slam.

After staring fixedly at the display, her husband put his cards face downwards upon the table and covered his eyes.

" I suppose," he said brokenly, " I suppose you had a reason for overbidding me. I confess I can't see it, but I expect that's because it's too subtle."

" What d'you mean ? " was the indignant reply. " Look at those "—and Betty pointed proudly to a queen-high flush of six diamonds.

" But you called hearts ! "

Betty started. Then—

" So I did," she said guiltily. " I meant diamonds."

" I see," said her husband grimly. " After all, they're both red, aren't they ? "

Here the laughter which Anne and Anthony had been endeavouring to restrain broke out tempestuously. Betty's procedure and bearing at the Bridge table would have unhinged an enthusiast, but since the four domestics played for amusement and a penny a hundred her short-comings hurt nobody and were highly diverting.

With a sorrowful look at his opponents, George proceeded laboriously to amass three tricks.

With the game went the rubber, and by mutual consent the party broke up. It was half-past nine, and all had duties to do. Anne went singing to fill Mrs. Bumble's hot-water bottle, and Betty to heat the milk which it was her mistress's practice to consume at bed-time. Mr. Bumble, as became his sex, favoured something more substantial, and light refreshment in the shape of a ham sandwich and a bottle of beer before retiring suited him admirably. In Anthony he had a conscientious victualler. The sandwich was invariably fresh, the bottle of beer untasted, the glass clean. Mr. Bumble had marked these qualities and hugged himself.

This night, when Anthony entered the dressing-room, his master was sitting coatless upon a chair.

" I beg your pardon, sir," said Lyveden, " I hope you've not been waiting."

" No, no," was the cheery reply. " Not your fault, me boy. I'm early. There now ! Maria ! " Mrs Bumble appeared in her doorway in a red dressing-gown. " Look at that there tray, me dear. Ain't it a treat ? "

" Deluscious ! " said Mrs. Bumble.

" The very look," continued Mr. Bumble, " o' that sanwidge makes me that 'ungry you wouldden believe."

"May I cut you another one, sir?" said Anthony.

"'Ark at the boy," said his employer. "Wants ter kill me with kindness. Why, I could eat sixty, I could. But one's too many, reelly, at my time o' life."

"Joo drink beer, Tony?" inquired Mrs. Bumble.

"Yes, madam."

"Then go an' 'ave a nice bottle," she said, beaming.

"Thank you very much, madam."

"Yes, an' give George one," said Mr. Bumble, not to be outdone in generosity.

"Thank you, sir."

"Don't mention it," was the agreeable reply.

Anthony bade them "Good night" and left them breathing good-will.

As he descended the stairs, the particular verity of the adage which Valerie had quoted upon a memorable afternoon nearly three weeks ago appealed to him forcibly. "Better is a dinner of herbs where love is." Certainly he was leading the humble life. Born and educated to administer, if not to rule, here was he fetching and carrying, a hewer of ham and a drawer of corks. He wondered if there were any other footmen who were also Companions of the Distinguished Service Order. That there were no other footmen who were so comfortably housed, he was sure. And Patch was in clover. Anthony reflected that he had much to be thankful for. A dinner of herbs was infinitely better than none at all. He was, you observe, unconsciously converting the proverb to his own use. Stalled oxen, with or without hatred, were not nowadays in his line. He had quite forgotten what they were like, and cared as little. Indeed, but for Valerie, his Ambition would have been dead. Even now it lay very sick. High stomachs are easily upset. But a nodding acquaintance with Hunger will make Ambition turn her face to the wall.

The duty of George Alison at nine-thirty was to take

the dogs for a run.   When he returned this evening to find Anthony in the act of setting two bottles of beer upon the table, he lifted up his voice and thanked Heaven that he had at least one friend.

" Thirteen perishing months," he concluded, " have I been in this house, and this is the first time I've ever had an extra rum ration.   And that with my own flesh and blood, to say nothing of a lawful wife, running round the Bumbles from morning till night.   I admit that on two several occasions your predecessor produced to me my master's liquor, but his ribald reception of my inquiry whether such production was authorized left me no alternative but to refuse to consume it."

" What's that ? " said Betty, bustling into the room. " I recognized the tone of abuse, but I couldn't hear the words."

" My love," said George, " I was but remarking that beer is thicker than water.   And now will you take my boots off before you clean them ?   Or clean them first and take them off afterwards ? "

Betty Alison seated herself upon the table and raised her husband's glass to her lips.

" I looks," she said, " towards you."

When she set it down, the glass was half empty.

After a moment's silence—

" You've—you've left some," said her husband in a shaking voice.

" I know," she said.   " That's because I can't drink any more.   I hate beer."   She slipped off the table with a yawn.   " And now I'm going to bed.   Don't let him sit up, Anthony.   The car's ordered for nine, and he's got to get a new tire on."

" Where are we going ? " said Lyveden.

" First meet of the season," said George.   " I forgot to tell you.   Buck's Folly, the Bumbles think, but they're not certain.   Deuce of a job for me, I tell you. Everybody drives anywhere and anyhow.   You're backed into, you're always being called on to stop your engine, you're expected to be able to turn in a six-foot lane and to manoeuvre on a marsh as if it was wood pavement. To do any good, you want something between a gyroscope and a Tank. A car's useless."

"Stacks of people, obviously," said Anthony.

"Unfortunately, yes. Hardened as I am, I'm not looking forward to that side. I suppose you hunted—in the old days."

Anthony nodded.

"At Oxford, and sometimes with the Blackmore Vale. My uncle had a house in Dorset."

"Ah! We used to do a bit with the Pytchley before—before the War."

For a moment nobody spoke.

One and all they had stumbled into the closet of Memory. Pictures of dead days stared at them—days when they had come and gone as they pleased, before there had been a new earth and, seemingly, a new heaven. Old sounds rang in their wistful ears, forgotten scents came floating out of the darkness. . . . The closet grew into a gallery. . . .

"Good night," said Betty quietly. "Don't sit up late."

She slipped out of the room.

It was a tired face that George Alison raised to Anthony.

"Thank your stars," he said jerkily, "that you aren't married. I don't matter. I don't mean I like service, but I'm well enough off. But Bet—poor Bet. Think what her life should be, and then look at what it is. And her father's worth half a million. He cut her off when she married me. I had enough for two then, so it didn't much matter. But now. . . . She's wonderful—perfectly marvellous, but—it's hard to see her hands getting rough, man. Very hard. Her hands. . . ."

Anthony crossed the room and touched him upon the shoulder.

"If I were married," he said, "I should feel just the same. And then there'd be two fools instead of one. My dear fellow, if Betty regretted her bargain, then she'd need your sympathy. As it is, so long as she's got you, d'you think she cares whether she wears sables or an apron?"

"But you saw how she dried up just now."

"Shall I tell you why?" said Anthony.

"Why?"

"Because to-morrow morning you're going to a meet in blue, and she's sorry it can't be pink."

The two finished their beer, and George retired somewhat comforted.

As he had predicted, their attendance of the meet the next morning was only effected at the expense of more patience than Alison possessed. He was forced, in fact, to borrow from Anthony. Indeed, he afterwards confessed that, but for the latter's presence, he should undoubtedly have committed an aggravated assault.

The vicinity of Buck's Folly proved to be suspiciously vacant, and upon arrival at the standpoint itself it was instantly and painfully clear that the Bumbles had been mistaken. A passing butcher, when interrogated, grinningly vouchsafed the information that the meet was at Saddle Tree Cross, a spot of which all the occupants of the car had heard, but the way to which no one of them could tell.

Swelling with importance, Mr. Bumble produced a map, and George's face fell. He had seen that map before —from a distance. So had others. No one but Mr. Bumble had ever seen it at close quarters. Unhappily for all concerned, the latter's accomplishments did not include map-reading, an omission distressingly obvious to every one but himself. To follow his directions was fatal. Failure to appreciate his directions was at once

easier and more disastrous. What was still more unfav-
ourable was that, in possessing himself of the map, Mr.
Bumble became possessed of a devil. There was no
doubt about it. From being the most kindly of masters
he became a snarling absurdity, whose endeavours
simultaneously to study the canvas, observe the
configuration of the country-side, and rave into the
speaking-tube were consistently vain. George raised
his eyes to heaven and prepared for the worst. . . .

This came almost immediately.

After having obediently turned the car round, George
was peremptorily advised that, after all, he had been
facing the right way. Mr. Bumble rather unfairly
added that in his opinion the fool who had made the
map ought to be prosecuted. The warmth with which
he committed this belief to the speaking-tube rendered
it not so much inaudible as incoherent, and George,
who believed it to be a further direction, had to ask
him to repeat the remark. By the time Mr. Bumble had
realized that he was being addressed and had placed
his ear to the tube, George had concluded his inquiry
and was patiently listening at the opposite end. . . .

With such a beginning, the rest was easy. The wheels
of wrath were greased. Thereafter it was no longer a
question of revolution, but of speed. At times the
velocity attained was appalling.

Seven hideous miles slunk staggering by.

Mrs. Bumble, of course, had been in tears from the
outset. Anthony, as we know, was busily engaged in
administering comfort, temporal and spiritual. The
difficulty was to get George to take the nourishment.

"The fool's like a drowning man," he protested,
"with his arms round your neck. Your only chance
is to hit him under the jaw. Get out and do it."

Mr. Bumble had just formed and blasphemously
announced the horrifying resolve to return to Buck's
Folly and start all over again, when Anthony heard a

horse whinny. In a flash he was on the running-board
and touching his hat.

"I think we're just there, sir," he ventured.

Mr. Bumble hesitated, George set his foot upon the
accelerator, and a moment later they swept round a
bend to see the familiar medley of cars and dog-carts,
bicycles and phaetons, saddle-horses and governess-
cars, writhing below them upon a high-road into which
the lane they were using almost immediately debouched.

With a sigh of relief, Mr. Bumble dropped the map
and proceeded to mop his face. . . .

Comparatively, the chauffeur's troubles were over.
After such a drubbing, the nuisance of the congestion
to which they were soon contributing was like a flick on
the collar, and ten minutes later the car was berthed
safely with two or three others upon an apron of turf.

Mr. and Mrs. Bumble alighted, and George and
Anthony were left to themselves.

Then another car squirmed out of the ruck of vehicles
and came rolling on to the sward. The gentleman
ensconced upon its back seat was for the saddle, and
plainly glad of it. His careless, handsome face was
radiant, his manner full of an easy, inoffensive confidence, his gaiety—to judge from his companions' laughter—infectious. His turn-out was simple, but faultless. Despite the fact that he was sitting between
Lady Touchstone and Valerie, Anthony liked the look
of him.

Since their experience upon the edge of the cliff,
Lyveden had not till now set eyes upon the lady.
Unwilling to visit her home, he had inquired by letter
how she was doing. After receiving two little notes,
each of which assured him that she was not one penny
the worse, he wrote no more. Letters and notes were
sober and to the point. Any one might have read them.
The truth is, the two were love-shy.

Give to a dog a finer and meatier bone than he has

ever dreamed of, and mark his reception of your favour. Ten to one he will be afraid of it. He will walk about the fragment delicately ; possibly he will touch it with the tip of an envious tongue ; presently he will lie down at a respectful distance, watching it with big eyes. The thing is too vast for him. He must have time to become familiar with his stupendous luck.

So with Miss French and Lyveden. The gods had tossed the two title-deeds of a dream so wonderful that they were frightened. The gift was too precious to be handled at once. Like the poor dog they must have time. . . .

You will understand, gentlemen, that this was no ordinary affair of love. Convenience had had no hand in it. My tale had been shorter if she had thrust but the tip of a finger into the pie. Pity, Selfishness, Gratitude—none of the stock emotions went to the making of the foundations of this fabric. It was not founded at all. Neither had it grown out of friendship. It had no infancy. Had the two never met, it is probable that—circumstances permitting—each would some day have fallen in love with somebody else. And that would have been a regular business. Convenience, Friendship, and other hard-working matchmakers would all have put shoulders to the wheel and clapped one another on the back when the banns were published. The fact that the two had met saved, in a way, infinite trouble.

Valerie had many swains, and more than a few women had looked twice at Anthony. Such hearts, however, as had bleated for their sympathy had either bleated altogether in vain, or, finding the sympathy vouchsafed not at all what they wanted, bleated more fiercely than before. All the same, the two were not seraphim. They were mortal enough, and, if more than ordinarily attractive, revealed upon close examination a very ordinary collection of failings. The wonder was not in themselves. The fact that their natures were in just accord, was, at the most, curious. It was true, nevertheless. Each wanted precisely what the other was ready to give. Their personalities agreed like two indentures —proved themselves mutual elixirs. The wonder began and ended when they encountered one another. It was then that the seed of love flashed into bloom. Miracles alone beget miracles. Parallel lines had met.

The sight of Valerie gladdened Anthony's eyes. He sat very still in his seat, staring under the wind screen and wondering whether she would recognize his back. He hoped that it was not because of her mishap that she was not in a habit. He could hardly be expected to divine the true reason. This was, shortly, that the lady, who had expected to see him, could not enjoy a pastime from participation in which footmen are for a variety of reasons so rigorously debarred. Incidentally, she had seen Anthony before he had seen her, and the smile with which he had credited her companion's bonhomie was due to his presence alone. Had this been explained to the young sportsman, as one of Valerie's swains it would have spoiled his day. As it was, he emerged from the car with the genial air of one who is in high favour, and, after a word with a groom who had come up bustling, mounted a good-looking grey and, waving his hat to the ladies, proceeded to join his fellows with his eyes sparkling and his chin on his shoulder.

" Mason," said Lady Touchstone.

The chauffeur, who had descended, sprang to the door.

" Open the door." The man did so, and her ladyship alighted. " I'm going to look at the hounds. You'd better come with me."

" Very good, my lady."

The pair moved off in single file.

Though the office was new to him, the dignity of Mason's demeanour was irreproachable. It was clear that the blood of flunkeys was in his veins. As a matter of fact, one hundred years before, his grandfather had done much escort duty, with a band on his hat and a cane in his hand. Though Mason did not know it, the manner had been bred in his bone.

" 'Ere's a lady wants yer."

This was quite true. Miss French had not put it so bluntly, but it was not her fault that the messenger she had selected knew a footman when he saw one.

Major Anthony Lyveden thanked his informant with a smile. Had it been Caliban himself that had growled the message, the smile would have been as ready. Such a summons lost nothing in the telling.

George received the intimation that his colleague would be back in a minute apathetically. He was yet in some dudgeon. Beyond heaving a sigh charged with the resignation of a martyr who remembers that he has left his gloves in the torture-chamber, he evinced no interest at all.

Anthony crossed the turf to where Miss French sat smiling in a brown laudaulette, and touched his hat. Appearances had to be kept up. Valerie inclined her head gravely enough, but the look with which she honoured his action was not of this world. Anthony felt astoundingly rich.

" How are you ? " he asked anxiously.

" Perfectly all right."

" Sure ? "

Valerie nodded, smiling.

" I wasn't even tired the next day," she said. " Were your arms very stiff ? "

" Only for a day or two."

" And Patch ? "

" As right as rain."

" Will you be free on Sunday ? " said Valerie.

" From two o'clock on."

" Will you come to Bell Hammer ? "

" I will," said Anthony.

" I'll come to meet you with the two-seater. To-morrow I'm going away. Aunt Harriet has to go to London. Have—have you been back . . . since ? "

" To your window ? "

" To our window," said Valerie.

Anthony nodded.

" Yes," he said quietly. " I—I can't keep away."

It was true. The place fascinated him. Tremendous happenings had made it a shrine. Already worshipful as Valerie's bower, the ledge was freshly consecrate to two most excellent saints—Love Confessed and Life Triumphant.

" I thought you had," said Valerie. " I saw your footsteps. And—oh, please don't go so close to the edge, Anthony. Promise me you won't. It—it frightens me so."

Love lent the words an earnestness which there was no mistaking. My lady leaned forward, with her hand gripping the woodwork. There was a strained, pleading look upon the beautiful face, the proud lips humbling themselves, the glorious eyes beggars—Royalty upon its knees.

Quite naturally, Anthony's heart answered her.

" I promise, sweet," he said.

The vocative transfigured the lady. Anthony found himself mirrored in two dew-burning stars. To deck her favourite, Nature had robbed the firmament. To see such larceny, it is not surprising that the round world stood still. . . .

With a supreme effort Anthony pulled himself together.

" Patch is too funny," he said. " He'll come as far as the bank—you know, below the thicket—and not a step farther. He just stands there and wags his tail apologetically. And there at the foot of the bank he waits until I return."

Valerie laughed merrily.

" Poor little dog," she said. " It was enough to——"

" I say, Val, did I leave my flask in the car ? "

The two had been too much absorbed to observe the return of the fresh-faced youngster, and the latter's words cut their communion short, much as the sudden rasp of curtain-rings scatters the rear of slumber. It was providential that the world was moving again. The suspension of perpetual motion would have been bound to excite remark. As it was, the new-comer was upon the very edge of staring, when—

" Let me introduce Mr. Every—Major Lyveden," said Valerie. The two men nodded mechanically and murmured politeness. " Yes, you did, Peter. Here you are." She plucked the lost property from the bowels of the seat and rose to restore it. " By the way," she added adroitly, " now's your chance. Major Lyveden'll tell you whether you ought to wash a horse's legs."

Thus appealed to—

" Unless," said Anthony, " you've got a groom in a million, I shouldn't advise it. It means mud-fever."

" There you are," said Valerie, doubly triumphant.

The youth's face was a study. Respect was fairly bundling Astonishment out of the way. Anthony had spoken as one having authority, and Every was visibly impressed.

" You really think so, sir ? "

With one accord Valerie and Anthony smiled. The employment of the title was at once so irregular and so appropriate. Instinct had shown herself to be above raiment. Surely no manner of man ever was paid so exquisite a compliment.

A motor-horn coughed, and Anthony glanced over his shoulder. Then—

"I must go," he said quietly. "Good-bye."

He touched his cap with a smile and left them.

Every gazed after him with his hat in his hand. Then he looked at Valerie with wide eyes.

"But—but he's a footman," he said stupidly.

*   *   *   *   *

When upon the following day Anthony admitted that he had never seen the view from The Beacon, the Alisons, all three, cried out upon the omission with no uncertain voice.

The four were breakfasting.

"But," declared Anne, "you simply must see it. It's the most wonderful view in the world."

Anthony doubted this. He did not say so, of course, but he would have staked a month's wages that he could have shown them a finer. As it was, he expressed politely enthusiastic astonishment.

"It is, really," said Betty. "And the tints at this time of year—why, even George raves about it!"

"That's right," said her husband. "Never lose an opportunity of insult. Why 'even George'? Can't a chauffeur have a soul?"

"Who went to sleep at the Russian Ballet?" said Betty.

"Go on," said George. "Rake over the muck-heap. And what if I did? The music suggested slumber. I merely adopted the suggestion."

"Did it also suggest that you should snore?" said his wife. "Or was that your own idea?"

George touched Anthony on the arm and nodded towards the speaker.

"Look at the scorn in that eye," he said. "See? The one that's looking our way."

With an air of unutterable contempt, Betty lighted a cigarette and then hurled the matchbox at her unsuspecting spouse. The missile ricocheted off his chin and fell noisily into the cup of tea which was halfway to his lips. . . .

When order had been restored—

" He must see it at once," said Betty. " Before the leaves fall."

" The view, or the ballet ? " said George.

" Idiot ! " She turned to Anne. " Why don't you take him this afternoon ? It's his day out, and you know you can always go."

" Yes, please do," said Anthony.

He could not very well have said anything else. Besides, Anne was all right. He liked her. There was, of course, but one woman in the world. Still Anne was a good sort, and he would not have hurt her feelings for anything.

The matter was arranged then and there.

Seven hours later the two, with Patch, were tramping over a rising moor towards a dense promise of woodland which rose in a steep slope, jagged and tossing. This day the ragamuffin winds were out—a plaguy, blustering crew, driving hither and thither in a frolic that knew no law, buffeting either cheek, hustling bewildered vanes, cuffing the patient trees into a dull roar of protest that rose and fell, a sullen harmony, joyless and menacing. The skies were comfortless, and there was a sinister look about the cold grey pall that spoke of winter and the pitiless rain and the scream of the wind in tree-tops, and even remembered the existence of snow.

" I wish it was a better day," said Anne. " It's always worth seeing, but you won't see so far to-day, and there's no sun."

Anthony glanced at the sky.

" Unless," he said, " it's worth seeing when the trees are bare, it's just as well we're going there to-day. That sky means mischief. Are you sure you're warm enough ? "

Anne laughed.

" Supposing I said I wasn't," she said, " what would you do about it ? Give me your coat ? "

Anthony stood still.

" I should take you home—quick," he said gravely.

Honestly he hoped that she would waver. He had never wanted to come. Left to himself, he and Patch would have walked—elsewhither. Had he not known that Valerie was away, he would have excused himself at breakfast. Not for anything in the world would he have forfeited a chance of meeting her. Poor Anne's feelings would have had to rough it.

" I'm as warm as toast," said Miss Alison cheerfully. " And I know you don't want to come," she added, bubbling, " but you've just got to. You'll thank me afterwards."

Fiercely as he protested his innocence, Anthony felt extremely guilty. He had, it seemed, committed a breach of good taste, which must be repaired forthwith. He determined to be very nice to Anne. This should not have been difficult, for she was full of good points.

Fate had not been kind, but Anne found no fault with her heritage. Indeed, her temper was infectiously healthy. For years now Fortune had never piped to her, but that did not keep her from dancing. In the circumstances, that she should have been so good to look upon seemed almost hard. . . .

The two passed on.

It was a way Anthony had never gone, and, once in the thick of the woods, he could not have told where he was. Anne, apparently, knew her line backwards, for she climbed steadily, chattering all the time and taking odd paths and random grass-grown tracks with an unconscious confidence which was almost uncanny. More than once she turned to strike across some ground no foot had charted, each time unerringly to find the track upon the far side waiting to point them upward

—sometimes gently, and sometimes with a sharp rise, but always upward.

For all that, the pace his companion set was almost punishing, and Anthony was on the point of pleading a respite, when—

"Almost there now," panted Miss Alison. "Round to the right here, and——"

The rest of the sentence was lost upon Anthony, and is of no consequence to us.

As he was rounding the corner, he had turned to whistle for Patch. For two very excellent reasons the whistle was never delivered. The first was that the Sealyham was only five paces in rear. The second was that he was standing quite still in the middle of the path, wagging his tail apologetically.

For a moment Anthony stared at him. Then he swung round, to find himself face to face with a broad natural bank, some thirty feet high.

* * * * *

When Valerie French, who had come by way of the finger-post, saw Patch dormant at the foot of the broad bank, she could have jumped for joy.

At the last minute rheumatism had laid its irreverent hand upon the patrician muscles of Lady Touchstone's back, and the visit to Town had been summarily postponed. Valerie, who should have been sorry, was undeniably glad. She could not communicate with Anthony, but there was a bare chance that she might do better than that. What afternoons he had free she did not know. How he employed such as he had, he had told her in plain terms. She was, of course, to see him on Sunday, but that was four days away. Besides, she wanted to meet him upon that gravel cliff—that window-sill whose freehold they shared. High matters were on the edge of settlement. It was appropriate that they should there be settled where, in a mad moment, Fate had staked upon one cast all the kingdoms of the earth and their glory—staked them and lost them. That it was now but a question of taking possession of their inheritance, Valerie never doubted. In this she was right. The crooked way of Love had been made straight : only the treading of it remained—a simple business. That he had saved her life did not weigh with Anthony at all. That Death had summoned them, looked in their eyes, and let them go—together, made all the difference. It was as though a hand had written upon the wall. . . .

The sight, then, of the terrier verified hopes which she had been afraid to harbour. She had wanted so much, and it had all come to pass. She had wanted to meet her man, to see him ere he knew she was there, to find him there at the window, to come delicately behind him, to have him turn and see her, to mark the sudden gladdening of his dear grey eyes. . . .

Tremulously she ascended the tiny path and passed a-tiptoe into the thicket. . . .

You would have sworn it an elf that stole across the clearing beyond. . . .

As she glided into cover—

" Rain," said Anthony. " Now we're for it. No coats, no umbrella, no nothing. Anne, you're in for a wetting."

" Won't be the first time," said Anne cheerfully.

" Well, come on, any way," said Anthony. " The woods'll shelter us for a while, and then——"

" I shall have a bath," said Anne. " A nice hot bath directly I get in. You know, all steaming and——"

" Will you come on ? " said Anthony, laughing.

The two thrust through the screen and across the clearing. A moment later the thicket had swallowed them up.

As in a dream, Valerie heard their voices getting fainter and fainter. . . .

Presently they died altogether, and she was left

alone with the rain. This fairly pelted upon her, but she never moved. The truth is, she never noticed it.

A sudden rush of wind whipped a strand of her dark hair loose and flung it across her lips, but she never moved.

After a little while the wind died too, and for the second time she was left alone with the rain.

CHAPTER V

AN HIGH LOOK AND A PROUD HEART

HERE is a note, gentlemen, on its way to a lady. I have set it out now, that you may be wiser than she—by some twenty-four hours. Such as it is, I like my lookers-on to see the best of the game.

Rome,
14th November.

MY DEAR VALERIE,

I observe from your letter that you have lost faith in the man you love. Now, although I know him not, I trust him implicitly. I do not care what has happened. Shall I tell you why? Because I know that you would never have put your trust in him had he been unworthy.

Love plays such queer tricks with its victims, making the fearless timorous, the proud lowly, the trusting doubtful. Who was it coined that mischievous phrase, "Too good to be true"? He has much to answer for. Nothing is too good to be true. Not even the love of a man for a maid, Valerie. You found it so good that you were thoroughly prepared to find it false. And the moment you saw the clouds, you believed the sun to be dead. That is heathenish and the way of the people who imagine a vain thing.

His explanation will shame you, of course; but take the lesson to heart.

Your affectionate uncle,
JOHN FOREST.

*   *   *   *   *

The Assize Court was crowded. Even upon the Bench there was little room to spare ; and when the High Sheriff disappeared to return a moment later with two ladies, the Judge's clerk eyed the new-comers with something of that impotent indignation with which a first-class passenger regards the violation of his state by belated individuals whose possession of first-class tickets is highly dubious.

The calendar contained no case of unusual interest, but the Red Judge comes to Brooch but three times a year, and the old market-town makes the most of its gaol deliveries.

At the moment of the ladies' entering, Mr. Albert Morgan was in charge of the jury, and the twelve gentlemen were in course of hearkening to evidence which suggested with painful clarity that the prisoner's sins of commission included that of felony. That Mr. Morgan had been caught red-handed had not prevented the rogue from pleading " Not guilty." He had stood in docks before now. Besides, enough money had been found to instruct a member of the Bar—if not a solicitor—to argue his impudent case. . . .

" Anthony Lyveden," said counsel for the Crown.

" Anthony Lyveden ! " cried the constable-usher.

" Anthony Lyveden ! " bawled his colleague, opening the door of the Court.

Anthony, who was pacing the hall, came quickly. A moment later he had entered the box.

His footman's overcoat accentuated at once his height and his breeding. It suited the figure admirably, but not the man. The handsome, clean-cut face, the excellence of his speech—above all, the personality of the witness—gave the lie to his garb. Moreover, he displayed a quiet dignity of manner which was as different from that of the most exquisite lackey as is sable from civet. From resting upon him the eyes of the Court began to stare.

Lest their owners be thought unmannerly, it is fair to record that the last witness, whilst swearing that he was a chauffeur, had resembled one of the landed gentry of the Edwardian Age, and that the last but one—to wit, the chauffeur's employer—had sworn that he was a retired grocer, and looked exactly like one.

Anthony took the oath and glanced about him.

From the dock Mr. Morgan was regarding him with a malevolent glare. Farther back sat George Alison, upon his face an expression of profound resignation, which was plainly intended to indicate to his colleague the unpleasant nature of his late ordeal. And there, between the High Sheriff and Lady Touchstone, sat Miss Valerie French. . . .

With narrowed eyes and a face impassive as a mask she met the footman's look. By her side her aunt was smiling recognition, but Anthony never saw that. Gazing upon the beauty of that face which he had once transfigured, he found it frozen. That proud red bow of a mouth, that had been his for the taking, might have been graven of precious stone. Here was no vestige of Love. Tenderness was clean gone. Even as he looked, the blue eyes shifted casually to wander around the Court. . . . The cold wind of Indifference made Anthony's heart shiver within him.

Small wonder that he replied to counsel's questions mechanically, like a man in a dream.

He had, of course, known that he was out of favour.

One perfect Wednesday she had worshipped him to his face : upon the following Sabbath he had been turned away from her doors. For this mysterious fall from grace no reason had been vouchsafed. Moreover, so high was the favour, so eminent the grace, that Anthony had been desperately bruised. For a little he had been stunned. More than once, as he had walked dazedly home, he had tripped and stumbled. And, on reaching the house, he had done what he had never thought to do—surreptitiously poured and swallowed a glass of his master's brandy. As the days marched by, he had in some sort recovered—slowly, if for no other reason because Grief should have air and not be clapped under hatches. And now—here was the lady, pointing in person the unpleasant truth that she had no further use for him. . . .

Had they but told their love before his downfall, his course would have been simple. In that case, to ask an explanation of his dismissal would have been lawful enough. But things had not gone so far. It was while they were yet upon the threshold of harmony that the end had come. Of his honesty Anthony felt that he had no right to question her. The lady had not engaged herself : she was still free to do as she pleased. His cursed footmanhood was an additional embarrassment. To speak vulgarly, it put the lid on. And now—why was she here ?

Thus throughout his examination-in-chief the imps of Recollection and Speculation spun and whirled in his brain-pan.

Why on earth was she there ?

It is doubtful whether Miss French herself could have answered that question.

You will please believe, gentlemen, that her heart had brought her. It is the plain truth. Though Anthony did not know it, he had taken her faith in his hands and torn it across and across. For all that, she loved him still. She had a strange, pathetic longing to see him once more, and the case of " The King against Morgan " had offered her the chance. She had heard of the matter, and knew he must come to court to give his evidence. In such a place she would be able to study him undisturbed, and, most important of all, any speech between them would be safely impossible. A note to the High Sheriff had arranged her admission. . . . Incidentally, a burst tire on the way from Bell

Hammer had almost spoiled everything. As we have seen, however, the ladies were just in time. . . .

"Yes," purred counsel for the Crown. "And then?"

"Then the prisoner gave a cry and rushed into the drawing-room."

"What did you do?"

"I followed him and seized him. When assistance arrived, he was secured, and in the morning he was handed over to the police."

With a nod, counsel resumed his seat.

Mr. Morgan's representative got upon his feet with a truculent air. As he did so, somebody touched him upon the shoulder, and he turned to see his client leaning out of the dock. With an apologetic smirk at his lordship, the lawyer left his seat. . . .

"What is it? What is it?" he whispered testily.

Mr. Morgan breathed into his ear.

"This is the swine," he said evilly. "Put it acrost 'im. Arsk 'im——"

"You shut yer face," said his adviser. "An' don' try an' teach me my job, or I'll 'ave you in the box."

Before this threat Mr. Morgan subsided, muttering.

Impatiently counsel for the defence returned to his place. Once there, he adjusted his gown, consulted a blank sheet of paper with some acerbity, and then addressed himself to the witness.

"Why did you leave your last place?"

Anthony hesitated. Then—

"I was unable to get on with one member of the household," he said.

"Were you dismissed?"

"I was."

"Why?"

"As the result of a difference I had."

"Come, come, sir. That's no answer."

" The son of the house insulted me, and I knocked him down."

Such a sensational reply fairly took the wind out of counsel's sails.   Amid a stifled murmur of excitement he strove to collect himself.

" You—er—assaulted him ? "

" I did."

" Rather hasty, aren't you ? "

" I don't think so."

" We shall see.   Now, upon the night in question— the night of the burglary with which my client is charged—where had you been ? "

" To a private house."

" From which you, a footman, return at four in the morning ? "

" Yes," said Anthony.

" Did you have any drinks at the—er, private house?"

" I drank some wine."

" How many hours were you there ? "

" About five."

" You can drink a good deal in five hours ? "

" You can," said Anthony.

" How many drinks did you have ? "

" I drank two or three glasses of wine."

" What sort of wine ? "

" Champagne."

" In fact, you had a good evening ? "

" I enjoyed myself very much."

" Exactly.   And   you   returned—shall   we   say, 'happy'?"

" If you are suggesting that I was under the influence of drink——"

" Answer my question, sir."

The Judge interfered.

" Either, Mr. Blink, you are suggesting that the witness was under the influence of drink, or I fail to see the point of your questions."

Hurriedly counsel agreed, announced magnanimously that he would not pursue the matter, and plunged into a series of causeless and empty inquiries in the hope of stumbling upon an answer with which he might first of all hammer the witness and then erect a defence. His efforts went unrewarded, and behind him in the dock Mr. Morgan ground his teeth with vexation. That he was not getting his friends' money's worth was obvious. He did not expect to get off, but if he could have seen Lyveden discredited he would have taken his gruel with a grin. Venomously he gnawed his fingers. . . .

For the twentieth time counsel drew a bow at a venture.

" You're not under notice to leave your present place ? "

" Yes," said Anthony, " I am."

Despite herself, Valerie French started, and the chauffeur at the back of the court stared at the witness wide-eyed. The court, which had almost lost interest, pricked up its ears. Hardly disguising his relief, counsel proceeded to develop the impression in his own time-honoured way. Turning his back upon the witness, he elevated his eyebrows and then smiled very pleasantly upon a ventilator immediately above the jury-box.

" Really ? " he said. " This is most interesting. " Under notice, are you ? Dear me. . . . Why ? "

" I have given notice myself."

" Oh, indeed. Why ? "

" For private reasons."

Counsel appeared to find this answer so highly diverting that after a moment's hesitation the jury joined in his merriment. As the titter subsided—

" I'm afraid," said Mr. Blink apologetically, " I'm afraid I can't take that."

Anthony paled.

" I wish," he said, " to leave the neighbourhood."

" Why ? "

Anthony hesitated, and the Judge laid down his pen.

" Mr. Blink, I don't wish in any way to embarrass you, but can this affect your case ? "

An expert in impudence, Mr. Blink was well aware of the amazing possibilities of consummate audacity.

" My lord," he said solemnly, " my suggestion is that the witness knows considerably more about this burglary than he is willing to admit."

The improvised shaft went home.

For a moment there was dead silence. Then some one gasped audibly, a breeze of emotion rustled over the court, and the jury leaned forward. . . . Only the Judge, before him a list of the prisoner's previous convictions, sat like an image.

With a spiteful gleam in his eyes, Mr. Morgan moistened his lips. This was more like it.

Counsel, now in his element, addressed the witness.

" Whence," he demanded dramatically, " whence this sudden desire to make yourself scarce ? "

Breathlessly the reply was awaited. . . .

None came, however, and counsel took up the running with a dry laugh.

" Very good," he said. " I take your answer."

Anthony stepped down and joined the chauffeur without a word.

Ten minutes later Mr. Blink was fanning the flame of mistrust into a conflagration. What, he asked, did the jury think ? They were men of the world. Candidly, had they ever seen such a chauffeur and foot-man before ? Did they look like servants ? Of course they had Mr. Bumble's—their master's—confidence. *But had they the jury's ?* He did not wish to usurp the functions of the cinema or the stage, but it was his duty to remind them that sometimes Truth was stranger than Fiction. . . . Here were two servants, who were obviously not servants at all, giving such overwhelming satisfaction that they were allowed unheard-of liberty— liberty which afforded unrivalled opportunities. . . . "Out till four in the morning, gentlemen. A latch-key to let them in. A motor-car at their disposal. And now—leaving this comfortable—this perfect situation. Why? No answer. *Is it because the game is up, gentlemen?* . . ."

His lordship, who in his time had seen many juries befooled, summed up rather wearily, and at twenty-five minutes to one Mr. Morgan was found "Not guilty."

That the latter should greet the verdict with a gesture of derision verged, all things considered, upon indecency. It is good to think that the warder who hustled him from the dock, and played full-back for the prison, made this as clear as daylight.

* * * * *

Valerie left the court in some annoyance. She was annoyed that Anthony had been lessened, and she was annoyed to find that she cared whether he had been lessened or not. She would also have liked to know the reason for his proposed departure. Undoubtedly it had to do with Anne Alison. His very reticence proved it. Perhaps she was going, too. . . . Anne Alison. . . . At the very thought of the girl, Valerie's resentment welled up anew. Jealousy knows no law. The reflection that it was at her instance that Anthony had gone as footman to the house where Anne was housemaid rode her with a harsh and merciless hand. Often enough, sunk in most bitter contemplation of this fact, she got no further.

That she got no further to-day was due to a timely interruption—nothing less, in fact, than a snort of an intensity too clamorous to be ignored.

Valerie looked up.

"At last," said Lady Touchstone with some asperity. "That's the fourth."

" The fourth what ? " said Valerie.

" The fourth snort," said her aunt. " I don't know what's the matter with you nowadays. To snort at all, I must be profoundly moved. You know that as well as I do."

" What's the matter ? " said Valerie.

Lady Touchstone stared at her.

" My dear," she said, " what you want is a change. You have just witnessed what I hope is the most flagrant miscarriage of justice of recent years, you have seen twelve fools bamboozled by a knave, you have heard a friend of yours grossly insulted, and you ask me what's the matter." The car swung round a corner, and Lady Touchstone, who was unready, heeled over with a cry. " I wish Mason wouldn't do that," she added testily, dabbing at her *toque*. " So subversive of dignity. What was I saying ? Oh yes. A change. We'd better go to Nice."

Before Miss French could reply, a deafening report from beneath them announced the dissolution of another tire.

Mason brought the car to the side of the road. Then he applied the hand-brake and alighted heavily to inspect the damage.

With a resigned air, Lady Touchstone sat awaiting his report.

Valerie began to laugh.

" Shall I tell you what he's doing ? " she said.

Her aunt regarded her.

" I presume he's staring at the wheel," she said shortly. " Though of what interest a deflated tire can be to anybody passes my comprehension."

" Not at all," said her niece. " Mason is trying to make up his mind to tell you that we shall have to walk home. He only brought one spare cover, and we've used that."

Lady Touchstone glanced at her watch.

" And the Billows," she said grimly, " are coming to lunch in twenty minutes." She raised her voice. " All right, Mason. Miss Valerie's broken it to me. Stop the first vehicle that approaches and ask them to give us a lift."

" Very good, my lady."

" Supposing," said Valerie, " it's a milk-float."

" So much the better," replied her aunt. " I've always wanted to ride in a milk-float. It's the survival of the Roman chariot." Placidly she settled herself in her corner and closed her eyes. " Dear me. What a relief it is not to be moving ! If only the Billows weren't coming. . . ."

Neither she nor Valerie heard the approach of the Rolls. Indeed, it was not until George Alison, in response to Mason's signals, was bringing the great blue car actually alongside that the ladies realized that help was at hand.

The sight of Anthony Lyveden alighting to take his master's orders chilled Valerie as the breath of a crypt. Her aunt, on the contrary, was plainly as pleased as Punch at the encounter. . . .

So soon as Mr. Bumble appreciated that it was the quality of Bell Hammer who sought his assistance, he took appropriate action. Hat in hand, he descended into the road and, speaking with grave civility, put his car at the ladies' disposal. This being accepted, he handed them out of their own and ushered them into the Rolls. Then he bowed very pleasantly and closed the door.

Valerie started to her feet.

" But, Mr. Bumble," she cried, " of course you're coming. Aunt Harriet, we can't. . . ."

" Of course we can't," said Lady Touchstone. " Mr. Bumble, get in at once."

Humbly their host shook his head.

" Bell 'Ammer is no distance, me lady, an' the car

K

can come back. I shouldden dream o' takin' advantage of an acciden', me lady."

Regretting very much that she had never noticed the ex-grocer before, Lady Touchstone sought desperately to pull the position round.

"Mr. Bumble," she said, "we cannot use your car without you. That we do not know one another is my fault. Please get in. I want to tell you how very sorry we are about your case."

Again Mr. Bumble bowed.

"Your ladyship is most kind. If Mrs. Bumble was 'ere, it'd be different. . . . But we're both of us proud, me lady, fer you to 'ave the car. An'—an' please don' put yerself out, m'm. I'm in no 'urry."

The quiet determination of his tone was unmistakable. The little man was clearly stoutly resolved not to improve an acquaintance which his wife did not share. Wealth had not clouded his memory nor corrupted his simple heart.

Lady Touchstone hauled down her flag.

"You're one of the old school, Mr. Bumble," she said, "so we won't argue. Will you tell Mrs. Bumble that, if Thursday's quite convenient, we shall call at The Shrubbery and ask her to give us some tea?"

And Valerie put out her hand.

"Good-bye for the present," she said. "Thank you so very much."

The next moment they were gone.

Hat still in hand, the ex-grocer looked after the car.

"Lady by name an' lady by nature," he said softly. Then he put on his hat and turned to Mason. "'Ave a cigar, boy. I 'ate smokin' alone."

As they swept out of sight, Lady Touchstone picked up the speaking tube.

"George Alison!" she cried. Up went the chauffeur's head. "Stop the car, please. Valerie and Major

Lyveden will change places. We want to discuss the trial."

George slowed up with a grin.

Jack opened the door for Jill, who descended with an airy nod of greeting which hurt him more than the stoniest disregard. With her head high, she stepped to the seat he had left. As he was closing the high side door upon her, her fur coat intervened, and Jack set it gently aside. Jill felt the touch, turned, glanced down and twitched the garment away. . . .

Anthony's eyes blazed. A short six inches away, Valerie's blazed back. . . .

On the opposite side of the car George and Lady Touchstone were hanging out of their seats, raving concurrent invective against the Laws of England.

For a moment eyes searched eyes steadily. Then, with a faint smile, Anthony leaned forward and kissed the proud red lips. Then he shut the door with infinite care. . . .

Had Miss French's fur coat been less voluminous, the gulf which Error had set between the lovers might have been bridged within the week. But it was a fine wrap, and ample. In an instant the gulf had become a sea of troubles, with the house that Jack had built upon one side, and the castle which Jill had raised upon the other. And, as for a bridge, their labour now was lost that sought to build one. It had become a case for a causeway.

As the car slid forward—

"And why," said Lady Touchstone, "are you going away?"

Anthony laughed jerkily.

"Have a heart, Lady Touchstone," he cried. "I've already risked imprisonment to save my secret."

Her ladyship looked about her.

"This," she said, "appears to be the interior of an expensive limousine landaulette. Very different from

a court-house. The seats are softer, for one thing.
Besides, from his adviser the client should conceal
nothing."

" Are you my adviser ? "

" That," said Lady Touchstone, " is my rôle."

" But am I your client ? "

" I advise you to be."

For a long moment Lyveden stared straight ahead.
Upon the front seat Miss French was chattering to
George Alison with an unwonted liveliness, punctuated
with little bursts of merriment. All the while she
kept her head so turned that Anthony might miss not
a jot of her gaiety. . . .

" I'm sorry," said Lyveden quietly. " You're very
kind, Lady Touchstone, and I'm properly grateful.
But I can't tell you."

He was, of course, perfectly right. Intervention was
not to be thought of, much less encouraged. For one
thing, to mutter that Valerie and he were estranged
would be to proclaim a previous intimacy. For another,
it was an affair, not of hearts only, but of deeps calling.
Each lifting up the other's heart, the twain had distilled
a music that is not of this world : it was unthinkable
that an outsider should be shown a single note of the
score. Finally, Anthony wanted no peace-making.
What had he to do with peace ?

The silver cord was loosed, but he had not loosed it.
The golden bowl was broken, but not at his hand. It
was she—Valerie French—that had wrought the havoc.
That cord and bowl were the property as much of
Anthony as of her had not weighed with the lady.
As if this were not enough, he was to be used like a leper.
. . . What had he to do with peace ?

The thought that he had been able to pick up the
glove she had thrown down with such a flourish elated
him strangely. To kiss My Lady Disdain upon the
mouth—that was an answer. That would teach her

to draw upon an unarmed man. For she had thought
him weaponless. What footman carries a sword?
And then, in the nick of time, Fate had thrust a rapier
into the flunkey's hand. . . .

Lady Touchstone was speaking. . . .

"Well, well," she said gently, "perhaps you're right.
I'm sorry, you know. I saw two lives smashed once
by a clerical error on the part of a florist's assistant.
I knew them both, too, but neither would speak. When
it was just too late, Eleanor opened her mouth. . . .
Unknown to her, I went to the florist's shop and looked
at their order-book. Sure enough, there was the trouble.
I never told her, of course. But it's haunted me ever
since. Two lives . . . smashed. . . . And they say
that silence is golden. . . . When you do go, will you
let me have your address?"

"I can imagine nothing more worthless," said
Anthony. "But I think I've been rude enough.
I promise to send it you."

For no apparent reason he laughed bitterly.

His companion shuddered.

"Don't laugh like that, Major Lyveden. It's bad
for my heart. Oh, dear. How fast George is driving!
We shall be at Bell Hammer before we know where we
are." Suddenly she leaned forward and caught at the
footman's sleeve. "Anthony Lyveden, I've shown
you my hand. As you love my niece, what is the
trouble?"

Anthony set his teeth.

"Can't be done," he said, "Lady Touchstone.
We've got to work it out for ourselves."

"Curse your pride," said that lady. "There.
Now I've sworn at you. But it's your own fault. And
how are you two goats going to work it out for yourselves? With one of you bleating at Nice, and the
other—Heaven knows where—in England? D'you go
to church, Anthony Lyveden?"

" I used to."

" Then go again. Get to your knees and pray.
Pray to be delivered from blindness of heart, Anthony
Lyveden. D'you hear ? Blindness of heart. From
pride, vainglory and hypocrisy. Not that you're
hypocritical, but they go together, and it'll do no harm.
And I shall make Valerie go, and—and I shall pray for
you both."

Anthony slid off his hat and put her hand to his
lips. . . .

As he did so, the car sped past a red lodge and into
a curling drive.

Lady Touchstone sought for a pocket-handkerchief.

" There's a tear on my nose," she explained.   " I can
feel it. It's a real compliment, Anthony Lyveden.
You're the very first man that's ever made Harriet
Touchstone cry."

The car swept to the steps.

Anthony was down in a flash.   Tenderly he handed
her out. . . .

By the time her aunt had alighted, Valerie was at
the top of the steps.   Anthony walked up to her steadily.
Then he took off his hat.

" I humbly apologize," he said.   " It was unpardon-
able."

" You're right," said Valerie quietly.   " That's just
what it was."

As she spoke, a servant opened the door.

Valerie turned on her heel and walked into the
house.

That same evening, when the others had gone to
bed, Anthony called his terrier and set him upon his
knee.

" Patch," he said, " I've come back to the fold."   As
was his habit when mystified, the terrier swallowed
apologetically.   " Is that too hard for you, my fellow ?
Let me put it like this.   Once there were just you and

I, weren't there? A fool and his dog. Caring for nobody, nobody caring for them, but to each other—just everything." The Sealyham licked his face. "Then one day she came . . . She. A wonderful, peerless creature, to dazzle the poor fool's eyes. And the fool just fell down and worshipped her. He didn't forget his little dog, Patch. He never did that. But—well, it wasn't the same. Of course not. You must have felt it sometimes. . . . But you're a good little chap. And I couldn't help it, Patch. She—seemed—so—very—sweet. . . . I risked your life for her once. I did, really." He paused to stare into the fire. Then he took a deep breath. " By Jove, if you'd gone . . . I should have been left now, shouldn't I? Properly carted. Well, well, old fellow, it's over now. Never again, Patch. The fool's learned his lesson. You'd never let me down, would you? No. But she has. They say it's a way women have. And I'm going to wash her right out of my life, Patch. Right out. Now."

He set the dog down, stretched out his arms wearily, and got upon his feet. The terrier leaped up and down as if he had been promised a walk.

Anthony laughed.

"So? You're pleased, are you? Ah, well . . ."

He turned out the gas, and the two passed upstairs.

Anthony was as good as his word.

You cannot kill Memory, but you can send the jade packing. That he did faithfully. By sheer force of will he thrust all thoughts of Valerie out of his head. They returned ceaselessly, to be as ceaselessly rejected. Their rejection took the form of displacement. They were, so to speak, crowded out. All day long he was for ever forcing his attention upon some matter or other to the exclusion of the lady. A thousand times she came tripping—always he fobbed her off. Considering how much of late he had been content to drift

with the stream, the way in which his mind bent to
the oars was amazing. His output of mental energy
was extraordinary. Will rode Brain with a bloody
spur. When night came, the man was worn out. . . .

In the circumstances it was hard, though not
surprising, that he should have dreamed so persistently
of the tall, dark girl. It suggests that Nature is an
unscrupulous opponent. Be that as it may, night after
night, while the man slept, the tares were sown. Sleep,
whom he had counted his ally, proved herself neutral.
She was content to knit up the sleeve of care. That her
handmaidens as fast unravelled it was none of her
business. After a week of this devilry, Anthony groaned.
Then he set his teeth, and, pleading insomnia, obtained
permission to walk abroad after supper. With Patch
at his heels, he covered mile after mile. So, though
the mental strain was prolonged, he became physically
played out. His determination had its reward. He
came to sleep like the dead.

With a sigh for his simplicity, Nature plucked another
iron out of the fire. . . .

Anthony began to lose weight.

*   *   *   *   *

Thursday afternoon came and went, and with it
Lady Touchstone and Valerie. The Bumbles were
duly overwhelmed, treating their visitors with an
embarrassing deference which nothing could induce
them to discard : out of pure courtesy Lady Touchstone ate enough for a schoolboy, thereby doing much
to atone for Valerie, who ate nothing at all : the Alisons
respectfully observed the saturnalia and solemnly
reduced Mason to a state of nervous disorder by entertaining him in the servants' hall : Anthony kept out of
the way.

Not so Patch, however, who must, of course, put his
small foot into it with a splash.

The visitors were in the act of emerging from the

front door, Mrs. Bumble was dropping the second of three tremulous curtsies, and Mr. Bumble was offering the stirrup-cup of humble duty, when the terrier emerged from some laurels and, recognizing Valerie, rushed delightedly to her side. Before she was aware of his presence, he was leaping to lick her face. . . .

To disregard such unaffected benevolence would have been worse than churlish, and Valerie stooped to the Sealyham and gave him her cheek. Patch lay down on his back and put his legs in the air. His tail was going, and there was a shy invitation in the bright brown eyes which was irresistible. Valerie hesitated. Then, on a sudden impulse, she picked up the little white dog and held him close.

" Good-bye, Patch," she whispered. " Good-bye."

She kissed the rough white head and put him down tenderly. Then she stepped into the car with a quivering lip.

It was as the car was turning out of the drive that she burst into tears. . . .

Such consolation as Lady Touchstone sought to administer was gently but firmly declined : and, since her niece would have none of it, neither, gentlemen, shall you.

It was a few hours later—to be exact, at a quarter before ten o'clock—that a gentleman of some distinction laid down *The Times*.

For a moment or two he sat still, looking into the fire. Then he picked up a pile of depositions and drew a pencil-case from his pocket. For a while the occasional flick of a page argued his awful attention to the recital of crime : then the keen grey eyes slid back to the glowing coals, and the longhand went by the board. It was evident that there was some extraneous matter soliciting his lordship's regard, and in some sort gaining the same because of its importunity.

Mr. Justice Molehill was all alone. He had sent his

marshal to the cinema, " lest the boy should grow dull,"
and, except for the servants, somewhere below stairs,
the great gaunt mansion used as the Judge's Lodging,
lodged for the nonce no other inmate.

The room in which the Judge sat was enormous.
Indeed, the shaded lamp, set upon a table close to his
shoulder, did little more than insist upon the depths of
the chamber, which to illumine effectively you would
have needed a score of lamps slung from the ceiling.
For all its size, however, the room was sparsely furnished. At the far end a huge carved writing-table
loomed out of the shadows ; six high-backed chairs
reared themselves here and there against the walls ;
between prodigious windows a gigantic press lifted its
massive head. Reckoning the little table bearing the
lamp, and a pair of easy-chairs, that is a ready inven-
tory. A heavy carpet and curtains of the same dull red
certainly excluded the draughts. For all that, it was
not a chamber in which to sit apart from the fire. The
marshal hated the place openly, and, on being rallied
by the Judge, had confessed that it " got on his nerves."
He had even suggested that it was haunted. Mr.
Justice Molehill had laughed him to scorn.

His lordship, then, was gazing upon the fire. After,
perhaps, about two minutes of time, he crossed his
knees suddenly and flung up his hand in a little gesture
of impatience.

" Anthony Lyveden," he muttered. " Where on
earth have I heard that name ? "

The expression upon his face was that of a man
absorbed in searching his memory. He was, indeed,
so much engrossed in this occupation that the keen grey
eyes went straying whither they listed.

Let us follow those eyes.

From the light of the fire in its cage to the toe of
his lordship's pump, up to the chiselled mantel and the
cigarette-box—the marshal's—perched on the narrow

ledge, down to the heavy bell-pull by the side of the
hearth, on to a high-backed chair against the wall,
down again to the floor—all black here, for the light is
too distant to show the carpet's hue—on into the
shadows, where something—the table, of course—shows
like a grim bas-relief hewn out of the darkness, on to
its ponderous top, where the candles . . .

It was upon the top of the table that the keen grey
eyes came to rest—idly. The next moment his
lordship's frame stiffened with a shock.

The radiance of two wax candles was illuminating
the bitterness of death upon a man's face. It was an
old face, long, gaunt, clean-shaven, and the ill-fitting
wig that gaped about the shrunken temples gave it the
queer pinched look which tells of a starved belly.
Eyes red-rimmed and staring, a long thin nose, and an
unearthly pallor made it displeasing: the dropped jaw,
showing the toothless gums, made it repulsive.

The hair upon Mr. Justice Molehill's head began to
rise.

For a moment the face stayed motionless. Then
the grey lids flickered, and a trembling hand stole up out
of the darkness to twitch at the lower lip. A paper
upon the table appeared to claim the attention of those
horrible eyes. . . . But not for long. Indeed, they
had subjected the document to the very barest perusal,
when, with a convulsive movement, the creature clawed
at the paper, tore it with ravening hands and, clapping
the fragments to its distorted mouth, bit and savaged
it like a demoniac. . . .

Hardened as he was to the spectacle of Rage dominant
his lordship paled before this paroxysm of unearthly
passion. All the agony of disappointed avarice, all
the torment of mortification in defeat, all the frenzy of
impotent fury, blazed in one hideous blend out of that
frightful countenance. Could he have moved, the
Judge would have crossed himself.

Then suddenly came a change. The passion ebbed out of the face, the paper fluttered out of the loosened fingers, the red-rimmed eyes took on another look. Snail-slow the trembling hand was travelling across the table. . . .

Immediately between the silver candle-sticks lay a horse-pistol. As the fingers approached it, their trembling increased. Twice they hesitated, craven flesh rebelling against a recreant will. They shook so frightfully upon encountering the butt that it seemed as if to grasp it were beyond their power. Once they had seized it, however, the trembling left them and passed into the hand. . . .

With the approach of the weapon, the horror upon the face became unspeakable. The eyes were starting, the mouth working painfully. Resolved to be rid of life, yet terrified to die, the wretch was writhing. There never was seen so loathsome a paradox. Cowardice was gone crusading.

The Judge's tongue clove to the roof of his mouth. With the assistance of the other hand, the pistol had been turned about, but head and hands were all shaking so violently that the introduction of the muzzle into the gaping mouth was hardly accomplished. Twice cup missed lip, and the steel went jabbing against the ashen cheek. The next moment gums drummed on the metal with a hideous vibration.

With a shock his lordship recognized the sound as one which he and the marshal had heard more than once at this hour, and, after discussion, had attributed to an idiosyncrasy of water under the influence of heat.

That the supreme moment had arrived would have been patent from the eyes alone. Riveted upon the trigger-finger, squinting until the pupils were almost lost to view, they were the orbs of a fiend. Even as the Judge gazed, the light of Insanity took flaming possession. Hell, grown impatient, had sent a sheriff for the usurer's soul. . . .

With a dull crash the fire fell in, and the Judge started to his feet with an oath.

The candles were gone.

The first thing which Mr. Justice Molehill did was to wipe the sweat from his face, and the second, to mix himself and consume the strongest whisky and soda he had swallowed for years. Then, being a man of stout heart, he picked up the lamp and walked to the writing-table at the end of the room. Here all was in order, and the closest scrutiny failed to reveal any trace of the vision. The chair was there, certainly, but its seat was dusty, and upon the table itself there was nothing at all. The curtain behind the chair, when disarranged, disclosed a window, heavily shuttered as usual, but nothing more.

Now, his lordship disliked defeat as much as anybody, but if there was one thing which he detested more than another, it was an inability to prove an excellent case. Looking at it from his point of view, he had here a personal experience at once as interesting and incredible as a man could fairly be expected to relate. The reflection was most provoking. So much so, indeed, that, after a moment's hesitation, the Judge picked up the chair and placed it upon the table. Then he bent down and, thrusting his hands beneath the edge of the carpet, lifted this up from the floor. The fabric was heavy, but he hauled with a will, and a moment later he was standing upon the boards he had uncovered. Thereafter, at the cost of a good deal of exertion, he managed to roll it back from the window as far as the table itself. Holding it in place with his knee, his lordship reached for the lamp. . . .

It was his intention to discover whether the boards did not afford some real evidence of the crime, and it is a matter for regret that, upon perceiving that the floor had been diligently stained all over with some coffee-coloured preparation, for the second time in the evening his lordship swore. He was, in fact, in some dudgeon about to replace the lamp, when the torn edge of paper, showing between two boards, caught his observant eye. . . .

The fine handwriting was faded, but still quite legible.

10*th Jan.*, 1789.

Sir,

Your letter leaves me no hope but that you have been most grossly betrayed. Should you so desire, I will render you indisputable proofs that the Marquess of Bedlington hath no need of funds, much less hath delivered in any's favour a bond for the vast sum declared in your letter. In a word, though the name subscribed to the bond be that of Bedlington, it was not the Marquess' hand that set it there. Who hath done you this injury, I know not, but Time hath shown that his lordship's twin brother, Lord Stephen Rome, lately decd., with whom the Marquess was justly at variance, more than once scrupled not to assume his brother's person and title to compass his own ends. . . .

At the mention of the twin brother, Mr. Justice Molehill raised his keen grey eyes to stare at the lamp.

"Rome," he said softly. "Rome. That's right. It was at the *Grand Hotel*. And Anthony Lyveden was the name of the sole legatee. I knew I'd heard it before."

*   *   *   *   *

Mrs. Bumble's parlourmaid was counting upon her pink fingers.

"Sunday twenty-eight, Monday twenty-nine, to-day thirty. . . . Yes. To-morrow's the first of December."

George Alison regarded his wife.

"Let us hope," he said gloomily, "that it's a better

month. In the course of the last four weeks I've had seventeen punctures, I've endured a miscarriage of justice which has undoubtedly shortened my life, and I've lost as good a pal as ever I struck."

" To hear you speak," said Betty, " any one would think that Anne and I had enjoyed ourselves. It's been just as bad for us."

The chauffeur shook his head.

" You rave," he said shortly. " In the first place, what have you to do with tires ? "

" If we haven't had the punctures," was the reply, " we've heard enough about them."

" Yes," said Anne. " It's been almost as bad as golf. ' What I did at the fourteenth hole.' "

" In the second place," said George, " women adore irregularity. I can conceive nothing more delectable to the feminine appetite than the spectacle of Justice derailed. The apotheosis of our esteemed friend and late colleague, Mr. Albert Morgan, has afforded you two more indirect gratification than anything I can remember."

"Gratification ? " almost screamed the two girls.

" Gratification," said George. " If I'd come home and said he'd pleaded guilty and been sent down for five years, you'd have been all depressed. In the third place——"

" Monstrous," said Betty. " Don't laugh, Anne. As if the very thought of that man walking about free didn't make my blood boil."

" It made it run cold last time," observed her husband. " Same principle as a geyser, I suppose. . . . Well, as I was saying, in the third place, what was Anthony to you ? "

" One of the best," said Betty stoutly. " That's what he was."

Her husband wrinkled his nose.

" My point is that he was a man's pal. He was nice

to you because he'd been properly brought up, but . . ."

Mournfully he passed his cup to be refilled.

" Go on," said Betty silkily.   " I wouldn't miss this for anything."

Suspiciously George regarded her.

" Well," he said defiantly, " he hadn't much use for women."

Mrs. Alison turned to her sister-in-law and nodded scornfully at her husband.

" Our wiseacre," she said.

" All right," said the chauffeur.   " Don't you believe me.   He as good as told me so the day before he left, but I suppose that doesn't count."

Gurgling with merriment, his sister rose from the table and, coming behind the speaker, set her hands on his shoulders.

" And I suppose that's why he ' wished to leave the neighbourhood,' " she said, laying her cheek against his.   " Betty and I were too much for him.   Which reminds me, Bet, you and I ought to go to Bell Hammer and take those books back."

Her brother screwed his head round and looked at her.

" You're not suggesting that Valerie——"

" Sent him away ? " said Anne.   " Heaven knows. But he's just crazy about her, isn't he, Bet ? "

The parlourmaid nodded.

" And she ? " queried Alison.

" Loves him to distraction," said Anne.

" Which is why she lets him push off ? " said George. " I see.   And I suppose, if they'd hated one another like poison, they'd have been married by now.   You know, this is too easy."

" Ah," said Betty, with a dazzling smile, " but then, you see, women adore irregularity."

Her husband, who was in the act of drinking, choked with emotion.

That the household was once more without a footman was a hard fact. Major Anthony Lyveden, D.S.O., was gone. His period of service at The Shrubbery had come to an abrupt end upon the previous day. His notice had not expired, but when he received an offer which was conditional upon his immediate departure from Hawthorne, he had laid the facts before Mr. Bumble and left two days later. All efforts to persuade him to leave an address were unavailing. This was a pity, for, ten minutes after he and Patch had left for the station, there had arrived for him a letter from a firm of solicitors that numbered many distinguished clients, and The Honourable Mr. Justice Molehill among them.

Since Anthony will never read that letter, neither will we. We will leave it where it is now, where it will lie, I dare say, until the crack of doom—behind the overmantel in the servants' parlour, gentlemen, with its back to the wall.

Anthony, then, was gone, and Patch with him. The Judge had been gone some time. Mr. Morgan also had left the neighbourhood, and was earning good money in the West End by the simple expedient of wearing the Mons medal, to which, never having seen " service,' he was not entitled, and perambulating the gutters of South Kensington with a child in his arms. The child was heavy and cost him sixpence a day, but, as an incentive to charity, it left the rendering of " Abide with Me," upon which Mr. Morgan had previously relied, simply nowhere.

Lady Touchstone and Valerie were still at Bell Hammer. More than once the latter had revived her suggestion of a visit to the South of France. Each time Valerie had applauded the idea and then promptly switched the conversation on to another topic. . . . Women understand women, and with a sigh her aunt resigned herself to the prospect of a winter in Hamp-

shire. Return to Town she would not. London was
not what it had been, and the vanities of the metropolis
fell dismally short of the old pre-War standard. You
were robbed, too, openly, wherever you went. With
tears in their eyes, shopkeepers offered you stones
instead of bread, and charged you for fishes. Besides,
unemployment was booming, routs were frequent,
rioting was in the air. . . . Lady Touchstone decided
that, if she was not to snuff the zephyrs of Nice, the
smell of the woods of Bell Hammer was good enough for
her nostrils.

If Lyveden had lost weight, Miss French had gained
none. The blow that had fallen all but a month ago
had hit her as hard as him. Yet, of the two, her plight
was less evil. Each of them had dropped in their
tracks, which is to say that, while Lyveden had fallen
upon the rough ground of bare existence, Miss French
had fallen into the lap of luxury.

I am prepared to be told that this should have made
no difference—that creature comforts cannot minister
to a broken heart. But, sirs, the flesh and the spirit
are thicker than that. The iron must have entered
uncommon deep into the soul for the body no longer
to care whether the bath-water run hot or cold.

For all that, the girl was desperately unhappy.
That she should have been bracketed with Anne was
bad enough ; that they should have been wooed in the
same nest, to say the least, smacked more of business
than of love : that it was her nest, of which, of her love,
she had made the man free, was infamous. It was such
treatment as she would not have expected at the hands
of a counter-jumper—a deserter—a satyr. Possibly a
satyr in a weak moment might have fallen so low. But
Anthony was not a satyr. And deserters are not, as a
rule, recommended for the D.S.O. To suggest that
he was a counter-jumper was equally ridiculous. He
was a most attractive gallant gentleman. This made

his behaviour infinitely more discreditable.   It was a sordid, demoralizing business. . . .

And that, gentlemen, is what a hot bath will do.

Now look on this picture.

Valerie lay as she had flung herself, face downward upon the bed.   Save that one satin slipper had fallen off, she was fully dressed.   One bare white arm pillowed her brow, covering her eyes—mercifully.   Let us touch that gleaming shoulder.   See?   It is cold as ice.   That little slipperless foot. . . .   Cold as any stone.   But then it is the month of December, and she has lain so for two hours.   Two hours of agony.   She can remember every look those steady grey eyes of Lyveden's have ever given her, and in the last two hours she has remembered them all.   Inch by inch she has gone over the playground of their hearts : word by word she has recited their conversations : she has gathered great posies of dead blossoms, because they once smelled so sweet : she has trodden the lanes of Memory to her most grievous wounding, because they are still so dear. . . .

Then there were other times, when Pride had her in a strait-jacket, and the very thought of Anthony made her eyes blaze.

She had been walking herself out of one of these moods, and was tramping rather wearily through the twilight and up the long drive, when the cough of a motor-horn behind her made her start to one side.   The next moment a car flashed past. . . .

It was the local doctor's Renault.

Valerie's heart stood still.

The next moment she was running like a deer. . . .

The car beat her all ends up, and by the time she had reached the steps, the front door was shut.   She pealed the bell frantically. . . .

To the footman who answered it—

" What's the matter ? " she panted.   " Who's ill ? "

"Miss Alison, miss. I think it's a broken leg. She an' Mrs. Alison 'ad been to tea with 'er ladyship, an', as she was leavin', she——"

"Don't keep saying ' she,' " snapped Valerie. "Say ' Miss Alison.' And—and bring me some fresh tea. In the library."

She swept past the bewildered servant and disappeared.

The mills of God were off.

*   *   *   *   *

Twenty-four hours had gone by.

All this time the mills had been grinding steadily, and the grain, which had been awaiting their pleasure for exactly one calendar month, was beginning to disappear. After a while Valerie had come to realize that her pride was to be reduced to powder, and that there was nothing for it but to submit to the process with the best grace she could. Not every woman would have reasoned so wisely : few would have given to their decision such faithful effect. You will please remember that any reduction of her pride seemed to Valerie extraordinarily unjust. That there was stuff other than pride in the grist never occurred to her.

It was the evening, then, of the day after the accident, and the two girls were alone in the pleasant bedroom whither Anne had been carried the day before, and where she was like to spend the next six weeks of her existence. The patient was wearing one of Valerie's night-gowns and looking very nice in it. She was also smoking one of Valerie's cigarettes, and, so resilient is youth, chattering merrily between the puffs.

"Lady Touchstone was wonderful. She knew my leg was broken before I did. Almost before I knew where I was, she had my head in her lap and was telling me to lie quite still and hang on to her hand for all I was worth. ' You'll find it a great help,' she said. ' I know I did. And if you know any bad words, say them.'

For all the pain, I couldn't help laughing. And then she told me how she'd broken her leg in the hunting field, and the vicar was the first to get to her, and how she hung on to him and made him feed her with bad language till help arrived. And, when I tried to say I was sorry, she said the butler deserved six months for not having the steps sanded, and asked me, if you and she tried to make me comfortable while I was your guest, if I'd try to forgive you. . . ."

"That's the only possible way to look at it," said Valerie. " It's all our servants' fault, and we're only too thankful to be able——"

"You're very sweet," said Anne wistfully. " But to be saddled with me for six weeks——"

"Hush!" said Valerie, with a grave smile. " You promised not to talk like that."

Anne Alison sighed.

"It is unfortunate, though," she said. " I can't think what they'll do at The Shrubbery. If only Anthony hadn't just left. . . . You knew he'd gone, didn't you? "

Valerie shook her head.

"I knew he was going," she said.

"He left on Monday," said Anne. " We're all heart-broken. He was wonderful to work with, and nobody could help liking him. George is desperate about it. Being a man, you see. . . . Besides, they were a lot together. On the car, I mean. Off duty we never saw much of him. He liked being alone. I think I'm the only one he went for a walk with all the time he was there. And then Betty sent him. He'd never seen the view from The Beacon, so I took him. He was bored stiff, and we got soaked coming home, but he was very nice and polite about it. He always was. And now, I suppose——"

"The Beacon? " said Valerie faintly. " Where— where's The Beacon? "

"I don't know what its real name is," said Anne.
"We always call it 'The Beacon.' You must know it.
That very high place in Red King Walk, where the cliff
goes sheer down. . . ."

Valerie tried to speak, but no words would come.
Something seemed to be gripping her by the throat.
The walls of the room, too, were closing in, and
there was a strange, roaring noise—like that of mills
working. . . .

With a terrific effort she fought unconsciousness
away. . . .

*Her—their nest then, was, after all, inviolate. He
had never taken Anne there. Betty had sent him. And
—he had—been bored—stiff. . . .*

It was as if a mine had been sprung beneath the
spot upon which had been dumped her emotions of the
last two months, blowing some to atoms, bringing
to light others that had lain buried. Out of the wrack,
joy, shame, fear fell at her feet—and a sentence out of
a letter was staring her in the face.

"*His explanation will shame you, of course, but take
the lesson to heart.*"

"I wonder," she said shakily, "if you could give me
Major Lyveden's address."

"I would, like a shot," said Anne heartily, "but he
wouldn't leave one."

Again the rumble of those labouring mills came swelling out of the silence into a roar that was thunderous,
brain-shaking. . . . For a moment of time they
pounded the understanding mercilessly. . . . Then,
all of a sudden, the machinery stopped.

The corn was ground.

CHAPTER VI

THE COMFORT OF APPLES

ANTHONY was healthily tired. So much so, in fact, that he was sorely tempted to retire to bed without more ado. On reflecting, however, that at least twenty minutes must elapse before his faithful digestion could also rest from its labours, he lighted a pipe slowly and then —afraid to sit down, lest he should fall asleep—leaned his tired back against a side of the enormous fireplace and folded his arms.

It is probable that the chamber which his eyes surveyed was more than four hundred years old. That it was at once his hall, kitchen, and parlour, is undeniable. One small stout wall contained the front door and the window, a third part of which could be induced to open, but was to-night fast shut. Another hoisted the breakneck staircase which led to the room above. A third stood blank, while the fourth was just wide enough to frame the tremendous fireplace, which, with its two chimney-corners, made up a bay nearly one half the size of the little room it served. The ceiling, itself none too high, was heavy with punishing beams, so that a tall man must pick and choose his station if he would stand upright ; and the floor was of soft red brick, a little sunken in places, but, on the whole, well and truly laid.

A cupboard under the stairs served as a larder and store-room ; a flap beneath the window made a firm table ; in spite of their age, a Windsor and a basket chair, when called upon, satisfactorily discharged the duties for which they were contrived. A battered foot-bath did more. In a word, it received platters and knives and forks which needed cleansing, and in due season delivered them cleansed; of a Sunday morning it became a terrier's tub; and upon one afternoon in the week a vessel in which clothes were washed.

Since this was all the furniture, the place looked bare. As a living-room it left much to be desired; but, since Major Anthony Lyveden did not live in it, that did not trouble him. He used the room, certainly—he was using it now; nightly he slept above it—but he lived in the open air.

This was patent from the look of him.

Wind, rain, and sun set upon their favourites a mark which there is no mistaking. Under the treatment of these three bluff specialists the handsome face had in a short month become a picture. In all his life the ex-officer had never looked so well.

It was when he had given his late master notice and had twenty-one pounds in the world that Lyveden had seen the advertisement—

A solitary existence, hard work, long hours, £3 a week, fuel, a bachelor's unfurnished lodging, and an open-air life is offered to an ex-officer : the job has been considered and abusively rejected by five ex-other ranks on the score that it is " not good enough " ; as an ex-officer myself, I disagree with them ; incidentally, I can pay no more ; sorry to have to add that applicants must be physically fit. Write, Box 1078, *c/o " The Times," E.C.*4.

Immediately he had applied by telegram, paying for a reply. . . .

Three days later he and Patch had emerged from the London train into the keen night air of Chipping Norton.

There on the platform to meet him had stood his new employer—a tremendous figure of a man, with the eyes of an explorer and the physique of an Atlas, and, after a little delay, Lyveden had found himself seated in a high dog-cart, which, in the wake of an impatient roan, was bowling along over the cold white roads, listening to the steady deep voice foretelling his fate.

"We're going to Girdle. I've taken a room at the inn there for you to-night. Your cottage is two miles from there. I'll show you the way and meet you there in the morning—at half-past eight, please. It's water-tight—I had the thatch tended this year—and it's got its own well—good water. It's in the park, by the side of the London road, so you won't be too lonely. Now, your work. Woodman, road-maker, joiner, keeper, forester, gardener—that's what I want." Anthony's brain reeled. "That's what I am myself. Listen. I've inherited this estate, which has been let go for over a hundred years. There isn't a foot of fencing that isn't rotten, a road that you can walk on, a bridge that is safe. The woods—it's all woodland—have gone to blazes. I want to pull it round. . . . Fifty R.E.'s and a Labour Battalion is what it wants, but that's a dream. I've tried the obvious way. I asked for tenders for mending a twelve-foot bridge. The lowest was seventy pounds. I did it myself, single-handed, in seven days. . . . I've saved my stamps since then. Well, I've got a small staff." Anthony heaved a sigh of relief. "Two old carters, two carpenters, three magnificent sailors—all deaf, poor chaps—and a little lame engineer. But I haven't an understudy. . . . I hope you'll like it, and stay. It's a man's life."

"I like the sound of it," said Lyveden. "What are you on now?"

"Road-making at the moment. The fence is the most important, but the roads are so bad we can't get the timber through. It's all sawn ready—we've got a toy saw-mill—but we can't carry it. You see . . ."

The speaker's enthusiasm had been infectious. Lyveden had found himself violently interested in his new life before he had entered upon it.

The next day he had accepted the tiny cabin as his future home, and had had a fire roaring upon the hearth before nine o'clock. Colonel Winchester, who had expected to lodge him at Girdle for the best part of a week, had abetted his determination to take immediate possession with a grateful heart, presenting his new tenant with some blankets and an excellent camp-bed, and putting a waggon at his disposal for the rest of the day. Seven o'clock that evening had found Anthony and his dog fairly installed in their new quarters.

And now a month had gone by—to be exact, some thirty-four days, the biggest ones, perhaps, in all Lyveden's life. In that short space of time the man whose faith had frozen had become a zealot.

Five thousand acres of woodland and the fine frenzy of an Homeric Quixote had wrought the miracle. Of course the soil was good, and had been ruthlessly harrowed and ploughed into the very pink of condition to receive such seed. For months Lyveden's enterprise had been stifled : for months Necessity had kept his intellect chained to a pantry-sink : such ambition as he had had was famished. To crown it all, Love had lugged him into the very porch of Paradise, to slam the gates in his face. . . . Mind and body alike were craving for some immense distraction. In return for board and lodging for his terrier and himself, the man would have picked oakum—furiously : but not in Hampshire. That was the county of Paradise— Paradise Lost.

As we have seen, the bare idea of the employment had found favour in Lyveden's eyes, and, before they had been together for half an hour, the personality of

Winchester had taken him by the arm. When, two days later, master and man strode through the splendid havoc of the woods, where the dead lay where they had fallen, and the quick were wrestling for life, where the bastard was bullying the true-born, and kings were mobbed by an unruly rabble—dogs with their paws upon the table, eating the children's bread—where avenues and glades were choked with thickets, where clearings had become brakes, and vistas and prospects were screened by aged upstarts that knew no law ; when they followed the broken roads, where fallen banks sprawled on the fairway, and the laborious rain had worn ruts into straggling ditches, where culverts had given way and the dammed streams had spread the track with wasting pools, where sometimes time-honoured weeds blotted the very memory of the trail into oblivion ; when they stood before an old grey mansion, with what had once been lawns about it and the ruin of a great cedar hard by its side, its many windows surveying with a grave stare the wreck and riot of the court it kept—then for the first time Anthony Lyveden heard the sound of the trumpets.

The physical attraction, no doubt, of the work to be done was crooking a beckoning finger. To pass his time among these glorious woods, to have a healthy occupation which would never be gone, to enjoy and provide for his dog a peaceful possession of the necessities of life, was an alluring prospect.

Yet this was not the call the trumpets had wound.

That distant silvery flourish was not of the flesh. It was the same fanfare that has sent men to lessen the mysteries of the unknown world, travel the trackless earth, sail on uncharted seas, trudge on eternal snows, to sweat and shiver under strange heavens, grapple with Nature upon the Dame's own ground and try a fall with the Amazon—with none to see fair play—for the tale of her secrets.

Anthony's imagination pricked up its flattened ears. . . .

Gazing upon the crookedness about him, he saw it straightened : looking upon the rough places, he saw them made plain. He saw the desolation banished, the wilderness made glad. He saw the woods ordered, the broken roads mended, the bridges rebuilt, streams back in their beds, vistas unshuttered, avenues cleared. . . . He saw himself striving, one of a little company sworn to redeem the stolen property. Man had won it by the sweat of his brow—his seal was on it yet— that great receiver Nature must give it up. It was not the repair of an estate that they would compass : it was the restoration of the kingdom of man.

Marking the light in his employee's eyes, Colonel Winchester could have flung up his cap. Opening his heart, he spoke with a rough eloquence of the great days the place had seen, of lords and ladies who had slept at the house, of coaches that had rumbled over that broken bridge, of a troop ambushed at the bend of the avenue, of a duel fought upon that sometime sward. . . .

" The world 'd think me mad. In the clubs I used to belong to they'd remember that I was always a bit of a crank. To the Press I should be a curio worth three lines and a photograph of the ' Brigadier Breaks Stones ' order. But there's a zest to the job you won't find in Pall Mall. There's an encouragement to go ahead that you seldom strike in this world. There's a gratitude the old place'll hand you that no reporter could ever understand. . . ."

It was true.

As the short days went tearing by, the spirit of the place entered into Anthony's soul. He laboured thirstily, yet not so much laboured as laid his labour as a thank-offering at his goddess's feet. He counted himself happy, plumed himself on his selection for the

office, thanked God nightly. But that he needed the
pay, he would not have touched it. As it was, a third
of it went into his tool-bag. The appalling magnitude
of the task never worried him—nor, for the matter of
that, his fellow-workers. Master and men went toiling
from dawn to dusk under a spell, busy, tireless as gnomes,
faithful as knights to their trust. Their zeal was quick
with the devotion to a cause that went out with coat-
armour. Rough weather might chill one iron, but
another was plucked from the fire ere the first was cold.
There never was seen such energy. Place and purpose
together held them in thrall. Had encouragement
been needed, the death of every day showed some
material gain. Foot by foot the kingdom was being
restored.

Whether the goddess of the estate had charmed
Patch also, it is not for me to say. He was certainly
a happy fellow. Life had apparently developed into
one long, glorious ramble, which nothing but nightfall
could curtail. To his delight, too, Anthony and the
other men showed an unexpected and eventful interest
in stones and boughs and ditches and drains, and sometimes they even dragged trees along the ground for him
to bark at. It is to be hoped that he also expressed
his gratitude of nights. . . .

If he has not done so this night, it is too late now,
for he is stretched upon the warm bricks in a slumber
which will allow of no orisons this side of to-morrow.

Let us take his tip, gentlemen. The night is young,
I know, but Anthony has been abroad since cock-crow.
Besides, I have led you a pretty dance. You have, in
fact, tramped for miles—'tis two and an odd furlong
to the old grey house alone—and the going is ill, as
you know, and the night, if young, is evil. A whole gale
is coming, and the woods are beside themselves. The
thrash of a million branches, the hoarse booming of
the wind, lend to the tiny chamber an air of comfort

such as no carpets nor arras could induce. The rain, too, is hastening to add its insolence to the stew. That stutter upon the pane is its advance-guard. . . .

Did you hear that dull crash, gentlemen? Or are your ears not practised enough to pluck it out of the welter of rugged harmony? It was an elm, sirs, an old fellow, full of years, gone to his long home. For the last time the squirrels have swung from his boughs : for the last time the rooks have sailed and cawed about his proud old head. To-morrow there will be another empty stall in that majestic quire which it has taken Time six hundred years to fill. . . .

The distant crash brought Lyveden out of a sleep-ridden reverie. For a second he listened intently, as if he hoped that he had been mistaken, and that the sound he had heard had been but a trick of the wind. Then he gave a short sigh and knocked out his pipe.

*　　*　　*　　*　　*

"And you've had no answer?" said the Judge, snapping a wafer betwixt his fingers and thumb.

His guest shook his head. Then he hastened to enlighten the wine-waiter, who had been about to refill his glass with port and had construed the gesture as a declension of the nectar.

"Never a line," he said shortly. "Of course the letter may never have reached him. But, if it did, he may not have thought it worth while . . . I mean, I wrote very guardedly."

"Naturally," said the Judge, "naturally. Still, I should have thought . . ."

The two men sat facing each other across a small mahogany table from which the cloth had been drawn. The surface thus exposed gave back such light as fell upon it enriched and mellowed. In this it was typical of the room, which turned the common air into an odour of luxury.

Servants, perfectly trained, faultlessly groomed, stepped noiselessly to and fro, handing dishes, replenishing glasses, anticipating desires. A tremendous fire glowed in its massive cage ; a crimson carpet and curtains of almost barbaric gravity contributed to the admirable temperature and deadened unruly noise. A brace of shaded candles to each small table made up nine several nebulæ, whose common radiance provoked an atmosphere of sober mystery, dim and convenient. Light so subdued subdued in turn the tones of the company of hosts and visitors. Conversation became an exchange of confidences ; laughter was soft and low ; the murmurous blend of talk flowed unremarked, yet comforted the ear. The flash of silver, the sparkle of glass, the snow of napery, gladdened the eye. No single circumstance of expediency was unobserved, no detail of propriety was overlooked. Pomp lay in a litter which he had borrowed of Ease.

" Shall I write again ? " said the solicitor.

Mr. Justice Molehill stared at his port. After a moment—

" No," he said slowly. " Not at present, at any rate. I don't want to push the matter, because I've got so very little to go on. In moving at all, I'm laying myself open to the very deuce of a snub."

" I shall get the snub," said his guest. " But that's what I'm paid for. Besides, I'm fairly hardened."

That he evinced not the slightest curiosity regarding his mysterious instructions argued a distinction between the individual and the adviser, firmly drawn and religiously observed. For a Justice of the King's Bench suddenly to be consumed by a desire to know the names of the uncles of somebody else's footman smacked of collaboration by Gilbert and Chardenal. Once, however, the solicitor knew his client, he asked no questions. Reticence and confidence were in his eyes equally venerable. Usually he had his reward. He had it now.

"In the spring," said his companion, "of 1914 I went to Sicily. On my way back I stopped for one night at Rome. The day I left, while I was resting after luncheon, the manager of the hotel brought a priest to my room—a Catholic priest of some position, I fancy—an Englishman. I can't remember his name. He spoke very civilly, and begged my instant attention.

"An old Englishman, it seemed, lay dying upon the first floor. He was all alone—no relations—no servant. He could speak no Italian. Realizing that he was dying, he was frantic to make a will. His frenzied attempts to convey this desire to the attendant doctor had resulted in the latter dashing into the street and stopping and returning with the first priest he encountered. This happened to be my friend. Upon beholding him, the patient, who had hoped for a lawyer, had turned his face to the wall. Then, to his relief, he found that, though a priest, yet he was English, and begged him to fetch an attorney. The priest hurried to the manager, and the manager brought him to me. . . .

"You know how much I know about wills. All the same, argument was not to be thought of. To the laity, solicitor, lawyer, barrister, and attorney are synonymous terms. Moreover, they are all will-wrights. A judge is a sort of shop-steward. . . .

"Well, I drew one. To tell you the truth, I don't think it was so bad. I attended the poor man. I took his instructions. And there and then in the sick-room I drew the will upon a sheet of notepaper. He signed it in my presence and that of the priest. The latter then took charge of it, with a view to getting it stamped next morning at the British Consulate. We both had some hazy idea that that was desirable.

"I left Rome the same night.

"Gradually—we've all had a lot to think about in

the last seven years—I forgot the whole incident. Then, some two months ago, when I was at Brooch, a fellow gives evidence before me in a burglary case. A footman called Anthony Lyveden. For a long time I couldn't imagine where I'd heard the names before. Then something—I'll tell you what in the smoking-room —brought it all back. Anthony Lyveden was the nephew of the man whose will I made, and he was named as the sole legatee.

"In a way it's no affair of mine, and yet I feel concerned. I'll tell you why. That footman was a gentleman born. Moreover, he was down on his luck. He didn't look like a fellow who'd run through money, and I think the old testator was pretty rich. He gave that impression. And for a will made in such circumstances to go astray it would be easy enough—obviously. The devil of it is, except for the name of Lyveden, I can remember nothing else."

The solicitor sipped his port. Then—

"A search at Somerset House," he said slowly, "should give us the maiden surname of Anthony Lyveden's mother. If she had a brother. . . ."

Sir Giles Molehill raised his eyes and sighed.

"And it never occurred to me," he said. "It's high time I went to the Court of Appeal."

Two days later his lordship received a letter informing him that a search at Somerset House had revealed the fact that a son named Anthony had been born upon the fourteenth of January, 1891, to a Mrs. Katharine Lyveden, formerly *Roach*.

As he read it, the Judge exclaimed audibly.

The note which he wrote there and then shall speak for itself.

DEAR BLITHE,
Roach was the surname of the testator. Please go on. When you can submit a Christian name to my memory,

please do so.   I am not sure that it will respond, but we can try.

> *Yours sincerely,*
> GILES MOLEHILL.

*   *   *   *   *

When Anthony Lyveden had been for a week at Gramarye, he had reluctantly posted a letter containing his new address.   This he had done because he had promised to do it.   As the letter had fallen into the box, he had prayed fervently, but without the faintest hope, that it might never be delivered.   A galley-slave who has broken ship and won sanctuary does not advertise his whereabouts with a light heart.   He may be beyond pursuit, yet—he and the galley are both of this world ; things temporal only keep them apart, and if the master came pricking, with a whip in his belt. . . .   You must remember that Anthony had been used very ill.   At first, bound to the oar of Love, he had pulled vigorously and found the sea silken, his chains baubles.   Then a storm had arisen.   In his hands the docile oar had become a raging termagant, and, when he would have been rid of it, the baubles had opposed his will.   He had been dragged and battered unspeakably.   Over all, the lash had been laid upon his bare shoulders ; and that with a nicety of judgment which should have been foreign to so white a wrist and to eyes that could look so tender. Now that he had escaped out of hell, it was not surprising that he was loth to discover his refuge.   Still, a promise must be respected. . . .

For that matter, supplications do not always go empty away.   The answer to Anthony's came in the shape of a fire which attacked the last coach but one upon a London train and partially destroyed two mailbags before its flames were subdued.   It follows that, though he did not know it, such friends as the

ex-officer had knew no more where he was than did the
man in the moon.

It is here convenient, believe me, to go imagining.

We have looked into Anthony's mind at the hour
when he posted his letter.   Had he posted it this nine-
teenth day of January, instead of six weeks ago, and
we, as before, peered into his brain-pan, we should
have found his supplication that the missive might go
astray even more urgent.   We should have noted that,
while he was just as fearful to be reminded of the galley
and the tall dark ganger with the red, red mouth and
the merciless thong, he also viewed with alarm the
possibility of any distraction from his work.   The
galley-slave was become a votary.

Let us be quite clear about it.

Anthony had come to Gramarye to try to forget.
In this he was steadily unsuccessful.   At the end of a
month he had not advanced one inch.   His love for
Valerie was as breathless, haunting, wistful as it had
ever been.   The whole of the kingdom of his heart
was hers alone, and, so far as he could see, like to remain
hers only for the rest of his life.   Since, therefore, he
could not dispatch Memory, he sought to immure her.
Since Valerie's sovereignty was so fast stablished that
it could not be moved, he sought to rule his heart out
of his system.   Had it been possible, he would, like
Æsop's Beaver, have ripped the member from him
and gone heartless ever after.   The Fabulous Age
being dead, Anthony made the best shift he could, and
strove to bury kingdom and queen together so deep
within him that their existence should not trouble his
life.   If he could not put out the light, he would hide
it under a bushel.   It occurred to him that his mind,
appropriately occupied, should make an excellent bushel
—appropriately occupied. . . .   He resolved that
Gramarye should have his mind.   Of this he would
make a kingdom, mightier and more material than

that of his heart. The trouble was, his mind, though more tractable, liked Valerie's occupation, found it desirable, and clung to its present tenant for all it was worth. By no means dismayed, Anthony, as before, had recourse to ejection by crowding out. . . . Two things, however, made this attempt more formidable. First, he did not have to be for ever scouring the highways and hedges for a new tenantry; Gramarye was always at hand. Secondly, though Anthony did not know it, *there was no need for Gramarye to be compelled to come in.* He was pressing an invitation upon one who had invited herself. The hooded personality of the place had stolen up to the door : already its pale fingers were lifting the latch. . . . Before he had been in the Cotswolds for seven weeks, she had thrust and been thrust into the doorway.

It was the thin end of the wedge.

Each passing day fell upon the wedge like the stroke of a hammer. Sometimes they drove it : oftener the wedge stayed still where it was. But it never slipped back. When it was stubbornest, and the days seemed to lose their weight, when Valerie's hold seemed indefeasible, when the woods were quick with memory, when Anthony heard an old faint sigh in the wind, and the laughter of a brook fluted the note of a soft familiar voice, then more than once that strange, cool, silvery call had stolen out of the distance, to melt upon the air as soon as uttered and leave its echoes at play upon the edge of earshot. . . . Before the echoes had died, the wedge would have moved.

For a master at once so tireless and so devotedly served, Colonel Winchester handled his team with a prudence which must have chafed his infatuation to the bone. Of every week, five and a half days did they labour and not an hour more. No matter how loudly a chore called for completion, no matter how blackly wind and weather were threatening the half-done work,

upon Wednesday afternoon and Sunday not an axe
was lifted, not a cord hitched, not a nail driven. It
was a wise rule and fruitful. The Sabbath rest leavened
the labour of the week. As for the midweek breathing
space, the men were not monks ; however zealous their
studies of the lilies of the field, the provision of meat
and raiment must have some crumbs of consideration. . .

It was, indeed, these two commodities which had
taken Lyveden to Girdle this January day. The milk-
man, the baker, the grocer, had all to be interviewed
and paid. A kindly farmer's wife, who baked fresh meat
for him and sent it thrice a week to his cottage in the
shape of a cold pasty, had to be visited and made to
accept payment for a slab of sweet fresh butter he had
not asked for. A little linen had to be picked up. . . .

By half-past three Anthony's errands were run.
He had dealt with them quickly, for there was work
waiting at the cottage ; a load of fuel had to be stacked,
and Patch had been bogged that morning and was,
consequently, fit neither to be seen nor smelt. Besides,
there was a book about forestry which Winchester had
lent him. . . . Anthony bent his steps homeward
eagerly enough.

As he left the village, a horsewoman overtook him,
shot him a sharp glance, and passed ahead. Her habit
was mired, and it was evident that she had had a fall
hunting. That Anthony did not remark this was because
he was regarding her horse. There was nothing unusual
about the animal, but of the two beings it alone touched
his attention. If Valerie was like to be buried, at
least she had killed all other women stone dead.

It was consequently in some annoyance that, upon
rounding the second bend of the infamous Gallowstree
Hill, he saw the lady before him with her mount across
the road, placidly regarding a hunting-crop which lay
upon the highway. As he came up—

"Would you be so good ? " said the girl.

" With pleasure."

Anthony picked up the crop and offered it. As he did so, the horse became restive, and there was quite a substantial bickering before his mistress could accept the whip. Anthony, if he thought about it at all, attributed the scene to caprice. In this he was right, yet wrong. Caprice was the indirect reason. The direct cause was the heel of a little hunting-boot adroitly applied to a somewhat sensitive flank. There is no doubt at all that Anthony had a lot to learn.

Out of the broil stepped Conversation lightly enough.

" You must forgive us both," said the lady, turning her mount towards Gramarye. " We've had a bad day. Quite early on we took the deuce of a toss, and I lost him. A labourer caught him, and then let him go again. By the time I'd got him, the hounds were miles away. I'd never 've believed it was possible to go so fast or so far as I did and never hear of them. After two solid hours I gave it up."

Anthony was walking by her side, listening gravely.

" What a shame ! " he said. Then : " I hope you weren't hurt."

" Shoulder's a bit stiff. I fell on the point. But a hot bath'll put that right. D'you live here ? "

" About a mile on. At Gramarye."

The girl stared at him.

" Gramarye ? "

" Not at the house," said Anthony. " I live in the cottage at the south-west end of the park."

" Oh, I know. D'you work there, then ? "

Anthony nodded.

" That's my job."

" So you're Major Lyveden ? " said the girl.

Anthony looked up.

" How did you know ? " he said.

A pair of large brown eyes regarded him steadily.

Then the red lips parted, and André Strongi'th'arm
flung back her handsome head and laughed merrily.

"Did you think," she said, panting, "did you really
think that you could come to dwell in the parish of
Girdle, and the fact escape the notice of the other parish-
ioners?" She hesitated, and a suggestion of mockery
crept into her voice. "Or are you too wrapped up
in the estate to think about anything else?"

"I believe I am," said Anthony.

"I beg your pardon," said Miss Strongi'th'arm with
an elaborate courtesy. "Thank you very much for
enduring me for three minutes. If I'd——"

Her hunter broke into a trot.

"No, no," cried Anthony, running beside her.
"Please walk again." She pulled the horse up. "I
didn't mean to be rude. I meant——"

"I should leave it alone," said André. "You'll
only make it worse. You're much too honest. Besides,
I love the country, and I—I think," she added dreamily,
"I can understand."

"Can you?"

The eagerness in Anthony's voice was arrestingly
pathetic, and André started at the effect of her idle
words.

"I—I think so. I've given water to a thirsty plant.
. . . I suppose the gratitude of a landscape . . ."

"That's it," said Lyveden excitedly. "You've got
it in one. The place is so pathetically grateful for
every stock and stone you set straight, that you just
can't hold your hand. And all the time the work's so
fascinating that you don't deserve any thanks. You
seem to get deeper in debt every day. You're credited
with every cheque you draw. If I stopped, it'd haunt
me."

"It is plain," said André, "that, when you die,
'Gramarye' will be graven upon your heart. All
the same, are you sure you were meant for this?

Aren't there things in life besides the straightening of stocks and stones ? "

" The War's over," said Lyveden.

" I know. But there was a world before 1914. I think your occupation's wonderful, but isn't it a little unnatural—unfair to yourself and others—to give it the whole of your life ? As estates go, I fancy the possibilities of Eden were even more amazing than those of Gramarye—I daresay you won't admit that, but then you're biassed—and yet the introduction of Eve was considered advisable."

" With the result that . . ."

Miss Strongi'th'arm laughed.

" With the result that you and I are alive this glorious day, with our destinies in our pockets and the great round world at our feet. I wonder whether I ought to go into a nunnery."

" I've tried kicking the world," said Anthony, " and I'm still lame from it. And Fate picked my pocket months and months ago."

" So Faint Heart turned into the first monastery he came to," said André, leaning forward and caressing her hunter's neck. " What d'you think of that, Joshua ? "

As if by way of comment, the horse snorted, and Anthony found himself joining in Miss Strongi'th'arm's mirth.

" There's hope for you yet," gurgled that lady. " Your sense of humour is still kicking. And that under the mud appears to be a scrap of a dog. When you take your final vows, will you give him to me ? "

" In my monastery," said Lyveden, " monks are allowed to keep dogs. There is also no rule against laughter."

" Isn't there, now ? " flashed André. " I wonder why? There's no rule against idleness either, is there ? " She laughed bitterly. " Rules are made to cope with inclinations. Where there's no inclination——" She

broke off suddenly and checked her horse. Setting
her hand upon Lyveden's shoulder, she looked into
his eyes. "You laughed just now, didn't you?
When did you last laugh before that?"

Anthony stared back. The girl's intuition was
uncanny. Now that he came to think of it, Winchester
and his little band never laughed over their work—
never. There was—she was perfectly right—there
was no inclination. Eagerness, presumably, left no
room for Merriment. Or else the matter was too high,
too thoughtful. Not that they laboured sadly—far
from it. Indeed, their daily round was one long festival. But Laughter was not at the board. Neither
forbidden, nor bidden to the feast, she just stayed
away. Yet Mirth was no hang-back. . . . Anthony
found himself marvelling.

"Who are you?" he said suddenly.

For a second the brown eyes danced; then their
lids hid them. With flushed cheeks the girl sat up
on her horse.

"Who am I? I'm a daughter of Eve, Major Lyveden. Eve, who cost Adam his Gramarye. So you
be careful. Bar your door of nights. Frame rules
against laughter and idleness—just to be on the safe
side. And next time a girl drops her crop——"

"I hope," said Anthony gravely, "I hope I shall
be behind her to pick it up and have the honour of her
company to turn a mile into a furlong."

"O-o-oh, blasphemy!" cried André, pretending to
stop her ears. "Whatever would Gramarye say?
Come on, Joshua."

The next moment she was cantering up the broad
white way. . . .

As she rounded a bend, she flung up an arm and
waved her crop cheerily.

Anthony waved back.

*   *   *   *   *

Miss Valerie French sat in her library at Bell Hammer, with her elbows propped on the writing-table and her head in her hands. She had been free of the great room ever since she could remember. Long before her father's death she had been accustomed to sit curled in its great chairs, to lie upon the huge tiger-skin before the hearth, or gravely to face her father across that very table and draw houses and flights of steps and stiff-legged men and women with flat feet upon his notepaper, while Mr. French dealt with his correspondence. Always, when the picture was completed, it would be passed to him for his approval and acceptance ; and he would smile and thank her and audibly identify the objects portrayed ; and, if he were not too busy, they would remind him of a tale, the better to follow which she must leave her chair and climb on to his knee. . . .

Then he had died—ten years after her birth, nine years after her mother's death. There were who said he had died of a broken heart—a heart broken nine years before. It may have been true. Valerie loved the room more than ever. . . .

When she was come of age, she made it her boudoir. Flowers and silks and silver lit up its stateliness. Beneath the influence of a grand piano and the soft-toned cretonnes upon the leather chairs, the solemnity of the chamber melted into peace. The walls of literature, once so severe, became a kindly background, wearing a wise, grave smile.

Such comfort, however, as the room extended was to-day lost upon Valerie. Beyond the fact that it was neither noisome nor full of uproar, Miss French derived no consolation from an atmosphere to which she had confidently carried her troubles for at least twenty years. The truth is, she was sick at heart. There was no health in her. She had been given a talent and had cast it into the sea. She had stumbled

upon a jewel, more lustrous than any she had dreamed
this earth could render, and of her folly she had flung
it into the draught. She had suspected him who was
above suspicion, treated her king like a cur, unwarrant-
ably whipped from her doors the very finest gentleman
in all the world. What was a thousand times worse,
he had completely vanished. Had she known where
he was, she would have gone straight to him and, kneeling upon her knees, begged his forgiveness. Her pride
was already in tatters, her vanity in rags : could she
have found him, she would have stripped the two
mother-naked. In a word, she would have done
anything which it is in the power of a mortal to do to
win back that wonder of happiness which they had
together built up. It must be remembered that Valerie
was no fool. She realized wholly that without Anthony Lyveden Life meant nothing at all. She had
very grave doubts whether it would, without him,
ever mean anything again. And so, to recover her loss,
she was quite prepared to pay to the uttermost farthing.
The trouble, was, the wares were no longer for sale ;
at any rate, they were not exposed to her eyes. The
reflection that, after a little, they might be offered
elsewhere and somebody else secure them, sent Valerie
almost out of her mind. And it might happen any day
—easily. The wares were so very attractive. . . .
Moreover, if their recovery was to beggar her, by a
hideous paradox, failure to repurchase the wares meant
ruin absolute. . . .

When Valerie French had discovered that her jealousy
of her lover was utterly baseless, she had had the sense
to make no bones about it, but to strike her colours at
once. That Anthony was not there to witness her
capitulation did not affect her decision. If she was
to have their intelligent assistance, the sooner others
saw it and appreciated her plight, so much the better
for her. Only her aunt and the Alisons could possibly

help at all ; to those four she spoke plainly, telling
the cold facts and feeling the warmth of well-doing in
tearing her pride to tatters.   Then she rent her vanity
and begged their services to find and, if necessary, plead
for her with the ex-officer.   The Alisons had promised
readily, but there was no confidence in their eyes.
Lady Touchstone, however, had sent her niece's hopes
soaring.   She had reason, it seemed, to expect a letter.
Major Lyveden had promised to let her have his address.
And, he being a man of his word, it was bound to come
—bound to come. . . .

For more than a month Valerie hung upon every
incoming post.   Then she knew that the letter had gone
astray.

For the hundredth time Miss French read through
the three letters which lay before her upon the table,
written in the firm, clear hand of Anthony Lyveden.
Except she drew upon the store of Memory, she had
nothing else at all that spoke of him.   Hence the common envelopes became three reliquaries, the cheap thin
notepaper relics above all price, piteously hallowed by
the translation of the scribe.

The letters affording no comfort, Valerie rose and
moved to a great window which looked on to the terrace
and thence into the park.   Instantly the memory
of one sweet September night rose up before her—a
night when he and she had paced those flags together,
while music had floated out of the gallery, and the stars
had leaped in the heavens, and the darkness had
quivered at the breath of the cool night air ; when he
had wrapped his love in a fairy tale and she had
listened with a hammering heart . . . when he at last
had put her hand to his lips, and she had given back
the homage before he could draw away. . . .

The terrace was worse than the letters, and Valerie
turned to the books.   Idly she moved along the wall,
reading the names upon the calf bindings and not

knowing whether she read them or no. A sudden
desire to look at the topmost shelves made her cross
to the great step-ladder and climb to its balustered
pulpit. Before she was half-way there the desire had
faded, but she went listlessly on. Come to the top, she
turned to let her eye wander over the nearest shelf.
Old, little-read volumes only met her gaze—Hoole's
works, Jessey, John Sadler, Manley. . . . Of the ten
small volumes containing Miss Manley's outpourings,
the seventh was out of place, and Valerie stretched out
a hand to straighten it. As she did so, she saw the
title—*The Lost Lover*. For a moment she stared at
it. Then she turned and, descending one step of the
ladder, sat down on the edge of the pulpit and buried
her face in her hands.

We will leave her there with her beauty, her shapely
head bowed, her exquisite figure hunched with despair,
her cold, white, pointed fingers pressed tight upon
those glorious temples, her little palms hiding the
misery of that striking face, her knees convulsively
closed, that shining foot tucked beneath the other in
the contortion of grief. We will leave her there on the
ladder, learning that sorry lesson which Great Love
only will set its favourites when they have gone
a-whoring after false gods in whom is no faith.

*   *   *   *   *

At half-past six upon the following Monday evening
Lyveden returned to his cottage with Patch at his
heels. In spite of the hard frost, the work had gone
well. A bridge had been finished which should laugh
to scorn the elements for a long century ; a sore-needed
staff had been set beneath the arm-pit of a patriarch
oak ; a truant stream had been tucked into its rightful
bed. It had been a good day.

Arrived at his door, Anthony turned and looked
upward. The cold white brilliance of the stars stared

winking back ; the frozen silence of the firmament hung like a magic cloak upon the shoulders of darkness ; the pool of Night lay in a breathless trance, ice-cold and fathomless. Anthony opened the door and passed in.

Within three minutes the lamp and lantern were lighted and a fire was crackling upon the hearth ; within ten, fuel had been fetched and water drawn from the well ; within twenty, the few odd jobs on whose performance the comfort of regularity depended, had been disposed of ; and by seven o'clock the Sealyham had had his dinner, and his master, washed and groomed, was free to sit down to a substantial meal.

At the first glance, the latter's dress was highly reminiscent of the warfare so lately dead. The shade and stuff of the stout breeches, the heavy ankle boots, the grey shirt-cuff emerging from the sleeve of the coarse cardigan, were old familiar friends. The fact that Lyveden had laid aside his collar heightened the comparison. Only his gaiters struck a discordant note. These were of good box-cloth and buttoned from knee to ankle. Tight-fitting about the calf, but not shaped to the leg, they fell well over the tops of the heavy boots, resting, indeed, upon the insteps. They suited Anthony, for whom they might have been made, admirably. They were, moreover, a wholly redeeming feature, and turned his garb from that of a thousand corporals into the homely attire of a gentleman farmer. So soon as you saw them, you forgot the War. The style of them was most effective. It beat the spear into a pruning hook. With this to leaven them, the rough habiliments were most becoming. In a word, they supplied the very setting which manhood should have ; and since Anthony, sitting there at his meat, was the personification of virility, they served, as all true settings should, by self-effacement to magnify their treasure. The ex-officer might have stepped out of Virgil's *Eclogues*.

He had finished his meal, cleared away the remains, set the table for breakfast, and was in the act of filling his pipe, when the Sealyham growled. Anthony, whose ears were becoming sharper every day, listened intently. The next moment came a sharp tapping upon the door. In an instant Patch was across the room, barking furiously. . . .

Laying down his pipe and tobacco, Anthony followed the terrier and, picking him up in his arms, threw open the door.

" So you didn't bar it, after all," said a mocking voice. " Well, my conscience is clear. I warned you. And since you are at home and the door is open, will you extend your hospitality to a benighted Eve ? "

Anthony stepped to one side.

" I'm all alone," he said hesitatingly.

" So am I," said André, entering. " Oh, what a lovely fire ! I'm just perished," she added, crossing to spread her hands to the blaze. " It's not a night to be motoring."

Anthony shut the door and put the terrier down. The latter ran to the lady and sniffed the hem of her garments. After a careful scrutiny he turned away. . . .

" It's not a night," said Anthony, " to be walking the countryside in evening dress. Have you had a breakdown ? "

" Not that I know of," replied Miss Strongi'th'arm. " Don't be so modest. I happened to be passing and I happened to see your light, so I thought I'd come and see how Adam was getting on. Is it against the rules ? "

" I'm all alone," said Lyveden steadily.

" Is that an order to quit ? "

" I'm only thinking of you," said Anthony. " I know I've dropped out of things lately, and the world goes pretty fast, but I'd hate people to talk about you." He felt himself flushing, and went on jerkily : " I mean, I don't honestly know what's done nowadays and what

isn't. If you're quite easy . . . you see, I'm older
than you," he added desperately.

There was a little silence.   Then—

"Don't stop," said André, with a mischievous smile.
"I've never been lectured by a monk before.   Besides,
I collect points of view."

"Is mine extraordinary ? "

"An exceptionally rare specimen. I shall always
treasure it."   She produced a cigarette case.   "May
I smoke a cigarette ?   Or is that also against the rules ? "

Without a word Anthony struck a match. . . .

"Thanks," said the lady.   She unbuttoned her
coat.   "It's nice and warm in here," she added comfortably.   "Oh, please don't look so reproachful !   I just
can't bear it.   I'm not doing anything wrong, and it
makes me feel awful.   Of course, if you don't want
me . . ."

"You know it isn't that," he protested.   "I only
thought possibly—I mean . . ."   He broke off helplessly and touched the back of a chair.   "Wouldn't
you like to sit down ? "

"Shall you sit down if I do ? "   Anthony shook
his head.   "Then I shan't either.   I'd much rather
stand."   And, with that, my lady set her back against
the side of the fireplace and crossed her shapely ankles.

It must be confessed that she made an arresting
picture.   Mean as the light was, it woke the luminous
beauty of her auburn hair ;   a sprinkling of freckles
gave to her exquisite complexion a jolly look ;   the
bright brown eyes and the merry mouth were those
of a Bacchante.   Above her plain black frock her
throat and chest showed dazzling white ;   below, the
black silk stockings shone with a lustre which was not
that of silk alone ;   over all, the voluminous mink coat
framed her from head to toe with a rich luxury.

"And how," said André, "is Gramarye ?   Have you
finished the bridge ? "

Anthony stared at her.

" How did you know ? " he said.

Miss Strongi'th'arm shrugged her fair shoulders.

" What does it matter ? " she said. " Let's talk about something else—if you can. Have you thought over what I said ? No. I can see you haven't. Well, well. . . . Have you laughed since we met ? "

" I—I don't think I have."

" Ah. . . . Why not ? "

" There's been nothing to laugh at. The work's big —serious."

" Wasn't the War serious ? "

Anthony crossed to the hearth and kicked a log into flame.

" I suppose so," he said reluctantly.

" Yet you laughed every day."

" Yes, but——"

" But what ? "

" The War was different. You can't compare the two. Then you laughed because it was better than crying. Now there's no reason for it. There's no time on your hands. The work's too urgent—too solemn. It's like restoring a cathedral. You don't feel you want to laugh." He swung round and faced her. " There's a religion in the atmosphere ; Gramarye's a sort of temple ; when you're in the woods, instinctively you lower your voice ; there's something sacred about the place ; there's——"

Miss Strongi'th'arm dropped her cigarette and caught her *vis-à-vis* by the shoulders.

" Don't ! " she cried. " Don't ! It's all wrong ! The place isn't sacred. It's absurd. You're infatuated. Gramarye's getting into your blood. Soon you won't be able to think of anything else. And gradually it'll eat up your life—your splendid, glorious life. I know what I'm talking about. D'you hear ? I say I *know* ! I've seen one man go under, and now

N

you're going—*you !* " The flame died out of her voice leaving it tender and passionate. " And you're too wonderful a thing, lad ; you're too perfect a specimen ; you're too strong and gentle . . . too honest. . . . Ah "—her hands slipped from his shoulders and her eyes dropped—" you needn't look so reproachful. I know I'm a rotter. I dropped my crop on purpose the other day, because I wanted to talk to you ; and I lied to my mother and said I was dining out to-night, and then came here, because . . ." Anthony put out an appealing hand. The girl laughed bitterly. " All right. I won't say it." She started feverishly to fasten her coat. " It's about time I was going, isn't it ? About time. . . ."

In silence Anthony passed with her to the door. There was simply nothing to say.

Together they walked to her car, a well-found coupé standing dark and silent upon the wasted track, facing the London road. André opened its door, thrust in a groping hand. . . . For a moment her fingers hunted. Then two shafts of light leaped from the head-lamps. A second later the near side-lamp showed Anthony how pale was her face. . . .

The lights in the car went up, and André picked up her gloves. Standing with her back to Lyveden, she pulled them on fiercely, but her hands were shaking, and the fastening of the straps was a difficult business.

Patch, who had come with them and was facing the opposite way, put his head on one side and stared up the line of the track. Then he trotted off into the darkness. . . .

The straps fastened, André turned about.

Anthony put out his hand.

" Good-bye," he said gently.

For a moment the girl looked at him. Then she gave a little sob, and, putting her arms about his neck, drew down his head and kissed him frantically. A moment later she was leaning wearily against the car, with the sleeve of her right arm across her eyes. As she let it fall, Winchester stepped out of the darkness with Patch at his heels.

" André ? " he said. And then again, " André ? " Anthony swung on his heel and faced the speaker. The latter stared at him with smouldering eyes. " Lyveden ? " he said hoarsely.

There was an electric silence.

Then Anthony turned to Miss Strongi'th'arm.

" I most humbly apologize," he said. " My feelings got the better of me. I pray that you will try to forgive me." He turned to Winchester. " This lady needed some water for her radiator, and came to my door——"

" You blackguard ! " said Winchester. " You——"

" It's a lie ! " flamed André.

The cold steel of her tone fairly whistled. Instinctively both men started.

" It's a lie, Richard. He's the cleanest, straightest man that ever breathed. He'd no idea who I was. He hasn't now. He never knew my name till you said it. I forced myself upon him the other day. I forced myself upon him to-night. And he's—he's just turned me down. . . . He said what he did just now to try and shield me. But he's blameless. It was I who—made the running. And I'm glad you saw it. *Glad !* " She tore off her left glove. " Because it's your own fault. It's eighteen months since I promised to be your wife. Eighteen solid months. And I'm tired—sick of waiting —fed up. First it was Russia : then the North of France : then—Gramarye. *Gramarye !* " She flung back her head and laughed wildly. Then she snatched a ring from her finger and hurled it on to the ground. " There's the ring you gave me. God knows why I didn't give it you back yesterday—months ago. I'd reason enough. I suppose I still hoped. . . . But now you've killed it. I don't even care what happens to you. You've messed up my life, you've messed up your own, and, what's a million times worse, you're doing your level best to mess up his."

Upon the last words her voice broke piteously, and André covered her eyes. So she stood for a moment, white-faced, her lips trembling. . . . Then she whipped into the car and slammed the door. A moment later the engine was running. She let in the clutch, and the car moved forward. . . .

As she turned on to the London road, she changed into second speed . . . into third . . . top. . . .

The two men stood as she had left them, motionless, the little white dog eyeing them curiously.

The steady purr of the engine grew fainter and fainter.

When it had quite died, Anthony turned and touched the other upon the shoulder.

"There's always Gramarye," he said.

For a moment the giant peered at him. Then he straightened his bowed shoulders and threw up his head.

"Yes," he shouted, "yes. There's always Gramarye!"

CHAPTER VII

NEHUSHTAN

" **I** T is only right, Lyveden," said Colonel Winchester, "that you should know that I am losing my mind."

The steady, measured tone of the speaker invested this bald statement with a significance which paralyzed.

Anthony stood as if rooted to the floor.

" Yes," said the other, " it was bound to shake you up. But I want you to realize it. Sit down for a minute and think what it means."

Anthony did as he was bid—dazedly. His employer turned his back and stared into the fire.

The silence which ensued was painful. So much so, that Mr. Samuel Plowman, Solicitor and Commissioner for Oaths, whose nerves were less subordinate than those of the two ex-officers, was hard put to it not to scream.

It must be confessed that in the last twenty-five minutes the poor gentleman had encountered a whole pack of things, none of which had been dreamt of in his philosophy. Little had he imagined, when he was desired to attend professionally at Gramarye " precisely at half-past ten on Sunday morning," what that attendance would bring forth. Colonel Winchester had certainly a reputation for eccentricity. His letter was undoubtedly—well, peculiar. Mr. Plowman had smiled upon his finger-nails—a sapient, indulgent smile. He had dealt with eccentricity

197

before. Witness Miss Sinister of Mallwood, who had summoned him in just such a way, but more peremptorily. Then he had been desired to superintend the cremation of a favourite cat. That was nine years ago. For the last eight years he had superintended Mallwood. Mr. Plowman had smiled more than ever. . . .

At twenty-six minutes past ten that February morning he had ascended the broken steps of the old grey mansion, a little curious, perhaps, but, as he would have told you, "ready for anything." There being no bell, he had raised and let fall the great knocker, and then stood still in the sunshine looking placidly about him. The desolation of the park left him unmoved. Money, judiciously expended, could rectify that. And the house seemed sound enough. They knew how to build in the old days. Colonel Winchester was probably using only one wing for the present. In time to come, possibly . . . Mr. Plowman had straightened his tie.

Then the door had opened.

Clad like a husbandman, his shirt open at the neck, his sleeves rolled to his elbows, the biggest man Mr. Plowman had ever seen had stood regarding him. The cold majesty of a lion had looked out of those terrible eyes ; neck, chest, and arms proclaimed the strength of a Hercules ; the pose was that of a demi-god at bay. The carelessly brushed fair hair, the broad forehead, the unusual distance between those steel-grey eyes, the fine colour of the cheeks, the fair, close-cut beard, contributed to make the fellow unearthly handsome. But there was something behind it all —a dominating irresistible force, which rose up in a great wave, monstrous and menacing.

Mr. Plowman, who knew little of personality, felt as if he had been suddenly disembowelled. . . .

Thereafter he had been led stumbling through the

semi-darkness of a stark hall, by gaunt mouldering passages to the servants' quarters. A fair-sized parlour, looking upon a courtyard, carpetless, curtainless, and something suggestive of an " Orderly Room," had presently received him.

There a deep bass voice had bade him be seated, and he had been told quite dispassionately that he was present to assist the speaker to prepare for insanity.

All things considered, it is to Mr. Plowman's credit that he was able to appreciate and answer coherently quite a number of questions which his client had put to him upon matters of law. The strain, however, was severe, and he was unutterably relieved when he was directed to move to a table, where paper and ink were waiting, and take down the explicit instructions which the voice would dictate. He had obeyed parrot-wise.

The dictation was hardly over when Lyveden had appeared at the window and, at a nod from Winchester, walked to a side-door and entered the room a moment later. . . .

What immediately followed his entrance, gentlemen, we have already seen. Your time being precious, I have but made use of the silence which poor Mr. Plowman found so distressful.

The great figure before the fire turned slowly about and, folding its mighty arms, leaned against the mantelpiece.

" When it will happen," said the deep voice, " I have no idea. Sometimes it seems very near ; at others, as if it may never come. Yet I know it will. So I must be prepared. . . . Mr. Plowman is here to assist me in this preparation.

" I've tried to tell him, Lyveden, about the estate. I've tried to explain what it means to me. I feel that I've failed." Mr. Plowman was physically unable to utter the deprecative ejaculation which he knew should have been here inserted. His lips framed it, but it was never expressed. "I have, however, explained that I am engaged upon its restoration, and that you are my second-in-command. I have told him that when I—when my call comes, I wish the work to go on. This is where you come in. I have given him certain instructions, all of which depend upon you." The speaker unfolded his arms and stood upright. *"When I'm gone, are you willing to carry on?"*

Before Anthony could answer, the other had lifted his hand.

"Wait. Don't answer till you know where you are.

"You'll have a Power of Attorney and absolute control. The moment I'm certified, you'll stand in my shoes. Some of my income must be set aside —I shall have to be looked after, you know—the rest you will administer as if you were me. You'll be the master of the other men. Your word will be law. The future of Gramarye will be in your hands. You can follow the line I've taken, or you can strike off on your own. You'll have absolute power. I'm ready to give it you, if you're ready to take it. But you must wash sentiment out. The question of my helplessness mustn't weigh with you. You mustn't consider anything except yourself. If Gramarye means enough to you——"

"It does," said Lyveden.

"Are you sure?"

"There's nothing else in my life."

"Ah!"

His keen grey eyes glowing with the light of a visionary, Winchester stepped forward, and Lyveden got upon his feet. For a moment the two men looked one another in the face. Then Winchester shivered suddenly, put a hand to his head, and turned away. . . .

The pathos of the gesture loosened Anthony's tongue.

"You know best, sir, and it isn't my place to try to dissuade you. Let the business go through. Once for all, whatever happens to you, I'll carry on. I'll do everything exactly as if you were there. You can rest easy. But—— Oh, how can you think such a thing? I never in all my life saw any one less likely to go under. You're not the type, sir. It's—it's laughable." The words came tumbling out of an honest heart. "I saw men go mad in France, but they were hardly your sort. Perhaps you're too much alone. Will you let me live with you? Or, if it's insomnia——"

"It isn't insomnia," said the giant. "It's insanity."

Mr. Plowman, who was picking up the pen which for the second time had escaped the play of his trembling fingers, started violently and struck his head against the table. The absurd action attracting annoyed attention, he broke into a cold sweat.

"But you can't know that!" cried Anthony. "Only a doctor can——"

"What doctor would tell me the truth?"

"You needn't ask him. You can ask to be told the symptoms, and then compare them with yours. If they tally——"

"You speak as a child," said Winchester. "Insanity's not like chicken-pox. There's no book of the rules."

"I don't care. You can't possibly know. On a matter like this your own opinion's worthless. It's the one thing no man can say of himself. You can't judge your own judgment." Staring into the fire, Winchester began to tap the floor with his toe. "I've said I'll carry on, and you can put my name in, but I'm sorry I was so quick."

"Why?"

" Because I oughtn't to subscribe to this belief. It's all wrong. I'm admitting a possibility which doesn't exist. I'm humouring a dangerous whim. For over two months I've spent ten hours a day in your company —I've sat at your feet—I've marvelled at your wisdom —I've envied your instinct—I've been dazed by your amazing efficiency—and now I'm to put on record——"

With a stifled roar, Winchester threw back his head and beat with his fists upon his temples.

" You fool ! " he raved. " Out of your own mouth. . . . The very wisdom you marvel at has shown me what you can't see. That instinct you say you envy has opened my eyes. I tell you I'm going *mad*. Time and again I've seen the writing upon the wall. I walk with Insanity of nights. Three months ago I chucked my revolver into the lake, or I shouldn't be here to-day. You babble of madness ; I tell you I *know* the jade. Why, there are nights when the stars slip and the world lies on her side, and only the woods of Gramarye keep me from falling off. I climb from tree to tree, man. They're like the rungs of a ladder, with their tops swaying in the wind over eternity and their roots stuck fast in a gigantic wall —that's the earth . . . on her side . . . They're sticking straight out like pegs. And sometimes I hear a roar coming, and the trees are bent like reeds, and the wind screams to glory, and the whole world turns turtle—swings right over and round. Think of it, man. Twelve thousand miles in a second of time. And there are the stars on my right, and I'm climbing the wrong way up. . . . But Gramarye holds me fast. As long as I'm in the woods—— But the roads are the devil. They make such a gap. You have to climb them to get to the other side. The trees are child's play—they help you. But the roads . . . I shall meet it on one of those roads . . . one day . . . one day. . . ."

The deep sonorous voice faded, and with a whimper Mr. Plowman slid on to the floor.

It was Anthony who picked him up and carried the unconscious lawyer into the open air. As he was helping him to his feet, Winchester appeared with brandy.

" I was so engrossed," he said quietly, " that I never saw you go down. Was the room too hot ? "

Mr. Plowman gulped down some spirit before replying. Then—

"Yes," he said jerkily. " I—I think perhaps it was. I must apologize, sir."

Winchester inclined his head.

" You have your instructions," he said. " And you have seen Major Lyveden, and heard him consent to act. Prepare the necessary papers immediately and send them to me for signature. If any question arises, lay it before me by letter. If you must see me "—the unfortunate attorney blenched—" write and say so. I need hardly add that, with regard to what has passed between us, I expect your observation of the strictest confidence."

" M-most certainly, sir."

" One thing more." An envelope passed. " There is a cheque on account. If on reflection you wish to take counsel's opinion, and that is not enough, write and say so." He put out his hand. " Good-bye. I'm much obliged to you for coming. I hope you'll be none the worse."

With starting eyes Mr. Plowman touched the great palm. Then his client turned, and, clapping a hat on his head, strode off into the wilderness.

As the sound of his footsteps died—

" There's a paper—in there—on the table," said Mr. Plowman. " And my hat and coat—and bag . . ."

" I'll get them," said Anthony.

" It's—it's very good of you."

When he returned, the lawyer had fastened his collar and was nervously bullying his tie into place.

" Have you a conveyance ? " said Anthony.

" N-no, sir. I sent the fly away. I had thought I would walk back," he added miserably.

Clearly the chance of encountering Winchester was not at all to his taste.

" You'd better come with me," said Lyveden. " It's the quickest way to Girdle. I live in the cottage close to the London road."

Mr. Plowman felt inclined to put his arms round Anthony's neck. . . .

Three-quarters of an hour later the little attorney stepped, with a sigh of relief, on to the King's highway. Going and pace had tried him pretty hard, and he was simply streaming with sweat. He pushed back his hat and blew out his cheeks comically. Then he set down his bag and started to mop his face.

" By Jove ! " he said, panting. " By Jove, I'm glad to be——" His eyes resting upon Anthony, he broke off and fell a-staring. " Why," he cried, " you haven't turned a hair ! "

Anthony smiled.

" I take a lot of hard exercise," he explained.

" By Jove ! " said Mr. Plowman, wide-eyed. " Well, I'm awfully obliged to you."

" You've nothing to thank me for." Lyveden pointed to the cottage. " That's where I live." He put out his hand. " Are you all right now ? "

" Splendid, thanks. Can't think how I came to faint like that. Of course . . ."

He took the outstretched hand meditatively.

" The room was unusually hot," said Anthony.

The other stared at him.

" Yes," he said slowly. " By Jove, yes. . . ." With a sudden movement he picked up his bag. " Good-bye."

The next moment he was plodding down the broad white road.

Anthony watched him till he could see him no more. Then he turned on his heel and whistled to his dog.

As he did so, the purr of an engine rose out of the distance, and he turned to see a large touring-car sailing towards him from the direction of Town.

" Come on, Patch ! " he cried quickly.

The approach of the car made him anxious. The terrier, he knew, had crossed the road, and there was something about this particular reach of metalling that tempted motorists to pass at the deuce of a pace.

The car sailed on.

It was fifty paces away, when Anthony heard Patch flouncing through the undergrowth in response to his call. In another second the terrier would take his customary flying leap from the bank on to the road—on the same side as the car. . . .

In a flash, Anthony was full in its path, spreading out signalling arms.

The tires were tearing at the macadam as Patch leaped into the road and, missing his footing, stumbled on to his nose twenty-five paces ahead.

Anthony ran up to the car, hat in hand.

" I'm awfully sorry," he said. " My dog was coming, and I couldn't stop him. I'd called him before I saw you. I was afraid he'd be run over."

The fresh-faced youth at the wheel stared at him.

" That's all right, sir," he grinned. " How are you ? You don't remember me, Every. Met you at Saddle Tree Cross—huntin'. Valerie French introduced us."

" Of course," said Anthony. " I remember you perfectly. Are you all right ? "

" Goin' strong, thanks." He turned to a girl at

his side. " Joan, let me introduce Major Lyveden—
my sister." Anthony bowed. " We're goin' down to
Evesham to see some spaniel pups. Are you livin'
down here, sir ? "

Anthony indicated his cabin with a smile.

" That's my house," he said. " I've turned forester,
and I'm working on this estate."

" But how priceless," said Joan. " If I were a man,
that's just what I'd——"

" Yes," said her brother. " I can see you gettin'
up at dawn an' hewin' down trees an' things with
a bead-bag on your wrist an'——"

" I said ' if I was a man,' " protested Joan. " I
said . . ."

The argument waxed, and Anthony began to
laugh. So soon as he could get a word in—

" I mustn't keep you," he said.

Peter Every glanced at his watch.

" Twenty-past twelve ! " he cried. " George, no !
I'll have to put her along. I suppose you won't come
on and lunch with us, sir ? We'd love it, and we can
drop you here on the way back."

" Yes, do," urged Joan.

Anthony shook his head.

" You're very kind," he said, smiling, " but I've
any amount to do. When you live alone, and you've
only one day a week . . ."

" I'm sorry," said Every. " Still, if you won't . . ."
He let in the clutch.

" Good-bye," said Anthony.

" Good-bye," cried the others.

The car slid forward.

A moment later, arrived at the top of the hill,
it dropped over the crest and sank out of sight.

*   *   *   *   *

It was twelve days later that Mr. Peter Every found
his cake to be dough.

Taking advantage of a general invitation, issued
when he was six years old, he had asked himself to
Bell Hammer ostensibly to enjoy a day's hunting, but
in reality with the express intention of inviting Miss
Valerie French to become his lady-wife.

All things considered, it was rather hard that before
he had been in the house for an hour and a half he
should himself have pulled his airy castle incontinently
about his ears.

This was the way of it.

It was that soft insidious hour which begins when
it is time to dress for dinner and ends in horrified
exclamation and a rush for the bath. Valerie, seated
at the piano, was playing Massenet's *Elégie*, and Every
was lolling in a deep chair before the fire, studying
a map of the county and thinking upon the morrow's
hunt. In such circumstances it is not surprising that
the printed appearance of Saddle Tree Cross should
have remembered Lyveden.

" By the way, Val," he said, raising his voice to
override the music, " I met a pal of yours the other
day."

Valerie raised her eyebrows and continued to play.

" Did you ? " she said, without turning. " Who
was that ? "

" Major Lyveden."

The *Elégie* died a sudden discordant death, and
Valerie started to her feet.

" *Where ?* "

The flame of the inquiry scorched Peter Every's
ears.

Dropping the map and getting uncertainly upon
his feet, he demanded aggrievedly to be told what on
earth was the matter. . . .

On trying subsequently coherently to recall what
had happened in the next five minutes, he found his
memory pardonably confused.

Valerie had taken him by the shoulders and shaken him like a rat : she had hurled at his head an unending stream of questions—all about Lyveden, and, when he had hesitated, had shaken him again ; when he had tried to protest, she had put her hand over his mouth ; when she had clearly exhausted his memory, she had announced that they would go up to Town the next day, and that on Sunday morning, sun, rain, or snow, he would motor her down to where Lyveden dwelt ; then she had said she was sorry she'd shaken him, smiled him a maddening smile, told him, with a rare blush, that Anthony Lyveden was " the most wonderful man in the world," kissed him between the eyes, and then darted out of the room, calling for Lady Touchstone. . . .

Sitting that night upon the edge of his bed, with his hands in his pockets and a pipe in his mouth, staring moodily upon the carpet, Peter had thought ruefully upon his shattered fortune.

" Blinkin' fine week-end," he muttered, " I don't think. I roll up for a hunt an' a dart at the most priceless girl that ever was foaled, an' I lose the one an' am roped in to help the other to another cove." He laughed bitterly. " 'Minds me of a drama-play. S'pose I'm cast for the perishin' strong man wot 'ides 'is bleedin' 'eart." He flung out a dramatic arm. " ' Reenunciation, 'Erbert, 'ath its reeward.' (Loud and prolonged cheers.) Well, well. . . ." He rose to his feet and stretched luxuriously. " It's all the same in a hundred years, and so long as she's happy . . ." And with that little candle of truly handsome philosophy Mr. Peter Every lighted himself to bed.

Upon the following Sunday, at a quarter before midday, he set Miss French down upon the London road at the spot at which he and Joan had met Lyveden a fortnight before.

" I'll wait till you've seen if he's in," he said, nodding

towards the cottage. " If he is, I'll come back in an hour. That do ? "

Valerie smiled and nodded. She was just twittering. Then she flung her veil back over her shoulder and stepped off the road on to the wasted track. . . .

It was a beautiful day—a handful of sweet-smelling hours filched by Winter out of the wallet of Spring. The wet earth seemed drenched with perfume ; the winds kept holy-day ; the sun, like a giant surprisedly refreshed, beamed with benevolence.

Her knocking upon the door of the cottage evoking no answer, Miss French decided to try the back.

The venture was fruitful.

There upon the red-brick pavement stood a small snow-white dog, whom Major Anthony Lyveden, seated upon a soap-box, was towelling vigorously.

Between the fuss of the operation and the amicable wrangle which it induced, neither of the parties heard the lady's approach. For a moment she stood spell-bound. Then she turned and waved her arm to Every, sitting still in the car fifty odd paces away. Intelligently the latter waved back. . . .

As Valerie turned, there was a scrabble of paws. Followed a sharp exclamation, and the next moment Patch was leaping frantically to lick her face, while Anthony Lyveden, who had risen to his feet, was staring at her and recoiling, towel in hand, as if he had perceived an apparition.

For the two, who had shared big moments, it was the most tremendous of all. Upon a sudden impulse that black king Fate had flung his warder up. Instantly the barriers of Time and Distance had been swept away, and Love, Shame, Fear, and a whole host of Emotions had come swarming pell-mell back into the lists—a surging, leaderless mob, thirsty to flesh their swords, quarrelling amongst themselves. . . .

Sit you there by the king, sirs, if you will watch the

tourney. Climb up into his pavilion ; make his grim
equerries give place. I will answer for their black looks.
And the king will laugh at their discomfiture. His
jester for the length of my tale, I can twist the tyrant
about my little finger.

See, then, the wrangling press take order of battle.
Observe the clamorous throng split into two rival
companies, each of them captained by Love, with
Hope and Shame on one side, and Fear and Mistrust
upon the other. These six are the most notable ;
the rest you shall discover for yourselves, when issue
is joined. One other knight only I beg you will
remark—him in the cold grey harness, knee to knee
with Mistrust, whose device is a broken bough, sirs,
whom there is none to counter upon the opposite
side. . . . That is no one of the Emotions, but something less honest—a free-lance, gentlemen, that has
ridden unasked to the jousting and cares for neither
cause, but, because he will grind his own axe, ranged
against Valerie. There is a fell influence behind that
vizor that will play a big part this February day.

When Valerie French looked upon her lost lover,
she could have wept for joy. The sight of him,
indeed, rendered her inarticulate, and, before she had
found her voice, came Shyness to tie up her tongue.
This is important, because her sudden inability to
speak upset everything.

For a month after she had known the man faithful
and herself for a fool, Miss French had constantly
rehearsed this meeting. Then, when she had almost
lost hope that it would ever take place, the rehearsals
had lost their savour. . . . Forty hours ago they had
been revived and conducted feverishly by day and
night. She had a score of entrances, and humble
opening lines to suit them all. Before Anthony could
speak, she would have disarmed him by kneeling in
the dust. The most submissive sentences her love

could utter were to be laid at his feet—calls which, if his love were yet alive, must wake some echoes. Too honest, however, to make a play-actress, Valerie had reckoned without stage-fright. . . .

Lyveden was the first to recover.

"Why, Miss—Valerie," he said, "where have you sprung from ?" He came to her smiling and put out his hand. "I can see by your face that I'm forgiven. I'm so glad. I hate to be at variance." Mechanically Valerie laid her hand in his. "I've got such a wonderful job here," he went on easily. "Are you just passing ? Or have I time to tell you about it ?"

"I'd—I'd love to hear," stammered the girl.

Things were going all wrong. There had been nothing like this in any of her scenes.

"I'm restoring an estate," said Anthony. "When you knew me, I was a footman. Now I'm something between a forester, a landscape-gardener, and a roadman. This "—he lifted an indicating arm—" this belongs to a Colonel Winchester. It's been let go for over a hundred years, and he and I and a few others are working to pull it round. It's just fascinating."

Valerie nodded.

"I'm glad you're happy," she said, and wondered whether that was the moment to speak her unspoken lines. Surely a better opening would present itself. Now that they could not come first, it seemed so awkward to thrust them in without any introduction. While she hesitated, the chance passed.

"I'm sure you are. Would you care to see something of the park ? I'd like you to. It'll make it easier for you to understand what we're up against and what an amazing attraction there is in the work." Together they left the cottage and made for the track. "If we go down here for a bit, you'll get an idea of the condition of things, and then I'll show you some of the work we've done. Of course it goes slow. Five thousand acres aren't reclaimed in a day. You see. . . ."

The steady, even tone flowed with a surprising ease. Anthony could hardly believe his ears. How on earth he was able to talk so naturally he could not divine. He was, of course, putting up a tremendous fight. The sudden appearance of Valerie had fairly staggered him. Then instinctively he had pulled himself together, and, with his head still singing from the blow, striven dazedly to ward her off. The great thing, he felt, was to keep talking. . . .

Ever since his dismissal he had fought unceasingly to thrust the lady out of his mind : latterly his efforts had met with a halting success. Now, not only was all this labour utterly lost, but he was faced with a peril more terrifying than death. The prospect of being haled once more unto Pisgah, the hell of viewing once again that exquisite land of promise unfulfilled, loomed big with torment. He simply could not suffer it all again. The path, no doubt, would be made more specious than ever. Oh, indubitably. And the whips which were waiting at the end of it would have become scorpions. . . . Anthony had braced himself for an immense resistance.

The devil of it was, he loved the girl so desperately that resistance pure and simple would be of no avail. He knew he could never hope to parry the thrusts those beautiful eyes, that gentle voice, were there to offer him. Once before he had tried, and failed signally. It was plain that his only chance of safety lay in attack. He must press her tirelessly. The great thing was to keep talking. . . .

Thank God, there was a subject to hand. Gramarye made a wonderful topic, inviting, inexhaustible. Her blessed woods and streams, her poor blurred avenues, her crumbling roads, the piteous havoc of the proud estate stood him in splendid stead. Anthony found himself not only talking, but waxing enthusiastic. The queer conceit that Gramarye had responded to his cry for help filled him with exultation. Out of his grateful mouth her praise came bubbling. . . .

Settling himself in his saddle with a slow smile, the Knight of the Broken Bough laid on more lustily than before.

It was Patch who unwittingly put a spoke in the latter's wheel.

Miss French's reappearance had affected the dog powerfully. One October day he had known her for Anthony's darling, and as such had become her vassal. He had since seen no reason to withdraw his fealty. As we have seen, at her coming he had leaped for joy. Occasion and personage, however, deserved more honour than that. Ever since the three had begun their ramble, he had been scouring the undergrowth for an offering meet to be laid at the lady's shining feet. It was the way of his heart.

Not until Miss French and Lyveden were standing beside a tottering bridge, and the latter was pointing the traces of a vista which once had gladdened all eyes with its sweetness, but was now itself blind, did the little squire happen upon a treasure worthy in his sight to be bestowed. At this juncture, however, a particularly unsavoury smell attracted his straining nostrils. . . . A moment later what was, despite the ravages of decomposition, still recognizable as the corpse of a large black bird was deposited with every circumstance of cheerful devotion immediately at Valerie's feet.

To ignore such a gift was impossible. Its nature and condition saw to that. To accept it was equally out of the question. But tacitly to reject such a love-token needed a harder heart than Valerie's or, for the matter of that, than Anthony's, either.

Miss French gave a queer little cry of mingled distaste and appreciation, and Anthony hesitated, lost the thread of his discourse, and stopped.

"How very sweet of you, Patch! No, I mustn't touch it because I'm not allowed dead birds. But I do thank you." She patted the panting head. "Look. Here's a stone I'll throw for you—down into the brook. I'm sure it'll be good for you to wash your mouth." She flung the pebble, and the dog went flying. Valerie turned to Lyveden with a glowing face. "Don't think I'm fishing for another dead bird, but I wish I could feel you'd forgiven me as truly as Patch. Oh, Anthony, I just can't tell you how deadly ashamed I feel, how——"

"My dear girl, you mustn't talk like this. I knew there was some misunderstanding—I didn't know what—and I——"

"I thought you cared for Anne Alison."

"Oh, Valerie. . . ." The wistful reproach of his tone, the sad-faced ghost of a protesting smile hovering about his lips, brought tears to Valerie's eyes. "Well, well. . . . I'm so glad I'm cleared in your eyes. I'd 've hated you to go through life thinking that I— was like that. . . ." Suddenly he caught at her arm and pointed to the ramshackle bridge. "There's another instance of the rot we're out to stop. Another winter, and that bridge 'd be in the stream, damming it at the deepest and narrowest point. Result, the water's diverted and spreads all over the road, trying to find another way into its channel. No road can stand that, of course. Gradually——"

"Tell me more of yourself," said Valerie.

Anthony let go her arm and put a hand to his head. "Myself?" he said slowly. "Well, this is my life. I live in the cottage, you know—very simply. It was a wonderful stroke of luck—getting the job. I saw it in the Agony Column."

" Before or after you'd given notice ? "

" After. I tell you, I was thankful. And now
—I little dreamed what a wonderful billet it was.
Living in these beautiful woods, with nothing to——"

" Why did you give notice ? " said Valerie.

" Oh, I don't know. I think I was unsettled.
After all, a footman's job——"

" Was it because of me ? "

There was a long silence. Then—

" Yes," said Anthony. " But that's ancient history,"
he added quickly. " It wasn't your fault if I chose
to take that line. Besides "—he flung out demon-
strative arms—" see what you've brought me, Valerie.
When I think that less than three months ago I was
carrying coals and washing up glasses and waiting at
table——"

" And in love with me," said Valerie.

Lyveden's outstretched arms fell to his side.

The worst had happened. Valerie was under his
guard. . . .

A pitiful hunted look came into the steady grey
eyes. Slowly the brown right hand stole up to his
forehead.

" I never ought to have been," he said dully. " I
ought to have had more sense. It was always—
out of the question . . . utterly. I think perhaps
if I'd had a job to put my back into, I'd 've——"

He hesitated, at a loss for an expression which would
not be ungallant.

Instantly Valerie lunged.

" You'd 've what ? "

" Behaved better," he said desperately, turning
back the way they had come.

Head back, eyes closed, lips parted, Valerie stood
like a statue.

" Behaved . . . better ? " she whispered. " Behaved . . . better ? " She shivered, and, when the

blue eyes opened, there was the flash of tears springing. "When you talk like that," she said quietly, "you make me feel like death. I deserve it, I know. I deserve anything. But, if you knew how it hurt, I think you'd spare me." Staring into the distance, Anthony dug his nails into his palms. "I came here to-day to pray your forgiveness. Since I—found I was wrong, I've been more utterly wretched than I thought a woman could be. I didn't know there was such agony in this world. Aunt Harriet'll bear me out, and so will the Alisons. I told them the truth. And when, after all these weeks, I found where you were, I just thanked God. . . . You and I know what we were to each other. Try and put yourself in my place. Supposing you'd turned me down —because you were rotten. . . ." Anthony winced. "Yes, rotten. There's no other word. And then you'd found out your mistake. How would you feel?"

"I'm sure you had cause," blurted Lyveden. "It was a mistake, of course. But you couldn't know that. And I—I've nothing to forgive, dear. I've never thought ill of you—never once. I can't pretend I wasn't shaken, but I always knew there was some mix-up."

"You were—shaken?" said Valerie.

Anthony nodded.

"You see," he explained, "I was terribly——"

"Have you got over it?" said Valerie.

With the point at his throat, Anthony did the only possible thing, and threw down his arms.

"No," he said steadily, "I haven't, and I don't think I ever shall."

There was a long, long silence, which the suck and gurgle of water fretting a crazy sluice-gate had to themselves. Then—

"What d'you mean?" breathed Valerie.

" I think," said Lyveden, " that I shall love you as long as I live."

Valerie just sighed very happily.

" I think," she said, standing a-tiptoe, " I'm the luckiest woman of all the ages."

Then she slid an arm through Anthony's, and they started back. . . .

Anthony's brain was whirling. He did not know what to think. What was worse, he did not know what to do. Did she think he had called back Time? That he had asked her to marry him? *Had* he? Were his words tantamount to that? Was he prepared to marry her—this wonderful, glorious creature stepping so joyously beside him—this peerless queen, who had wronged him, yet in his eyes could do no wrong? As once before, that touch upon his arm sent the blood singing through his veins. His pulses leaped and danced. An old strange joy came welling. . . . It was as if a fountain within him had begun to play—an old forgotten fountain, long dry—and the sun was turning its delicate spray to a flourish of sprinkled silver. Against his better judgment he turned and looked at her. My lady felt his gaze, and turned to meet it with a swift smile. All the beauty of youth, all the tenderness of love, all the shyness of maidenhood hung in that glowing countenance. As once before, twin stars had come to light the gentle gravity of those dark blue eyes. The mouth he had kissed in anger was a red flower. . . .

The memory of that kiss came back to him with a rush. He had forgotten it, somehow. He was forgiven, of course. Still, it was only right to speak of it—she had confessed her trespasses so very handsomely.

Standing still, he took hold of her hand.

" Valerie, I quite forgot. The kiss I gave you that day was the kiss of a bully. I've never——"

A small cool hand covered his lips.

"Hush, lad. You mustn't say it. I know you were angry, or you'd never have done it. But that was my fault. You know it was. And "—she hesitated, and a blush came stealing to paint the wild rose red—" it's the only kiss you've ever given me, and—since then—I've been very glad of it."

For a moment Anthony stood trembling. Then he put his arm about Valerie and held her close. There was the whisper of a tremulous sigh in his ears, the warm fragrance of quick-coming breath beat upon his nostrils, the radiance of love-lit beauty flooded his eyes. Slowly he bent his head. . . .

A wandering breeze swept out of the distance, brushed past the leafless woods, set the curtain of silence swaying, and—was gone.

Anthony started violently and threw up his head, listening. . . .

Imagination lent him her ears.

The faintest silvery ripple, the liquid echo of a cool clear call went floating out of audience. . . .

In an instant the man was transfigured.

"The trumpets!" he cried hoarsely. "The trumpets! Didn't you hear them?" The light in his eyes was fanatic. Instinctively Valerie shrank away. Regardless, he let her go. "I forgot. Gramarye—I'm pledged to her. It's too late, Valerie. Oh, why did you come?" He buried his face in his hands. "You'll never understand," he muttered. "I know you never will. It's no good—no good. . . ." Suddenly he stood upright and took off his hat. Then he smiled very tenderly and shook his head. "It's too late, Valerie—my sweet—my darling. . . . Too late. . . ."

He turned and strode down the track towards the tottering bridge.

For a moment Patch stood looking from him to the

girl, uncertain and puzzled. Then he went scampering in Anthony's wake.

* * * * *

" As soon as you've finished, Lyveden, we'll have that fir down. It's the only way. With that list on her, she may go any day. And, when she does, as like as not she'll push half the bank into the road."

Anthony, who was munching bread and meat, nodded agreement. His employer got up and strolled in the direction from which the crunch of wheels upon a rough road argued the approach of a supply of posts and rails.

The fence about the estate was going up.

It was indeed high time. What was left of the old paling was in evil case. Worm and rot had corrupted with a free hand. There was hardly a chain, all told, that merited repair. So Gramarye was to have a new girdle. For the last week Winchester and his little band had been working at nothing else. A spell of fine weather favouring them, the work flew. Master and men worked feverishly, but for once in a way, without relish. The industry of the gnome was still there, but it had become nervous.

The reason for this must be made clear.

Always, till now, the little company had laboured in secret. The thick, dark, lonely woods of Gramarye had sheltered all they did. No strange, unsympathetic eyes had ever peered at their zeal, curious and hostile. This was as well. They had—all ten of them—a freemasonry which the World would not understand. They were observing rites which it was not seemly that the World should watch. Hitherto they had toiled in a harbour at which the World did not touch. Knowing naught else, they had come to take their privacy for granted. Now suddenly this precious postulate had been withdrawn. Since wellnigh the whole of the estate was edged by road, the erection of the fence at once cost them seclusion and showed them how dear they valued it.

All day long the World and his Wife passed by, kindly, mocking, or silent—but always curious. The little fellowship became resentfully self-conscious. . . . Old wounds reopened ; forgotten infirmities lifted up their heads. The three great sailors remembered that they were deaf. The little engineer noticed his trailing leg. The lean, grey-headed joiner thought of the wife who had left him : his fellow recalled the cries of a dying child. Anthony minded Miss French. Only the two old carters were spared the ordeal, their labour keeping them busy under the cover of the woods. Winchester himself felt the unusual exposure most of all. But that the fence was to give them the fee-simple of privacy, he would have abandoned the enterprise. It was not that he was ashamed, but, as an *atelier*, he had no use for a house-top. " Working in a shop-window," he styled it. If he detested publicity, his resentment of idle curiosity was painfully apparent. Once or twice, indeed, he had broken out and, in a voice of thunder, bade loiterers begone. Happily they had always obeyed. . . .

Anthony finished his lunch, gave a few pieces to Patch, quenched his thirst with a draught of well-water out of an old beer-bottle, and got upon his feet. Winchester had not reappeared, so he strolled across to the fir-tree which had been marked for destruction. As usual, his employer was perfectly right. It would be idle to carry the paling along this piece of bank and leave the tree standing to menace fence and foundation. The sooner it was out of the way, the better.

He crossed to where the sailors were crowded about the engineer, who was drawing a rough diagram upon the sawn face of timber to illustrate some argument. Hard by, upon a log, the joiners were smoking and conversing in a low tone.

" Where are the axes, Blake ? The Colonel and I are going to fell that fir."

The grey-headed joiner rose and stepped to a rough litter covered by a tarpaulin. The latter, being turned back, displayed a travelling armoury of tools. As he lifted two axes out of their slots, Winchester came thrusting out of the undergrowth.

" Ready, Lyveden ? " he queried. " Right."

Anthony flung off his coat, made Patch fast to a convenient bush—you could not be too careful when trees were falling—and took an axe out of the carpenter's hand. The sailors had disappeared in the direction of the waggon. A moment later the two ex-officers were felling the tree.

It was Winchester's whim to use an axe where he could. He delighted in the pastime, and his tremendous physique enabled him to make such play with the tool as could few men who were not experts. Under his guidance, Anthony had proved an apt pupil, and the two, working together, could send a soft-wood tree toppling in no time. So engaged, they made a wonderful picture. Had any passed by at this moment, they might have been pardoned for staring.

At his fourth stroke Anthony misjudged the angle, and his axe stuck. As he leaned forward to lever it out of the wood, there was the whirr of steel falling, and he flung himself back with a cry. The other had struck without waiting for him to get clear.

As an error of judgment, the thing was inexplicable. A child of six would have known better. And an axe was no pop-gun.

For a moment he stared at Winchester like a man in a dream.

His employer blinked back. . . .

Then his eyes narrowed.

" *You're* getting curious, are you ? " he said thickly.

In spite of himself, Anthony started.

Loosely nursing his implement, the other took a step to one side. There was not much in the movement, but it placed him between Lyveden and the road.

Anthony kept his eyes riveted upon the powerful hands playing with the haft of the axe. . . .

Twenty paces away a saw was going. Raised above the din could be heard the engineer's voice calling for the return of his pencil. A distant clatter of timber told that the waggon was being unloaded.

Anthony moistened his lips.

For another pair of eyes he would have given anything. Any moment now he would have to jump —one way or the other. It did not matter which. The going was equally bad. But if he met an obstruction—caught his foot in a root—fell among briers at the outset, he knew he was doomed. The impulse to glance to one side was terrible. Yet he dared not take his eyes from those terrible itching fingers. If only one of the men——

The noise of the saw stopped, and a piece of wood fell with a thud. Blake's voice was heard asking the whereabouts of his rule. The answer was inaudible, but the next moment somebody started to move in the direction of the fir. As they passed Patch, they chirruped.

In an instant the axe leapt to Winchester's shoulder, and Anthony jumped. . . .

A moment later Blake parted the bushes, to see his employer wrench free an axe which had bitten into the ground, and hurl himself after Lyveden, who was on his feet again and running steadily about six paces ahead.

For a second the fellow stared stupidly. Then he let out a yell and started in pursuit.

The two ex-officers were evenly matched. If Anthony was the lighter and younger, Winchester had run for Oxford. Moreover, the latter knew the woods like the back of his hand. Anthony, who did not, ran blindly. This was not a moment to pick and choose. All the time he was desperately afraid of mire. . . .

Briers tore at his legs, saplings whipped him across the face, a bough stabbed at his eyes and, as he turned, scored his brow savagely ; a rabbit-hole trapped his foot and sent him flying, but he caught at a friendly trunk and swung round to find his balance and a new line before him. So quick was the turn, that the giant behind him lost the yard he had gained. Down through a grey beechwood, over a teeming brook, into a sodden drift of leaves, up through a welter of bracken, on to the silence of pine-needles, over the top of the ridge into the cursed undergrowth again, panting, straining, sobbing for breath, his temples bursting, his hands and arms bleeding, unutterable agony in his side, Lyveden tore like a madman. The pace was too awful to last. Always the terror behind clung to his heels.

They were flying downhill now, and the giant's weight was telling. On the opposite side of the valley was another pinewood. If he could only reach that, between the good going and the up-gradient Anthony felt that there was a bare chance. The thing behind, however, was coming up.

The slope grew steeper . . . precipitous . . . With a shock, Lyveden realized that the giant must be almost above him, that he had only to drop. . . . With a frightful effort he swerved. A tangle of matted thorn bushes opposed him. Frantically he smashed his way through, kicking desperately at the suckers, plunging to find a footing—a holding—anything. For a moment he trod the air. Then he fell heavily, head first, into a ditch. . . .

Only the sight of the road before him and the firm

brown carpet beyond could have got him upon his feet. Dazed and winded, he staggered across into the pinewood and started to struggle up the slope. . . .

A sudden thought came to him, and he glanced over his shoulder. The next moment he was leaning against a tree-trunk, gazing down into the road.

Winchester was flat upon his face, spread-eagled, scrabbling with his nails upon the roadway and cursing horribly. He seemed to be endeavouring to haul himself across. Had the road been a wall, you would have said he was trying to scale it. . . .

He had made no progress by the time the others arrived, and was easily secured. Then ropes were sent for, and two of his magnificent sailors lashed his arms to his sides.

* * * * *

The end of a conversation held this same evening in the hall of Bell Hammer may be recorded.

" He's not himself, Aunt Harriet. There's something wrong. Nobody could have been more gentle— or handsome. He was just wonderful. And then . . ." Valerie broke off and shrugged her shoulders helplessly. " His work and the place itself—Gramarye, he calls it —seem to have got into his blood. You never saw such enthusiasm. It was unnatural."

" Anthony Lyveden," said Lady Touchstone, " is not the man to go mad."

" I know. But he ought to see somebody—a doctor. There was the queerest light in his eyes. . . . And he spoke strangely, as if he heard things. Who's the great man for—for brain trouble ? "

" Sperm," said Lady Touchstone placidly. " But you're racking my brains for nothing. Anthony Lyveden's not——"

" I know he isn't ! " cried Valerie. " That's what makes me certain there's something wrong. He's doing something, or taking something, or being given something, that's affecting his mind. It's not internal ; it's some outside influence. If he didn't care, it'd be different. But he does. He said so. But he didn't seem to have room for me and the estate at the same time. It had to be one or the other. It was like a bad dream —past dispute, but illogical."

"I should write to John Forest," said her aunt. "Ask him to come and stay. He's a wise man. I don't feel equal to telling you what to do. I don't know what to tell you. If you'd come back and said that he wouldn't see you, I was going to Chorley Wood ——"

"Chipping Norton," corrected Valerie.

"Well, Chipping Norton—myself. I was going to kneel down in the mud and refuse to get up. I was going to wear that blue face-cloth that we both hate. I'd got it all worked out. But, from what you tell me, there's apparently nothing for me to kneel for."

"Nothing whatever," said her niece. "He's given me everything, and—I've come empty away," she added miserably.

Lady Touchstone rose and stooped to kiss the girl tenderly.

"Take my advice," she said, "and write to John Forest to-night. And now don't fret. You're a thousand times better off than you were four days ago. For one thing, you know where he is. What's more, he's content to let bygones be bygones. My darling, you've much to be thankful for. And now go and take a hot bath, and try and get a nap before dinner. Poor child, you must be dead tired."

With a sudden movement Valerie threw her arms about her aunt's neck.

"I don't know why you're so good to me," she said.

Then she kissed her swiftly and, getting upon her feet, passed up the broad stairs.

P

For a moment Lady Touchstone stood looking after her niece. Then she put a hand to her head and sank into a chair. She was profoundly worried. If any girl other than Valerie had come to her with such an account, she would have been less troubled. But Valerie was so very clear-headed. True, her love had got away with her, and she had had the very deuce of a fall. But she was up again now, and nothing like that would ever happen again. Her judgment was back in its seat as firm as ever. And when she said that something was wrong with Anthony, that he seemed to hear things, that there was " the queerest light in his eyes," Lady Touchstone knew that it was perfectly true. What was worse, she was entirely satisfied that these things meant brain trouble. For three months after his wife had died, Valerie's own father had been under surveillance for precisely similar symptoms. She remembered them fearfully And this Major Lyveden was so reminiscent of poor Oliver. His voice, his manner, the very way his hair grew about his temples, reminded her strangely of her dead brother. It was not surprising that she attributed Anthony's condition to a somewhat similar cause. What troubled her most was her conscience. She had set her heart upon the match, and she was now uncertain whether it was not her clear duty to try to call it off.

After a little she rose and crossed to a table. Taking a sheet of notepaper, she began to write.

DEAR WILLOUGHBY,

I think it probable that within a few days your secretary will make an appointment for you to see a Miss Valerie French. This is my niece. She does not know we are friends. When she tells you her tale, you need make no allowance for hysteria. Believe every word she says. She will not exaggerate. And please remember this. It is most desirable that she should marry the man about whom

*she will consult you. But it is still more desirable that
she should not marry a madman.*

Yours always sincerely,
HARRIET TOUCHSTONE.

Then she selected an envelope and addressed it to

Sir Willoughby Sperm, Bart.,
55 Upper Brook Street,
Mayfair.

*   *   *   *   *

After a nightmare three days, work at Gramarye
was again in full swing. Anthony's succession to
Winchester had been accepted without a murmur. If
the men displayed any feeling, it was that of relief.
When he had told them that nothing whatever would
be changed, shown them his Power of Attorney,
explained that he was a steward sworn to continue the
work till—till his employer should have recovered,
they had stared upon the ground like schoolboys and
stammeringly requested an assurance that things would
go just the same. Reassured, they had nodded approval
and exchanged gratulatory glances. Then they had
gone about their business.

Anthony's task was less simple. Apart from his
compliance with the Law—a painful and embarrassing
ordeal, which Mr. Plowman fussily stage-managed,
dressing every detail with such importance that the
layman's wonder melted gradually to a profound contempt—there was much to be learned. That all was in
beautiful order saved the situation. And a letter,
addressed to him in Winchester's bold handwriting,
proved a master-key to the mysteries of income and
outgoings.

*. . . There's three hundred on deposit at the Bank.
That's to cover the immediate expense of putting me away.*

*Now look at Sheet 7. That's last year's balance-sheet.
That'll show you I was well within my income. All the
same, expenses will have to be cut—to provide for me.
The wages must stand, and so must the " Horses and
Stabling " (Book 2). Don't part with the roan. There'll
be times when you'll have to go to Town, as I did, for odd
accessories. " Tools and Materials " (Book 3) will have
to suffer, but we're well set up now, so you ought to pull
through. . . .*

There was an invitation, too, to live at the mansion,
which Anthony did not accept. Twice a week he
would visit the office and work there faithfully, but he
could not bring himself to live in the house.

Apart from the manner in which the blow had been
dealt him, he felt the loss of his employer most bitterly.
He found the tragedy even more piteous than terrible.
That so rude an axe should have been laid so untimely
to the root of so glorious a tree filled him with sorrow.
That the tree should have heard the step of the woodman on his way to the felling, haunted his memory.

So far, however, as Lyveden's health of mind was concerned, itself grievously inopportune, the catastrophe
could not have happened at a more opportune moment.
Trading upon the heels of his encounter with Valerie,
it made a terrific counter-irritant to the violent inflam-
mation which that meeting had set up. Yet if the
back of the sickness was broken, disorder and corrective,
alike so drastic, were bound seriously to lower the
patient's tone. His splendid physical condition supported its brother Mind and saw him well of his faint-
ness, but the two red days left their mark. Looking
back upon them later, Anthony found them made of
the stuff of which dreams are woven—bitter, monstrous
dreams, wherein the impossible must be performed lest a
worse thing befall and a malignant eye peers beneath
stones which even Misery herself would leave unturned.
How he had parted with Valerie he was uncertain.

He could not remember her going. Of her coming he knew nothing at all. She had appeared and, he supposed, disappeared. Of Winchester's attack upon him, and the subsequent chase, his memory was clearer. How he had escaped, however, at the foot of the brier-clad slope, he could not conceive. He could have sworn that for the last thirty paces the man was not three feet behind. . . .

He was thankful to get back to work, and plainly immensely relieved to find that, during his absence, the others had made such progress with the paling that the scene of his employer's seizure had been left well behind.

A week had elapsed since that cloud-burst, and, as before, Lyveden was finishing his lunch, when he noticed that Stokes, the second carpenter, had not returned. The fellow had gone to his quarters, to fetch some implement, nearly an hour before. When another half-hour had gone by, Anthony, in some impatience, dispatched Blake for the tool. Twenty minutes later the latter returned, chisel in hand, but with no news of his mate. When it was five o'clock and there was still no sign of Stokes, Anthony struck work and ordered an organized search. It seemed rather hopeless, but, on the whole, the best thing to do. The man was missing. If possible, more zealous than any, it was unthinkable that he was playing truant. He could not have been spirited away. Anthony supposed gloomily that he had met with a mishap. There was, indeed, no other solution.

It was getting quite dark when they found him down in a little dell upon a patch of greensward. Considering that he was a joiner, and not a sexton, he had made remarkable progress with a very creditable grave, which, he explained, was to receive the dead with which the woods were distributed. He added that it was a disgrace to leave so many corpses lying about, and pointed out that he had removed his boots for fear of treading upon them.

When they sought to humour him, he became suspicious and violent, and there was quite a struggle before he was overpowered.

CHAPTER VIII

THE POWER OF THE DOG

THE accident was inevitable.

Everybody present, except the driver of the green taxi, saw that. And he was so fearful lest the driver of the red omnibus should lose one withering participle of the apostrophe he had provoked, that he could not be bothered with the exigencies of traffic and the Rule of the Road.

Everybody, including Mr. Justice Molehill, shouted impotently; a small page, on his way to the post-office, stood agonizedly upon one leg; and a moment later there was a splintering crash, the blue taxi shed a cabin-trunk and a suit-case on to the pavement, and then, after a paralyzing moment of indecision, came heavily to rest against the panels of its aggressor.

Now, his lordship had no desire to become embroiled in a dispute which might easily beget a *subpœna*. Still, because of his elevation to the Bench, he had not resigned the fellowship of Man, and, since he was the nearest individual to the blue taxi, he stepped to it quickly and opened the door.

A man of about sixty years emerged gratefully. His cassock and the purple about his hat argued him a prelate of the Catholic Church.

" Thank you so much . . . No, I'm not hurt at all. I sat still because——"

" Good heavens ! " cried the Judge. " I know you."

The other peered at him in the half-light. " My name's Molehill. We met at Rome—over a death-bed will."

The prelate started. Then recollection came twink-ling into his gentle eyes.

" Of course," he said, putting out his hand. " I remember perfectly. Before the War. How very strange that——"

" It's Fate," said the Judge excitedly. " Or Pro-vidence. For the last three months I've been racking my brain for your name, so that I could get into——"

" Forest," said the other.

Sir Giles Molehill slapped himself upon the thigh.

" That's right ! " he cried. " Forest ! John Forest ! "

The presence of a rapidly increasing crowd and four constables at once discountenanced any further ebullition of glee, and emphasized the discretion of withdrawal.

The Judge thought rapidly.

" Look here," he continued, " my club's just over there." He nodded across the street. " If you'll wait a moment, I'll fetch the commissionaire. He can take charge of your luggage, and then, if you'll come in and have some tea with me, I shall be delighted."

" You're very good," said the other.

Mr. Justice Molehill hastened away. . . .

Ten minutes later the two men were seated before a comfortable fire, absorbed in each other's conversa-tion.

" That will," said the Judge, " which you and I witnessed in 1914 has never been proved."

" That," said his guest, " is, I fear, my fault. At the present moment it's lying in a drawer of my writing-table at Rome."

" No ? " cried his lordship, twittering.

Monseigneur Forest nodded.

"If you remember," he said, "after you and I had witnessed the old gentleman's signature, I took charge of it."

"That's right. You were going to take it to the British Consulate, to see if——"

"They'd stamp it. Exactly. Well, I was too late that day. I attended the next morning, and, after a little difficulty, they consented, for what it was worth, to put a seal on it. Then I went back to the hotel. When I asked whether the testator was still alive, they told me he'd gone."

"Gone?" cried the Judge incredulously. "But the man was dying."

"Dying or not, he'd left for Paris that morning. To the amazement of the manager he had quietly walked into the office, asked for his bill, and ordered a cab to be sent for and his luggage to be brought down. Apparently the doctor attending him had tried to protest, and had been sent away with a flea in his ear. I can only assume that the old fellow was subject to some violent malady, which comes and goes suddenly, one of whose attacks he has been warned will prove fatal."

"What an amazing thing!" said his lordship. "It never occurred to me that he would survive the night. However, as it happens, it doesn't affect the validity of that will. He's dead now. He died in 1917. But the will that was proved and is lying at Somerset House was made in 1910."

"You mean to say that the will we witnessed supersedes it?"

"Undoubtedly."

The prelate covered his eyes.

"Dear me," he said. "Dear me. I blame myself very much. I should have sent the document after him, of course. His address was there. I quite intended to. But I had to leave for Vienna very suddenly upon the next day. Instead of the days I had expected, I was away for months. I only returned upon the eve of the explosion——"

" And, naturally, you forgot all about it. So did I. The merest accident brought the whole thing to my mind."

" Accidents all the way," said the priest.

The Judge smiled.

" It looks like it," he agreed. " To be short, I came across the man in whose favour our will was made. Such a nice-looking fellow—obviously without a penny. Earning his living as a servant. Lyveden, his name was —Anthony Lyveden. Don't let me raise your hopes. I've lost him again—utterly. But everything's happening in the right order. It was no good finding him just to make his mouth water."

" But the other will," said his guest. " What about that ? Haven't its provisions been given effect to ? "

" That," said Sir Giles, tapping him on the shoulder, " is the beauty of it. We're upsetting nobody. The other will leaves Lyveden every penny, *provided he becomes a Knight.*"

" What an infamous condition ! "

" There you have the story. Upon what he believes to be his deathbed, the old fellow repents his harshness. Recovered, our Pharaoh hardens his heart and lets the old will stand. ' The Devil was sick, the Devil a monk would be.' "

" *De mortuis,*" said the prelate. " Besides, now we're going to canonize him, willy nilly."

" With any luck," smiled the Judge. " Can you send for the document ? "

Ruefully Monseigneur Forest shook his head.

" I must go for it," he said. " I must return at once. It's the least I can do. ' Without a penny,' you said ? Poor fellow. I was going into the country to-morrow, to stay with my niece. But that must wait."

" We haven't found him yet," said his lordship.
" That may be the deuce of a business.   Of course, now
our hands are free.   With the will located, we can
advertise.   I think, perhaps, though, we'd better wait
till we've produced it to the solicitors."

The priest agreed heartily.   Then he counted upon his
fingers.   After a moment's ca'culation—

" I'm not as young as I was," he said, " but, if all
goes well, I'll meet you here a week from to-day with
the will in my pocket."

Tea and the comparison of notes upon matters of
moment, other than the fortunes of Anthony, occupied
another half-hour, when, after exchanging addresses,
the two men parted, pledged to meet again in seven
days' time.

The Judge walked home thoughtfully.

The queer little play was almost over.   The strange
human document which it had pleased him to piece
together was almost whole.   He found himself wondering why he had shown such solicitude.   After all, who
was this Anthony Lyveden ?   Why had he been at such
pains to set this beggar upon horseback ?   Perhaps
Fate had meant him to walk. . . .   If she had, she was
playing a curious game.   Thanks to her efforts, the
fellow's toe was practically in the stirrup.   And he
himself—Lyveden—had no idea of it. . . .

Mr. Justice Molehill smiled.

It was really an entertaining little play.   Until it was
time for his entrance, the leading character would not
even know that he was taking part.   There he was——

The smile died suddenly, as the reflection lost its
savour.

Where ?   Where was the leading character ?   Supposing, when the time came, he could not be found. . . .
Into what a dismal fiasco the play would turn.   All his
interest would have been thrown away.   His solicitors
would have been investigating a lost cause.   Forest

would have been sent packing back to Rome upon a fool's errand. . . .

Mr. Justice Molehill gnawed at his lower lip.

There was no doubt about it. For some reason which, for all his prudence, he could not perceive, this Hecuba was a great deal to him.

His bewilderment may be excused. The reason was out of his ken. The truth is, there was a ghost to be laid, and Fate had chosen him for the job. Judge or corner-boy, the man himself did not matter. The lot falling upon him, he had become in this adventure the particular agent of Fate.

King or herdsman, jester or sage, croupier or harridan —lend her what personality you please—Fate hath the reins and so the laugh of the universe. Ever at its rump, her pricks are insensible alike to kicks or kisses. Folly, sceptre or rake in hand, she stands or sprawls upon Eternity, bending the ages to her whim. And we, poor things, at once her instruments and butts, stumble about her business, thinking it ours, setting each other up, bringing each other low, spoking each other's wheels and all the time, wise in our own conceit, basking in the sunshine of our fine free-will, like lack-brains toasting their shanks before an empty cage.

A Napoleon is still-born ; a Medici never survives his swaddling-clothes. Into the tiny graves are huddled a million destinies. The sexton's shovel smothers up a Renaissance ; soon the daisies will blow above History. Those eyebrows are lifted, that lip curls, and two fair homes go down in sorrow. This man misses a train, to travel with Fortune in the one that follows. A horse is beaten on the post, and the frantic clerk who has backed it goes for five years to gaol. Five years. . . . What are five years to Fate ? A cable-operator nods over the Wheatstone, and a king loses his crown. A witness hesitates, and an estate passes to the bastard and to his heirs for ever. . . .

And so the game goes on.

The living grains of sand go slipping and sliding into place in that gigantic hour-glass, striving and fretting in their vanity, but always impotently falling towards that thin neck, where days are numbered and the punctilious turnstile ushers to those mysterious marches where there is no more Time.

Look at them here.

Judge and maiden jostling a prelate—one upon either side—each of them in a toss about the same Anthony Lyveden, yet neither aware of the other's existence, and all four falling, while they fret, first into place and presently, one by one, towards that thin neck where days are numbered. . . .

What? Have I whipped up a puppet without advising you? Bear with me, sirs. 'Tis but the rustle of a gown—a silk knee against satin—upon the staircase. In another moment I shall have opened the door.

The more Monseigneur Forest thought upon the matter, so suddenly thrust smoking before him, the more uneasy he became. The kindest of men, he found the picture of the poor legatee fighting for existence when, but for another's remissness, he would have had a goodly heritage, inexpressibly distressing. Indeed, could he have started for Rome that night he would have done so. But for the knowledge that he was about to do all in his power to rectify the wrong, he could not have slept. As it was, the reflection that Anthony Lyveden had yet to be found worried him greatly. It was, of course, most unfortunate that the business had not cropped up before. Here he was on his way to Hampshire, in response to a cry so instant that he had set everything on one side, and now, however sore her need of him, his niece, Miss Valerie French, would have to wait. Blood might be thicker than water, but the poor pinched ghost that had been knocking so long upon his door took vaulting precedence of any flesh and blood. In the good man's eyes this stranger, Anthony Lyveden, had earned and must be accorded the privileges of the dead.

Directly he reached his hotel he sat down at his bedroom table and indited a letter.

1st *March*, 1921.

My Dear Valerie,

I am, as you see, in London.

Till an hour ago I was on my way to you. Now I must leave again for Rome to-morrow morning.

By accident there has come to me the knowledge of a grievous wrong, for which I am largely responsible. This, mercifully, it may be in my power to repair. To attempt to do so, however, necessitates my immediate return in quest of a paper which none but I can procure.

You can guess, my dear, how very much distressed I am that I must keep you waiting, but, if I told you the case, you would be the first to hale me to the station.

I shall return straightway to England—that is, so soon as my years permit—and, all being well, I shall be here again one week from to-day, and with you at Bell Hammer one week from to-morrow.

You did not tell me the nature of your trouble, so that I can offer no counsel; if, as I suspect, it concerns the man of whom you have already written to me, remember, for what it is worth, that my faith in him has never wavered from the moment you told me that he had won your love.

Your affectionate uncle,

John Forest.

To the prelate, who framed it, that letter was the best he could do : to Miss Valerie French, who received it, it was a great disappointment : and to an eminent brain-specialist, who had never heard of it, it was worth exactly three guineas.

*   *   *   *   *

" I should have come to you before," said Valerie, " but I was expecting my uncle, and wanted to ask his advice before I took such a step. But now he's delayed, and I can't wait any longer."

Sir Willoughby Sperm leaned forward and picked up a pen.

" One moment," he said, taking a sheet from a drawer. " Now then. What is the patient's name ? "

" Major Anthony Lyveden, D.S.O.," said Valerie. " L-Y-V-E-D-E-N."

The name was entered.

" Yes. Address ? "

Valerie hesitated. Then—

" Gramarye, Chipping Norton," she said.

The address went down.

" Age ? "

" I think about thirty."

" Wounded ? "

" Not that I know of."

" When did you see him last ? "

" Eleven days ago."

" And before that ? "

" Not for three months."

" And his demeanour had changed in the interval ? "

" Exactly."

" Are you engaged to him ? "

" No."

" Were you engaged to him ? "

" Practically."

" And it was broken off ? "

" I broke it off."

" Why ? "

" I suspected him of inconstancy."

" Did you tell him so ? "

" No."

" And he ? "

" He left the neighbourhood."

" That was three months ago ? "

" Yes."

" Was your meeting eleven days ago accidental or by arrangement ? "

" I visited him unexpectedly."

" In the hope of reconciliation ? "

" Yes."

" How did he take it ? "

" Most handsomely."

" The reconciliation was effected ? "

" Yes."

" But his demeanour has changed ? "

" Yes."

" In what way ? "

" He seems infatuated with his work."

" To the exclusion of you ? "

" Exactly. It's as if in the interval he'd become a priest, and, although he still loved me, he was no longer free."

" What is his work ? "

" Restoring an estate—the place he lives at—Gramarye. It's a very large estate—nearly all woods—and it's been entirely neglected for a number of years. He and some others, including the owner, are working to get it straight—re-making roads, building bridges, cutting down trees. It sounds Quixotic, but I can see the fascination. Besides, he took the work of necessity. He's very poor."

" He seemed to consider himself devoted to the service of the estate ? "

" Exactly."

" Did he exhibit any one particular mental symptom ? "

" He heard things which I could not hear."

" Did he say what they were ? "

" Trumpets."

" Anything else ? "

" When he heard them, his eyes . . ."

Valerie hesitated.

" Yes ? "

"—were the eyes of a fanatic."

There was a long silence, while the pen was busy upon the broad sheet. Then—

" He should be seen," said Sir Willoughby, " by a specialist without his knowing it. I can't go down. Later, I may be of use. I hope you won't need me. The obvious thing to do is to get him away. But, if you can't do that, no one can—peaceably. D'you think you could try again ? "

" I feel it would be waste of time," said Valerie. " You say some one should see him. Can you tell me who to go to ? "

" D'you know Dr. Heron ? " Valerie shook her head. " He assists me a lot. If he can go, I know of no one better. Would you like me to speak to him ? "

" I should be very grateful."

Sir Willoughby pressed a bell. To his secretary, who answered the summons—

" I want to speak to Dr. Heron," he said.

In silence the girl withdrew.

Whilst the two were waiting, the physician spoke very kindly.

" I'm not going to express any opinion, because it would be valueless. It's clear that there's something wrong, but I've seen so many recoveries."

" Which you have brought about," smiled Valerie.

" I can never do more than contribute. I can only advise. It is the executive that works the cure. That's why I'm so hopeful about Major Lyveden."

" The executive ? "

" Such as the devotion of relatives."

" He has no relatives."

" Or, better still," said the doctor, " the love of a great-hearted lady." The muffled bell of a telephone interrupted. " Excuse me." He picked up the receiver. " Is that you, Heron ? . . . Can you see a friend of mine this afternoon ? . . . At four-thirty ? " Sir Willoughby looked at Valerie with raised eyebrows. She nodded quickly. " Yes. That'll do . . . Miss French. Miss Valerie French . . . A case in the country . . . Urgent . . . She wants your report. I won't say any more. She'll tell you better than I. Ring me up, if you like, before you go. Good-bye." He pushed the instrument away and turned to Valerie. " I'll have another word with him when you've told him your tale."

" Thank you so very much."

Having laid three guineas upon the table under the decent cover of a photograph frame, Valerie rose to her feet. Sir Willoughby rose also and passed to the door. As he held it open, he put out his hand.

Valerie took it and held it.

" Nobody could have been kinder," she said.

The physician smiled.

" Try not to worry," he said. " I haven't seen Gramarye, but I don't think she'll stay the course. Not if you set the pace. . . ."

* * * * *

It was the following Sunday morning that, after considerable hesitation, Lyveden issued an order which he could well have spared. The instruction was addressed to the younger of his two carters, and was touching the roan and the dog-cart and a seven-mile drive. In a word, it had become expedient that Major Anthony Lyveden should go up to Town.

His employer had warned him that periodical visits
to London would be found indispensable.   For all his
dislike of the world, Winchester had had to pay them
from time to time.   Now that the latter was gone
from Gramarye, and Anthony reigned in his stead, the
duty, when it arose, fell to his lot.   Never relishing the
idea, he would not have believed that it could become
so odious.   Ere it had taken shape, it loomed vexatious.
Looking it in the face, he found it repulsive.   No
recluse could have been more reluctant to leave his
hermitage.   Major Anthony Lyveden felt positively
nervous.

Since he had been in charge the man had altered.

He, who in the old days had shouldered with a smile
responsibilities which would have set his elders sweating
with apprehension, found the light weight of Gramarye
a fardel to make him stagger.   This was out of all
order.   Had he lain sick for a month, the work would
have gone as steadily.   The truth is, he was investing
the conduct of a waggoner's team with the nicety
requisite to the control of a tandem of thoroughbreds.
That Lyveden of all men in the world should make such
a costly mistake showed that his nerves were hag-
ridden.

For all his dread of it, however, the visit to London
could not conveniently be postponed.   The need of
some of the items upon his little list of accessories had
become urgent, imperilling the work upon the estate.
A few hours in the Metropolis would be enough.   He
knew where to go.   Two addresses in the City and
another in Drury Lane would see the whole of his
pilgrimage. . . .

With a sigh, the ex-officer had locked up the safe
and, leaving the cold grey parlour, whence he administered, passed out of the echoing mansion into
the careless frolic of a fine March morning.

As he had expected, the younger of the two carters

was in the stables, and Anthony gave his order without more ado. Then he whistled to his Sealyham and started for home.

After a wild night the unrepentant winds were full of mischief. A monstrous dignity of fleecy clouds scudded undignified across the blue. The precious park became a tossing waste of woodland, teased into flurried liveliness, full of false starts and misdirection, instantly buffeted for every blunder and bellowing good-natured protests at every cuff. Respectable brown leaves chased one another down the tracks ; dark sober pools slapped their confining banks ; the steady flow of brooks faltered irresolute.

Nature herself being so roughly used, be sure that man and beast were plagued unconscionably. Anthony's hat was sent whirling, and his terrier's ears were flicked inside out at the first corner. Not that they cared—either of them—for the sunlight leapt with a joy that took the sting out of the horseplay and turned the edge of the devilment. The day was as good as a tonic. By the time they had sighted their cabin the two were revelling.

Not until he was on the point of entering the cottage did Anthony notice the artist. Seated upon the traditional camp-stool, the latter was sketching busily some twenty-five paces away. Apparently absorbed in his work, he never so much as threw the newcomers a glance, and Lyveden was more than half minded to let him be. Patch, however, thought differently. Even as his master turned to the door, there was a low growl, and a moment later the Sealyham was baying the intruder as if he had been a convict.

Calling the dog sharply, Lyveden advanced to apologize.

The lazy brown eyes hardly looked at him, and the slender fingers never left their work for an instant ; but a pleasant smile leapt into the stranger's face, and, ere the apology was voiced, he spoke with the utmost good humour.

"Please don't scold him. He's perfectly right. I'm a trespasser and a vagabond. I have no visible means of subsistence, and, if these things are crimes, I'm an habitual criminal. If you really don't want me to draw your cottage, I'll stop. But you must say so right out. And it isn't the cottage so much as the background I'm after. To be frank, this looks a promising place. I'm out for woodland—something that's not too tidy."

Anthony smiled grimly.

"Orderliness," he said, "is hardly our forte at present. The park's been Nature's playground for over a century, and she's made the most of her time."

"You sound," said the other, "as if you had authority. Am I free of the place, or not?"

For a second Anthony hesitated. Strangers were not to his taste. There was, however, a quiet careless indifference about the fellow's manner which was reassuring. Moreover, he liked the look of him, there was nothing monstrous about his attire—he might have stepped off a golf-course—and there was a kindly expression upon the intellectual face. Somehow the droop of a fair moustache subscribed to the suggestion of laziness which the eyes had put forward. Indeed, his whole demeanour argued the simple creed "Live, and let live."

Lyveden had just decided to give the required encouragement when the other knocked out his pipe.

"That's all right," he said lightly. "I never take offence. And I'm a rare believer in privacy. If I had a place in the country I should have a ten-foot wall about it and a guard-room at every lodge. It's not that I'm a misanthrope, but to my mind there's not much point in ownership if you don't——"

" I expect you'd issue some passports," said Anthony.
" Any way, please don't go.   And, if Gramarye's what
you want, you're free to come and work whenever you
like.   Nobody'll say anything to you; but if they
did—I'm going to Town to-morrow—my name's
Lyveden, and I'm the—the agent here."

" You're very good," said the artist ; and with that
he filled his pipe and set to work again.

Anthony went about his business.

By the time he had washed Patch, the stranger was
gone.

Dusk was falling ere Lyveden saw him again—a tall,
thin figure striding up the track from the depths of
Gramarye.   As he passed the cottage, the ex-officer
hailed him, offering to house his paraphernalia for
the night.   After a moment's hesitation, the other
accepted. . . .   With the interior of the cabin he was
plainly delighted, pointing his host a score of engaging
features which only an antiquary would have recognized.
Anthony gave him some tea, and the two sat smoking
for the inside of an hour.

At length the artist rose.

" I must get back to Girdle," he said.   " About two
miles, isn't it ? "

"About that.   I won't say ' Good-bye.'   If Gramarye suits you, perhaps I shall see you again."

"Thanks to your *laisser passer*, you may.   I want
to get on to Woodstock, really ; but your woods are
worth a day or two.   Good night."

He swung off into the darkness, and a minute later
Anthony heard his steps upon the metalling of the
London road.

It was upon the following afternoon that Lyveden
swore under his breath.   At the time in question he
was standing in a large efficient-looking shop which
smelt strongly of cordage and was situate in Drury
Lane.

The manager was nervously apologetic.

"They've bin on order a week now, sir, but I can't honestly say as I expects them under three. You know what labour is now. In the ole days it was a matter o' 'phonin', an' hanythin' you liked 'd be 'ere by special messenger in 'alf an hour. But now. . . ."

He threw up his hands helplessly.

"Where else can I try?" said Lyveden.

The man mentioned two or three stores—each of them in the City.

"But I don' think you'll get 'em, sir. You might get an hodd one, but 'alf a dozen o' 'Lightnin'' mattocks at the moment is worth their weight."

With a sigh Anthony bowed to the inevitable.

"There's my address," he said, handing the man a slip of paper. "Send me a card the moment they come in."

"I'll set six aside for you, sir."

"All right."

He paid for the goods he had purchased, had them placed in a taxi, and drove to Paddington.

He was so ridiculously glad to see the station again that the ordinarily provoking discovery that he had lost the return half of his ticket but twitched the hem of his temper. With a rueful smile he determined to deduct the price of his carelessness from his next week's wages.

The fact that he had broken no bread since breakfast never occurred to him. His one idea was to get back to Gramarye. Not that the dreaded visit had proved exacting. Indeed, as was to be expected, London had roared as gently as any sucking dove. It was with no true sense of relief that he watched the bustling platforms recede. Them and their fellows, the streets, he bore no grudge. Hideously crowded as they were, he felt almost kindly disposed towards them. He could afford to be magnanimous. He was on his way back. An hour or so, and he would stand once more under the grateful shadow of his sanctuary. . . .

He had no newspaper, nor any need of one. The flitting landscape, the regular pounding of the wheels were declaring tidings precious beyond price. A hundred times he wished the compartment empty save for himself, that he might have exulted openly. As it was, he was reduced to hugging himself surreptitiously, to staring upon the window and winking at his elusive reflection, which he could dimly focus in the stout pane. After a while he became pitiful of his fellow-travellers. As like as not, poor devils, they thought they were well off. And here beside them sat one who was bound for Gramarye. Anthony hugged himself anew. Then another station flashed by, before his feverish eyes could read the name, to set him twittering with speculation. . . .

By the time the train steamed into Chipping Norton, the ex-officer was trembling all over.

To Patch, who had spent the day in the wood-shed, his master's return to the cottage was the signal for an undisguised explosion of ecstasy. Herein, as the noise of the roan's hoofs died away, he was unexpectedly joined by Anthony, and for a long two minutes the two wallowed in a pure paroxysm of glee.

It is to be noted, however, that while the terrier presently dispatched a generous supper with every indication of relish, his master left his untasted. Of the cold well-water the latter was undeniably glad, drinking great draughts and presently drawing more and washing luxuriously. Then he drew more and drank again, but he could touch no food. Neither, tired as he was, could he sit still before the fire. . . .

Two hours later he stumbled across his threshold like a drunken man. Another draught of water revived him somewhat, and, after resting a little in the

Windsor chair, he mounted the tiny staircase and went
shakily to bed.

* * * * *

Eight days later the artist with the lazy eyes rose
from his leather-topped table to greet Miss Valerie
French.

Handing her to a chair, he resumed his seat, and,
after a word or two upon the weather, turned straight
to the point.

" I saw Major Lyveden for the first time last Sunday
week.   We met in the morning, and he gave me tea the
same afternoon.   The next day he went up to London
—on business of some sort—but I saw him on Tuesday
and again on Friday and Saturday.

" I don't propose to trouble you with technical
terms.   All the same, it's not always possible for a
medical man to render his language literally into the
King's English.   Now and again I shall give you rather
a free translation, so you mustn't hold me too tight to
anything I may say.   I tell you this, because I'm
going to state facts and not hand you mere expressions
of opinion."

Valerie nodded intelligently, and the speaker cleared
his throat.

" Now, Miss French, one thing is manifest.   If
Major Lyveden remains at Gramarye, he will lose his
reason."   The doctor paused, and for the first time
Valerie noticed the sober, methodical tick of a grandfather's clock.   This, so far from spoiling, served to
enrich the silence investing the latter with an air of
couchant dignity which was most compelling.   " He is
at present the prey of certain malignant forces—the
more immediate of them natural ; some, I believe,
unnatural—and nothing short of his removal from
where he is now can set him free.   I'm not certain that
even removal will be entirely effective.   But it's
obviously the first step.   If a man is down with malaria,

the first thing to do is to get him out of the swamp."

Valerie was very pale, but her voice did not tremble.

"And supposing he won't leave . . . ? "

"He must be taken away—forcibly. Listen. At the village inn I picked up a lot of news. All sorts of rumours are current—all touching Gramarye. Most of them are nonsense, and I won't repeat them. Others are founded on hard fact. Have you heard of a Colonel Winchester ? "

Valerie nodded.

"Major Lyveden spoke of him as his employer."

"That's right. He owns the estate, and was the working manager of this restoration business."

"*Was?*" breathed the girl.

"Was. Three weeks ago he went mad." Valerie started violently. "It's said that he tried to kill Lyveden. That I can't answer for, but he's in a private asylum for dangerous lunatics."

There was a painful silence. Then—

"Is—is it the place ? " said Valerie faintly.

The specialist rose to his feet and started to pace the room.

"As a doctor, I ought to say ' No ' ; as a man who has spent the inside of a week there, I'm moved to say ' Yes.' Surroundings can depress or elevate, of course. That's common knowledge. But there's something more than that here. In the village they told me the place was accursed. Nonsense, of course. Yet—— Honestly, Miss French, I don't know how to tell you . . . There's—there's a dreadful sinister attraction about the park : there's an unearthly magnetism about the woods—a queer, wistful fascination about the wilderness. At Girdle they swore it was birdless. It may be. There are such places. I certainly saw neither bird nor beast while I was there. And that's not natural. But it's not what you see and hear : it's what you feel. It's terribly hard to explain, but the place appeals most powerfully to the emotions. You feel an irresistible impulse to go to *Something's* assistance. Of course my eyes were skinned, so I saw the treachery. But I felt the appeal." He halted and threw out a hand. " Imagine a serpent disguised as a beautiful woman in distress—*that's* Gramarye. And if I'd been there a month, instead of a week——" He stopped suddenly, like a man whose tongue has run away and made a fool of its governor. "And now please forget what I've said. It doesn't affect the case. I went down to see whether there was reason to fear for Major Lyveden's sanity. I've found that there is. And I advise that he be taken away forthwith."

" To a home ? "

" A private house would be better. If it became necessary, he could be moved. But he shouldn't be allowed to have an inkling that his mind is in danger."

" I'd be thankful to have him at Bell Hammer."

" Your home ? "

" Yes," said Valerie. " In Hampshire."

The doctor resumed his seat and crossed his legs.

" You're prepared to undertake it ? " he said. " I mean, it may be a very trying responsibility."

" Dr. Heron, I hope to become Major Lyveden's wife."

The specialist nodded.

" Good. Do you wish me to arrange his removal ? "

" Oh, please."

" Very well. Have you a closed car ? "

" Yes."

" Any brothers ? "

Valerie shook her head.

" Why, doctor ? "

" Because," said Heron, " he will resist. It doesn't matter."

" I've two friends who will help me."

' Young strong men ? "

Valerie shivered.

" Yes."

" Can you trust your chauffeur ? "

" Implicitly."

" Good. Now let's see." He turned the page of a diary and then returned it. " To-morrow's Tuesday. I don't want to waste any time, but we can't rush things. Please have a room at Bell Hammer ready on Friday. I'll arrange for two nurses to go to you that afternoon. I shall go back to Girdle to-morrow evening. I hope I shall want your two friends and the chauffeur with the car during the week-end, but I may have to wait. In any event, I shall wire to you at Bell Hammer, giving them twenty-four hours' notice and telling them where to come. Please tell the chauffeur to have enough petrol and spares to go from Girdle to Hampshire without a break."

" Is that everything ? " said Valerie.

" Almost. There's just this. We ought to arrive by night ; but I want you to leave all instructions and go to bed."

" I can't do that, doctor. I'll promise not to appear, until you send for me, but——"

" That'll do. That's what I want. Don't think I'm being professional. Remember, I've taken Sperm at his word, and spoken more frankly to you than ever I've done in my life."

" I'm more than content," said Valerie. " You and Sir Willoughby have been just wonderful."

" That's the epithet he and I keep for you, Miss French." They rose and shook hands. " And since of your amazing self-control you've asked no questions, I'll make you a present of an answer. In my opinion, he will recover completely."

Valerie caught her breath sharply, began to tremble violently, and then burst into tears.

* * * * *

Order means much to me, gentlemen. Indeed, I believe in the dame. To fall foul of her ruling does not like me at all. Unless, however, I am to play the diarist, there are times when I have no choice but to retrace my steps. This is one of them. Four windy days must be clapped back on to the hasty calendar— four days, sirs, of which three do not matter, while the fourth, or first—whichever way you look at it—concerns us mightily. In a word, it was upon the eleventh day of March that poor Mr. Slumper was also among the prophets.

> 66 *Bedford Row,*
> *London,* W.C.
> 11*th March,* 1921.

Dear Sir,

Anthony Lyveden, Esq.

We understand that this gentleman was recently in your service.

We have to make to him a communication of the utmost importance, and one which it will be to his great advantage to receive.

Since, however, we have already addressed to him one letter c/o yourself, to which we have had no reply, and since we have reason to believe that he has quitted your service, we shall be much obliged if you will be so good as to inform us where he may now be found, or, failing that, the address to which he proceeded on leaving your house. If you should be unable to give us this information, we shall be grateful for any suggestion you may be in a position to make as to the probability of his present whereabouts.

> *We are, dear sir,*
> *Yours faithfully,*
> Bulrush & Co.

Joseph Bumble, Esq.,
The Shrubbery,
Hawthorne,
Hants.

Mr. Slumper was in the act of preparing to fold the letter before inserting it in the envelope which he had carefully addressed, when he saw the words " Anthony Lyveden."

For a moment he stared at them. Then, glancing furtively round, for it was no business of his to read the letters for whose dispatch he was responsible, he subjected the sheet to a hurried perusal.

What he read excited him. There was no doubt about that. In a moment his nerves were at leapfrog. Fingers and lips and eyelids all flickered and fidgeted in a manner painful to see. Twice he half rose from his chair, only to sink back upon the edge, twittering. . . . Here was an intention with no drive behind it. The truth is, the back of Mr. Slumper's will was broken in twain.

The exact moment at which the fracture had occurred cannot be stated with any certainty. A sentence of three months' imprisonment in the second division was not responsible. The smash was before that. Probably it came with the realization that he stood beneath the shadow of the Criminal Law. Be that as it may, the ex-financier emerged from prison a broken man. But for the interest of Mr. Blithe, the senior partner of Bulrush & Co., who had had him met at the gates and straightway sent him for a month to the seaside, poor Mr. Slumper must have sunk like a stone. When he was fit to follow an occupation, he was encouraged to accept a living wage, the work of an office-boy, and a tiny room to himself. . . .

Here, then, it was that Mr. Slumper was doing battle.

How much it cost the poor sinner to pick up the letter, emerge from his closet, and make his way upstairs to Mr. Blithe's ante-chamber will never be known. That it reduced his overdraft in Heaven goes without saying. Curiously enough, the penetration of the barrier erected upon the obnoxious personality of a managing clerk proved a less formidable business than Mr. Slumper had expected. The very truculence of the fellow stung the derelict to a sudden defiance. This was but a flash in the pan—yet enough for a bully. . . . After a moment's delay, Mr. Slumper was admitted into the senior partner's room.

Blithe looked up with a kindly smile.

" Yes, Mr. Slumper ? You want to see me ? "

All his nervousness returned with such a rush as to make the ex-financier break into a sweat. But he found his voice somehow, and fell a-wondering who it was that was speaking his thoughts.

" If you please, sir. It's—it's about this letter." He laid the sheet upon his employer's table. " I was— thanks to your goodness—addressing the envelope. I take a great interest in the work, sir : and I don't, of course, read the letters, except to obtain the addresses. But the heading of this one, sir, happened to catch my eye. The name being familiar, I took the liberty of reading the text. And—and—I'm very loth to step out of my place, sir, but, if you are seeking the where- abouts of a footman called Lyveden, sir, Anthony Lyveden, I hardly think there can be two of that name. I mean . . ."

The solicitor smiled encouragingly.

" Go on, Mr. Slumper," he said.

Mr. Slumper moistened his lips.

" It will seem strange to you, sir, but he—if it is he— was in my service last summer." He passed a trem- bling hand across his mouth. " He left me right at the last. He was very good to—to us. . . . And I used to wonder sometimes what had become of him—he was a gentleman, you know. And then I saw him again. . . ."

Blithe leaned forward.

" Yes ? "

" Last Monday, sir. At Paddington Station. I had

the pleasure of fetching a bag for you, sir, from the cloakroom that afternoon." (It may be mentioned that this particular commission should have been executed by the commissionaire attached to the office. As, however, it was raining at the time, that gentleman and the managing clerk aforesaid had seen no good reason why " old Slumper " should not satisfactorily perform the duty and save his betters a wetting. Both paid for their blindness in due season. The principal was dismissed, with the result that, after a heated argument, the accessory before the fact was hit first upon the nose and then upon the left eye with all the principal's might.) " He was having some luggage labelled to go with him by train. There seemed to be some question of over-weight. I was quite close to him. Indeed, it was hearing a voice I knew that made me look at him. I heard him say, ' I'm going to Chipping Norton and on to Girdle.' I very nearly spoke to him, but——"

" You're quite sure it was he, Mr. Slumper ? "

" Oh, yes, sir. I've no doubt at all."

" Splendid," said Blithe. " I'm extremely obliged to you. I shall write to Girdle at once. If, as I verily believe, you've found us our man, we shan't forget it. Of course I'll let you know as soon as I hear." The speaker rose to his feet. " So you're getting on all right, are you ? I'm so glad. And keeping fairly well ? That's right. Come out this way." He opened a private door. " Good morning, and thank you so much."

With a full heart Mr. Slumper passed humbly down the stairs. . . .

Within the hour another letter came to his desk for direction. This he read without any hesitation. Indeed, the pleasurable glow of achievement which it induced ushered a gleam into the dull brown eyes such as they had not known for many a day.

CONFIDENTIAL.

> 66 *Bedford Row,*
> *London, W.C.,*
> 11*th March,* 1921.

Dear Sir,

We have reason to believe that a gentleman of the name of "Anthony Lyveden" is residing in your neighbourhood. We are anxious to obtain his address in order that we may make to him a communication of the highest importance, and one which it will be to his great financial advantage to receive.

If you can furnish us with his address by return of post we shall be greatly obliged ; but, if you are unable to do so, kindly cause immediate inquiries to be instituted with a view to locating him, and advise us accordingly.

Our information is that Mr. Lyveden left London for Chipping Norton en route for Girdle on Monday last, the 7*th inst.*

> *Yours faithfully,*
> Bulrush & Co.

S. Plowman, Esq.,
    Solicitor,
        Girdle,
            Oxon.

If to be told that the Probate Divorce and Admiralty Division of the High Court of Justice will be prepared to award you a mansion in Town, an estate in Dorsetshire —each of them, as they say, ready to walk into—and nearly three-quarters of a million of money, is to receive a communication to your great financial advantage, then Bulrush & Co. had not overstated their case.

There was no doubt about it. Anthony's ship was signalled. The pilot was going aboard. Very soon the galleon would be in the stream.

If the double journey had proved too much for John

R

Forest, so that the prelate was compelled to rest before returning to England, at least he had sent the will by registered post.   This in due season had been produced to the testator's solicitor, a benevolent gentleman of the Old School, who, after an interview with Sir Giles Molehill and Blithe at the Royal Courts of Justice, was entirely satisfied regarding its validity.   Indeed, his anxiety to wash his hands of the usurper was almost voluble.

"And I may say, my lord, that I more than once spoke very warmly to my client about that iniquitous proviso which he made me insert.   But, as your lordship knows, a testator has always been permitted to indulge his utmost eccentricity, and my words fell upon deaf ears.   He was a difficult man, sir, was Jonathan Roach.   But when the time came, and I had to break the news to young Lyveden, it was a sorry business. I'm heartily thankful it's going to be put right."

"I hope it is, Mr. Orphan," had replied the Judge. "But we've still got to find our protégé.   That I must leave to you and Blithe to pull off.   I've done my part. But you must keep me informed, for I'm determined to be in at the death."

The two attorneys had promised faithfully, and left the Judge smiling.   Benevolence and shrewdness seldom go hand-in-hand, and his lordship's words had contained a subtle instruction to Blithe to shepherd his elderly brother and not to retire from the case.   The flick of an eyelid had disclosed Blithe's reception of the hint.

With what result, we know.

And that is the sum of my arrears, gentlemen. Henceforth, if you please, you shall find the street of narrative straight as a French highway, with hill and dale certainly, but none of your hairpin corners to send you doubling upon your tracks.

*   *   *   *   *

It was eleven o'clock of a Sunday morning.

Never was an hour more melodiously announced. The diverse tongues of Oxford insisted upon its arrival for fully five minutes. Indeed, the harmonious argument, which had begun as his lordship's car was nearing Magdalen Bridge, was still in progress when the great grey limousine swung out of St. Giles's and on to the Woodstock road.

All three of its occupants were in a holiday humour. The Judge was radiant; Orphan proved splendid company; while Blithe, a brilliant talker, kept the two bubbling with merriment upon a fire of delicate wit. The miles fairly melted beneath their gaiety. Indeed, it was not until the Judge's eye caught the message of an odd finger-post that any one of the three realized that they had passed Blenheim.

" CHIPPING NORTON 8 ! " cried his lordship. " Gad, gentlemen, we're nearly there. Blithe, you're a stage-manager in a million. The thing's going to pan out like a well-written play. What time did you tell Plowman to expect us ? "

" At twelve o'clock," said Blithe. " With any luck we shall just do it nicely."

" Good ! " said the Judge. Then : " I think we'd better pick up Plowman and take him with us, don't you, Orphan ? "

" I think so. For one thing, he knows Lyveden and can introduce us."

" Quite so." His lordship consulted his watch. " We ought to have landed our fish by a quarter to one. We'd better mark down an hotel and carry him off to lunch. You'd better speak to him first and just make sure he's our man."

" Certainly," said Orphan. " I think if I ask him his mother's maiden name, where he was born, his age, and the name of his uncle's butler, that ought to do."

"Why the name of the butler?" said Blithe. "Is that a catch?"

"Quite right," said Orphan. "Just to make doubly sure. Old Jonathan Roach never would have a man-servant in the house. It was a whim of his. If I get the right answer, I shall be easy for ever. But I don't want to take any risks with the best part of a million at stake."

"I agree," said Sir. Giles. "Have you got some cash for him?"

The other nodded and touched his coat.

"One hundred in notes and a cheque-book. I'll take his specimen signature, and put a thousand to his credit to-morrow."

"Good!" said the Judge. "That's the style. I wish poor Forest was here. He'd 've enjoyed it thoroughly. Such a pathetic letter he wrote me when he sent the will. Blames himself out of all reason for keeping the document so long. I sent him a line on Friday to say that we'd found our man. I admit it was rather precipitate, but, all things considered, I think I was justified. By the time the letter reaches him it will be a *fait accompli*—and I wanted to ease his mind."

"If you ask me," said Blithe, "it's all over but the shouting. The talk I had with Plowman over the telephone settled it. In fact, that was when the shouting began. Which reminds me that the trunk line from London to Girdle requires attention. It was not a conversation at all. It was a joint rhapsody."

"Personally," said the Judge, "I detest the telephone. It's a pomp and a vanity of a wicked world. You can never be sure who you're talking to, nor how many people are listening; there's no record of what you've said and no evidence that you've even said it. The invention is a convenient nuisance, conducive to blasphemy, and should be abated."

The car rolled on.

Presently, though none of them knew it, they slipped past Anthony's cottage and so down Gallowstree Hill to the village they sought.

To say that Mr. Samuel Plowman was ready and waiting in no way describes his condition. The little lawyer was wellnigh beside himself with expectation. The prospect of meeting a Justice of the King's Bench intoxicated. The possibility of entertaining such a one in the flesh and the dining-room of The Nook, Girdle, made tales of Paradise seem tame. A burning discussion with Mrs. Plowman had resulted in a decision not to offer his lordship lunch. That would be attempting too much. Cakes and ale, however, flanked by a dish of sandwiches and a tantalus, made a collation at once independent of service and adaptable to every appetite. Furniture was moved, rugs were transferred, the first floor was spoiled to turn the spare bedroom into Mr. Plowman's conception of a Judge's lavatory. It had been mutually agreed that Mrs. Plowman's presence would be intrusive, but, in the circumstances, to go soberly to church was more than the good lady could stomach. An O. P. was therefore established in the bathroom beside the geyser, to which point of vantage Mrs. Plowman undertook to repair the moment the car was heard. . . .

The Nook standing close to a corner of the London road, seven times was the O. P. occupied and evacuated between half-past eleven and twelve, and three times did Mr. Plowman actually throw open his door and advance, nervous but beaming, into the drive, only to hear the deceitful engine once more gathering speed. The fourth time, however, the purr of the engine fell to a steady mutter, which was maintained. The car was not at the gate, but it was not moving. Possibly its occupants were inquiring for The Nook. . . . Mr. Plowman tried not to run down the drive. With her heart in her mouth, Mrs. Plowman peered past the geyser to where the branches of a monkey-puzzler maddeningly obstructed her view of the front gate. . . .

Two minutes later the little solicitor reappeared, walking most delicately and attending a tall, distinguished-looking man with every circumstance of veneration. Behind them came two other strangers, who might have been equerries. That, for all his ecstasy, Mr. Plowman remembered to throw a smile up to the bathroom window, literally reduced Mrs. Plowman to tears of joy.

It was no desire for refreshment, but pure kindness of heart that moved Sir Giles Molehill to accept the attorney's invitation. And, as was his way in life, he did the thing handsomely. Did he see beer? Splendid. He would have a bottle of beer. Yes, and a sandwich. Excellent. Just the thing after an eighty-mile run. What excellent roads they kept in Oxfordshire! He never remembered better. And the Cotswold air was magnificent. Really, one had to spend one's days in a stuffy Court in Town to appreciate the country as it deserved.

"Yet we thrive on the atmosphere, bad as it is. Look at the time we live, Mr. Plowman. Who ever heard of a Judge dying? Yes. I really must have another sandwich. They're so excellent. And now we want you to come with us in the car and take us to Mr. Lyveden . . . *Major* Lyveden, is he? Right . . . D.S.O. ? Good fellow. Wonder what he got that for. And then you'll come on to lunch. . . ."

By the time they were back in the car, Mr. Plowman was upon the edge of praying for an occasion of saving his lordship's life at the expense of his own. . . .

At the south-west corner of Gramarye the guide gave the signal, and the car was stopped. Then Plowman and Orphan alighted and passed up the wasted track.

Except for a wreath of smoke curling from the chimney, the cottage might have been deserted. . . .

" I rather expect," said Plowman, " he'll be having his dinner. . . ."

A second later he was tapping upon the door.

For a moment there was a dead silence. Then a stealthy movement made itself heard. . . .

The two men listened intently.

From the London road the Judge and Blithe were watching them closely.

The door remaining fast shut, Mr. Plowman knocked again.

Instantly the movement ceased. After perhaps twenty seconds it was renewed, but with a difference. The stealth had become hasty.

The two men stared at one another. Then—

" Better go in," said Orphan, with his hand on the latch.

This yielded to pressure, and the next moment the door was open.

The atmosphere prevailing in the little chamber was uninviting. There was a fire glowing upon the hearth, and the room was unpleasantly hot. From the reek of a pungent tobacco emerged an unsavoury smell of something which was not fuel, burning. Scattered about the red-brick floor were black feathers without number, and here and there amid the plumage appeared the muddy print of feet. Perched upon the logs was a pot bubbling, and by the side of the hearth an old pair of boots emitted wisps of steam. Lyveden himself was nowhere to be seen.

Plowman looked round wide-eyed, and Orphan blew disgustedly through his nose.

The former raised his voice.

" Major Lyveden," he called, smiling, " may I come in ? "

There was no answer.

The two conferred in a whisper. Then Plowman cleared his throat.

" Major Lyveden ! " he called. " It's Plowman speaking—Plowman, of Girdle. Can you spare me a moment ? "

Still no reply was vouchsafed.

Followed by the other, Orphan advanced into the room and looked behind the door. There was no one there.

He stepped to the foot of the flight of stairs and spoke upward.

" Is Major Lyveden there ? "

For a moment it seemed as if he, too, was to go unanswered. Then—

" Nao," said a voice thickly, " 'e ain't. 'E's gorn aout, 'e 'as. An' won' be beck till ter-morrer."

Orphan looked sharply at Plowman. The latter shook his head, frowning, as if in denial, and lifted his voice.

" Who's that ? " he snapped.

Somebody was heard to swallow. Then—

" I tell yer 'e ain't 'ere," said the voice. " 'E's— 'e's gorn aout."

" Who has ? " said Orphan.

" Majer "—the speaker hesitated—" Majer Dibdin."

The hesitancy alone would have proclaimed the impostor, and, while Plowman ran for the others, Orphan told the occupant of the bedroom, first that he was an infernal liar, secondly that he was being addressed by a magistrate, and thirdly that, unless he desired to be given into custody for stealing poultry and housebreaking, he had better descend forthwith and tell the whole truth.

As the Judge and Blithe came up, with Plowman behind them, Orphan stepped backwards out of the doorway.

" Come on," he said roughly. " Out in the air."

Barefoot, of his trepidation still grasping the carcass of what had been a black Orpington, there emerged from the cottage a filthy and evil-smelling tramp. A week's sandy stubble bristled upon his chin, the pendulous lips were twitching, the crafty eyes shifted uneasily from side to side.

The four lawyers stared upon the beastly apparition in disgusted dismay.

The sickly smile of guilty embarrassment upon their *vis-à-vis'* face had begun to swell into the cringing leer familiarly precedent to an appeal for leniency, when the fellow leaned forward, stared fearfully at the Judge, and, dropping the pullet with a screech, recoiled against the wall.

" I ain't done no 'arm," he cried, whimpering. " I ain't done no 'arm. I never stole that there 'en. She were dead in the way, me lord. Runned over by a cyar, she were. I only come aout last Toosday, me lord, an' tryin' ter run strite an' git a good job o' work, like wot you said, sir. It's gauze trewth I never stole that there bird. She was layin' . . ."

Out of a bad business the queer recognition stood solitarily opportune. Rhadamanthus' own promise of clemency in return for the truth could not have been more effective. The plain facts, however, were wofully bitter to hear.

The tramp had taken undisputed possession at eight o'clock that morning. The cottage was then empty. The fire was out and the bed in order. Upon the floor of the living-room lay the fragments of a pitcher, with the water, which this had held, settled in a pool upon the bricks. A Windsor chair was fallen, Dagon-like, upon its face, with its legs in the air. What no one could understand was the fact that the lamp, which hung from the ceiling, was still burning.

* * * * *

More or less recovered, but profoundly depressed,

Monseigneur Forest reached Hampshire upon the following Thursday. He had visited the Judge in London, and learned from his mouth first the news and then the details of the unpleasant truth. His lordship's contention that Fate was opposed to their endeavours, he found it difficult to dispute. Believing that he was on his way to a triumph, he had come breathless to participate in a rout. For three days he had dandled a new-born joy, to find it stark upon the fourth. . . .

Valerie was not at the station, but Mason was there with the car, and the poor man was glad to be alone. He was mourning a stolen opportunity to repair a great wrong, and would not be comforted. The lost legatee haunted him more tragically than ever.

As the car swept to the house he noticed two girls upon the steps.

They were interrogating the butler.

Observing his arrival they cut their inquiries short.

The prelate emerged, however, in time to hear the servant's concluding words.

" No, madam. Only that the improvement was maintained. Thank you, madam."

" Who's ill ? " cried Forest sharply.

The butler inclined his head.

" Major Lyveden, sir—a friend of Miss Valerie's. He——"

" *Who ?* "

For all his training the servant jumped.

" Major Lyveden, sir. Major Anthony Lyveden."

Monseigneur Forest looked round helplessly. Then he put a hand to his head and sat down on the steps.

CHAPTER IX

VANITY OF VANITIES

IN a quiet, even tone Lyveden was talking.

The pleasant voice went steadily on, now reciting, now commenting, now lending argument, a cool dispassionate gravity that forced the ear. Facts were so clearly stated, conclusions so reasonably drawn, points so firmly made—all without a trace of emotion, yet seriously offered in the most conspicuous good faith—that it was almost impossible to realize that the speaker was insensible. But that is the way of brain-fever. . . .

The voice faltered and stopped.

Fervently Miss French prayed that it and the frantic brain might rest from their labours. She wanted desperately to think—to be mistress of her thoughts—but, so long as the voice prevailed, the impression that she was being addressed prevented her, first because it was so vivid, and then because of its importunity.

It was half an hour since Sir Willoughby Sperm's car had rolled down the curling avenue and slipped past the tall lodge-gates. If all went well, another fortnight would elapse before the great specialist saw the patient again.

The silence continuing, Valerie fell to wondering what the two weeks would bring forth. That the fever would presently abate, and the ex-officer be spared his life, seemed highly probable. In fact, Valerie steadily refused to consider that he might weaken and die.

What she was eternally asking was what would happen when the engine of the brain, at present running free, was once more engaged with the system it was used to control. Would the coupling break suddenly, and her man go an idiot for life? That she could not believe. Or would the old balance be restored, perfect as ever? There was doubt in the doctor's eyes. Was he, then, to wake stumbling upon that No Man's Land which lies between sense and idiocy? And, if so, how were his trembling steps to be guided aright? Carefully she started to weigh Sir Willoughby's words. . . .

"What concerns me most is how to deal with his condition of mind when the fever has run its course. From what I've seen, and from what Heron has told me, I'm satisfied that it is vital that Gramarye should never again enter into his life. That park, or estate, or whatever it is, had taken such an unhealthy hold upon his imagination, that he was half-way to insanity. If Gramarye is permitted again to take the helm. . . . Well, the ship is half-way across—half-way across those narrow straits which divide reason from lunacy. We've got to take the helm and put it over just as hard as ever we can. You understand? In a word, if, for instance, Major Lyveden were to revisit Gramarye, I think the game would be up. That, of course, can't happen. But it is, in my opinion, of the highest importance, not only that no reference to the place should be made before him, but that we should do our utmost to direct his attention to other matters. We can't expunge the last four months from his memory—I wish we could. Half the asylums in England would be empty if we could do that. But we can avert our eyes from the record, and we can try to avert his."

'Try to avert his.' How? Anthony was not an infant, to be beguiled with a rattle when he cried for a blade. And if Gramarye was proposing 'again to take the helm,' who was to stop her? Had Miss French put that question to Sir Willoughby, he would have replied, "Yourself." For that reason she had not asked him. Again and again he had insisted that, if the mischief was to be mended at all, it would be at her hand. . . .

There were times when the thought terrified her, when the panic fear of the condemned sat in her eyes. For Valerie knew it was just. It was she who had brought a gallant gentleman to this pass—she who had smashed the exquisite wonder of melody their hearts had danced to—she who had hacked asunder the silken bridge of love and sent her lover into the arms of Gramarye.

Gramarye!

Her solitary visit to the park stood out of the girl's memory like a snow-covered peak, vivid and frozen. There was no mercy there. What was far worse, there was an unearthly appeal. Flesh and blood were one thing, but a wild mystery of woodland, the desolate grandeur of a ruined park, the majestic havoc of a proud estate—these were another matter. Looking upon her rival's face, she found it notable. . . . Valerie set her white teeth. That its beauty was a mask hiding some dreadful influence, made her heart faint within her. . . .

Yet, if this fainted, it always revived. Valerie French was well-plucked. If it was ordained that she should fight with Black Magic, with Black Magic she would fight. It was her own fault. . . . It was typical of the girl that the fact that she had already paid very heavily never once occurred to her. She had called the tune without asking how much it would cost. That the piper's bill was so long was due to her recklessness. She did not dispute the account.

For the hundredth time she wondered what line Gramarye would take. . . .

It seemed, mercifully, that the fell influence of the

estate was not to have things all its own way. While
the sick man in his delirium talked much of Gramarye, he
spoke of Valerie too—frequently. For hours together,
sometimes, he dwelt upon their love. As a rule, he
debated with himself whether it was fair to her to let
her see him again. (Listening to these heart-searchings,
Valerie's heart burned within her.) Then he would
call his Sealyham and speak to him of the lady, asking
if she were not wonderful and a sight for sore eyes.
" When she calls you, Patch, aren't you proud of your
name ? And she took your head in her hands to-day.
I saw her. Such sweet, pretty hands. . . . And you
looked in her eyes, Patch, and then you licked her nose
—very gently, like a good little dog. . . ." Then,
again, Anthony's life as a footman was often remembered.
Mr. and Mrs. Bumble were gratefully discussed. The
Alisons—George especially—figured constantly. Even
his life in the Army was sometimes mentioned, and other
older days, hard to identify. . . . Gramarye held a
good hand—undoubtedly : but there were other cards
in the pack.

The door opened noiselessly, and a fresh-faced nurse
stole into the darkened room. Valerie and she exchanged
whispers, and, after another glance at the silent figure
upon the bed, the lady of Bell Hammer gave place to
the professional and made her way slowly downstairs.

*   *   *   *   *

It was past three o'clock of a sullen March afternoon
when Mr. Peter Every dismissed his parade.

The men turned away listlessly, hollow-eyed.

Only the little lame engineer said anything at all,
and that was an inaudible communication to the three
great sailors, whose hearing was gone. Gloomily the
latter watched his fingers stumble over their rude
translation of Every's last words. . . .

" So there you are. Colonel Winchester's gone.

Major Lyveden's too ill to ever come back. Without the authority of one of these two, not another penny can be spent on this estate. Obviously the work's got to stop. I know you don't want wages, but you've got to live. . . . And I've come, as Major Lyveden's friend, to tell you this before the Law steps in—as it will—and does it more bluntly.

" I know it's rough on you, and I'm devilish sorry, but it's got to be faced. . . . And, as I say, I'm commissioned to offer you all your passage to Canada and fifty pounds apiece to tide you over there till you can get going.

" You chaps think it over.

" I'm staying at *The Rose* at Girdle, and those who want to accept, report to me there to-morrow morning at ten o'clock. Then I'll tell you the details and fix everything up. Right."

Leaning against the trunk of a fallen beech, Every watched his little audience wade through the weathered fringe of bracken and turn on to the rough brown road that dipped and curled into the heart of Gramarye.

The droop of their shoulders, the heaviness of their steps, the silence in which they went, trumpeted misery. Anything, however, was better than the dull sightless stares with which the news that their work was over had been received. Every, who was no coward, had been prepared for suspicion, defiance, violence. Instead, his service of the warrant had been accepted without a word. He had no shred of authority, but not the slightest attempt had been made to call his bluff. It had been, in fact, a painful walk-over. The seven labourers seemed to expect a death-blow. When it fell, they met it with the apathy of despair. Every felt as though he were sentencing a bunch of forest ponies to the pits, and the dumb hopelessness of their demeanour plucked at his young heart-strings. . . .

For two or three minutes after the little group had
passed out of sight the young man stood motionless.
Presently his eyes wandered from the trail up a rude
bank, all starred with primroses, through the dim
breathless magic of a pinewood on to a peering screen
of new-born leaves, pale-faced and trembling. After a
moment's rest, they turned southward to where the
lean brown road went paving a deep corridor, straight,
silent, its black walls towering. Distance and gloom
lent these a grim symmetry, suggestive of duress ;
above, a grey ribbon of sky issued a stony comfort,
such as prisoners use. . . . With a shiver, Every turned
away his head. To the north the ground fell sharply,
and the cut of the road vouchsafed a glimpse of what
it led to—woods, woods, woods, swelling, rising, tumbling, bolstering one another up, shouldering one
another aside, some with their limbs still bare, others
laced with the pale pinafore of spring, all of them dense
and orderless, composite regiments of timber, where
squire and skip-jack stood back to back, and the whelps
of both thrust and quarrelled for a place in the bulging
ranks.

Every became suddenly conscious of a silence more
tense and death-like than he had ever dreamed of. . . .

Then a wind breathed—miles away . . . to the
north.   He could hear the breath coming, a mere whimper among the tree-tops. The whimper became a
whine. . . . Reaching the pinewood, the note slid into
a moan, that rose slowly to a thin wail as the breath
fled up the corridor with the towering walls. The wail
fell to a sigh. . . .

With straining ears, the man waited for this to
fade. . . .

" Mopping up ? " said a quiet voice.

Every started violently and turned right about.

Ten paces distant, within the shadow of the beechwood, was a big upstanding grey, with ears pricked,

vigilant. Square in the saddle sat a girl, in a habit of dark blue cloth. So dim was the light that Every could not distinguish her features, but he marked how the eyes burned out of a pale face and noted the glint of copper beneath the hard felt hat.

" Mopping up ? " she repeated quietly, but this time there was a silkiness in the tone that put the man on his guard.

" That's one way of puttin' it," he said lightly. " I'm sort of windin' up the Company."

" The Garden of Eden Limited," flashed the girl. " History repeats itself." For a moment she hesitated. Then—" Where's Adam ? " she said carelessly.

" Done a bunk," said Every, with no idea of what she meant. " Are you a creditor ? "

Miss Strongi'th'arm regarded him.

" Either," she said coldly, " you are a liar or else a fool."

Every stared at her speechless. . . . After a moment the girl shrugged her shoulders. Then a riding-boot flashed, and the grey sprang forward.

As she pulled up beside him—

" By what authority do you dismiss these men ? "

Every looked up steadily into the angry eyes. Then he took off his hat.

" Forgive me," he said quietly, " but by what authority do you ask ? "

For a second he thought she would strike him. The cold fury of the pale peaked face, the haughty set of the lips, the blaze of the great brown eyes, heralded violence. . . .

Every never moved.

With a sudden movement André turned her head to stare into the distance. At length—

" I've lost all I had in this estate—this venture . . . and a lot that—that wasn't mine," she said slowly. " Is that good enough ? "

s

Before the weariness of her tone, Every's resentment
went down with a rush.

"I'm most awfully sorry," he said gently. "I'd no
idea of this. I don't think any one has. Of course, if
I'd known for a moment that you were—er—interested,
I shouldn't have dreamed of moving in the matter without your consent." He hesitated. Then—"But surely
you can recover something. I mean, the place can be
sold, and I'm sure the solicitors would see to it that
you——"

André gave a dry laugh.

"I hardly think they'd allow my claim," she said
shortly.

Every swallowed before replying.

"You could try," he said desperately.

"Fool," said the girl contemptuously. "It's not a
question of money. It's a question of men." And
with that she fell to whistling under her breath.

Every decided that she was mad.

"I'm afraid I don't understand," he said stiffly.
"What I'm doing, I'm doing with the approval of Mr.
Plowman, solicitor to Colonel Winchester—he's the
owner of this park : and, if you apply——"

"Yes, I know that," said André quietly. "But
for this park, I should be Mrs. Winchester."

The scales fell from Every's eyes. The picture of
the giant, of whom Plowman had told him, pacing a
madman's cage, rose up before him, and a great wave
of pity for his companion swept into his heart. It
occurred to him suddenly that, but for the grace of
God, Valerie French would stand by this strange girl's
side. . . .

"Think you understand, don't you ? " sneered André.
She laughed shortly. "You've got a lot to learn yet.
First of all, my friend, this isn't a park. It's a temple.
The very place you're standing on is holy ground. And
those clowns you're sacking are priests—sworn to moil

and toil for Gramarye until she's sucked the brains out
of their heads. And you're spoiling her game . . . I
should go carefully, if I were you, my friend. And if
you get safe out of her to-day, I shouldn't come back
—*if you can help it* . . . I don't want to be rude, but
she's brought down bigger game than you—far bigger.
. . . And they were her *favourites*."

" I'm not afraid," said Every.

" Of course you aren't. If you were, you'd be safe.
If Samson had feared Delilah, he wouldn't have lost his
eyes." She broke off and shrugged her shoulders.
Then—" And now, if you're satisfied with my authority
to question you, what's yours for dismissing these
men? "

" I have none," said Every. " But the chap who
was here—Lyveden——"

" Yes ? " breathed André.

" Well, he's too ill to——"

With a moan, the girl dropped the reins, flung back
her head, and clapped her hands to her temples.

" I knew it," she wailed, " I knew it ! First Richard
Winchester, and then Anthony . . . my darling . . .
Anthony Lyveden . . ."

Every stood spellbound. The tragedy had taken a
new—a frightful turn. Valerie—trustful, unsuspecting
Valerie—was hideously involved. He wondered if
Lyveden delirious would babble of this strange girl.
If he did. . . . And when he recovered—what then ?

Hurriedly he reviewed the position.

Under Dr. Heron's direction, Lyveden had been
drugged here, at Gramarye, and brought to Bell
Hammer. The whole object of his removal was to smash
his infatuation for Gramarye, so that he might feel free
to worship Valerie. On their joint love the whole thing
was founded. Everything had been arranged on that
basis. And now . . . if Lyveden had been consulted,
perhaps he would not have come—not because of

Gramarye, but because of a girl—a girl with auburn hair. . . .

" Where is he ? "

The words cut his reflections with a clean slash.

" Who ? "

André Strongi'th'arm's eyes narrowed.

" The high priest," she said.

" D'you mean Major Lyveden ? "

" I do."

Every paled. Whatever might be the other's standing, with him Valerie came first. It might be rough on the girl, but that could not be helped, and would eventually, he supposed, be mended. One thing was plain. Not at any price must she go to Bell Hammer.

" I'm afraid I'm not at liberty to tell you."

" Why ? "

" If you're thinking of visiting him, I assure you——"

" I wish to know where Major Lyveden is."

Every drew himself up.

" I'm very sorry," he said, " but until I've seen those in charge of him, and have their permission to tell you——"

" I have a right to know."

Every winced. Then he looked up boldly.

" As Colonel Winchester's *fiancée* ? " he said.

André caught her breath. Then she bowed her head.

" As a most miserable woman," she said brokenly. " Somewhere it says, ' From him that hath not shall be taken away even that which he hath.' . . . Well, it's as one of those outcasts . . . one of those hopeless double bankrupts——"

" Stop ! " cried Every, aghast. " Stop ! I don't want to hear. . . . Listen. I'll be at Girdle till Friday. That day I'll leave a note for you at the inn, with Lyveden's address inside."

He had, I suppose, some vague idea of getting to Hampshire before her.

For a second the girl stared at him with knitted brows. Then—

"You appear," she said coldly, "to be not only a fool, but a poisonous fool. After all, if you won't tell me, I suppose there are other ways. . . ." She picked up the reins. "And so you're a friend of Major Lyveden's ? To tell you the truth, I shouldn't have thought he'd have had much use for you."

With her words, the hunter moved forward. . . .

Dazedly Every watched the two pass at a walk into the gloomy corridor and dwindle slowly to a mere blur of blue and grey under the shadow of the towering walls. At last distance and dusk swallowed them, and he could see them no more.

By the evening of the following Thursday the young man's work was gone, and by ten o'clock on Friday morning his car had left Girdle and was flying up Gallowstree Hill.

Provision had been made for the men ; the horses in the stables at Gramarye had been disposed of. He had only come, with Valerie's approval, out of sheer pity for helpless men and beasts. His unexpected interview with André Strongi'th'arm worried him sorely. He was convinced that between her and Anthony there had been a serious affair. Himself devoted to Valerie, this made him furious ; remembering her devotion to Lyveden, it scared him. If, after all that had happened, Valerie was to find, not only that her cake was dough, but that it was not even her cake, but another's, Every verily believed the shock would send her out of her mind. The mortification alone would be enough to unhinge any woman. . . .

The sight of Anthony's cottage at the edge of the park reminded him of his proposal to recover his tobacco-pouch. He had laid it down on the tree-trunk whilst he was addressing the men that memorable Monday afternoon.

Not daring, for fear of thieves, to leave the car upon the highway, he drove her gently on to the wasted track. Even then he was not comfortable, for she could be seen from the road. After a moment's hesitation, he decided to risk it. He could not drive to the spot, for from here, for a furlong or so, the road was in ribbons. They seemed to have been hauling timber. The only thing to do was to be as quick as he could and hope for the best. Going fast, he should be back again in twenty minutes. . . .

There had blown a gale in the night, and Every was not surprised to find one of the tall dark pillars of the gigantic corridor fallen across the lean brown road. It was his haste in surmounting this obstacle that was responsible for the simple but painful fracture of his left leg. The trunk was slippery, and he had jumped untimely to save a fall. Two stout boughs had been waiting, and the rest was easy. . . .

Now, Peter Every was, as we know, no coward ; but when, lying there, he reflected that, thanks to his efforts, the estate was now deserted, he became extremely uneasy. And presently, when he remembered Miss Strongi'th'arm's words, he broke into a cold sweat.

' If you get safe out of her to-day, I shouldn't come back—*if you can help it.*'

* * * * *

" I'm told," said Anthony weakly, " that I'm at Bell Hammer."

Lady Touchstone smiled and nodded.

" That's right," she said gently. " And Valerie should be here to welcome you, but she's asleep. So you must make shift with me."

The truth was, Valerie French had broken down. The strain of waiting and watching for the hour for which she longed, yet dreaded, had proved too much. Only the day before she had fainted suddenly, and, honestly glad of an excuse, the local doctor had ordered her to bed forthwith. Valerie had obeyed dumbly. She knew that she had come to the end of her tether, and so to that of her wit ; and since, to deal at all hopefully with Anthony's return to consciousness, her understanding must be on tiptoe, she knew that she was better away. If the change was to come before she was fit for duty, it could not be helped. In her present condition she was, she felt, worse than useless.

Two hours later Anthony had tried to sit up, failed, looked dazedly about him, and when the fresh-faced nurse stole to his side, asked first for some water and then, shakily, to be told where he was. He had promised, in return for the answer, to ask no more questions, but to go quietly to sleep. This promise he had immediately broken by asking anxiously for news of his dog. Learning that Patch was below, and well and happy, he had spoken no more. After eighteen hours he had awaked, greatly refreshed, to find himself the cynosure of three pairs of eyes. These were all kindly and full of cheer. Two pairs were contributed respectively by the nurse and Lady Touchstone, while the third was set in the face of an overgrown cherub, who smelt agreeably of Harris tweed and was gently furbishing his *pince-nez* with an enormous handkerchief.

" This," continued Lady Touchstone, " is Dr. Gilpin." The cherub grinned reassuringly. " He's extremely pleased with you, and, when you're better, I think you'll return the compliment."

" I've been ill," said the patient stupidly.

The cherub nodded.

" Gave us quite a turn once or twice," he said, smiling. " But you're all right now. And if you'll promise to obey orders, I'll have you out of bed in a fortnight."

Anthony's face fell. Then—

" I'm in your hands, sir," he said. " And I'm very, very grateful for all you've done." His eyes turned to

Lady Touchstone. "And you. I don't understand anything yet," he added plaintively.

"Good," said the doctor. "Now we know where we are." He took out his watch. "If you would like it, you and your hostess can have a little chat —for ten minutes only—just to clear matters up. Then Nurse Ford will take over."

"Please," said Anthony.

A moment later the two were alone.

"I don't know how I come to be here," said the patient slowly, "but I'm afraid it must have been a terrible inconvenience and—and expense. You know I've no money."

Subduing an inclination to burst into tears—

"On the contrary," said Lady Touchstone, "you're quite respectably off. Since you've been ill, you've come into money—more than enough to pay for everything. So don't let that worry you."

She felt that it was not the moment to tell him that he was virtually a millionaire.

For a moment the man did not speak. Then—

"How did I get here ? " he said.

"You may well ask," was the reply. "If I hadn't seen it with my own eyes, I wouldn't have believed it possible for George Alison to lift a man of your inches and carry him single-handed right from the front door. I know he rowed for Cambridge, but, all the same, it was the act of a fool. And I told him so. Of course, he only grinned. You know that inane, irresistible grin of his when he's done something he knows is——"

"George Alison ? " said Anthony. "George Alison ? How on earth——" He stopped short and started up on an elbow. "What month is it ? "

"April," said Lady Touchstone. "And now lie down again, there's a dear boy. . . . And why shouldn't Alison have——"

"But if it's April—— *Good God !* " he cried hoarsely,

raising a trembling hand. *" D'you mean to say I've lain here in this house for six months ? "*

The woman's heart leaped into her mouth.

" And why not ? " she said quietly. " I know a case of a man who lay unconscious for over two years—the result of a fall hunting. And when he came to——"

She stopped to peer at the patient.

Then she rang for the nurse—instantly.

Anthony had fainted.

* * * * *

Thus fell that formidable position upon whose delicate reduction all the science of physic, the love of women, the wisdom of friends, had been feverishly concentrated by day and night for nearly three weeks.

Chance and a woman's instinct had done the trick. As by a miracle the hopeless had come to pass. The helm had been put hard over, and the craft had answered as sweetly as any swish-tailed circus nag. Gramarye and all her works, if not forgotten, had in the twinkling of an eye become the fabric of a dream—mere relics of a fantastic age for a sane mind to marvel at.

For two or three days after the momentous interview Anthony said very little. When he had again seen Lady Touchstone, and the two—blind leading the blind —had satisfactorily fixed the very date of his collapse, George Alison was sent for. Carefully schooled, the latter spent a fruitful five minutes by the sick man's side. Upon the third day came Valerie. . . .

The girl was exalted. Gratitude had set the crown upon the glory of her array. No one had ever seen her look so beautiful. Out of the furnace the fine gold had come refined, dazzling.

My gross pen cannot picture her.

The dark lustre of her hair, the exquisite curve of her lips, her pride of carriage, were things for sonnets. Her small firm hands, the white column of her neck, the colour springing in her cheeks, made three sweet won-

ders. The style of her was superb. Tall, straight, clean-
limbed, her figure remembered graces of a younger age.
The simple flowered-silk dress looked as though all
who put it on must go in elegance. Silk and satin
covered her precious feet. A nosegay of violets,
brooched to her gown, echoed the hue, but not the
magic of her eyes. Had the poor flowers been blowing
still upon their mother bank, all wet with dew, and
had a star stooped to prove how sweet they smelled,
then, sirs, they should have rendered more faithfully
my lady's eyes.

Anthony had wondered when she would come. . . .

A breath of perfume, a swift whisper, the rustle of
silk—and there was Valerie by his side.

" Oh, Valerie ! "

Miss French fell upon her knees.

Very gently Lyveden put her hand to his lips. Then
he turned away his head and began to cry.

With a bursting heart, Valerie almost gathered him
in her arms.

" D'you love me, Anthony ? "

By way of answer he just clung to her. At length—
" I'm—I'm sorry, my sweet. . . . It's—I think it's
just because . . . I love you so much." With an effort
he mastered his lips. " And I'm so very sorry, dear, I
kissed you like that—the day I went down. I dreamed
about it. I dreamed you came to me, and I apologized."
With her heart in her mouth, Valerie smoothed his
brow. " And you were—so very sweet. You said "—
he hesitated—" you spoke so very handsomely."

" I'm so glad, darling."

" And, oh, Valerie,"—he was himself again now—
" I've had such a wonderful dream. I've been waiting
for you, my darling, before I spoke of it."

" What did you dream, lad ? "

" I dreamed that I'd left the Bumbles—I had given
notice, you know—and gone, in answer to an advertise-

ment, to a place in the Cotswolds. It's all so real, so
vivid, that it's almost impossible to appreciate that
it's all a dream. I can remember every detail of the
journey—I had Patch with me—down to the faces of
my fellow-passengers. A woman with a baby got out
at Oxford and left a parcel behind. And I ran after
her with it. I can see her scared face now, poor soul,
when I touched her on the shoulder. . . ."

The story of the last four months came pelting.
Anthony fairly opened his heart. At first, listening
to the bare truth told with the confident naïveté of dis-
belief, Valerie felt as though she were cheating the
blind. After a little, this sense of shabbiness was
suddenly supplanted by a perfect torment of apprehension lest Anthony should detect her hypocrisy.
Presently, before her breathless interest in the narrative, the girl's uneasiness slipped unremarked away,
and, when the door opened and the gentle nurse
appeared to part them, she was following the ingenuous
recital with unaffected eagerness.

Valerie nodded her acquiescence in the unspoken
order, and the nurse withdrew. As the former rose to
her feet—

" Ah, must you go, my lady ? "

" Till this evening, dear lad."

Anthony sighed fretfully.

" And I've wasted all our precious time with my old
dream. I've hardly spoken of you, and there's so much
I want to know."

" We've plenty of time, darling. Think of it. Once
we never knew when—if, even, we should ever see one
another again. Now . . . Oh, Anthony, we're very
rich."

" I am," said Anthony, smiling. " And when you
say you are—why, then I feel like a king."

Valerie flung up her head. An instant. and she was
singing. . . .

> " *If I were a queen,*
>   *What would I do?*
> *I'd make you a king*
>   *And I'd wait upon you—*
> *If I were a queen.*"

Never melody knew such tenderness.   Poor Anthony
could not trust himself to speak. . . .

Valerie stooped and laid a soft cheek against his.
Then she pressed his hand to her lips.

The next moment she was gone.

*   *   *   *   *

When Sir Willoughby Sperm learned of his patient's
progress, he struck the words " Major Lyveden " out
of his diary.   The action cost him exactly one hundred
guineas, and the secretary by his side bit her lip.   To
keep that Saturday free for his visit to Hampshire, she
had refused nine appointments.   But, if he was a bad
business man, Sperm was a good doctor.   Anthony was
out of the wood.   Very well.   Considering the nature
of the peril with which the wood had been quick, the
less the fugitive saw of strange doctors, the better for
him.   To insist upon the gravity of his late disorder
was most undesirable.   Besides, if at this juncture a
specialist's visit to Bell Hammer could serve any useful
purpose, Heron was the man to pay it.   It was he who
had walked and talked with Lyveden when the latter's
brain had been sick.   So he alone of the doctors could
compare Philip drunk with Philip sober.   Happily no
such comparison was necessary.   Had it been vital, it
could not have been made.   For the patient to renew
the acquaintance of the artist he had met at Gramarye
—and that in the person of a distinguished brain
specialist—would hardly have conduced to his health
of mind.   Indeed, from the moment that Anthony had
reached Bell Hammer in safety, so far as the inmates
of that house were concerned, the very name of Dr.

Heron was, by his own advice, religiously forgotten as though the man had never been. It was natural, however, that one who had done so much to arrest the disorder should care to hear how Anthony was faring. By a mutual arrangement the cherubic Dr. Gilpin wrote to the former faithfully three times a week.

Similar, though less frequent, reports were regularly rendered to Mr. Justice Molehill.

One of these latter I will set out, for it was a wise man that wrote it, and the matter is to the point. I would, sirs, that I could show you the handwriting, so fine and easy to read.

> *Bell Hammer,*
> *nr. Brooch,*
> *Hants.*
> *April 11th, 1921.*

Dear Sir Giles,

Major Lyveden continues mercifully to make good progress.

I saw him myself yesterday for the first time, and must make haste to confess that I am overjoyed. When I say this, you will understand that he is not only the stranger whom we are helping to the acquisition of a great fortune, but the man whom my niece is delighting to honour. Lyveden is a man of great personal charm and fine character, and I am sure that he will administer his heritage wisely and faithfully, and that he will make Valerie a proud and happy woman. I am glad to say, too, that your memory of his appearance is as true as your judgment. In short, he is a splendid specimen of manhood.

There is, of course, no doubt at all that he is our man, i.e. the only nephew of the late Jonathan Roach. Boldly advancing out of my province, I begged leave to ask him a question or two, to which the most exacting of opponents could not in decency have objected. His replies made me ashamed of the doubts which I never—even officially— harboured.

Of the nature of his brain trouble and of his escape I have already told you. Enough that that wondrous bridge which an Omnipotent Providence threw across the river, while we stood gaping upon the other bank, stands fixed as any rock. As often as he will revisit Gramarye, the patient treads it with a firm, confident step. I do not matter—besides, I must soon return to Rome—but, by my advice, Valerie and those who are and are to be about him are schooling themselves to use this same strange bridge. Future safety, I contend, lies in making it a thoroughfare. So only approached, Gramarye will indeed become 'such stuff as dreams are made on,' and the four months he spent there be 'rounded with a sleep,' for ever.

I have told Major Lyveden the story of the lost will, and of your close interest, to which alone he owes his fortune. His great desire is to thank you personally. My own remissness he forgave in undeservedly generous terms.

I expect to leave for Italy early next week, and while I shall write again before that, I shall hope, if you are then in London, to visit you on my way.

Believe me,

Yours very truly,

JOHN FOREST.

The prelate was not the man to exaggerate. Anthony's recovery went on amain. His state of independence had, as we know, been broached by Lady Touchstone : it was becoming that the true extent of his fortune should be disclosed by Monseigneur Forest himself.

The sick man received the news with some emotion.

He felt as though suddenly a wand had been set in his hand—a wand beneath whose careless touch the shifting flux of wishes must set and crystallize. For more than eighteen months he had "thought in pennies." Henceforth it would be unnecessary to think at all. The spectre of Ways and Means was laid for ever. Often, when his purse had been lightest— when he had been forced to eat sparingly of the cheapest food—he had been used to remember an old fragment of Virgil that he had learned as a boy. *Forsan et haec olim meminisse iuvabit.* Times without number he had been glad of the tag. And now it had served its turn. . . . Looking back upon his penury, he could not wish that he had been spared those lean, ill-favoured days. And when, because of these, Monseigneur Forest reviled himself, Lyveden refused to listen, declaring that the experience had been invaluable, and must surely stand the camel in good stead when the time came for him to negotiate the needle's eye. For a prelate to withstand such a contention was more than difficult. . . . Yet if the patient spoke to the point, it was by accident. His thoughts were elsewhere. Childishly excited, he was wanting to use his wand. Ridiculously enough, his romping brain could not furnish a wish to be converted. . . . Suddenly an idea came to him. His dog, his little faithful dog, had gone in need of a collar for over nine months. . . .

Patch !

Mercifully the terrier was dumb. Otherwise the prelate's " Bridge of Providence " must have returned unto the air whence it came. As it was, the dog was brought to the sick-room twice every day. The tenderness with which he treated Anthony was wonderful to see. Naturally boisterous, the efforts with which he mastered the frenzy these interviews provoked, were manifest. He knew that Lyveden had been dangerously ill. He knew that he was mending. The twofold consideration set the flame of his devotion flaring. Yet, when he visited his master, the jet must be reduced to a pilot. . . . The marvel is the dog did not burst. Instead, placed within reach, he would set a quivering foot upon the bed and lick the caressing hand with a touch that would not have broken a bubble. Presently, whimpering with excitement, he would post about the chamber, seeking an object to present to his lord. Of such, the choice which the room afforded was straitly limited, and when for the second time he had selected one of the knobs of a chest of drawers, endeavouring to detach this by dint of biting it off, the fresh-faced nurse was advised of his intention, and a log of wood was procured to be kept in a corner. Thereafter twice a day the billet was brought reverently to the bedside.

Poor Patch! It was the best his dull wit could devise.

Oh, Patch, could you but see how idle and clumsy is your act, you would hang your small head. Could you perceive the vanity of repetition, your bright brown eyes would fill with tears. Could you be told whence comes the gift which you give Anthony, your little tail would be clapped between your legs. . . . Yet have I heard tell of a ram caught in a thicket by his horns; of altar steps worn thin by the observance of the same offices ; of spikenard that might have been sold and given to the poor. . . .

Sirs, this poor scrap of a dog errs in good company.

The April days slipped by, smiling, or shrill, or tearful, as the mood took them.

A letter which Valerie had received from Peter Every, written and posted at Girdle upon the last day of March, had set her mind at rest about Anthony's stewardship of Gramarye. Apart from the action of the Law, that book had been closed as gently and firmly as mortal man could close it. By the removal of the steward, neither men nor beasts engaged there had been left one penny the worse. The former, indeed, were well out of a bad business. Incidentally, they would very soon be well out of Anthony's way. Never had money been so advantageously spent. Valerie had written to Every a letter of heartfelt thanks.

By the courtesy of the Bumbles, their chauffeur came to Bell Hammer two or three times a week. He did not always see his late colleague, but Alison was no fool, and points were constantly arising upon which Valerie was glad of his advice. It was he who went through Anthony's wardrobe with the utmost care, saying which of the garments he had seen before and which had been acquired since their owner's departure from Hawthorne. The latter were carefully destroyed. Lyveden's few personal effects were subjected to a similar scrutiny and partial destruction. Nothing was left to chance. If George was uncertain, Betty and Anne were sent for. If no one could be sure, whatever it was, the article in question went to the furnace. Never was the high-road of convalescence more faithfully reconnoitred.

Less actively, Lady Touchstone and Forest contributed according to their means. These were substantial. The electric personality of the one, the gentle charm of the other, were better than physic. The one stimulated; the other composed. A twinkling hour of Lady Touchstone's company was like a glass of champagne. A talk with the Monseigneur rivalled the quality of old Madeira. Wisely administered, the wine built up the wasted tissues of the mind. The latter's digestion being sound, Lyveden throve upon the diet. His brain put on weight daily.

So far as his body was concerned, no one had any anxiety at all. Anthony's fine constitution and the open-air life which he had led at Gramarye stood him in splendid stead. So much so, that when, upon St. George's Day, Patch came trotting with a red rose in his mouth, he found the bed empty and his master sitting cheerfully upon a sofa before the fuss and worry of a bright wood fire. It was clear that a new era had

begun. Patch dropped the rose and fairly hurled himself
at a small log lying conveniently in a corner beside an
old *prie-Dieu*.

*   *   *   *   *

A mischievous look came into Valerie's eyes.

" You haven't heard a word," she said, bubbling,
" of what I've been saying. You know you haven't."

Anthony laughed guiltily.

" Yes, I have," he protested. " You were saying
you'd half a mind to give up having hydrangeas and
—and—er—not have them at all," he concluded
lamely.

Valerie uttered a little crow of triumph.

" Scandalous," she said. " Simply scandalous. It's
no good pretending. I know perfectly well what
you were thinking about. You were thinking of
Gramarye. That old dream of yours . . ."

Mark, sirs, how the mighty may fall and how
familiarity may breed contempt. Gramarye had
lost her sting. Spoiled of her puissance, she had
sunk to the level of " Boney "—fare for the ears of
children, food for a jest.

" No, I wasn't," said Anthony, smiling. " At
least, not directly. I was thinking of an argument
the Monseigneur put up about my dream."

" What did he say ? "

" Well, his contention was this. You know, if,
for instance, a bell rings when you're asleep and
dreaming, as likely as not the noise is introduced
—not necessarily in the same form—into your dream,
isn't it ? Very well. That shows the senses are
working. The message arrives distorted, but it arrives.
Well, he said that in his opinion practically everything
that came to pass in my dream was originally suggested
by some outside influence. Water being poured into
a basin suggests a brook. A sewing-machine becomes
a train. The hiss of a burning log escaping steam.

So much for the ears. Now for the eyes. A maid helps the nurse to move a sofa—I see timber being hauled. The doctor shakes his thermometer, and there's Winchester wielding an axe. . . . It's a pretty theory, and the more you study it, the sounder it seems." He crossed his legs and started to fill a pipe. " All the same, I must have a fertile imagination. I think I always had. As a child I was left alone a great deal, and I fancy that helped."

It was a lazy Sunday morning—the fourth in the month of May. John Forest had been gone a month, and Lady Touchstone was properly at church. Greenwich would have told you that it was ten o'clock, and the gorgeous tapestry of Summer was still wrought with the brilliant embroidery of a heavy dew. Lawns, flower-borders, and stiff box charactery sparkled and shone in the hot sunshine. The sky was cloudless : a haze kept to itself the distant promise of the park : there was no wind. The sleepy hum of insects, a rare contented melody, tilted the hat of Silence over that watchman's eyes. The wandering scent of hawthorns offered the faultless day a precious buttonhole.

Sitting easily among the cushions of a teak-wood chair, Anthony let his eyes ramble luxuriously over the prospect. In a *chaise longue* by his side Valerie was engaged in the desultory composition of a letter to her uncle in Rome. Stretched blinking upon the warm flags, Patch watched the two vigilantly for any sign of movement.

" Did I ever have a red-haired nurse ? " said Anthony suddenly.

Valerie shook her head.

" No," she said. " You had the same two all the time. Why ? "

" I dreamed of a red-haired girl." Valerie sat very still. " André, her name was. I met her first in

the road . . . I remember she knew me. She'd been
hunting and looked like a Bacchanal. She turned
up again later on—one night. I was just going to
bed." He frowned at the recollection. " I wonder
I didn't chatter about that. I was worried to
blazes. . . ."

" That—that's the worst of dreams," said Valerie
slowly. " You're impotent."

With a shock she realized that she had written
ANDRÉ in capitals in the middle of her letter, and,
below it again, BACCHANAL. Casually she scratched
out the words till her pen ploughed up the sodden
paper.

" It's a wretched feeling," said Anthony. " I
dreamt she—cared for me. And I—I never got
there. She had to tell me right out. . . . Oh, Valerie,
it was awful."

Miss French felt as though her heart had stopped
beating. She could have screamed to Anthony to go
on. Instead—

" Poor old chap," she said gently.

She had her reward.

" When she saw there was nothing doing, she went.
. . . And then Winchester appeared with Patch,
as I was putting her into her car. I remember he
called her ' André '—that's how I knew her name. . . .
And then he cursed me, because she was his *fiancée*,
and she fairly tore him up. Then she chucked down
his ring and drove off. There must have been a car
leaving Bell Hammer just then. I can hear her
changing the gears now." He passed a hand over his
eyes. " I can't remember any more, except that
Winchester was shouting. . . ."

For a long moment the two sat very still. Then
Valerie scrambled to her feet and put her head on
one side. Her eyes were just dancing.

" You and your red-haired sirens," she said

reproachfully. "And now come along, and I'll pick you a buttonhole."

The cloud poor Peter Every had found so menacing had discharged rain of pure gold. Love had emerged from the shower, refreshed, glistening. The two could not know that, while they passed down the steps into the sunlit flower-garden, a girl with auburn hair was pushing a frantic three-year-old through the Scotch mist of Donegal, and wondering at every bank whether she would have the good fortune to break her neck.

Still, though their rain be golden, clouds beget shadows. If Lyveden responded to Valerie's invitation, he did not rise to her mood. The throwback to Gramarye had set him thinking. . . .

"Valerie," he said slowly, knitting his brows.

The girl had been upon the point of stopping to pick a rose. His serious tone, however, made her look up. The bloom was spared.

"Yes."

"When I went down—in November—there was something wrong. I mean, we were at variance."

With difficulty the girl repressed a shiver.

For a while she had hourly dreaded an allusion to the grim episode. Then, when the weeks went by and none was made, she began, at first feebly, to hope that it was buried. Gradually the hope had swelled into belief. Lately she had made sure that upon the first day, when Anthony had wept in her arms, he and she had been treading upon its grave. And now here it was—like a river full in their path, a swift-flowing treacherous stream which they must ford together. She would have given anything for a moment to collect her thoughts, but Anthony had started across. Already he was up to his knees. . . .

To be frank, she was in a tight place. The issues she had to deal with were clogged. Her treatment of them was to be governed by ruthless premises. Finally, if she made a false step, her fortunes and those of Anthony would be again in the melting-pot.

For an instant her brain zig-zagged. The next moment she had it in hand.

" Yes," she said slowly, " we were. I hoped you'd forgotten. You see, I'm very much ashamed. And, when my eyes were opened, I was just terrified. I felt as if I'd committed murder."

As she spoke, her brain fairly flashed through the rules which must govern this talk.

Everything hinged upon one mighty postulate —that *Anthony had collapsed precisely at one-fifteen upon the* 16*th of November*. He had, of course, done nothing of the sort. But that did not matter.

From that hour, for four months and a half, he had lain in a trance. This was the second article, which except Anthony believed, he could not be saved.

Anthony's memory, however, was a faithful servant —not to be tampered with. To reconcile the servant's report with the articles of his faith, a third tenet became essential. This was that *what Anthony remembered was the burthen of a dream*.

There go the governing principles.

Now for the issues.

Her sudden—perhaps excusable—jealousy of Anne Alison, her barbarous dismissal of Anthony, her quite inexcusable failure to give any reason for such treatment, her subsequent enlightenment by Anne herself —there is the skeleton whose dry bones he and she are to pick over—a gruesome business *which has already been dispatched* . . . upon the twentieth day of February, gentlemen, up in the Cotswold Hills. They both remember it perfectly. Yet Valerie must forget it, while Anthony must think it was a dream . . . *must*. . . .

Neither by word nor look must Valerie suggest

that the highly delicate ground she knows so well has ever been broken before.

Think, sirs, what a slip on her part will do.

It will plainly knock the three precious articles aforementioned into a cocked hat. Thence they will be retrieved to be turned against her—used to her condemnation by Anthony frantic. As for their love, the fragments of this that remain will not be worth taking up. . . .

Anthony passed a hand across his forehead.

" Shall I tell you what I dreamed ? "

" Yes," said Valerie.

" I dreamed that you came to me to make it up. And I was afraid. I tried to keep off the subject. I'd come such an awful cropper that I didn't want any more falls. But you would have it out. . . . And you said—don't laugh—that you'd turned me down because of Anne Alison." He stopped still and looked at her. " What was the real reason ? "

Leaning her back against a green box wall, Valerie moistened her lips. Then—

" It's perfectly true," she said quietly.

Anthony stared.

" What's true ? "

" Listen. You remember the meet at Saddle Tree Cross ? "

" Yes."

" When we spoke of my ' window,' and you said the spot meant so much to you that you couldn't keep away ? "

Anthony nodded.

" D'you remember I said I was going away the next day ? "

" Perfectly."

" It fell through, and I didn't go. There wasn't time to tell you, so I went—to the ' window.' "

Anthony started. " That's right. I found you there with Anne Alison."

" But, Valerie——"

" I know, I know. Anne told me, after you'd gone—*down*." The slip she had so nearly made set the girl sweating—literally. " I was mad, Anthony, mad," she panted. " I couldn't think straight. I nearly jumped over the cliff. I think the shock sent me blind. I'd always grudged her being so much with you. I want you to know the truth. She was always at the back of my mind. And when I saw you together—there, at our window——" She buried her face in her hands. " I know it was vile of me, dear. You see what I'm like. And if, now that you know, you'd like to go to an hotel . . ."

" But, Valerie, why didn't you give me a chance ? "

" I was mad," she wailed, " mad. I loved you so wildly, Anthony, that I was stunned. And, in spite of it all, I loved you just as much. And that made me so furious, I could have torn my hair. I wanted to hurt you cruelly, and when I did, I bruised my own heart."

" But why——"

" I was too proud. You'd dared to touch my pride " —she laughed hysterically—" my precious, sacred pride —my Ark of the Covenant. D'you remember how Uzzah died because he touched the Ark ? Well, you had to die. . . . And now "—she spread out her arms pathetically—" it's the pride that's dead, Anthony. Dead . . . dried up . . . shrivelled. . . . And I know what I'm worth."

She stopped.

Out of the neighbouring silence floated the comfortable note of a wood-pigeon. Clear of the shadow of the green box wall two butterflies flitted and whirled in the hot sunshine, while a fat bumble-bee hummed with excitement before the promise of a tall blue flag.

With his face in his hands, Anthony never moved.

" And that's all I've got to say. When I found I was wrong—well, I didn't know there was such agony in this world. . . . I deserved it, I know. Don't think I'm complaining. I deserve anything. But . . . if tears count, then I've paid—some of the score. . . ."

The man's hands were quivering.

Looking upon him, Valerie could see that he was gazing between his fingers.

" I'm afraid to speak," he said uncertainly. His voice was trembling with excitement. " I'm afraid to go on. Don't think I haven't forgiven you. I have, Valerie. I did—oh, ages ago. But . . . we're skating on terribly thin ice—terribly thin. We must go frightfully carefully, Valerie. You've no idea how carefully." The girl stared at him. This was uncanny —as if he could read her thoughts. He went on breathlessly. " My dream, dear. This is what happened in my dream. . . . You reproached yourself in just the same handsome way. You used the same phrases." Valerie started. " And then—after all— *something went wrong*. . . . What it was, I don't know. I can't remember. And that's the trouble. I can't remember what happened. But it's been the same so far, and then—*something went wrong*. . . ."

Valerie stood paralyzed. If Anthony was afraid to continue, she was terrified.

With an ungracious buzz the fat bee emerged clumsily from the tall blue flag and sailed noisily out of earshot. The sudden snap of jaws suggested that Patch, who was waiting patiently for the walk to proceed, forgave the flies no trespasses.

" You can't understand, dear. But you must take my word for it. I've trodden this way before. And presently—very soon now—there's a snare—a hole in the road. And if we go in, Valerie, it's—it's all

up. I know it. It happened in my dream. . . . And
I'm afraid to go on."

The tremulous misery of his tone wrung the girl's
heart.

Instinctively she stretched out a hand.

Anthony recoiled with a cry.

" Don't ! Don't touch me ! I remember. You
took my arm." Head back, he clawed at his temples.
" That's right. And we started to walk. We had
been standing. We started to walk back towards the
cottage. And I felt absurdly happy—all of a sudden.
. . . That was just before the end. And then——
Oh, if I could *only* remember. . . ."

The agony of desire in his tone seared Valerie's brain
into action. With a shock she realized that there she
was standing like a dolt, *quietly watching Lyveden
cudgelling his brains for the password back to Insanity*.
Any second he might stumble upon it. For once,
mercifully, his memory was sluggish—would not
respond. And there he was flogging it, to extract
that hideous fatal delusion that he was pledged to
Gramarye. . . .

Frantically she sought for a distraction. Her
brain, however, was away, with the bit in its teeth.
She could do nothing with it. The only thing she
could think of was that dreadful pass, which Anthony
was straining every nerve to recall. This rose up
vivid. His reference to the kiss he had given her
—her soft reply—the way he had taken her in his
arms—then that mischievous breeze that had come
whispering out of the silence, remindful, suggestive
—the start he had given at its touch—the hoarse
cry—the terrible light in his eyes. . . .

Anthony gave a great shout.

" *I* know," he panted jubilantly. " *I* know. . . .
It's coming back, darling, it's coming back—bit by
bit. Then I spoke of that kiss. I said how sorry I

was and asked your forgiveness. And you said——"
He stopped suddenly and clapped a hand over his
mouth. After a moment, " 'Sh," he said shakily.
" I mustn't repeat your words. That'd be moving.
And we mustn't move, Valerie. We're just at the
edge of the pit. We mustn't move an inch till I can
see where it is. Don't be frightened, dear. It's all
right. All our happiness depends upon my remembering, and—it's coming back. . . ."

His voice faded, and in an instant he was deep in
thought.

Eyes narrowed, his under-lip caught between his
teeth, he stared fixedly ahead, making a supreme
effort—plainly.

Valerie stood spellbound.

A pompous hum argued that the fat bee had decided
to revisit the vicinity.

Far in the distance there was a movement—leaves
shaken with the wind. A breeze was passing. The
timber of the park murmured the news faintly. . . .
With a sigh the tall elms of the avenue confirmed the
park's report. A breeze was passing . . . coming . . .
a little mischievous breeze. . . .

For one long moment Valerie's heart stood still.
Then she threw back her head and began to sing.

> " *Where the bee sucks, there suck I ;*
>   *In a cowslip's bell I lie. . . .*"

Anthony stared at her open-mouthed. Her throat
felt as though it had steel bands about it. She just
smiled and sang on.

> " *There I couch when owls do cry,*
>   *When owls do cry,*
>   *When owls do cry. . . .*"

The leaves of the lime-trees beyond the green box
wall were trembling—she could see them—beginning

to bob up and down. The boughs themselves were
beginning to sway elastically. Valerie sang like a
book.

> " On a bat's back do I fly,
>   After sunset, merrily, merrily,
>   After sunset merrily. . . ."

The lime-trees had stopped trembling. The breeze
had passed. . . . An exultant note swept into the
melody.

> " Merrily, merrily, shall I live now,
> Under the blossom that hangs on the bough—
>   Merrily, merrily, shall I live now,
> Under the blossom that hangs on the bough—
> Under the blossom that hangs on the bough."

With a fine, happy smile, Lyveden heard the song
out.

Then he stepped to my lady and caught her two
hands.

" Exquisite," he said, glowing. " Exquisite, Valerie.
I never knew you had such a lovely voice."

As he spoke, the girl's knees sagged, and he was
just in time to catch her before she fell. . . .

Her collapse was momentary. She was not, I
suppose, unconscious for more than five seconds. It
was, indeed, at her bidding that Anthony set her down
upon a low stone seat.

It was natural that he should be greatly concerned.

" Oh, my sweet, it was my fault. I frightened you.
I know I did. Lean your head back. That's right.
I was all worked up about that rotten dream. I'll
never mention it again. I'm so very sorry, dear.
I wouldn't have upset you for anything. And you
sang so beautifully. . . . Why did you sing, Valerie ? "

" I—I don't know. I heard a bee humming, and
that made me think of the song. It was very silly."

" It was very sweet, lass. And I just loved it. And, oh, my lady, please never think of our misunderstanding again. I felt I wanted just to know, but that was all. D'you feel better now? " Valerie nodded. " Are you sure? "

" Quite."

" Shall I get you some water? "

" No, thanks, lad. I'm all right now."

Kneeling on one knee beside her, Anthony patted her hand.

" I'm so thankful. . . . I can't get over your singing like that . . . I felt—carried away. I shall remember it always." He sighed happily. " I've got so many happy memories to take away."

Valerie sat up straight.

" To take away? " she breathed.

" My dear, I've been here nearly six months already. It's only with an effort that I can remember that I'm your guest. I don't want to go. Drifting along like this is simply perfect, but . . . there's such a lot to be done . . . heaps."

" There's plenty of time."

" I know, but—well, look at my clothes, for one thing. I'm not fit to be seen."

The girl breathed again. Then—

" Oh, yes, you are, old chap. Fitter than you think. Besides, you don't have to stay in London because you're going to a tailor."

" I know," said Anthony slowly. " I know. But it isn't only that. You see, my lady, when I came here to your house, it was as a footman. . . . And I think I'd better leave it as—well, no more than a friend. That's a big enough step, in all conscience. After a little—a very little—I shall come again, Valerie. . . ."

His fingers closed about hers.

" You never came here as a footman," said the

girl. " You came as my beloved. You went out of
the garden of *The Leather Bottel* that very first day
—my lord. What does it matter what else you
were—are—will be ? Oh, Anthony, you dear, honourable child. . . ."

With his disengaged hand Lyveden covered his eyes.

" I meant to be so strong," he said humbly. " God
forgive me, I'm very weak. You see—I love you so."
His head bowed, he took hold of her other hand.
" My lady, my beautiful lady, will you marry this
lover of yours—this irresolute child ? "

" Yes," said Valerie, " I will."

Anthony fell upon both knees.

" I worship you," he said simply. " Ever since that
first day at the inn, you've had my heart in your
hands. Sleeping, waking, your voice has rung in my
ears ; and my eyes have seen you in the background
—a tall dark girl, with the air of a queen . . . always
. . . always. . . . You've lighted pantries, you've
honoured servants' halls, you've turned a third-class
carriage into a bower. . . . And, when I came to know
you, the face of the earth was changed. I didn't
know there was such a being in all the world. I don't
think you ever were born : I think you stepped out
of a fairy tale some midsummer eve." He stopped to
lay his head reverently upon the blue silk knees.
" And you—are—to be—my wife. . . . In a few
short weeks' time you're going to take my name—
stand all in white by my side—put off your glorious
girlhood for the last time, and go away—to live with
me—for ever. . . ." The cool firm fingers laid hold
of his. " Wherever I am, your footfalls will be about
me, your perfume will be in the air, your smile will
gladden my eyes. . . . Oh, Valerie, my love, my
darling, my queen—you've made me a king. . . ."

Slowly Valerie led the strong rough palms up to her
throat.

" If I've made you a king, lad," she breathed,
" you mustn't kneel to me."

Getting upon his feet, Anthony pressed his lips to
the slight fingers.

Valerie rose also.

" If I've made you a king, lad, you mustn't kiss my
hand."

Anthony took her in his arms and looked into her
eyes.

" I was wrong," he said, smiling. " You didn't
step out of your fairy tale. You never left it. You've
just invited me in."

Valerie put up her mouth.

*　　*　　*　　*　　*

Nineteen days had slipped by—careless, halcyon
days, the matchless morning of a golden festival.

Jack and Jill were beyond imagination happy.

Lyveden had been prevailed upon to stay in Hampshire, and when he must visit London, to return the
same night. I am not certain that these days were
not the best of all. Valerie saw him off in the morning :
the two had all day to think upon their state ; his
home-coming at even delivered a perfect reverie.

The last of these flying visits must be recorded, for
it was unlike its fellows, and, though I cannot answer
for Lyveden, Valerie will remember it always.

There is no doubt at all that Anthony was growing
quite accustomed to the liberal atmosphere of Lincoln's
Inn Fields. As he bent his steps westward, he
found the huge square admirable. For comfortable
dignity, no other square he could remember compared
with it. This, he decided, was because its sides were
not too high for its area. London, as a whole, had
grown up. Had she grown outward instead, perhaps
. . . He remembered suddenly that she had grown
outward as well—out of all conscience, since Pepys
had taken pleasure in Lincoln's Inn Fields. With a

contented sigh Lyveden reflected that by nine-thirty
that evening he would be back at Bell Hammer. The
sweet smell of the country, the song of the wind in
tree-tops—above all, the abundance of cool soft air,
seemed to have become essential to his life. For the
present, at any rate, he had no use for Town. It
choked him. He was glad, however, that his solicitor's
office was in Lincoln's Inn Fields. . . .

Some clock announced the hour—a quarter to four.
The ex-officer quickened his pace. Savile Row had
to be visited, and Pall Mall. Most important of all, a
coupé had to be proved. . . . Anthony's heart beat
faster. The car was for Valerie.

As he left Kingsway behind, the gross belch of an
' Alarum ' demanded passage. Anthony fell to wondering whether his sweet would not prefer some other
usher. An ' Alarum ' got there, of course ; but it was
Rabelaisian. Perhaps . . .

The sound of a collision between two pedestrians
disturbed his musing.

It was nothing. Chin on shoulder, an errand-boy
had collided with a man in a silk hat. Anthony
was so close to the latter he could have touched him.

The boy muttered an apology, and the man laughed.

" My fault as much as yours," he said lazily, and
passed on.

It was Dr. Heron.

Anthony reeled against the wall.

Observing his movement, two typists squeaked
with pretended alarm, and then, giving him a wide
berth, lurched on, convulsed with mirth and clutching
one another.

To the poor woman who approached him and asked
if he were ill, Anthony at first said nothing at all.
Then he replied dazedly that he was " all right,"
and moved uncertainly away.

Arrived at the corner of Drury Lane, he hesitated,

looking round helplessly, as if he were not sure of his way. Immediately opposite, a large efficient-looking ironmonger's shop presented a plain, well-kept, *familiar* face. . . .

Anthony stared at it with a dropped jaw.

The errand-boy, who had found his demeanour promising, and had been loitering in the hope of developments, took up a good position in the gutter and fairly drank Lyveden in. Almost at once another of his species joined him.

After a prolonged stare—

" Wot's 'e doin' of ? " said the new-comer. " Sayin' 'is prares ? "

The other sniggered.

The noise aroused Anthony. With an effort he straightened himself. . . . Then he walked unsteadily across the street and into the shop.

The manager came forward.

" Have those mattocks come in ? "

For a second the man peered at him. Then—

" Oh, Major Lyveden, isn't it ? Yes, sir. Six ' Lightnin' ' mattocks, it was. I sent you a card, sir, three weeks ago. I've got the six on one side for you, sir."

" I'll take them now."

" Certainly, sir." He turned to an assistant and gave directions. Then : " Excuse me, sir. Jim ! "

A boy came at a run.

" Fetch me that envelope off of the top o' my blottin'-pad. It's pinned there." He turned to Lyveden. " When you was 'ere last time, sir, you dropped your ticket. I kept it by, in case you come in again, thinkin' you might be glad of it. It ain't six months yet, sir, since you was 'ere, so it's still good."

A moment later Lyveden was looking fixedly at the return half of a third-class ticket which had been issued at Chipping Norton.

" Thanks," he said slowly, slipping it into his pocket. " I'm much obliged."

He paid for the goods and waited whilst a taxi was fetched.

Then he followed the mattocks into the cab, and told the surly driver to go to Paddington. . . .

Five hours later he staggered, rather than walked, along the wasted track and up to the cottage door.

There had been no roan to meet him, and the mattocks had made their weight felt after the first two miles. He laid them down thankfully.

For a moment he looked about him.

Behind him—over towards Girdle—the sun had just gone down. And Gramarye . . . Gramarye had never looked one half so beautiful. . . . All her hard lines were gone. Every sacred twig of her had put on a wedding garment. The wild mystery of the place had been exquisitely veiled. The majesty of desolation was in full dress. Far as the eye could reach, the toss of the glorious woods had become unspeakably enriched . . . maddening. . . .

His eyes glittering, Lyveden hugged himself in a paroxysm of glee. The man was just gloating. . . .

Then he strode to the wood-shed.

" Well, Patch," he said cheerily. " Has Patch been a good little——"

The sentence snapped off short.

For a moment Anthony stared at the empty staple. Then he turned on his heel.

" Patch ! " he cried sharply. " Patch ! "

After listening intently for a moment, he stepped hastily on to the wasted track and began to whistle. . . .

Presently, trembling with anxiety, he started to stumble along the trail, whistling frantically. . . .

*　　　*　　　*　　　*　　　*

Seated in the hall at Bell Hammer, Valerie looked at the clock. As she did so, the faint crunch of wheels upon gravel told that the car was leaving to meet the down train. An instant later the clock struck nine. Miss French threaded her needle thoughtfully. . . .

Curled by her side upon the sofa, a little white dog with a black patch breathed stertorously.

A door opened, and a servant appeared with a letter. This had been expressed. Valerie laid down her work, and, after a glance at the envelope, opened it curiously.

DEAREST VALERIE,

Do you know anything of Peter? We only got back from America two days ago, and when we rang up his club—he was living there while we were away—they said they hadn't seen him since March. Of course we're frightfully worried. He had the car with him, and we're trying to trace that. Oh, Valerie, father's just come in and said that the car's been found at Carlisle. In a garage there, and that two men left it to be seen to a month ago, but the police think he bought it from them and is afraid. Please wire if you——

With a crash the small table by her side upset its complement of violets on to the parquet, there was a wild scrabble of paws, and Patch was at the front door, snuffing the sill and whining tremulously. . . .

Valerie got upon her feet.

" What is it, Patch ? " she said. " He isn't here yet."

For a second the terrier listened.

The next moment he was almost beating himself against the woodwork.

Letter in hand, Valerie crossed the hall and opened the door.

The dog rushed out into the drive.

For a moment he stood there, plainly straining his ears.

An instant later he was flying down the avenue. . . .

     *   *   *   *   *

The glow of the sunset faded. Evening gave way to dusk. Night stole into her throne-room. . . . One by one, men, spent with their labour, went to their rest. Pillowed upon the bosom of the country-side, villages fell asleep. And through them, while they slept, a little white dog went pelting breathlessly under the cold moonlight—now running, now dropping to a fast walk, now hesitating, now plunging on desperately, sometimes to the east, sometimes to the west, but in the main northward . . . due north, sirs . . . in the direction of the Cotswold Hills.

THE END

OTHER NOVELS BY DORNFORD YATES

ANTHONY LYVEDEN

" Behind Mr. Yates's grace of style is real power. Successive scenes of real comedy and tragedy show an equal mastery. The humour of the ' Berry ' books, sometimes whimsical, sometimes scintillating, is still there, and the author here unmistakably shows his ability to write a novel that will hold and delight the reader all the way through."
—*Sheffield Independent.*

VALERIE FRENCH

" An unusual story marked by considerable powers of imagination."
—*Liverpool Post.*

" One of the best novels we have come across this winter. A pretty story, and shows Dornford Yates in his breeziest style."—*Belfast Telegraph.*

AND FIVE WERE FOOLISH

" The book deserves a host of readers. Extraordinarily powerful and intriguing."—*Daily Telegraph.*

" Hit off with strength and that indefinable quality called style."
—*Tatler.*

AS OTHER MEN ARE

" As light and diverting as any novel we have read, and, be sure of this, there is a ' Yates ' touch, an unexpected vivid phrase, a wonderful adjective, that gives colour to page after page."—*The Sketch.*

" When Mr. Yates pauses in his stream of witty things, pauses but for a moment to describe a scene or a woman, in a few sentences he paints such a picture that the lover of fine words and phrases must need go over it again for the sheer joy of reading it."—*Glasgow Citizen.*

THE STOLEN MARCH

" The author is in his most humorous vein, the dialogue is brilliantly witty and clever, and humorous happenings and situations abound."
—*Time and Tide.*

" A tale of wild fancy and sparkling wit. Everybody is delightful. The book is one for the holidays."—*Irish Times.*

MAIDEN STAKES

" Mr. Dornford Yates has a style which is inimitable. His stories are full of laughter and sunshine and a spirit which few authors are able to capture."—*Eastern Morning News.*

" Mr. Yates is an extraordinarily pleasant novelist. His flair for dramatic thrills and clever dialogue is extraordinary."—*Liverpool Courier.*

WARD, LOCK & CO., LTD., LONDON AND MELBOURNE

OTHER NOVELS BY DORNFORD YATES

SHE PAINTED HER FACE

" Mr. Yates is at the top of his form. A tale of strife and cunning, wild adventure and sweet romance, in his best style. . . . Thank goodness for Mr. Dornford Yates."—*Nottingham Guardian.*

THIS PUBLICAN

" Mr. Yates tells his story in his usual entertaining, witty way, and brilliantly succeeds in making his somewhat difficult characters appear real."—*Liverpool Daily Post.*

GALE WARNING

" In addition to giving his characters all sorts of exciting things to do, Mr. Yates makes them talk like human beings, often uncommonly amusing human beings at that. ' Gale Warning ' has every attribute a novel of this type should possess. Most refreshing entertainment from first to last, with the spice of adventure and not a touch of the morbid."

—*Daily Mail.*

SHOAL WATER

" Worked out with Mr. Yates's accustomed ingenuity. The action is quick and the dialogue in his best vein."—*Sunday Times.*

PERIOD STUFF

" ' Period Stuff ' is the chocolate-cream of fiction, and very enjoyable in these rationed days."—*Punch.*

SAFE CUSTODY

" Amazing and breathless incidents . . . Mr. Yates at the top of his form . . . a most capital yarn."—*The Sphere.*

" An entirely delicious ' thriller '."—Norman Collins in the *News Chronicle.*

STORM MUSIC

" Dornford Yates is a clever story-teller, and his skill is cleverly revealed in this adventurous romance."—*Punch.*

" There is no lack of either excitement or mystery in this breathless story."—*Sunday Times.*

WARD, LOCK & CO., LTD., LONDON AND MELBOURNE